The Wolves of War:

The Beckoning

By T.L. Campbell

To request permissions, contact the publisher
at tcampbellauthor@gmail.com

Paperback: 978-1-5272-8666-5

First paperback edition 2021

Edited by Christina Kaye - Writeyourbestbook.com
Map design by Rebecca Vanette
- www.instagram.com/r.joys_fantasy_cartography
Formatting by Ellie Lewis – ellieml@hotmail.co.uk

Facebook: Tommy L Campbell Author
Instagram: @tl.campbellauthor

In memory of my Dad, Ian Campbell. My biggest hero.

And a big thank you to my Mum, Nat, Bill and Stace, for always being there and believing in me.

I love you all.

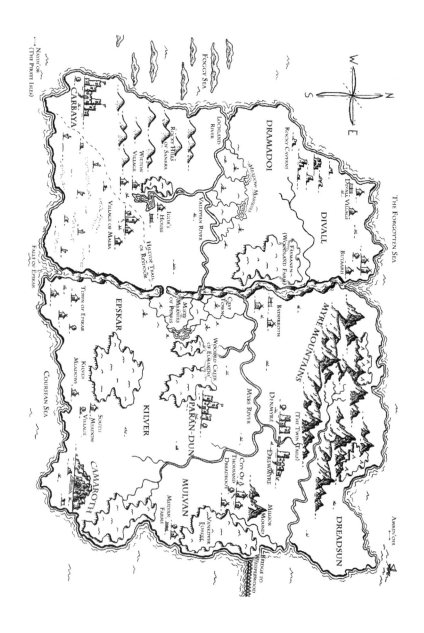

INTRODUCTION

Stories never go untold, and lands never go untouched.
From the whispering cacti trees of Divall to the magnificent glow upon the water within the falls of Epskar, the Kingdom of Ar'Gurd wasn't always so tropical and tranquil.

Once a kingdom which thrived upon the strength of its armies and the strange laws they lived upon, it soon became a kingdom enthralled by hate and anguish.

Its cities burned, and great families became great enemies.

Villages from each corner of the land were raided and ransacked whilst the plumage that beautified them were soiled.

Men, Elves, Wizards, and Dwarves co-existed during a time when it was not thought possible, whilst two royal brothers once with the strongest of bonds became the greatest of foes.

The War of the Wolves from the yesteryear is a legendary tale of deception, pride, honour, and freedom, but every great war has a beginning.
But this story takes you back, not just to the beginning, but back to *The Beckoning*.

CHAPTER ONE

THE BECKONING

Belthran

"Can we go now, Father? We've been out here all day; I've much to be getting on with," said Belthran as he hurled a heavy rock across the wasteland of Ar'Gurd.

"Not much longer, my son, your brother still has much to learn ahead of his birthday; is there nothing you'd like to share with him?" King Armish replied as he pulled his embedded sword with ease from the downed Zarnick's beastly skull.

"Yes, I do have some advice for you, Brother; when Father asks if you'd like to go on a trip, just say no."

Belthran muffled some more to himself as he hopped back on his horse, frustrated, and waiting to head back to the palace.

King Armish knelt in front of young Maxin and placed his heavy hand upon his small shoulders. "Maxin, my son, tomorrow is the day where you begin your search for your own ten-man army. Picking these ten men happens only once in your life, so you mustn't make mistakes; you must know what you're up against in this vast and open kingdom.

"As much as you're protected within the high walls of Carbaya, there're still dangers out in this land that will not hesitate to harm you, much like this Zarnick. You need good men to back you up, Son, and you must be able to do the same for them. Don't listen to Belthran, he took this trip days before his fourteenth birthday, too, and he was just the same then, stubborn and full of pride, but he turned out to be a great warrior who leads a great Unit, and I know you'll be the same."

Maxin looked back at his father with deep admiration, without taking his eyes off him for a second. He grabbed the handle of his father's sword that had been holstered back into its thick lizard skin casing.

"Someday, Father, I'll wield a sword as big as yours, I'll lead an army as powerful as yours, and I will rule a kingdom as great as yours."

A proud smile came upon the face of the king, though he could also hear Belthran yawning behind him.

"There's only one great kingdom, Maxin, and that is for Belthran to lead when the time comes. The others, well, the others are ruled by those who have never co-existed with men, so for you to be the ruler of Wizards, Elves, or even Dwarves, that'd be a great honour, indeed. As for wielding a great sword and leading a powerful army, that, my son, is all in your hands."

"Do you know what else is in your hands, Brother? Choosing to go home," interrupted Belthran as he continued to wait impatiently.

King Armish got back to his feet, keeping his hand rested upon Maxin's shoulder. He looked out upon the rocky hills of Sankra and watched the luminous sun as it began to head down behind the beautifully blossomed green woodland of Faymanen. "All of this *is* your home, Maxin, wherever in the kingdom you may find yourself, just remember you're *always* home."

"I don't see why we couldn't have just saved this little speech for when we got back to our *actual* home; you know, the one with thousands of villagers and a great white marble palace, the palace where I have many things to be taking care of," continued Belthran as he lay his head upon the back of his horses cushioned mane.

"Belthran, this is the start of your brother's future. You need to help guide him; you need to help prepare him and you need to hel—Belthran, watch out behind you!" cried King Armish suddenly as he pulled his sword from his case and ran toward Belthran.

Belthran, completely baffled by what was happening, turned his head to see a Zarnick leaping through the air toward him, its thick grey hair blowing through the wind as it soared along with its hundred razor-sharp teeth, glistening brightly from the sun that still peaked above the woodland.

The Zarnick barrelled into the side of Belthran's horse, sticking its two long, rhino-like horns into its abdomen and throwing Belthran to the ground with it, face-first into the rocky dirt, filling his mouth with sharp stone and mud.

Zarnicks never travelled in groups, so King Armish was stunned to see two so close to one another. He burst forward with the few inches that remained and stood over Belthran's grounded body to guard him.

The Zarnick began to slowly appear, creeping over the fallen horse. First came its bristled eyebrows and yellow snake-like eyes. It placed one giant paw on top of the horse and stood proud over its fresh kill. The Zarnick then looked King Armish dead in the eyes with no remorse nor sorrow, and with one objective in mind: to kill.

"You stay away from my son!" the king shouted with rage at the beast as both front paws of the Zarnick now lay indented into the body of the horse, its claws piercing its very skin with a mere touch.

Belthran spat the gritty dirt from his mouth as he began to rise to his feet, looking the beast dead in the eyes.

"Belthran, go and keep your brother safe," ordered King Armish as he shoved Belthran into Maxin's direction whilst keeping his sword held out toward the Zarnick.

"I can stay and fight, Father! That creature killed my horse; let me have this kill," demanded Belthran.

"This is not the time, Belthran, go to your brother and keep him safe."

"I do not need protecting, Father! We can fight this together," said Maxin as he pulled his sword from his holster.

"No, Maxin, you are not ready. Belthran, do as I say and protect your brother."

Then, the Zarnick suddenly bellowed out a deafening screech that would devastate the strongest of ears as it hopped over the horse and slowly marched its way toward King Armish, not taking its eyes off of him for a second.

Completely taken back by the screech of the Zarnick, Maxin moved a step backward whilst Belthran moved another step closer.

As the night air became stronger, the dirt and dust from the ground began to deviate and swirl around the armoured boots of the king; the whistling wind curdled through his well-groomed beard as he fixated his eyes on the approaching creature.

Suddenly, through the corner of his eye, he began to see Belthran move ever so slightly toward him.

"Belthran, get back now!" he ordered as he shoved Belthran back. And during that moment when the king's attention was diverted, the Zarnick seized its opportunity and sprinted at him with ferocity.

"Father!" bawled Maxin, looking on as the Zarnick pounced toward the king, just inches away.

The Zarnick mowed straight into King Armish. Its claws scraped brutally through the king's arm, smashing him to the ground as one of its horns narrowly avoided his neck, leaving him with a light scratch across his throat.

King Armish lay injured and beaten on the floor.

In complete shock and fear for his father's safety, Maxin pulled out his sword and ran toward the Zarnick.

At that point, he was unsure how he was ever going to take down this huge beast; he just knew he had to do something.

Sweat dripped from his brows as his hands began to shake, the look of determination upon his face looked somewhat overshadowed by a look of fear within his eyes.

Maxin came closer toward the Zarnick, who at that point was standing above King Armish.

The creature then raised one of its giant paws before very slowly and forcefully resting it down onto the king's head like a torture device.

With the Zarnick feeling in complete control, it stared down Maxin with deep predatory eyes awaiting his arrival.

Just feet away from one another, the Zarnick opened its mouth wide as drool began to ooze down the two large fangs within this beast's mouth and onto the face of the king.

King Armish used all the strength he could muster to try and wriggle free from the grasp of the beast, but he had no luck. And with this, the Zarnick applied more pressure; the creature's claws began to penetrate as the king tried desperately not to scream.

Maxin raised his sword as he ran the last few steps toward the Zarnick, when suddenly Belthran came running across with great speed, barrelling into Maxin, knocking him to the ground, and pushing him out of the way.

"This kill is mine!" exclaimed Belthran as he stood up tall with his sword hanging by his side; he slowly turned his head until his eyes locked onto the eyes of the beast once more.

With his skull being slowly crushed into the dirt, King Armish looked on as Belthran snarled and stared down the barrel of the Zarnick's nostrils.

"Belthran, get out of here! Get your brother home!" ordered King Armish through great stress, which was then met with a very disapproving screech from the Zarnick as its drool, once again, dripped down onto the face of the king.

Belthran had no response, nor no reaction to his father, he just continued to stare intently back at the Zarnick.

Once again, the Zarnick bellowed out another deafening screech, releasing its paw from the king's skull and stepping over his wounded body, but not before striking the king in the face with its back paw, knocking him unconscious.

Belthran screamed back at the Zarnick before charging toward it with great intensity.

Once the two were just yards away from one another, the Zarnick leapt through the air with its jaw wide open and its paws stretched out in front.

Quick to react, Belthran continued his run toward the Zarnick before skidding across the floor and rolling underneath the beast.

Belthran picked himself up quickly and swung his sword in the direction of the creature, who was now approaching from behind. Belthran was stunned and bewildered as his sword connected with the largest horn of the Zarnick, barely making a mark.

He quickly pulled back his sword in shock as the Zarnick, once again, stared down at him and growled; its eyes grew more bloodshot, and its spit became ravenous.

Belthran raised his sword to strike once more, but the beast was much quicker and much stronger to react.

The Zarnick lifted its front paws off the ground and stood up tall upon its hind legs before giving Belthran a swift strike across the face, once again knocking him straight to the dirt.

Belthran tried to raise himself from the stony ground, but his head felt weak, and his arms were like jelly. And through all of his tiresome efforts, he kept finding himself face-first back in the dirt.

As he lay helpless on the ground, the dirt around him became bright, and the aura surrounding him became somewhat calm, whether or not it being the knock to his head that caused this; it most certainly wasn't the case. Instead of brighter, the dirt had become darker, as the shadow of the Zarnick now lay upon him, and the aura that surrounded him could only have been described as a fly caught in a web, a web of certain death.

Belthran was dazed; he only came round once the warm oozing drool of the Zarnick's mouth streamed down his face. He took a look up to see the beast's jaw open wide, the creature's chilling breath stung his nostrils, and the hundreds of razor-sharp teeth stung his mind. The Zarnick was ready to rip him apart; all Belthran could do now was close his eyes and wait.

He closed his eyes and closed his mind. Then, everything went quiet.

Still able to feel the breath of the Zarnick resting on his nose, the end felt near, that was until the scent became weaker and the air became cooler. Sound around him slowly began to enter back into his ears, the sound of growling and the sound of struggle; he opened his eyes to a squint to see the Zarnick jumping aimlessly around.

His eyes began to focus as his lids curiously opened more. The Zarnick wasn't jumping alone; there was something hanging on to its back. Belthran's eyes opened wide when he realised it wasn't a something, but a someone, and that someone was his little brother, Maxin.

Belthran shot up from the ground regardless of any pain he was feeling, his adrenaline was urging him and pushing him forward.

He used his hands to dust the ground, searching for his sword, whilst his eyes remained fixated on Maxin.

Finally managing to grasp the brass handle of his sword, Belthran burst forward and raced toward the beast.

With Maxin still riding around the wasteland on the back of this Zarnick like a mechanical bull, Belthran was trying to keep up with them, not wanting himself to swing and miss at the wrong time.

Whilst hopping around the hard and cracked mud surface, the Zarnick spotted Belthran out of the corner of its eye, forcing it to a sudden halt.

Belthran continued to race toward the beast, brandishing his sword through the dusted wind.

The Zarnick, with a much quicker reaction, once again struck Belthran across the face with one of its great paws, knocking him straight back down to the dirt, right before leaning forward with force and flipping Maxin from its shoulders and on to the ground to join Belthran.

With the two brothers now on the ground, the Zarnick took a few steps back without taking its eyes off of them for a second. It scraped his two front paws through the concrete like mud, brushing the dust underneath its body. The Zarnick then lowered its posture and drew out a thick and steamy exhale.

The creature stared down both Belthran and Maxin with the most ferocious look before sprinting at full pace toward them.

Both dazed, Belthran and Maxin began to help each other up, unaware of the approaching beast.

Suddenly, they heard a screech, which forced them to push their hands into their ears; they both looked up and saw the Zarnick just yards away.

Maxin then grabbed hold of Belthran in fear as the horns of the beast glistened back at them through the declining sun.

Maxin closed his eyes, and Belthran, once again, waited for the inevitable.

Things went quiet as Maxin's eyes closed; he could hear nothing, but as more time passed, he could also feel nothing.

His eyes flickered open, and much to his surprise, he saw the decapitated body of the Zarnick laid down upon his feet whilst a battered King Armish stood above the creature with his bloodied sword draped and dripping down his leg.

Taking a deep breath, King Armish looked upon his two sons in great victory, but the same couldn't be said for Belthran and Maxin as they both drew vast sighs of relief. Armish took a cloth to his blade and wiped it clean of all the blood that stained it before he wearily hobbled over to the two young princes muttering to them. "Your mother isn't going to like hearing about this."

CHAPTER TWO

THE GREAT LAND

King Armish

Ar'Gurd was a sanctuary, a haven of a land. The days were hot, and the casualties were few, to say the least, and King Armish Hailguard ruled the kingdom as no king had before him.

He cared for the people, and they cared for him. He was gentle but rugged, calm but relentless, and above all else, he was passionate about the kingdom he was born to rule.

Helped along the way by the ever-beautiful Queen Neva Hailguard, the king made the land great; he made it blossom and thrive.

"Hard work pays off hard debts, and no hard debts allow for no hard life," he would say to the people, and that was a motto that a lot of them went on to live by.

King Armish was a man of many mottos, standing on the balcony of the Palace of Kings and speaking out to his many villagers across the courtyard. They were drawn to him with every word he spoke; each word in their ears felt more like treasure in their pockets.

The Palace of Kings stood tall within the city of Carbaya, the capital of Ar'Gurd. Built with rare white marble brick and stone, it had remained for hundreds of years being home to all royals who lived to see such days. It was within the Palace of Kings where Armish and Neva would create the laws and policies of the kingdom, but it was in the great hall of kings, situated in the centre of the city, where they would enforce them.

Villagers from all corners of the kingdom, from the city of Paran-Dun to the small town of Butaarh, would gather to hear the laws and policies of the land. As much as everyone agreed with King Armish being a great ruler, not all agreed with some of his laws.

As the law would have it, as soon as a villager reached the age of eighty, they were then classed as incapable and useless and would have to see out the foreseeable future at home. Some of the elderly embraced the years of relaxation whilst others wanted to continue doing their part for the kingdom.

However, there would always be jobs available to every man under the age of eighty. Deaf, blind, or limbless, there would always be a job suitable somewhere in Ar'Gurd. As for the women of the kingdom, they were known as keepers of the house; this meant that their job roles involved the upkeep and the daily running of their homes. There were those whose homes were built into local businesses or farms, which would allow for some women to expand their workloads into baking, farming, or even pouring pints of ale in the local taverns. Failure to commit to any of the land's declarations could result in imprisonment, or in some known cases, death.

There were many strange laws that folk had to abide by, but perhaps none stranger than the minimum child law.

The law was created many suns and moons ago by King Morlan II in a great attempt to keep the population high in Ar'Gurd, which had also proven to be very successful.

Each couple was ordered to have a minimum of two children per family. The only people who were exempt from this ruling would be those who were unable to conceive, from which they would then have to find another family willing to have more children for them to adopt.

Ar'Gurd was a very strange land with many strange laws.

King Armish was much like his father, King Hamus. He was handsome and stood tall over most; he had dark brown shoulder-length hair with a groomed beard the women just loved.

He took control of the kingdom at the very young age of twenty-three; his father had been struck by an illness called ground flu that had plagued the land and he died just days before a medicine was created.

With the child limitation law in play, King Armish wasn't an only child; he also had a younger brother, Clearus.

Being the oldest, Armish stepped forward on the day of his father's death and stood above the courtyard upon the balcony of the Palace of Kings and promised the people of the kingdom a leader, a ruler, a fighter, and a giver.

As Armish stood tall upon the balcony looking over at the people like a beacon of light, Clearus looked up at him in envy with jealous eyes and an angered smile, knowing that Armish had to have children himself, meaning Clearus's chances of ever becoming king looked very bleak.

Clearus wasn't much like his brother in looks; he had a clean-shaven face, short dark hair, and a nasty scar that ran down the right side of his face, which he picked up during a training session with Armish when they were but children.

Prince Clearus also had one child himself, a son, before his wife sadly passed away after giving birth to their second child, who also did not survive. Prince Clearus's son, Harnik, was what is known as a bad seed, a motherless child with a forever jealous father who knew he would never be king. Harnik had long dark hair and a slender build. He was cunning, much like his father, but his heart always remained true to his friends and his family; although his fondness for being a royal prince often outshone his true kindness.

Harnik would spend his days forcing others to do work for him, and he walked around like he was better than everyone else just because his blood was lined with royalty and gold. But other than being the king's nephew, King Armish never really worried about the boy, as he was too busy concentrating more on his own children; Belthran, Maxin, and Layna.

Belthran was the eldest of the three, and at seventeen years old, he was heir to the throne. Knowing he would be king someday made Belthran very cocky and stubborn. He was much like a body double of his father, minus the beard and his hair being slightly darker. He stood taller than most and was built like a man in his early twenties.

Although there were never really any full-scale battles in Ar'Gurd aside from the odd pirate attack every year or two, Belthran was already a very skilled fighter and was extremely talented with a blade. At such a young age, he was already one of the best fighters in the kingdom, and folk were ecstatic that someone so skilled was going to be king in time to come.

'The Coming King,' some folk would call him.

Although they were excited at the prospect of having a skilled fighter as king, there were still things about him that concerned them. They were unsure as to whether Belthran was smart or wise enough to lead a kingdom. Some folk were weary and uneasy about this, but others just could not wait to find out.

The old Whisper Baron of Carbaya used to speak of Belthran and his future on the throne; he was a careless old fool who spoke of coming days and rumours that surrounded the people of the city. Every great city or town in the land had a Whisper Baron, and Carbaya's was old man Kelby, who lived next door to the blacksmith's workshop down Waybury Way.

"Times of unease and uncertainty, the reign of a great king to be passed down to the coming king; what is it that awaits us?" He would cry out along the cobbled streets on a busy market morning. "Times of change, perhaps? Times of worry? The future has its path, and it all starts with the rise of a prince. He has strength, he has courage, but does he have the power to lead? Is Prince Maxin the future we desire?" He would continue as he created doubt and debate throughout not only the city but the whole kingdom.

Prince Maxin, however, was the second eldest of the two sons and therefore would not become king.

He was only thirteen years old, and he was already showing signs of becoming a bright child. Instead of being homeschooled, like Belthran was, Maxin chose to go to school with all the other children. He liked to be sociable and get involved in what all the other children of Ar'Gurd were doing.

As for his looks, Maxin took after his mother. For a child of thirteen, he was all fair-haired and freckle-faced; he didn't look much like a fighter.

Maxin *was* no fighter; he knew there were never many battles within the kingdom, so he never paid too much attention to it and thus decided to concentrate and focus more on the political side of things, and at just thirteen years old.

He had all the signs of being a great leader in the future, but people knew as long as Belthran was around, it was he who was going to lead.

As for the youngest of the children, Layna, she was just five years old and held the title of the only princess in the entire kingdom. Her birth struck a huge celebration throughout every city, town, village, or farm that Ar'Gurd had to offer. Men would travel from all over for a chance to wed their youngest sons to Layna when she came of age, but Armish and Neva did not care for that; they wanted Layna to be able to grow to make her own decisions in life.

"She will bring beauty to the kingdom. The princess will provide us with the fight and the belief to be the best we can be, and we will not have her look down on us," the Whisper Baron would cry, and the people of the city would listen. They did not want Layna to grow up and become embarrassed by the way the villagers lived or the way the villagers dressed; they wanted to make a good impression on her as she continued to grow and flourish.

Queen Neva and King Armish kept their children close and bonded to ensure those bonds would be unbreakable.

"An indestructible family rules an indestructible home; an indestructible home creates safe boundaries; safe boundaries form a safe haven; a safe haven brings people; people provide produce and produce creates a thriving community," King Armish once said to Neva.

They wanted to create an indestructible family to rule the entire kingdom, but before there were five, there were but two, and Neva and Armish met in the most unconventional way.

Neva was, in fact, hired by Prince Clearus twenty years ago to be his personal maid and clean his quarters.

Prince Clearus had kept quiet about this, as a law that had previously passed clearly stated that no woman should work, but instead, they should stay at home and care for their households.

However, Prince Clearus was a very proud man. He believed no man should be a cleaner; he believed they should be out in the farms, the barracks, and even the mines.

As careful as he tried to be, this secret lasted all but three months.

King Armish was informed of this deceit by his longest and most loyal friend, Payner, who was knighted a Sir when King Armish took his place as king. Payner spotted Neva leaving Prince Clearus's quarters late one night.

After several days of seeing the woman, Payner began to see a pattern form; he noticed that Neva had been going there twice a week on the same days and during the same times.

Payner informed Armish of the unusual activity he had been seeing over the last few weeks. He had told King Armish about how he saw this lady leave Clearus's quarters every Monday and every Friday.

"Maybe he just has a lady friend. I have been worrying about him a lot recently, and I must say it is about time, too," stated King Armish.

"No, my King, this was my initial thought, but this is something different," expressed Payner, who then went on to vent his views.

"I mean, say it was a lady, why the secrecy? And why is it he sees her on the same days at precisely the same time?"

***

The following Friday night soon came around, and King Armish and Sir Payner came up with a plan and decided to go to Clearus's quarters at a time when the woman would supposedly be there. They both hid outside the quarters for a short while before a woman eventually came along and went inside.

"That's her, my Lord," whispered Payner.

"Hmm. Well, I will tell you this much, my friend, if this is his special little lady, then he has done better than I ever expected him to," joked the king.

Upon seeing the woman enter his quarters, the two of them slowly walked up to the door for a closer look, from which both King Armish and Sir Payner tried to peer through a nearby window, but as the window was so small, they could not see a thing.

"This is hopeless. You and I know that there is only one sure way we can both find out what is really going on in there," stated Payner.

Before they knew it, both Payner and King Armish were sprinting toward the door in an attempt to break it down; with every step they took, they were getting faster and faster.

"Here we go," shouted the king.

Now both running as fast as they could about ten feet away from the collision, the door suddenly swung open.

Without hesitation, and in an act of desperation, Payner threw himself to the floor, thinking it was the only way of stopping himself in such a hurry, but King Armish, on the other hand, kept on running. Perhaps it was because he did not want to ruin his cloak on the gravel, but nevertheless, all Payner suddenly heard was a massive crash from within the quarters.

Payner picked himself up from the ground and brushed himself off. "My King, are you okay?" called Payner as he began to slowly move closer toward the open door.

Whilst holding onto his leg, Payner finally reached the door but saw nothing but a bunch of dirty bedsheets piled up in a big mound upon the floor.

"My King?" he called again from which he then began to hear a slight groan coming from the pile of sheets. Payner moved closer to the pile, as it then started to move. "Is that you, my Lord?" he asked. And this time, he got a response, as a muffled voice from the pile called out.

"Payner, help me up out of here, will you?"

Payner hobbled over to the sheets as quickly as he could and threw them on the floor behind him and then began to chuckle as he saw King Armish lying on the floor, also holding onto his leg.

"We are getting too old for this, my Lord," joked Payner as he grabbed onto the king's hand to pull him up.

"I think I landed on something hard," replied King Armish.

"Not something, my Lord, but someone," claimed Payner as he pointed toward a foot that was sticking out from underneath the sheets.

Payner cleared the remainder of the sheets only to find a stunning young lady lying helplessly on the floor.

King Armish moved toward her and offered his hand to help her up. "Are you okay?" he asked.

"Surprisingly unhurt, my Lord," replied the young woman who then added worriedly, "but I must say, I don't think Prince Clearus is going to be very happy that you came crashing in here."

"Do not worry. I am the king of this kingdom, which means I can handle my brother."

"I am sorry to cut this meet and greet short, my Lord, but I think we should talk to her about what we really came here for," suggested Payner as he turned his attention to the woman and asked, "what is it you are doing in here exactly?"

The woman began to nervously sweat and stutter, not quite knowing how to respond. She knew if she was to tell the truth, then she and Prince Clearus would get in a lot of trouble, but if she was to lie, then she would get in a lot more trouble for lying to a king.

She thought quietly for a second.

"Are you going to answer us?" asked Payner.

She stuttered again whilst trying to come up with a response but still had no idea what her response should be.

"Well?" continued Payner. And within seconds of him asking, he finally got a response, but it was not from the woman.

"What is going on in here?" came an angry, deep, and foul voice from behind them.

Sir Payner and King Armish quickly turned around to see none other than Prince Clearus standing in the doorway like an unwelcome guest.

"I demand an answer!" shouted the prince.

"You *do not* go throwing around demands here, Clearus. As king, that is my job. And with that being said, I demand *you* tell *me* what is going on here!"

"I will tell you what is going on here, *my Liege*, there are currently two bucket heads wandering around my private quarters and trying to attack my…lady."

That was then followed by a response from King Armish, who once again reminded Clearus who was king. "I am sorry, my brother, but I believe it is I who owns this property, and as the owner of the property, I am afraid I am allowed to come and go as much as I please. As for her being your…lady, is it? Tell me this, Brother, why keep it such a secret?"

Just like the woman had done before him, Clearus began to struggle for a response.

"Your hesitant response is not good, Brother; may I remind you, even as my brother, it is a great crime to lie to a king? Be truthful with me, Clearus, because I, too, am finding it extremely hard to believe that someone this beautiful is your lady," King Armish joked. "Let's face it, she is hardly going to be with you for your ravishing looks and your dashing personality now, is she?"

King Armish chuckled, and as Payner began to laugh along with him, Clearus responded rather abruptly, "Do not kid with me, Brother; a prince can have any woman he wants."

"So what is your excuse?" joked Payner this time as the king laughed along with him.

Prince Clearus suddenly became very red-faced and angry, still not quite knowing how to respond.

"Perhaps I should just go back and ask your 'lady' how you both met," suggested King Armish as he looked a panicked Clearus in the eyes.

King Armish knew he was lying; he was just waiting for him to admit it and was having plenty of fun in the meantime.

Although Prince Clearus was panicking, he was never going to crack, he was a stubborn and proud man, and he would tell twenty different stories before he ever told the truth if it meant not admitting he was in the wrong.

All of a sudden, a voice came from the woman whom the three men seemed to forget was still in the room with them.

"I will tell you, my Liege. I did not want to say anything as I thought I would be in much trouble, and I did not want the prince to be in trouble, either, but upon my head be it!" said the woman bravely. She then began to explain the situation.

"Prince Clearus and I met at the village festival three months ago. After he saw me, he approached me and asked if I would dine with him. Deep down, I knew he wasn't my type, but how could I say no? He is a prince, after all, so I reluctantly said yes. Later on that evening, he made a proposal to me, one that I could not possibly have turned down, as I am a single lady living alone in the city. He said he would pay me every Monday and Friday of each week to clean out his quarters, as he claimed the men had more important things to be getting on with.

"I knew it was wrong because the law clearly states otherwise, but as this proposal came from royalty itself, I only presumed that there was an exception in this case. I found out there was no such exception when Prince Clearus asked me not to mention this arrangement. I was being paid well and was able to afford to live a good life, but I know now that I shouldn't have let it go on; the laws are your laws, and there are no exceptions. Upon saying this, I am admitting that I have broken the law and am willingly accepting any punishment you hereby submit."

Silence filled the room for a matter of seconds before King Armish responded to the woman's confession. "First, I would like to thank you for your honesty; I know how hard that must've been for you. But as you so rightly stated, no matter what your thoughts and circumstances were at the time, you still broke the law. Considering everything you have said to me, and the laws that you broke, I'm going to make you a new proposal. We will discuss the proposal over something to eat. I will send a messenger with the arrangements shortly, but until then, I suggest you be on your way."

Without hesitation, the woman agreed to the king's commands and scarpered away from the prince's quarters.

King Armish then turned his attention back to his brother. "Now, Clearus, you have also broken the law by provoking that young lady to do so."

The king then looked round to Payner and asked him to leave them to it, as they had much to discuss.

Payner quickly left, and as soon as he did, the king and the prince were at each other's throats; they argued long into the night.

***

After several hours of arguing and discussing Clearus's crimes, King Armish finally decided on what his punishment should be. "So this is my final decision, Clearus, and you *will* respect it! From now on, you are in charge of cleaning your own quarters, and any decision you make in the future must be run by me. Is that clear?"

Prince Clearus was not happy with this decision, and it showed by the look of anger and disappointment on his face as he agreed to the terms and then watched Armish finally leave his quarters.

***

When the sun broke the following morning and the villagers began to open their market stalls for the busy morning ahead, the first thing on Armish's mind was to send a messenger to the woman's house with the arrangements for dinner.

The message was delivered, and later on that day, King Armish awaited her in the castle's mess hall.

After only a few minutes of waiting, the woman showed, and when King Armish laid eyes on her, his jaw just dropped at the pure beauty that stood before him. Standing in front of him was the most beautiful woman he had ever seen in the entire kingdom.

She arrived with the blondest of hair, the bluest of eyes, and the most stunning blue gown. King Armish was finding it hard to believe she was the same woman he saw in Clearus's quarters the night before.

She sat down with the king, and they proceeded to enjoy a nice meal together. He made her laugh, and she made him weak. He had not even asked her name, and there was, in fact, no discussion of the new proposal until later on that night; they were enjoying themselves together, and by the end of dinner, King Armish finally came out with his new proposal.

"First, I must ask your name."

"My name is Neva Thorn, my Lord."

"A beautiful name for a beautiful woman; but, please, call me Armish, and from this moment on, Neva Thorn, you shall be my Queen. You are spouseless, and so am I. We will have children together, and we will rule this kingdom, together. This is my proposal, do you accept?"

Neva didn't take too long to respond to the king; she saw this new proposal as more of a luxury than a punishment, so it wasn't a hard decision for Neva to make. She always believed the king was so handsome, and he was always so caring toward others.

Neva jumped straight from her chair and gave Armish a huge hug as she shouted her response to him. "Yes, yes, yes; of course, I accept your proposal!"

***

Two months later, Ar'Gurd was host to one of the grandest weddings the kingdom ever had. Celebrations lasted a whole week, all throughout each day and each night, as the people of the kingdom were now subjects to the ruling and power of King Armish and Queen Neva Hailguard.

***

Through centuries, Ar'Gurd was a very well-protected kingdom and gracefully stood the test of time.

Pirates were the only race to ever threaten the people of Ar'Gurd, travelling over from across the sea in a large fleet of finely crafted ships. They would occasionally attack Carbaya at times throughout the years to try and take the land for their own, but this would always result in a heavy defeat from which the pirates would have to retreat.

When the pirates did retreat, they would just go back onto their ships and sail back across the foggy sea, southwest of the capital. Nobody ever knew exactly where they were hiding and where they came from, and nobody ever dared to find out.

Nobody in Ar'Gurd was a good sailor, for they never had any reason to be. Ar'Gurd was their home, and that is where they liked to remain.

It always seemed like suicide to them if they were to chase down the pirates. There was only one time when the men dared to fight back, and it was a time that was not easily forgotten.

It was as normal as normal days go in Carbaya. Whilst under the ruling of King Hamus; the weather was hot, the fountains were sparkling, the markets were busy, and Lady Margreen was chasing the scallywags away from her flower garden.

It wasn't until mid-afternoon when the day soon became less ordinary. The pirates chose their moment, and they forced an attack upon the city; repel ropes were thrown over the walls, and arrows flew in by the hundreds.

After several hours of fighting and after taking a complete slaughtering from the men of Ar'Gurd, the pirates fled to the docks, and as usual, they jumped on their ships and began to sail away, but this time King Hamus sent some men after the pirates to chase them down; he sent enough men to find out where the pirates camped and to finish them off for good.

As the pirates sailed out, the men of Ar'Gurd climbed aboard a pirate ship that was left behind, and as bad as they were at sailing, the men still continued to sail in pursuit.

Just after they set away from the dock, the men looked over to the distance and saw the ship they were following just vanish into the fog.

They had no choice but to follow as they themselves were approaching the thickest of fog that lay across the sea.

Their boat eventually made it to the mist, and as they entered it, their boat, too, disappeared. But unlike the pirates, the men of Ar'Gurd never returned, and still to this day, nobody knows what happened to them. After this, nobody was ever again sent to follow the pirates.

Aside from the unlucky few following the attacks, the casualties on Carbaya were always minimal, but what King Armish was unaware of was that the biggest attack from the pirates was right around the corner, and it was heading straight for his doorstep.

It was also said and written that any king, prince, or sir of the kingdom should lead their own army. These armies would be formed of the leader and no more than ten handpicked warriors. The small, handpicked armies would be known as Units.

Armish commanded his own Unit, and when he became king, they became part of the city guard from which the king also led, but it also meant that Prince Clearus, Prince Belthran, Prince Harnik, and Sir Payner all had their own ten-man Units, and now it was time for Prince Maxin to command his own. As the requirement would have it, one must be at least fourteen years old before they could command their own Unit, and all warriors who were picked must be of the same age.

It was also said that if a Unit member dies, then they are not to be replaced. And if the leader of the Unit falls, then the Unit must disband. Those were crazy laws, but they were laws the people of Ar'Gurd would take very seriously.

***

Maxin

Prince Maxin's birthday was fast approaching, and it was to mark a tremendous occasion; there was to be a big celebration held within Carbaya. Fourteen was known as a coming of age for royal boys; it was the year from which they must train, control, command, and lead their own Unit.

The big day was just three days away, and Maxin was very excited. Even though he never saw himself as much of a fighter, he always knew he could be a great leader, and that is exactly what he wanted to be.

Although his birthday was still three days away, today would still be a big day for the young Prince, as on this day, he would be allowed to search every street, town, or local village for ten hand-picked boys of his own age to join his unit.

With Maxin finally being old enough to command his own Unit, it was said to make his birthday more of a celebratory event. As the last of the royal sons, this would be the final link in what was known as the Royal Units.

Maxin was soon to become the last royal member to be in command of his own Unit, thus making the link complete, and because of this, word was sent out across the land that Maxin would unveil the last link to the Royal Units on his birthday.

Wanting plenty of time to prepare for the big unveiling, Prince Maxin left the palace during the early hours and passed through a nearby village in his search for what he liked to call his 'Unity Subjects'.

People gathered that morning in the villages with their sons in the hope that the prince would pick them for his army.

From passing through the first village, Prince Maxin looked out amongst the gathered crowd and spoke aloud, "I am pleased to see such eager warriors. I see much talent and prospect within these villages, but choosing my first warrior is a big choice, and with that, I already know who I am to choose. I wanted to come down here this morning to tell you all to keep training hard, and once I have collected my first subject, I will be back to look for the remaining nine."

Following his speech, Maxin took to the stables to grab a horse before heading out on a mission outside of the castle to the house of his best friend, Igor.

Igor lived on the other side of a nearby lake. It was known as Hammerhead Lake, and as luck would have it, a hammer was Igor's favoured choice of weapon.

Two years ago, Igor killed an intruder in his house by shooting him with an arrow before taking the intruder's hammer and pummelling his skull to dust. Igor was big built for his age; he was the strongest child Maxin had ever known.

Since the attack, Igor had modified the hammer to suit his own personal build and strength, and because of his strength and size and also the fact they're best friends, this was exactly why he was Prince Maxin's first choice to join his Unit.

Along his travels and almost nearing Igor's house, Maxin began to slow down on his horse. Once he did, he began to hear a noise; it sounded like the breaking of sticks and the kicking of dirt.

He pulled his horse back and came to a complete halt. He took a quick look around, but there was nothing in sight.

Suddenly, he heard the sound again, coming from behind him. Quickly tossing his head around to see what it was, again he saw nothing there.

However, as Maxin turned his head back to face forward, he saw standing there right in front of him a vicious, vulture-like creature that preys on the innocent and the weak, a four-legged, grey-haired beast with a taste for blood, known only as a Zarnick.

Zarnick's rarely travelled with others; they were lone hunters but still lethal killing machines that any man would be smart to stay away from.

They were also very distinctive-looking creatures. Zarnick's all had two brown stripes on either side of their face, as well as a brown fluffy tip on their tails.

More importantly than that were their killing tools, the first being their two huge bone-crunching, flesh-devouring canine teeth, and the second being the two horns they had located on the top of their face, one big and one small, but both just as deadly as the other.

Maxin was frozen with fear as he looked into the Zarnick's yellow, snake-like eyes.

Not wanting to make any sudden movements, Maxin was very wary about reaching for his sword; he knew he could not just turn back and run away because Zarnicks were swift creatures, and they would catch him in no time at all.

As close as he was to Igor's house, he still couldn't shout for help as, again, he did not want to alarm the creature.

At that point, Maxin started to believe he was never going to make it back for his fourteenth birthday, or for any of his other birthdays at that. He was worried, puzzled, and not quite sure what he should do.

All of a sudden, the Zarnick bellowed out a massive screech before slowly moving toward him.

Without hesitation, Maxin pulled out his sword when the pace of the Zarnick began to quicken. "Igorrr!" he cried as he began to swing his sword in a panic, but unfortunately for him, he was swinging it every way but the right way.

And as the Zarnick's pace quickened once more, Maxin once again yelled, "Igorrr!" but still, there was no response.

Suddenly, the Zarnick charged straight toward Maxin's horse and stuck its horns right into the side of the horse's body.

Maxin fell straight from the horse upon impact. His sword falling loosely from his grasp as he hit the ground hard.

As his horse now lay dead, Maxin quickly picked himself up from the ground only to find the Zarnick pacing up and down, stalking him like easy prey.

He popped his head over the carcass of the fallen horse to see the Zarnick looking just about ready to feed. Maxin ducked back down behind his horse, and with his sword too far out of reach, he knew he had to act fast.

He looked left and right to see if there was anything he could possibly use to try and defend himself with when it suddenly hit him, the horse he took was from the city guard's stables, and the guards were forever leaving small weapons within the sacks that hung from their saddles.

As a brown leather sack dangled beside him, Maxin quickly pulled it open to have a look. He rummaged his hands around, pulling out maps, old bits of torn parchment and some stale bread, but not a single weapon. He desperately reached into the bag and dug as deep as he could, and that's when he felt something. He clutched onto a long cylindrical device, pulling it quickly from the sack. He couldn't believe his luck when he found himself holding onto a small stick of dynamite.

Maxin acted quickly and began to rub together two nearby rocks to try and create a spark to ignite the dynamite.

As he began to do this, he heard yet another deafening screech from the Zarnick. With panic rising, Maxin's pace quickened, and fortunately for him, he got the spark that he needed.

With the dynamite lit, Maxin stood up from behind the horse only to find that the Zarnick was no longer there. He let out a huge sigh of relief to see the that the beast had disappeared, but just as he was about to put out the dynamite, he heard another loud, ear-blowing screech coming from behind him; he quickly turned around only to see the creature now racing toward him.

At full pace, the Zarnick leapt into the air toward Maxin with his mouth wide open.

Acting upon pure instinct, Maxin, threw his stick of dynamite up in the air, as it was just about ready to explode.

The Zarnick caught the dynamite in his mouth on the way through.

Maxin instantly ducked out the way of the oncoming pounce and continued to run in the opposite direction. He ran as fast as he could without looking back until, suddenly, *boom*!

The explosion jolted Maxin, knocking him to the ground as he ran. Feeling dazed, he picked himself up and looked back around.

As the smoke and dust began to clear, Maxin saw the Zarnick was gone. All that remained were blood splatters, a handful of guts, and half a horn.

Maxin took a slow walk back to the area to reclaim his sword which he had previously dropped, but as he reached down and picked up his sword, he heard another screech from behind him. He quickly grasped his sword and spun around once more, only to find another Zarnick sprinting his way.

Maxin was speechless.

It was only the second time he ever saw two Zarnicks so close together, and this time, he did not have his father or brother to help him.

As the pace of the Zarnick quickened ever closer to Maxin, the young prince raised his sword with a strong firm double-handed grip around the hilt, ready to take on the approaching beast.

As the Zarnick grew closer with every step, the two were just about ready to collide. That was until a horse cut straight across their path, with the Zarnick taking a crunching blow to the head in the process, causing it to drop to the ground in a big heap.

The horse came to a sudden halt as its rider dismounted.

The rider came from around the back of the horse, only to be greeted warmly and with such delight. "Igor! Am I glad to see you!"

"I was just passing through," joked Igor as he walked across to the laid-out Zarnick who was still twitching from the strike to the head that it had just received. With his hammer still in his hand, Igor raised it high above his head, showing off his strength, before giving the hammer one more big swing and smashing it down onto the floored Zarnick's skull.

"There were two of them, Igor. I am lucky you were here. But did you not hear my cries?"

"I did not. There is nobody home. My mother is away visiting her family down south, and my father and brother are down helping with the construction of a new school in Wilton Village. I was down fishing by the lake."

"But I passed the lake; I did not see you there."

"There is more than one lake in this land, my friend. As a Prince of the Kingdom, you should know that," remarked Igor. "I was heading back this way when I heard a screech from beyond the hill. I rode over to take a look, and surprise, surprise, I see you having a catfight with a Zarnick! But now, come with me, my Prince, I will make a fresh brew and you can tell me why you and the Zarnick were having a falling out," Igor joked.

Igor climbed back up onto his horse, pulling Maxin up with him, but just as they began to ride off, out of nowhere again came a third Zarnick, barrelling into the horse and knocking both Maxin and Igor to the ground.

"Not again," huffed Maxin as he quickly picked himself up off the ground. He looked up to see the Zarnick standing just metres away from them both.

Fearlessly, Igor then took a step forward. "Let me handle this one!"

"That is fine by me, my friend," replied Maxin as he took a step back.

Igor dropped his hammer on the ground and moved another step toward the Zarnick. He then placed one hand behind his back.

The Zarnick growled back at Igor before running toward him with great pace.

As the Zarnick neared him, Igor pulled from behind his back a very small, but lethal, hammer, and with it, he cracked the Zarnick right in the face.

The creature fell to the ground and was dazed.

As the Zarnick began to rise, Maxin ran across with his sword and pierced the creature straight through its heart.

Igor walked over to pick up his hammer, but within seconds, the two boys heard several screeches coming from around them.

As Igor and Maxin looked around, they saw a total of six Zarnicks surrounding them.

"What is happening here? That's now nine of them in total," stated Maxin.

Maxin and Igor looked at one another before looking back at the group of surrounding beasts. They'd done this a few times before, eventually, one of the Zarnicks began to slowly move toward them.

Once again, Maxin held out his sword in front of him whilst Igor stood confidently, stroking his hammer.

Nerves of steel was one of the reasons why Igor was at the top of Maxin's list of recruits.

The Zarnicks began to surround and stalk the boys, growling and hissing intensely, and as Igor and Maxin faced five of them in front, Igor suddenly spotted the sixth hunched down and creeping around in an attempt to attack them from behind.

"Maxin, watch your back!!"

Maxin swung round quickly from Igor's warning, holding his sword awkwardly ahead of him, and with luck proving to be in favour of the young Prince on this day, he managed to slice the pouncing Zarnick's throat as he turned to face the beast.

After witnessing Maxin's fluke kill, Igor, with a proud grin on his face, turned back toward the other Zarnicks, only to see one racing in his direction.

but Igor was not afraid; with all his might, he ran ahead to meet it. The Zarnick pushed itself hard off the ground to attack, but the true warrior inside of Igor came rushing to the surface. He ducked and rolled underneath the body of the beast with great ease, in a way you wouldn't think possible for a boy of his stature.

The Zarnick landed firmly on the ground behind him, but as he turned back around to face Igor, he was met by a skull-crushing blow to the head.

Now four remained.

The largest of the beasts slowly stepped forward, one heavy paw after the other. This particular Zarnick looked as though it was the leader of the pack, which again was strange in the boys' eyes, as they were never known to travel in packs.

As the larger Zarnick steadily edged closer and closer toward Maxin and Igor, it attempted to intimidate them with every step it took. Bearing down each heavy paw into the dirt, leaving a trail of deep tracks behind it. When the Zarnick reached a few meters from the boys, it came to a complete halt. Its posture slowly changing with it. Its head lowered and its back arched. The boys were that close, they could see a small frown dawn on the face of the beast, along with a disturbingly deadly glare which caused the hairs on the back of their necks to raise.

Feeling as hough it lasted a lifetime, the chilling standoff soon came to and end when the large Zarnick screeched as loud as it could, the loudest screech Maxin or Igor had ever heard from one of those creatures.

With the deafening screech, Maxin and Igor had no choice but to place their hands over their ears, but that still wasn't enough to drown the sound out.

Suddenly, the screech was halted when an arrow came from out of nowhere and hit the Zarnick straight in between the eyes.

Igor and Maxin still with their hands over their ears, both looked around, but neither of them could see where the arrow had just flown from.

Almost instantly, the three remaining Zarnicks began making their way toward Igor and Maxin.

The pace of the two boys quickened as they split immediately, believing it was best to deal with each Zarnick individually. Igor split left as Maxin ran right. One Zarnick persued each of them.

Igor took care of the first Zarnick, making it look too easy. With one heavy swing of his hammer, he caught the oncoming creature in the side of the face. The Zarnick crashed heavily into the dirt twitching from the hit that it had just recieved. Igor moved over to it quickly, finishing the creature off in pure Igor fashion and putting it out of its misery with a second strike of the hammer, pummelling into its skull.

Just as this happened, the second Zarnick sprinted with more ferocity toward Maxin, the difference in abilities between the two boys was then shown as Maxin lost his footing slightly, shifting away from the Zarnick, causing him to fall to the ground, dropping his sword just to the side of him.

The Zarnick came to a sudden halt, stopping dead in his tracks. It edged closer to Maxin, eventually standing over him, growling menacingly as it showed off a mouth full of razor sharp teeth.

Igor, realising Maxin was in trouble, began to run to help him, but as he did, the forgotten third Zarnick came hurtling straight into him, knocking him straight to the ground.

The Zarnick standing above Maxin began to drool and growl at the mere sight of him, and soon enough, the Zarnick pounced at him, opening up it's claws as it leapt.

Maxin, in a state of bother, tried to keep himself composed as he scoured the floor around him, and luckily enough he was just able to reach his sword; he grabbed the handle tightly, and quickly held it out in front of him to skewer the Zarnick as it mounted him.

A few metres from Maxin and sprawled across the ground without his hammer, Igor was lying helplessly. The Zarnick pursuing him slowly walked over to his body and pressed its large paw down onto Igor's chest. The Zarnick snarled fiercely into the face of Igor, opening it's mouth wide, ready to feast on his flesh.

Igor could do nothing to stop it, and Maxin still lay under the body of a skewered Zarnick.

Igor knew he was about to meet his maker, the warm drool hitting his face and the stench of the Zarnick's horrible breath hitting his nose, and as a nervous sweat drizzled down the side of his face, he looked on in great solace as another arrow came from out of nowhere, hitting the Zarnick clean in the chest before a second arrow immediately followed catching it straight in the head.

CHAPTER THREE

SAVIOUR

Maxin

A cold breeze blew gently across Igor's face as he heard only the sounds of his own deep exhales.

Maxin shifted and scurried himself from under the Zarnick; he regained himself before taking a quick scour to look for any more wandering creatures.

"Igor, are you okay?" Maxin called over.

"I have had worse days, although I think I may have broken something," groaned Igor, clenching his arm around his abdomen. Much to Maxin's disbelief, Igor still carried a smile upon his face.

"What are you smiling about?"

"We took the fight to those balls of fluff; we showed them how real warriors fight. We won the battle, Maxin—our first battle!"

"Igor, as true as that is, you were almost eaten alive. The only reason you were not, is because of the arrows, from which we still do not know where they came from," stated Maxin.

His eyes scaled the distant lands that surrounded them, hills to the north, open green to the east and the west, and Igor's house toward the south. Although those arrows saved them, Maxin still had a panicked look about him.

What if the arrows were accidental misses? he thought, but his thoughts were soon scrambled by the ever-gloating voice of Igor and his own self credibility.

"Pfft, arrows. I had that Zarnick beat."

Maxin looked on as Igor stumbled back and forward on himself, just trying to keep himself from falling. Maxin chuckled to himself as he walked over to Igor and offered himself as an aid so he could stop himself from falling back down on the ground.

As expected from Maxin, Igor pushed his arm away and tried to stand up straight on his own whilst also trying to hide a slight groan of pain under his breath, attempting to try and keep his pride in front of the young prince.

Maxin chuckled to himself once more.

During the chuckling and Igor's struggle, another arrow appeared from nowhere, and this time landing directly into the ground, just inches from the feet of the two young boys.

There was a sudden sound of galloping in the distance, just one horse by the sound of it. Their eyes squinted as they gazed in the direction of the sound.

The sun began to near its peak above the hills, shining blazingly upon the faces of Maxin and Igor. They placed their hands over their eyebrows to try and block out the glare from the sun. They both looked on the best they could as they began to see the silhouette of a horse and what appeared to be a single rider gaining in on them at a fast speed.

At first glance, the rider looked small, younger than a full-grown man perhaps, with the outline of what appeared to be arrows hanging from his back.

"If you're here to kill us, then don't waste your time. Your face will be hanging off the end of my hammer before you can reach for another arrow!" warned Igor.

The two boys gripped their weapons tightly.

Eventually, the horse pulled up in front of Maxin; it had stopped directly in the way of the sun. With the light bouncing off the rider, it still made it difficult for the boys to identify who it was.

"Show yourself," ordered Igor.

The rider stepped off the horse, and the boys' gripped their weapons tighter. Once the rider had dismounted, he moved himself away from the rays of the sun and into clear view.

Maxin was stunned. He looked the rider dead in the eyes and saw none other than a young boy staring back at him.

"I am glad to have found you when and where I did, my Prince," spoke the rider.

"Who are you, stranger?"

"My name is Tamrin, my Lord. I rode this way regarding an audience with yourself, I had hoped for better circumstances, but then again, it did give me a chance to show you what skill I have."

"Skill? What are you talking about?"

"The skill I used to save your friend's life, of course, but there will be more time for that later. For now, you must get your friend home, he appears to be completely unconscious," claimed the rider, and much to Maxin's worry and slight amusement, he turned to his side to see Igor now lying flat out on the ground.

"It would be my great honour to escort you there, my Prince."

Maxin looked suspiciously across at Tamrin before looking down at the unconscious body of Igor.

"So be it, but once we get there, you are to tell me everything," stated Maxin.

After spending the next few minutes trying to get Igor's overweight frame onto the back of the Tamrin's horse, the boys then made their way south toward Igor's home, and with his home just metres beyond a small, bridged reservoir, it did not take them very long to get there. They burrowed inside and laid Igor on his bed and waited patiently for him to wake.

As they waited for Igor to regain consciousness, Maxin found it the perfect time to question Tamrin further.

Maxin walked over to a little basin in the corner of the room and filled up two small cups of water, which he then handed one over to Tamrin who sat on the end of an empty made-up bed.

Maxin sat himself upon a nearby stool. He looked into the big blue eyes of the young boy; there was not a scratch on him. He must have been around the same age with a clean face, rough blonde hair, and a slightly charming smile. He laid what looked like a very well looked after recurve bow atop of the bed.

Tamrin glared into an empty fireplace, the breeze from the cracks in the walls swept the ash across the oak floor between the feet of Maxin.

"You came to seek an audience with me, you wanted me to see your skills? Am I right in assuming this is about my royal Unit?"

Tamrin continued to stare into the darkened fireplace whilst responding. "My father, he spoke highly of the king and his two sons, Prince Belthran and the young Prince Maxin. He said to me that Carbaya was the strongest it has ever been, strong it remains, and even stronger it will become. Prince Belthran a born fighter, brute strength and courage, born and bred to rule with an iron fist and to be loved by many with a great Unit of men behind him. Prince Maxin, the younger, but smarter of the two, had all the traits of a true leader, and all he needs is the fighting power behind him.

"That's where I come in. I'm from the small village of Malba, just across the hill there. We don't have many fighters where I'm from, but we're a village of strong-hearted folk. We're brought up to believe that if you want to achieve something, then you need to be the best in that craft, and from the moment I first held a bow, I just knew that was my craft. I have worked so hard to become the best I could be. My father and I believe there is no better time, nor no better way, to excel with the skills I have gained than to fight behind a prince who is determined to be the best he can be in *his* craft. I want to fight for you, my Prince." Tamrin took his gaze away from the fireplace as he keenly looked Maxin square in the eye.

Before Maxin could say anything, another voice was heard coming from across the other side of the room, "How did you know where the prince was?"

"Igor, you're awake," said a relieved Maxin.

"Thank you for stating the obvious, Maxin," replied Igor as he pulled himself up slightly to rest his back against the pillows. Then, diverting his gaze back toward Tamrin, he said, "I began to wake when I heard *this* guy telling you his life story, but he just managed to miss out one important detail." He turned to face Tamrin. "How did you know where to find the prince?"

It was a question that escaped Maxin's mind, but it intrigued him just as much.

Feeling like he was on trial, Tamrin remained seated and very calmly stated his case. "It was pure luck. The open plains are not a route I like to travel alone, as you witnessed today; it brings nothing but danger, and it sets you open to become prey to the entire land around you. I was taking the trail of Reydoor across the hilltops to Carbaya when I heard the screeching of several Zarnicks and hearing several of them in close proximity to each other, I knew something wasn't right. I went to check it out, and by a stroke of luck I came across the two of you."

He then turned his attention back in the direction of Igor. "Does that answer your question?" he replied in a sarcastic tone.

Despite the pain he was feeling in his ribs, Igor sat himself forward as he proceeded to glare at Tamrin.

Maxin stood from his stool and took a small sip from his cup of water before placing it back on the table and walking across the room to Igor's bedside. He looked into the eyes of his best friend before smiling and placing his hand upon his shoulder, diverting his attention away from Tamrin.

"Igor, there is one reason and one reason alone that I came over here today to see you, and I think you know why that is. We've spoken of this day many times throughout the years, and now it is finally upon us. You're the strongest and bravest boy of my age I know. You're also my best friend, and I trust nobody in this world more than you, which is why I would like for you to be the first warrior in my Unit."

Igor smiled back at Maxin; he held his ribs even tighter as he pulled himself up from his bed and onto his feet. This time, he then placed his hand on Maxin's shoulder and replied, "There is only one answer I could ever give you; you are my brother and my friend. I would not want to fight alongside anybody else. Of course, I accept."

With a gaping smile on his face, Maxin swiftly turned his attention back over to Tamrin, who was looking on patiently. "Your skills have proved somewhat useful; you saved our lives with the way you handled yourself, and with great aim and accuracy. Skills like yours should not go unnoticed, Tamrin, and I believe that on my side you can become the greatest you can be, I'd be honoured if you were to join my Unit."

Tamrin let out a huge sigh of relief, as he heard the news he'd travelled all this way for.

"It's the reason I am here, my Prince, it's going to be my honour to serve and protect you from this point onward."

Upon selecting the first two warriors for his personal ten-man Unit, Maxin thought it would be in both their best interests if Igor and Tamrin had some extra bonding time to create a close Unity. Despite Igor's reluctance following the recent Zarnick attacks, Maxin ordered the two of them to stay where they were whilst he returned to Carbaya in search of more recruits.

He bid his momentary farewells to Tamrin and Igor as he borrowed Tamrin's horse and headed straight back for the city in haste.

After a much easier journey back to the city, Maxin was surprised to realise his brother Belthran was looking for him as he was met at the gate by his cousin, Harnik.

Looking beyond Harnik, he saw slightly panicked parents huddling their children together whilst city patrols ran from alleyway to alleyway.

"Cousin, where have you been? Belthran is looking for you! We have a thief and a killer on the loose."

"We do? Questioned Maxin. Do you know where my brother is?"

"I last saw him down by the barracks but an hour ago, you must go quickly, Maxin, and be careful."

Maxin dismounted Tamrin's horse and hitched it to a nearby post as he then ran off toward the barracks in search of Belthran.

As Maxin sprinted through the cobbled backstreets between the Thirsty Wench Pub and the beaten-down cottage on the corner of Poilerton Lane, he was suddenly dragged into an alleyway by a hooded figure as he ran past.

"Get your hands off me!"

"Please, I mean you no harm."

Maxin pushed the figure back with force before pulling out his sword from his holster and pointing it in the figure's direction, "Who are you?" questioned Maxin. "And what is it you want from me?"

"My name is Grendel, my Prince."

The name sounded highly familiar to Maxin, and a very intrigued look was bestowed upon the face of the young prince as he looked back at the hooded figure. Maxin tilted his head slightly to try and see underneath the hood, but he had no luck. "Grendel? I have heard that name somewhere before, but I can't for the life of me remember where."

Grendel stood the same height as Maxin, bloodshot eyes looking back at him.

Without taking his eyes off the prince for a second, Grendel let out a large exhale before pulling back his hood, only to reveal a hideous and deformed face. "Do you know of me now?" asked Grendel.

Maxin's eyes opened wide, and his jaw dropped; he'd never seen anything like it in all his life.

"I heard stories, whispers of your existence, sometimes I believed them to be true, and sometimes I believed them to be lies."

Grendel quickly pulled the hood back over his head in embarrassment. "As long as I can remember, anyone and everyone has made fun of my appearance, and no matter what I did to try and change it, I never could. My father, he's always working, and as for my mother, she died on the day of my birth. Because of my appearance, they believed my father's genes to be tainted and permitted him to have no more children with anyone else. But after all of that, I have still learnt to care, adapt, and grow for myself. I have stuck to spending my time in these dark halls they call alleyways, to hide my shame and disgust from the land."

He continued, "I have become stealthier than I could ever have imagined, killing small animals that scurry through the streets, just so I could eat whilst my father is at work. People go to my home just looking to see if the freak show is there, and that's why I don't stay there, and my father understands this. I have adapted to this style, and when I heard that Prince Maxin was looking for troops, I knew this was the perfect time to come forward and present myself and fight alongside the prince to earn the respect I have never earned before."

"You want to fight for me?" replied Maxin as he stood, shocked. "But how am I to know your skills are legitimate. How am I to know if you are a real cut above the rest?" he added.

Grendel glared at Maxin through the small gap in his worn-out hood and replied, "I can show you."

Maxin lowered his sword whilst seemingly confused by Grendel's response. Did he want to kill something or someone just to prove his worth?

Maxin's attention was diverted for a few moments when a handful of city guards hurried quickly past the alleyway. He looked back at Grendel and whispered assertively back to him, "Show me, how?"

"Perhaps, I could follow you, until an opportunity arises where I could show you my skill and my worth."

Maxin was unsure, he wanted to give Grendel a chance as he felt bad for him; but how long would he have to wait for a good opportunity to present itself? He didn't have much time left until his birthday and needed to find more fighters soon.

He looked down at the grimy ground for a few seconds, contemplating his response; his hesitance left Grendel with a level of uncertainty but a willingness to prove himself.

Grendel left himself on edge, waiting for Maxin to speak.

Eventually, Maxin raised his head and began to nod. "Very well, but I can only give you until the end of the day. If an opportunity for you to present your skill doesn't occur, then I'll have to say no; there're many others wanting this opportunity. With that being said, I need to find my brother. I hear there is a thieving murderer in the city, so we must move on."

"Right away, my Prince; and thank you for the opportunity, and if you don't mind, I would much rather follow you in the shadows, stick to the dark alleyways until I have proven my worth. I'd prefer it if I kept myself hidden, but I'll be behind you the whole time."

Maxin placed his sword back within his holster. Without uttering another word, he gave a nod toward Grendel and ran from the alleyway back in the direction of the barracks in search of Belthran.

***

Carbaya was panicked, some streets were filled with huddled villagers and other streets emptied with no sight nor sound of anyone.

"Who's caused all of this?" Maxin muttered to himself.

As he turned on to the street left of the blacksmiths, owned by Serdrick Dawne, the best blacksmith in all the kingdom, he was met by a man pushing his young son into him, muttering words so quickly that Maxin couldn't understand.

"I'm sorry, I cannot stop," claimed Maxin as he wormed around the man and his son. After a slight twist and turn, he then found himself within a large cluster of worried and freaked villagers, along with their kids, not knowing whether to run and hide or present their children to the prince.

Bells of the city rang loud and true as the group surged Maxin up against the wall of the Blacksmith's.

"Please, you must let me continue. I will come back, I promise."

The villagers heard nothing but the mumbles and advancements of their own voices, so caught up in the moment of everything. A couple of the parents grabbed onto the leather straps of Maxin's light-mail chestguard and began to tug and pull; more children were shoved in his direction as he tried to avoid the spit of the parents while they shouted and raved uncontrollably.

Another hand came from the crowd and grabbed Maxin by his pleated collar.

Maxin tried to pull away and push all the hands off of him until he was eventually dragged from the crowd by his collar and into an alleyway to the side of him. "Grendel!"

"Quick, my Prince, before they follow. I know a shortcut."

After escaping the panicked crowds with haste through the alleyways, Maxin eventually made it to the barracks, but

Belthran was nowhere to be seen. The streets were emptied; coins, bread, and broken bottles were scattered throughout the streets. He took a few minutes to catch his breath when, out of the corner of his eye, he suddenly saw one of Belthran's Unit warriors, Vinagey, running down a small street to his right, so Maxin decided to follow.

Pursuing Vinagey down the dark and secluded cobbled street, he eventually found himself outside one of the city's most popular taverns, The Barrell Inn. Not only that, but he finally saw his brother, Belthran, standing outside the tavern talking loudly to several villagers who had gathered round him.

"So if any of you see him, claim him! Dead or alive."

"Brother, what is going on here? Harnik tells me there is a criminal running loose, is that true?" questioned Maxin as he rambled up behind Belthran.

Belthran turned around with a look of joy upon his face. "Maxin, am I glad you're here! What you've heard is true; there is a killer on the loose, and the story behind it all is just as shocking," stated Belthran.

He then went on to explain what had happened. "Early on this morning, there was a call of a fire down on Millbury farms. My men and I were assigned to check it out, but when we got there, we just saw a woman, lying unconscious in the dirt, and the farm was already a pile of ash and wood on the floor. When the woman came around, she just cried; she broke down and told us that there was a one-year-old baby girl inside.

"The woman claimed the fire was no accident; she spoke of how she was outside picking some vegetables for her evening supper when she suddenly heard a crash coming from inside her home, along with the sound of her baby crying. As she went to enter the home, she saw a hooded male leap through the window, knocking her to the ground on his way past. She must have knocked her head on the way down because the next thing she knew she was being woken up by us.

"I have sent messengers to notify the child's father; it's news no man would like to hear. Along with this, my men and I had a sighting of the same man described, as we caught him attempting to break into another home. We shot at him with arrows, but he seemed to duck, dodge, and dive out the way of every one of them; he was very skilled. We continued to fire more arrows as he just continued to jump and bounce off of building walls before eventually throwing himself into a nearby alleyway. We chased after him, but he was gone. I have spoken to Father about the incident, and he has urged me to hand out posters of the figure to help try and catch him, but without seeing his face, we don't have a lot to go off."

Maxin just stood there, shocked, as in some way Belthran seemed to be describing the very boy who was trying to join his Unit. Grendel lived within the alleyways and claimed to be very stealthy and skilled. Maxin's suspicions grew until Belthran handed over to him a poster of the killer he had seen.

"This is him, Brother. He is out there somewhere—the arsonist, the thief, the child murderer! You must be careful."

Maxin was delighted to see the picture was not of Grendel but of another hooded figure.

"I will, Belthran. If I see this man, with the spirits as my witness, I will bring him down!"

"Good, Brother. Now, come with me as I have other matters to discuss with you."

So as Belthran's men continued to spread the word and hand out posters of the killer, Belthran took a short walk with Maxin to discuss some more business.

"Are you still looking for Unit warriors, Brother?"

"I am, I have two and a third one in line."

"One of them is Igor, no doubt? Either way, I may have found you a fourth, the younger brother of one of my own troops. He claims to be very skilled; his name is Scarlep, and he may be worth some of your attention."

"I will look into it, Brother, thank you. But for now, I am still considering my third warrior, and I could maybe use your help on how to resolve it, his name is Grendel, and he—"

But before Maxin could continue, the sounds of gut curdling screams behind him drew his and Belthran's attention.

"Watch out!"

"Behind you, my Lords!"

Upon hearing these screams, both Maxin and Belthran quickly turned around, but without even a moment to blink, Maxin found himself on the end of a vicious punch, knocking him straight to the ground.

Belthran looked up at the attacker only to see it was the hooded villain they were so desperate to find.

Following the punch, the villain ran straight past both princes and was once again heading for an alleyway.

Without hesitation, Belthran equipped his bow to take a shot at the runner, not wanting him to escape yet again.

He steadily took his aim and focused down the barrel of the arrow before taking his shot at the runner, who was fast approaching the alleyway.

The arrow flew from the bow and headed straight for the runner. But just as before, Belthran looked on as the runner bounced off of a wall and jumped over the arrow as it was just about to connect.

Belthran rapidly equipped yet another arrow before once again taking his aim and taking his shot. He fired the arrow quickly before the figure could escape, but much to Belthran's dismay, he looked on in frustration as he saw the runner duck into a nearby alleyway whilst his arrow stuck straight into an adjacent wall.

Maxin then slowly made his way back to his feet, holding his bloody nose from the punch he had just received.

"Are you okay, Brother?" asked Belthran.

Maxin did not say a word; he just nodded as he frustratedly stared toward the alleyway.

But that would not be the last they would see of the villain. As their eyes focused on the alleyway, they began to see a figure slowly backing out of it; it appeared to be the hooded thief.

Belthran quickly drew another arrow and aimed it toward him. "Stop there! Do not move another step!" he yelled.

The villain turned slowly to face them, appearing to be clutching his stomach and looking to be seriously hurt. Belthran, Maxin and other onlookers were even more surprised when they began to see blood seeping through his fingers as he applied pressure to his abdomen. Blood spilling into every fibre of his shirt around his hands. Looking as though he'd just been stabbed.

The villain suddenly dropped down to his knees before collapsing to the ground, face-first into the dirt; he was dead.

Maxin, Belthran, and the rest of the surrounding villagers and warriors looked on, confused. Suddenly, they began to see another hooded figure walk out from beyond the shadows of the alleyway, Belthran's aim still fixated on the spot.

The figure began to remove his hood slowly, revealing a face that caused gasps all around. But not for Prince Maxin.

Maxin, with a smile on his face, pulled his hands away from his bloody nose and turned to Belthran, saying, "Brother, this is Grendel."

Belthran and the other surrounding people looked on in awe at this hideous thing, but ever so slowly without realising, Belthran began to relax his arms.

Still in shock with his mouth and eyes wide open, he relaxed his arm too much, allowing the arrow to release from the bow. Suddenly, the arrow fired toward Grendel, and before anyone realised what had happened, the arrow flew straight through the top of Grendel's leg.

Grendel screamed at the top of his lungs as he dropped down to one knee.

"Grendel! Belthran, what have you done?"

Maxin and Belthran then sprint over to Grendel in a panic.

"I-I-I didn't mean to," stuttered Belthran as Grendel knelt in agony in front of him. Belthran then turned to two of his own men, Saxon and Belarear, and ordered them to take Grendel to the infirmary at once.

Belarear rushed over to Grendel and picked him up in his arms before heading off to the infirmary.

"Why did you do that?" questioned Maxin.

"I did not mean to, Brother. He caught me by surprise, and I accidentally released my arrow, I am so sorry. But you must go with him at once; be sure he gets the best care. I will deal with this body, and I will meet you there."

After taking a big, deep breath, Maxin then ran in the other direction toward the infirmary to help Grendel.

***

Belthran

Meanwhile, Belthran slowly walked over to the body of the villain, and soon enough, the villagers began to gather round.

Belthran knelt down in front of the body, turning him over and removing his hood, only to reveal what appeared to be a man, who couldn't have been any more than thirty.

He then called across to one of his most trusted troops, Danal.

Danal was somewhat of a genius, he knew everything there was to know about anyone whilst still being able to fight amongst the best of them.

"Danal, over here."

As Danal made his way over, Belthran shouted back across to his remaining troops with an order. "Vinagey, Kroyl, Angelio, Rekken, Anamaforth, Panagor, Maikin; get these villagers away from here at once. This is not a display."

Following orders, the troops then rounded up the gathering villagers before escorting them away from the scene.

Danal duly made his way across to Belthran and took a knee beside him.

"I want you to take a look, Danal. Do you know who he is? Or at the very least where he has come from?"

Danal began searching the body for clues of the villain's identity.

After searching for several minutes, he was running short on clues, that was until he decided to pull up the villain's sleeves and take a look at his arms, which is where he finally found one.

As he pulled up the sleeves, he instantly noticed a tattoo on the back of the right wrist. The tattoo was a small symbol that depicted a skull with an arrow pierced through the side of it and a sword through the top.

A look of shock came upon Danal's face.

"My Prince, you may want to take a look at this!"

"What is it, Danal? What have you found?"

Danal directed Belthran's attention toward the tattoo and explained to him what it meant. "This mark right here, this symbol, it is crafted onto those select few who choose nothing more in life than to steal, murder, and forever try to claim this land."

Suddenly, Belthran got the same stunned look on his face as he looked up at Danal. "You do not mean..."

"Yes, my Lord, this is the mark of a Pirate. They are back."

"It cannot be! Pirates never travel alone."

"This is what I fear, my Lord, he is not the only one in the city."

Belthran and Danal both picked themselves up off the ground and stared intently at one another.

"We must inform my father at once; the people of this city are in danger!"

"Right away. But first, my Prince, there is something else quite worrying you should know, too."

"What is it, Danal?" asked a worried but intrigued Belthran.

Danal opened his mouth to reveal this other piece of information, when out of nowhere, Belthran found himself blinded with blood in his eyes as another arrow came from out of nowhere and pierced straight through Danal's skull.

Everything from this point moved in slow motion through Belthran's eyes. With the blood of Danal splattered across his face, he watched on as his body crumbled to the ground like a sack of rocks.

After a very short while, reality returned to him, and he began to see panicked villagers running and screaming, not knowing what to do. He aimed his focus on the safety of the city and its people and rushed off to rally his troops, who were still nearby.

The local safety point for the villagers in an event like this would be the palace, but as they were too far away and were running out of time, Belthran ordered his troops to rally together and gather as many villagers as they could and move them into the barracks, which was only a few blocks away.

Including himself, there were eight men left within this section of the city to try and save as many villagers as they could as well as hold off the pirates from going any farther.

In a short amount of time, amongst managing to avoid several flying arrows, Belthran gathered six villagers together; three men, two women, and a child.

Belthran, using the skill he was known well for, desperately battled his way back to the barracks, where he found two of his troops, Vinagey and Kroyl, were already there.

Vinagey had managed to round up five men and two women, whilst Kroyl had gathered four women, three men, and two children.

Belthran and the villagers quickly ran into the barracks and joined the others, slamming the door closed behind them.

He had ordered the villagers to find somewhere safe to hide as he ran across to the wall and grabbed two bows and two quivers that were hanging up, throwing one to Vinagey and the other to Kroyl.

"We must do what we can to keep this city safe. We have done our best for these villagers, and now we must do more; we need to secure this building."

Belthran, along with Vinagey and Kroyl, proceeded back outside, equipped with their bows, to try and protect the villagers and fend off the Pirates for as long as they could.

***

After a few minutes had passed, Belthran suddenly spotted two more of his men making their way to the barracks in great haste. He ordered his men to hold fire as Angelio and Rekken approached. The two seemed to be working closely together as they each escorted three men and two women toward safety.

Belthran, Vinagey, and Kroyl then provided deep cover to allow them to pass through safely and unharmed.

"Angelio, Rekken. It is good to see you both and well done on the rescue, but there is still more work to be done. Get the villagers inside; grab yourselves a bow and then join us back out here."

Once Angelio and Rekken had led the villagers into the barracks, they collected their bows and headed back out the front, once again locking the barrack doors behind them.

Within a few seconds, another of Belthran's troops was seen running in the distance, carrying two children and being followed by two women and one man; it was Anamaforth, the scout of Belthran's Unit.

Once again under the protection from his fellow troops, Anamaforth was able to pass safely through the oncoming fire, and just like the others, he locked the villagers away in the barracks, grabbed a bow, and joined them out the front.

"My Prince, along with my gathering of villagers, I did a little scouting and noticed that the pirates were using the rooftops as high ground, something they have not done before. They now know they cannot defeat us on the ground, so they are attacking us from above. I saw at least thirty pirates, maybe more. There was also many innocent people dying out there, and I just couldn't reach them all."

"This is not good. Thank you for the report, Anamaforth, you could not have done any more. But where are the rest of the city guards? We seem to be alone out here."

Suddenly, in the distance, Belthran began to see his two remaining troops running for their lives, firstly there was Panagor followed by two children, four women, and four men, and following closely behind him was Maikin, who was in the company of four children, one man, and two women.

Again, under the protection from the rest of the Unit, Panagor was the first to make it back safely. Still following closely behind was Maikin, who was so close to making it; that was until a child who was running behind him tripped and fell.

Maikin looked back at the fallen child who lay on the floor screaming; he shouted at the villagers to keep heading for the barracks.

The Unit looked on in fear as Maikin then ran back in the other direction in an attempt to retrieve the child.

Once he made it to the child, he turned around to see the other villagers had safely made it back to the barracks.

With a smile and a sigh of relief, Maikin picked up the boy and told him everything was going to be okay, as he then continued to run back toward the barracks.

As he was running back, Maikin was struck in the calf from an oncoming arrow; immediately forcing him to drop down to one knee with a painful groan, and with the child still in hand, he heroically got back onto his feet and continued his objective, limping toward the barracks, much to the horror and dismay of his fellow troops who continued to provide support the best they could.

Belthran rose to his feet in an attempt to run and aid Maikin in his mission, but before Belthran could run anywhere, he was pulled back by Anamaforth.

"You will die out there, my Prince!"

"I cannot leave him! It only takes one more arrow."

"Please, my Prince, if that arrow hits Maikin, then it can just as easily hit you, and this kingdom needs its prince!"

Belthran said nothing more as he knew Anamaforth was right. He pulled back, equipped another arrow, and looked on in apprehension as he awaited Maikin's safe arrival.

It wasn't long until Belthran's look of worry turned to further dismay, as he devastatingly witnessed Maikin being struck with another arrow, this time piercing him straight through the middle of his back and forcing him to drop to one knee once again. As the child continued to scream in his arms, so to did his fellow unit members. Their cries echoed throughout the entire city, having no choice but to look on at the downfall of their fallen brethren.

Maikin failed to give up. With every ounce of strength he had left, he made his way back to his feet, but the second he did, he was soon taken down once again to both knees when a third arrow pierced his back, almost hitting him in the same spot.

Belthran's lips trembled as he cried out Maikin's name, looking on at his friend in great shock.

Maikin released the child and moved his face close to the boy's ear. Struggling with his remaining breath, he spoke the words, "Run, child," before gently pushing the child toward the barracks with whatever strength he had left.

As the child began to run, the others looked on in a final climax of sadness as a fourth arrow finally struck, this time going straight though Maikin's skull.

Belthran stood defeated as he looked on and saw the body of Maikin lying dead on the ground, but this view was shortly interrupted, as the small child Maikin had let go of had run straight into the line of Belthran's vision, taking him from his almost trance-like state.

Kroyl grabbed the young child as he made it to the safety of the barracks before then locking him inside with the other rescued villagers.

Anger and frustration clouded Belthran's mind, filling him with a rage he'd never quite felt before. He turned and looked at his men. "How many men did we rescue? Not the children, not the women, just the men?"

"Twenty-three, my Prince," answered Kroyl, reluctantly.

Belthran looked at them with an intense urge in his eye. By now, the arrows had stopped firing, giving Belthran plenty of time to plan his move.

"And seven of us make thirty, which means I want one of you to head back inside the barracks and arm every man with a sword. We take this fight straight to them!"

There was a large, "Yes, my Lord!" from the troops as Rekken volunteered and re-entered the barracks to arm every man with a sword. There were those who were willing and there were those who weren't, but after a few minutes, all twenty-three men were equipped with a weapon.

They all proceeded to make their way back out of the barracks to regroup with Belthran and the others.

Looking across the cobbled turf, the legs of the men began to tremble, and their palms began to sweat.

Belthran said nothing; he stood firm, still staring blankly at the body of his fallen friend.

He pulled his sword from his holster and gripped it tightly down his side as he began to speak aloud to all who stood behind him, still keeping his back to them.

"We didn't know this was coming. I'm as shocked as all of you by what has happened here today, but I am not surprised as to how it has turned out. These pirates have done what pirates do best; they sneak, they hunt, they surprise, and they kill, but they chose a bad day to attack, and they chose the wrong people to kill. Today, we do what our ancestors have done for many years, we beat them! But this time, we will not drive them out and force them to retreat to come back another day. After today, these pirates will sneak no more; they will hunt no more; they will surprise no more. No, after today, they will live *no more*!"

Belthran then gripped his sword tighter and raised it up in front of him before fearlessly running into the distance toward the pirates.

As the remaining troops and men of the village followed closely behind him with swords in hands, Anamaforth looked ahead, noticing the Pirates moving away from the rooftops.

They are going for a stealth attack, he thought as he continued to run behind the prince.

Anamaforth called over to Belthran for him to stop, but his mind was focused, and just continued on running, and everyone continued to follow.

The group suddenly found themselves in an empty street outside the Barrel Inn, right where it had all begun. The blood that spilled from the running Pirate and Grendel stained the cobbled streets, as did the body of Danal, enticing Belthran's rage further when he caught site of it once more.

The streets were empty and deathly quiet.

"Where is everybody; the pirates, the villagers, the guards?"

"I tried to warn you back there, my Prince, the pirates no longer sit amongst the rooftops, they—"

But before Anamaforth could finish, the pirates came flooding from all different streets and alleyways that surrounded them.

Belthran raised his sword once more. "Stand strong! Fight today to live tomorrow!" he screamed, shouting the quote of his ancestors as he ran toward the oncoming pirates.

Within quick succession, Belthran took down three of the pirates racing for him, once again showing his troops and the villagers his infamous skill in battle. He gave them all hope; he gave them something worth fighting for—a true leader.

Bethran's unit and the men of the village stood strong, holding their own well. The Pirates were dropping like flies and a victory seemed almost imminent. That was until, a second wave of Pirates joined the fight, storming in from the back alleys.

"There are more? Where did they come from?" shouted Kroyl as he struck down a pirate.

As villagers began to suffer injuries; it looked as though the pirates were beginning to turn the tables.

Belthran was fighting a losing battle as more villagers then fell to the sword.

**

Several more minutes had passed, and they were trying to remain strong, although by now, their legs were beginning to tire, and their breath was running short.

Belthran quickly struck down another Pirate who approached him. He turned quickly when he heard a struggle taking place behind him, only to be bumped to the ground by a nearby villager who was locked in a duel.

As Belthran tried to gather himself from the knock, he turned himself over, onto his back. He lifted his head from the ground, only to see two Pirates, walking intently toward him. He patted the floor around him to grab his sword but couldn't find it. His eyes grew in fear as the two Pirates now stood above him, smirking and sniggering to one another. One Pirate raised his sword to strike Belthran, and all the Prince could do was look on as a flurry of blood sprayed across his face.

Belthran didn't feel anything, not even a scratch, but knew he was still alive as he could still hear the clanging of steel above him. He began to slowly reopen his eyes. Suddenly he saw the face of someone he knew all too well; his cousin Harnik mounted on horseback, grinning back at him.

Harnik leant over his horse and held out his hand to Belthran. "Come on, Cousin, lying down there with your eyes closed, anyone would think you were napping."

As Belthran smiled back, he grabbed his sword that lay in the dirt next to him before giving his hand to Harnik.

Within a matter of minutes, along with help from Harnik and his troops, the pirates had fallen, quite admirably some might say, for they had not been this close to a victory in a long time.

CHAPTER FOUR

A JUSTIFICATION OF PEACE AND WAR

Maxin

Back within the infirmary and other parts of the palace, villagers and guards alike were unaware of anything that was happening out in the streets. All they knew was what Maxin had informed them about, the one man who had attacked.

"The doctor said you're going to be okay to walk in a few days, Grendel. I am sorry for all of this, and I'm sure Belthran is, too," apologised Maxin as he remained seated alongside Grendel's bed with Saxon and Belarear still accompanying them.

"How are you feeling?" he added, curiously.

Grendel looked down; he looked defeated and exhausted.

"I am feeling like this was no accident. I believe it when you say *Belthran* didn't mean to strike me. The spirits guided that arrow toward me, they took my looks, they took away my mother, and they make everyone look at me in disgust. It was them that forced Belthran to react to me the way he did; it was down to them that he released his arrow, and it was down to them that it hit me. Now, I don't know why they have targeted me since birth, but they have; they want me to suffer through life, they want everyone to hate me."

Maxin appeared shocked by Grendel's response. He stood up from his chair and placed his hand on his shoulder.

Grendel raised his head and looked back at him with a troubled look in his eyes.

"You cannot continue to feel this way, Grendel. It was unfortunate for you to have been born the way you were, but it also makes you individual. It's unfortunate that you lost your mother so young, but it's also made you strong. It's unfortunate that you've hidden yourself away from people for fear of them beating you, but this has also made you skilled. What I saw from you today wasn't someone who had been given a miserable life from spiteful spirits; I saw someone who has acquired skills, strength, and capability. And I saw someone who makes me want to hold out my hand to him and ask, will you become the third soldier of my Unit?"

That troubled look soon became a look of disbelief; nobody had ever been so nice to Grendel, and he wasn't expecting the prince to offer him a place in his Unit.

Grendel's disappointing frown became what looked very much like a smile on his face and he, once again, had a gleam in his eye.

"Me? You want me in your Unit? I cannot believe this, thank you so much, my Prince! I cannot wait to tell my father; he is going to be thrilled! There is nothing now that the spirits can do to me that will ruin this moment. Thank you, thank you, and thank you again!"

"Well done, lad," added Saxon from above him.

Maxin had a huge smile on his face at how happy he has made Grendel for possibly the first time in his life, his hand remained firmly on his shoulder.

"Well, I'm glad to have you on my side, Grendel; you are going to make a tremendous asset to the team. You mentioned your father. Tell me, where is he?"

"He will be out in the village somewhere, my Prince, it's hard to say where, he is the local messenger, you see."

The pleasantries were soon cut short when the doors to the infirmary flew open, almost knocking a doctor to the floor.

King Armish walked in assertively, marching over towards Grendel's bedside.

"Maxin, I heard word you were in here, and who is this?" as he looked over Maxin's shoulder toward Grendel.

"This is Grendel, Father. Belthran accidentally struck him with an arrow after Grendel killed the villain that Belthran was after, and he is also the newest member of my Unit."

"Very well, and very well done to you, too, boy; it is a great honour to be chosen."

King Armish squinted as he looked at Grendel. "What is wrong with his face?" he whispered gently into Maxin's ear.

He then switched his attention to Saxon and Belarear, who were still positioned next to him.

"And may I ask what you two are doing here?"

"We were ordered to escort Prince Maxin and young master Grendel here to the infirmary, my Liege," explained Belarear.

"Were you asked to nanny them?"

"No, my Liege."

"Then, get out of here and go and find something useful to do," ordered the king, and without hesitation, Saxon and Belarear scarpered.

They hurried toward the exit, but as they neared it, the doors flew open again, and this time, standing behind them was Prince Belthran, Prince Harnik, and their Units.

"Prince Belthran, myself, and Saxon were just comi—"

"Shut up, Belarear!" exclaimed Belthran as he stormed past Saxon and Belarear and toward his father.

"You! You! Are you not just a sight for sore eyes, Father? Tell me, where is Uncle Clearus and his troops? Where is Sir Payner and *his* troops? And where in this land is your army?"

Both Armish and Maxin looked on at Belthran, stunned by his actions.

"Son, what is going on here?"

There was a slight pause.

"Brother, is everything okay?"

Belthran looked up at his father with anger in his eyes, a small lump in his throat, and no fear, he replied to him with a deep passion in his lungs.

"Is everything okay? Is everything okay?" he cried, incredulously. "Answer me this, Father, why do all these troops standing behind me not only have blood seeping from their skin but have blood stains on their swords and armour, also? Answer me this, Father, how is it that without Harnik's help, you almost lost a son?"

The lump left his throat and his voice rose. "And answer me this, Father, how is it that two of my troops and nearly a quarter of the villagers in the south of the city are dead?"

The king opened his eyes wide, shocked by what he had just heard.

Other patients in the infirmary soon raised themselves from their beds the best they could and fixated on Belthran, whilst the doctors also listened in discretely.

"Belthran, I demand you tell me what is going on, at once!"

Still with a fiery glow in his eyes, Belthran replied with everyone still looking on intently.

"I will tell you, shall I, *King*? Earlier on, I took a walk past the throne room, and I saw you talking with an odd-looking fellow, all moustache and greasy hair; who was he? He was your royal decorator! And what was he assisting you with exactly? Was it about building a new throne for the throne room? Yeah, that's right, Father, I overheard you talking."

"So I was building a new throne. Please, explain to me how this is at all relevant to what has happened."

"Shall I tell you why? Because while you were getting your royal butt acquainted with the new royal highchair, the people you swore your life to protect were getting massacred, butchered like animals! And why were they getting butchered like animals, you ask? Because the man on the poster I was trying to catch, the man on the poster whom Grendel here killed, was a pirate."

The whole room drew silent. The doctors turned their heads, and the patients dropped their jaws.

King Armish looked round the room at the stunned faces and then back at the anger that was bestowed upon the face of his son.

"This is absurd; there is no way the man on the poster was a pirate. You seem to forget, Belthran, pirates do not travel alone."

"I did not forget; I had done well to remember it. Do you see Danal behind me? Because I do not. When Grendel took down the man on the poster, Danal and I went across to examine the body, and that is where Danal found it!"

"Found what?" intervened Maxin.

"A tattoo. Not just any tattoo—*the* tattoo. The skull with the bow and the sword, the tattoo that bares only one beholder, pirates! And upon discovering it, Danal was struck down by an arrow out of nowhere. Suddenly, we found ourselves being attacked from countless pirates; I took my men and as many villagers as we could and held them off at the barracks. Maikin fell trying to save a young child. We took the fight to the pirates, losing many valiant villagers in the process. I was knocked to the dirt and was one swing away from being beheaded, until Harnik came through with aid and helped us rid the city of attackers. So once again, Father, where in this land are all the city's troops?"

King Armish said nothing. He did not know what to say; his eyes opened wide as he looked up at his son and his blood-stained troops behind him.

The silence was tense. Belthran still waited on an answer from his father, and he was beginning to grow even more impatient. Belthran's mouth opened to speak but before he could Grendel's voice was heard first.

"Prince Belthran, pardon me, my Lord, but did you happen to see my father whilst you were out there? He is one of the city messengers; he has a big bushy beard and a lazy eye; I need to know he is okay."

"I am sorry, young Grendel; I saw no man of that description."

Grendel's head dropped in worry. Was it a good thing that Belthran hadn't seen his father? Or was it bad? Either way, Grendel didn't know what to think, that was until Anamaforth crept up from behind Belthran, stepping forward a few paces.

"Pardon my interruption, my Prince, but along my travels, I saw a man of this description. He had a small leather sack hanging from his cloth and big filthy boots that looked like they had seen a lot of ground in their time."

"Yes! That is him; that was my father. Is he okay?"

Anamaforth looked at Grendel with a saddened look in his eyes. "I saw your father running around outside the creepy wooden cottage that belongs to Old Lady Green. Arrows were flying. I'm not sure your father knew which direction to run; I tried to gather who I could. Honestly, I did..."

"Is my father okay?"

"He fell. I am so sorry, Grendel; there was nothing anyone could have done."

A tear strolled down Grendel's mutated and swollen cheek. "He died before I had a chance to tell him my news."

Maxin placed a comforting arm around him.

"The spirits have got me again, my Prince; I told you they want to make my life a misery."

Maxin was lost for words; all he could utter was an apology. But whilst Maxin was lost for words, Belthran wasn't.

"This is not the work of spirits, Grendel. This time, the fault lies solely on a king who would like nothing more than to know his arse is comfortable."

He looked back up at King Armish with a disgraced look upon his face. "Look at what you have done, Father! Just look at what you have caused, and yet you still cannot provide us with an answer."

King Armish opened his mouth to say something back to Belthran, but before he did, he paused and looked around the room once more. "I want everyone in this infirmary who is able to walk to get out. Leave me to speak with my two sons and my nephew."

Within seconds, the whole infirmary cleared, leaving behind only those who couldn't walk, Grendel being one of them.

This time, King Armish had words come to the tip of his tongue, and he was ready to explain where all the troops had gone, and Belthran eagerly awaited to hear what he had to say.

"First, I would just like to offer my deepest sympathy to Grendel. I am sorry to hear of your father's passing. I take complete responsibility for what has happened, and in light of this, I offer you our home to lay your head. We will add an extra quarter to the palace, and it will be yours. Anything you want, anything at all, do not be afraid to ask.

"I know this does not condone what has happened, but I will explain to you why. Belthran, Maxin, Harnik; I should have told you all what was happening and perhaps we would have been better prepared. As you know, over the last five years, Ar'Gurd has expanded and created more villages than ever before, but more villages means more protection, the kind of protection that uses the armies of other kingdoms. And as you know, we have three other kingdoms right on our doorstep; The Dwarven Kingdom, The Elven City, and The Wizard World.

"For many years, the Four Kingdoms have existed, and not once have we ever come in contact with any of the other three, whether that is a good thing or a bad thing, I do not know, but I thought it was about time we found out. I came up with the idea of organizing a peace treaty for all four kingdoms in the great hall, in the hope that we could be there for one another if one calls. I sent both Clearus, Payner, and their Units, along with city guards to assist them. They are walking into the unknown, and I would rather they had as much backup as they needed. I knew I still had you and Harnik around to cover the city grounds, so I did not think I had to worry, but I forgot the pirates. They had not threatened the city in so long that they were temporarily erased from my mind. I apologize to you all."

Maxin and Harnik did not know what to say; it was something that they never expected to hear. But, as usual, Belthran did not remain quiet.

"This is not over, Father! This is likely far from over. Say some of the pirates fled the city; they now know we are weak in number. They will go away today and come back in force tomorrow, or even tonight! We will fight to the death, you know that, but we will not be able to withstand them forever; this city will fall if the attacks keep up. You have to call half of the troops back, Father, or this land will not survive."

Armish's eyes welled up, he looked around the infirmary before looking back at his sons. He looked defeated, worried, and panicked; nothing had ever threatened the land like this before, and the fact that it was only mindless pirates made it worse. He took a few seconds to gather his thoughts. He looked back at Belthran; he had made his decision.

"Nothing will change; everything will remain as it is."

Looks of anger and hurt soon became looks of astonishment and glares of disbelief.

"But, Uncle, the city and its villages may not be able to hold off another attack!"

"Then, we make sure it does. I apologise for the problem I have caused, but the situation is just. Calling back our troops would be a waste of time and resources; it will take two days for the messenger to reach our troops. Having sent them out yesterday evening, they will already be more than halfway to their first destination, so if they make good time, give or take another day or two, then they will be back here, anyway."

"This is an outrage. We may not even have another day or two!" Argued Belthran.

"Please, Father, listen to Belthran."

"My decision is final, and I will hear no more on the matter! You boys must deploy your troops to the walls; I will send out word to Paran-Dun and to all the other villages in this land, making them aware of the attack. If we are not safe, then no city is. Now, you boys best get going. Once again, Grendel, I am deeply sorry about your father."

King Armish stayed for no reply, he had his final say, and that was that. He turned and left the infirmary without another thought.

Belthran was the next to leave, and he was far from pleased. He wasn't going to let this drop; he just huffed and stormed out of the infirmary.

Prince Harnik followed, walking soullessly to the door before turning around toward Grendel and saying, "I am sorry about your face."

Then, off he went to see what he could do to help with the defence of the city.

Which left Maxin and Grendel to look on at each other with great worry.

"Grendel, if everything they are saying is true, then this city needs me, and it needs as many men as it can get. I hope you understand that I must leave you now, and I must finish what I started; I need to complete my Unity!"

Grendel promptly grabbed hold of Maxin's hand, which still rested heavy upon his shoulder.

"Just know, Maxin, I understand what you must do and why you must do it. I don't blame your father for the death of mine, nor do I any longer blame the spirits. It was not their knife or arrow that took my father down, and I am going to take great honour in gutting as many of those filthy pirates as I can."

Maxin smiled and nodded back at Grendel before leaving the infirmary to carry on his mission.

Whilst walking through the long and narrow lit up palace hallways, Maxin came to his first stop on his quest, Belthran.

He made his way to Belthran's study, where he found him pacing up and down with his hands crossed behind his back, muttering words to himself that Maxin couldn't understand.

"Brother, are you okay? I need to talk with you."

Belthran continued to pace up and down muttering, but this time his words became clearer.

"This is absurd. I have never, ever seen or heard anything so foolish in my life. And father calls himself a great ruler! A great idiot, perhaps."

"Brother, I need to ask you something that will lead me on the right track."

Belthran stopped pacing and slowly looked up at Maxin. "What? What is it?"

Maxin moved toward his brother with urgency. "Before all of this occurred, you called upon me and you spoke to me of a young boy who could make a great addition to my Unit; may I have his name again?"

Belthran looked Maxin in the eye, and for the first time since the attack Maxin saw his brother smile.

"You are determined, Brother, I will give you that; I always knew you had it in you. His name is Scarlep, he is the younger brother of Rekken. Rekken is a loyal, trustworthy, and skilled fighter, and he speaks highly of his younger brother's talents. I have not met the boy myself, but he sounds like a worthwhile addition. I hear he hangs around at the stables a lot; it is probably best to start your search there."

"Thank you, Brother, I will try my best to gather as many troops as I can. And do not worry, we will prevail!"

Belthran's smile then turned into a wry laugh as he continued to pace up and down his study.

Maxin, on the other hand, left him to his business and continued on his own back down the palace hallways.

Before long, heading farther down the corridor, he heard raised voices coming from a nearby room—it was his mother and father. He moved in closely to the door before pushing his left lobe gently up against it to listen in closely to the back and forth arguing.

"You cannot honestly think that this is a good plan. Everything you and your ancestors before you have worked so hard to build is on the brink of being overrun, maybe even destroyed, and by what? One foolishly thought-out decision."

"Foolishly thought out? Do you think that this was an easy decision to make? You think I would make a decision without at least giving it a second of thought?"

"It was you not thinking about the consequences that got us into this mess. And how could you make such a decision without first consulting with me?"

"Consult with you? Why should I? I am the king, not you! It is I who runs this land; I am its protector, which means I make the tough choices."

"And it is I who takes care of this family. You are putting us all in danger. Do you not realise that you have children to protect?"

"Of course, I do. They are great fighters, and they will do us and Ar'Gurd proud!"

"You have three children, Armish! One of them, your only daughter and only five years old. Or have you forgotten? Or would you like to put a sword in her hand aswell?"

"I have not forgotten. And you are right; I do have children to protect and that is what I will do. I will be here; I will protect you all!"

"And how good are you against thirty pirates? Say you fail to protect us. If you die, are you willing to take the risk of your wife and children being slaughtered and butchered by pirates?

You think you're a great king, but great kings are known for the decisions they make, and I don't know of one person who agrees with this decision. If you don't recall the troops, we may not survive another onslaught."

"What do you know about kings? A great king is a great ruler, a man who can command any army, large or small, against any force. They make tough but right decisions when they need to, and they never change their minds. I am a great king, and I have made my decision! We will remain as we are, and this city will stand strong, just like it has done for many years. I will hear no more on the subject; my mind will not change."

At that moment, Maxin pulled his ear from the door, and it hit him that this was all really happening. The city was on the brink of war. He needed to find aid, and he needed to find it quick.

He ran down the remaining length of the corridor toward the main palace doors.

As he pushed them open, he was stunned by what he saw: something he truly thought he would never see—complete carnage. There was a sectioned off part of the palace courtyard where the bodies of the fallen villagers were carried and laid down upon the cobbled ground, so that the other villagers were able to pay their final respects, or in some cases, to see if a loved one had been caught in the crossfire.

The darkest clouds flooded the skies of Ar'Gurd on this day, and upon seeing the bodies and the smoke from the buildings in the distance, a look of fear came over Maxin's face, which seemed to say, *If this is what the pirates accomplished with their first attack, what would be the brutality and the consequence of their second?*

After standing upon the palace steps and staring solemnly at the fallen bodies for a short time, Maxin began to slowly make his way through the courtyard, seeing people break down in tears in front of his very eyes; mothers crying for their sons, husbands shedding tears for their wives, and other mourners grieving for their siblings. Maxin couldn't take any more, and he began to hurry through the crowds, many people oblivious to the fact that the young prince was walking amongst them.

As he hurried through the courtyard, in the corner of his eye amongst the fallen, he saw a very recognisable man. This particular man had big muddy boots, a huge bushy beard, and wore a sack around his neck; he was certain it was Grendel's father.

Maxin pulled a flower that had been growing through the crack of a nearby pillar and slowly walked over to the man, he stood above the body and closed his eyes. He muttered several words under his breath before reopening his eyes and resting the flower in between the man's hands.

After paying his respects, Maxin took a deep breath before heading off swiftly to continue his task.

***

Upon arriving at the stables, Maxin found himself looking up at a half empty and desolate barn. It was quiet, even the wind blew softly, lightly lifting the dirt from the ground.

He saw a young boy sitting on an upside-down steel bucket feeding one of the remaining horses that Payner or Clearus had left behind. The boy looked a few years younger than he expected, but Maxin gently called over to him regardless.

"Scarlep?"

The boy slowly turned his head round like a bewitched doll and just stared blankly back at him, so Maxin called over to him again.

"Scarlep?"

The boy just continued to stare.

After staring back at one another, Maxin was suddenly caught off guard by a fair voice that came from behind him.

"Do not mind Alma, my Prince, he is a very strange boy."

Maxin spun around quickly to see another young boy standing there, this one looking more of age. A rather small boy, fair-skinned, and slicked back fair hair, he was also equipped with daggers in either side of his belt. This had to be the boy Maxin was after.

"I am Scarlep. You're here looking for me?"

Maxin looked him up and down. "I'm glad that between the two of you, you're the one who answers to Scarlep, that boy over there was beginning to creep me out. But I am here on business, I know of your brother, Rekken, and he speaks highly of you. He claims you have great skill, perhaps great enough for a place in my Unit; would you agree?"

Without saying a word, Scarlep pulled out one of the daggers from his belt, flipped it up, and caught it on its point. He pulled his arm back before launching it toward Alma, and amazingly, as Alma was handing the horse a strip of hay, Scarlep's dagger sliced straight through the middle of it, cutting it in half and then wedging itself into a nearby wooden ledge. "I would agree!"

Scarlep was cocky, but Maxin liked it. He had a right to be cocky; he was talented, very talented.

"I'm impressed. But as impressive as that was, I have someone in my Unit who already has great aim and accuracy, so before I make my decision, I need to know, is there anything else that you can bring to my Unit better than anyone else can?"

"Apart from being lightning fast, able to handle multiple weapons, and being just as deadly with each, there is not really much else." Scarlep gloated.

Maxin didn't have to think for long; his mind was most likely made up before he even met the boy. He knew he needed warriors, and as he previously stated, he would rather it wasn't Alma with his bucket and hay.

"I think at this point in time, Scarlep, I can't afford to be picky. Word spreads, and I am sure being Rekken's brother you are aware of the situation we're in. I need troops, and you fit the persona that I am looking for. And as my father once said, great rulers sometimes have to make tough and quick decisions, and they never change their mind. So with that being said, Scarlep, it would be my honour if you would become troop number four in my Unity."

"The honour is all mine, my Prince; I accept."

"There are dark times ahead, Scarlep, I can feel it. But for now, I still have a duty to fulfil, so I will leave you with this; on the eve of my birthday, when the red sun sets and the blue moon rises, we will hold our first Unit meeting. I will send word to the other warriors that I have gathered so far; hopefully there will be more. So, for now, I must be on my way, and it's a pleasure to have you in my Unit."

And much like his father, Maxin left quickly without letting another word be said. Times were dark, and he could feel a change coming.

CHAPTER FIVE

WANDERING WORLDS

Prince Clearus

Meanwhile, in the far isles of the land heading toward their first destination and unaware of the situation in Carbaya was Prince Clearus, Sir Payner, both lots of their troops and the city guards.

King Armish had pulled out all the stops to assure safe passage and easy negotiations; there was no room for error on this mission.

They were but a few miles from their first destination, the Wizard World.

But during their journey, Prince Clearus had been thinking strongly about the elite force the king had sent to hand over the invitation to the meet.

"Sir Payner, this long ride has had me thinking, would it not be safer if only one of our Units travelled into these kingdoms?"

"What? Why do you say that?"

"My brother wanted us to enter these kingdoms with an army of soldiers all armoured up and raring to go; that is not the image that we want to present for a peaceful negotiation. Do you not think that this could cause them to feel threatened and overwhelmed? Do you not think that this approach has more cause for war? So what I am saying is, if only one of us is to enter each kingdom, then they may feel more like we have come to offer peace and less like we have come to offer battle."

Sir Payner sat upright on his horse and thought carefully about what Clearus was saying. "Do you know what, Clearus? For the first time in my life, I think I have heard you actually speak some sense, and do you know what? I agree with you. The king's intentions were genuine, but they lack realism. If we did enter and a battle occurred, I am sure our hundred plus men would not fare well against an entire kingdom. At least this way, less of us will die if such events take place."

"I guess that is one way of looking at it."

But the surprising thing was that Payner agreed with something Clearus was suggesting, but upon saying this, they still had another decision to make; which one of them would be the one to travel into the kingdoms?

The mission was a first of its kind; nobody had ever travelled to the other kingdoms before, and they all wanted to be the first to have a look inside. Fortunately, they came to a mutual decision on two of them, where Prince Clearus favoured taking a trip to the Wizard World, Sir Payner would just love to see the Elves.

Which then left just one question; which one of them would encounter the Dwarves?

But then again, it was Clearus who came up with another great idea, so that they would both see equal amounts of the new kingdoms, and as the Dwarven Kingdom would be the last one to visit, he decided it be best if they were to both enter it together.

Sir Payner, once again, found himself surprisingly agreeing with him.

Continuing on with their journey through the night, it wasn't much longer until Clearus and Payner found themselves on the edge of the north eastern land, which just so happened to be the gateway to the Wizard World.

The surrounding air was cavernous and ghostly. A small wooden raft floating upon the top of a crystal blue lake appeared to be the only way forward.

Drawing the short straw for himself, Prince Clearus stepped forward, mystified by the mysterious glow that surrounded the lake, and followed by his ten trusty companions; Azmar, Dentrol, Beena, Pinvar, Canel, Portran, Yaylmar, Thornas, and the two twin brothers, Kalim and Bempot.

Together, they all just managed to squeeze upon this small raft, holding on to each other for support and steadiness. As mentioned earlier, the Ar'Gurdian people did not have many dealings with travelling on water.

As they gathered on the raft, they slowly began to sail away, and all Sir Payner and the others could do was watch as the raft disappeared into the deep fog.

On the raft, Prince Clearus and his Unit were amazed by everything they began to see whilst in the fog.

In the distance, they could see a small forest on fire, but there was no smoke, nor were the trees burning to ash. This was magnificent magic, something no man had ever witnessed before. They were hypnotized by these beautiful bright flames.

As they sailed close toward the flames, the fog began to produce small lightning bolts that fired into the lake, sounding like small bombs as they hit the surface, but not one of them hit the raft.

Once they got to the flaming forest, the lake began to merge into a stream. They followed the stream downward, with the trees now on either side of them.

After a short sail down the stream, they could finally see the end; a large wooden gate stood in their way.

"How do you suppose we get in?" asked Pinvar.

As they approached farther toward the gate, they began to see a figure with its back turned.

Once they got to the end of the stream, not one of them, not even Clearus, dared to get off the raft.

The figure then slowly began to turn around to face them, moving his head first, and then his body. His eyes were pure white, and he stood about seven feet tall, holding a giant staff and looking as sturdy as a concrete pillar.

"Speak your name," came a deep voice from the figure.

"My name is Prince Clearus Hailguard of Ar'Gurd, son of Hamus, and these men here are my subjects. Who are you? Speak your name."

The Wizard ferociously slammed his staff to the ground, causing a thunderous thud. "I am a Guardian of the Night. What is your business here, stranger on the stream?"

"I am here on important business, sent by King Armish of Ar'Gurd himself to discuss great information of importance with your king."

"What information?"

"Our business is our own and is of no importance to you. Now, I demand to see your king at once!"

The Guardian slammed his staff down once more, this time disappearing within a puff of smoke.

Prince Clearus and his troops were speechless. They had never seen anyone disappear before, but then again, they had never seen a Wizard before.

"What is going on?" Thornas asked Clearus as he looked on through the gaps of his long blonde hair that covered his eyes.

"I have no idea."

"Then, what shall we do?" added Bempot.

"I don't know."

"Shall we turn back?" suggested Kalim.

"Will you all just stop talking for a moment. Nobody is to turn back; we are here to do a job by order of the king, and we *will* see it through, even if that does mean waiting here all night!"

And waiting is exactly what they done.

Time seemed to move slowly in this world; it felt like hours had passed when, in fact, only minutes had gone by. The troops remained sat on the raft, resting up against each other's backs.

Suddenly, they all heard a large familiar thud and stood back on their feet. They looked on as a puff of smoke soon became a Guardian of the Night, but this time, the Guardian was not alone; he was accompanied by another Wizard, a lot less fair, a lot less mystical and looking a lot more human.

"I hear from the Guardian that you wish to see the king?"

"Yes, that is right—I have an urgent matter that I must discuss with him."

"Well, we have no king."

Prince Clearus and his troops looked confused. "Then, who is in charge here?" the Prince asked.

"In charge of what? I am Florint, I oversee security."

"And who do you take orders from?" interrupted Bempot.

"The same person everyone in this land takes orders from."

"And who may that be?" asked Kalim.

"The Forcer, of course."

"Then, can you take me to him?" added Clearus.

"Who said it was a man?"

Clearus began to grow tired of the short, blunt answers. "Look, you know why I'm here. I told you I need to speak to the person in charge, and if the person in charge is the Forcer, then take me to her!"

"You!" replied Florint with some intensity.

"What?" a confused Clearus responded.

"I can take *you*, outsider, but just you. Your bodyguards will have to stay behind."

"They are not my bodyguards, Wizard. They are my troops. But if that is what it takes to get an audience with the Forcer, then so be it; take me to *her*."

Prince Clearus was wary about going in alone, but he knew it had to be done; the last thing he wanted was to go back to King Armish and say that not only did he fail but he didn't even try.

All of a sudden, clouds of smoke began to gather up around the raft; Clearus and his troops could see nothing around them. The smoke was soon followed by yet another thud. As soon as the thud hit, a lightning bolt came from the smoke and struck Clearus, and within a moment of it striking him, he just vaporized.

The smoke cleared for his Unit, only for them to find that Clearus and the Wizard were both gone, but the Guardian of the Night remained.

"I have just decided, I hate magic!" grunted Thornas.

After being vaporized, Prince Clearus suddenly began to wake on the other side, not sure how much time had passed. He looked around and found himself lying within a cushion-filled hole in the middle of an empty marble hall.

He sat up but began to feel dizzy and nauseous.

He also found himself in nothing but a velvet robe, stripped of his armour and his weaponry.

As he sat in this cushioned hole, a fly began to buzz quite irritatingly around his face. He swatted and swatted, but could not hit this fly, and everytime it would just keep coming back. The fly buzzed round his ear as he waved his hand some more, when suddenly, the fly just stopped, levitating dormantly in front of him, just hovering as still as he'd witnessed any fly do before. Clearus then looked on in complete ashtonishment as this fly exploded in front of his very eyes, and from it, emerged a beautiful young woman.

"Is that any way to treat your host?" asked the woman.

"What the..."

The prince's jaw just dropped. His eyes opened wide; he did not know what to say or what to think. Was he dreaming?

"Welcome to the Wizard World of Amren'oir, outsider. I'm Forcer Kandriel; I hear you seek my attention."

Still lost for words, Clearus couldn't find his tongue. Still not knowing what to make of what he saw, he was finding it more difficult to say what he came to say.

"Um, yes. I um, came to, um...Excuse me, can you first tell me, how did you turn from, um, you know, to um, well, you know?"

"You wish to know of my gift, outsider?"

"Please, call me Clearus."

"I am what is known as a Wizard Shape Shifter, Outsider Clearus."

"Good enough," said Clearus in a sarcastic tone under his breath.

"There are but five of us in all the land. I am the only female, and I have the ability to transform myself into any living creature at any given time. But enough about me, I wish to know why you are here?"

"I was sent by King Armish of Ar'Gurd from the land of man. He is asking for members or councils of the Wizard, Elven, and Dwarven Kingdoms to travel to Ar'Gurd for a meet between all four kingdoms to discuss a parlay. For the first time in history, we will all come together in the great hall of our greatest city, and the king insists that you attend; it is a week from today. Can I give him your word?"

"This is a most intriguing offer, Outsider Clearus—the four most powerful descendants from all four kingdoms, never been done before; it could end badly. But as the *most powerful*, I'm more intrigued to find out, you have my word. But before I let you go, Outsider Clearus, you make sure that you tell your king that if he is planning something, then we are not the *race* to mess with!"

"That I will. So, I guess now I will, um, be on my way, Lady Forcer. But before I do, can you just tell me...w-w-where are my clothes?"

"Head for the quilted archway, you will find what you are looking for there. Until we meet again, Outsider Clearus."

Suddenly, Kandriel once again exploded back into a fly and flew off, away from the marble hall.

Prince Clearus, still not yet quite used to the whole magic thing, picked himself up out of the cushioned hole and stumbled over to the quilted archway. As he walked through the archway, smoke began to gather around him once more, but this time, for only a split second, and when the smoke cleared, he found himself standing back on the raft with his Unit, fully clothed and fully armed.

"Prince Clearus. What happened?" asked Azmar.

"I don't know, Azmar. Something...magical."

"Is she coming to the meet?" added Thornas.

"Yes, she agreed. Now, can we please just get back to Ar'Gurd?"

And off they sailed back toward Ar'Gurd, without another word being said along the way.

***

As Payner, his troops, and all the other guards tirelessly lay waiting, they suddenly began to see the raft sail back through the fog.

"They're back!" signalled one of the guards.

"It doesn't seem like any of them are hurt or missing," claimed another.

"Although Prince Clearus is looking rather pale, wouldn't you say?" the first guard replied.

As the raft pulled into the bank, Clearus and his men steadily and graciously stepped back onto the great land they like to call home.

"Clearus, are you okay there?" asked Payner, worryingly, as he looked on at Clearus's vacant and very pale expression.

"Let me just tell you something, Payner, for someone who has never seen magic with his naked eye before, that my, friend, was way too much."

"Hahaha. But I thought you really wanted to see the magical Wizards and their *mystical* land. You must tell me all about it."

"Later. But for now, all I will say is this—I never knew one single person could make you feel so small and powerless."

"Well, as long as you enjoyed yourself, my friend," joked Payner. "So, is he coming?" he added.

"She," corrected Clearus.

"I'm sorry?"

"The *he* whom you're asking about is in fact a *she*," Clearus clarified. *"Or is 'she' a fly?"* he added under his breath.

"A she? Well, that was unexpected."

"You can say that again, Payner. Her name is Kandriel, she calls herself the Forcer."

"What does she look like?"

"Her appearance somewhat…changes," stated Clearus as he walked past Payner, leaving him with a very confused and wondrous look on his face.

As it was too late to move forward toward the Elven Kingdom, the group set up camp for the night, down by the mystic lake.

After his strange encounter with Kandriel, Clearus just couldn't sleep, tossing and turning; he couldn't get Kandriel out of his head.

This lasted for around an hour, until the image of the Wizard Queen began to fade from his mind, eventually allowing him to fall into a deep sleep. However his precious sleep didn't last for long, as seconds later he felt the whole tent light up around him. He shot open his eyes and saw nothing but the darkness of the night. From this point on, every time he closed his eyes, he felt the light. And every time he opened them, he saw the dark.

In his head, he thought the guys in the camp were messing with him, as it happened once more.

This time, Clearus sat up with his tired, bloodshot eyes. "Whoever is doing that, I'm warning you, stop it now, or you will be sorry!"

He laid his head back down and closed his eyes. And within seconds, the same thing happened again. His eyes shot open once more as he sat straight back up into the darkness, but again, he couldn't see light. But this time around, he began to hear something; the sound of fighting, the struggle of battle, and the patter of armoured boots on the ground.

"We're under attack!" he heard a man warn from the outside.

Clearus got to his knees, as he then saw a shadowed figure stalking the tent; it growled with every step it took.

He couldn't take his eyes off the figure for a second.

"There are too many of them!" another voice cried as Clearus remained fixated on the shadow as it crept ever closer toward the tent door.

His vision was limited inside the tent. He began to patter his hands around the floor, trying to locate his sword. All he could find was what felt like empty wine bottles, wash rags and his helmet.

Still unable to take his eyes off the shadow, he saw the figure finally reach the front of the tent.

Slowly, a small creature began to climb through the door, one small paw at a time, until Clearus found himself face to face with a Nawg, small fuzzy beings who are more vicious and deadly than they look.

Still unable to see much, Clearus saw the creature through a reflection of light from a campfire that beamed through the door when the Nawg came through.

Nawgs were very territorial creatures, and it appeared as though the group had set up camp in Nawg country.

The small Nawg looked back at Clearus with its big pointy ears and large snout, growling back at him as it crept ever so slowly toward him.

Breathing heavily, Clearus once again began to scour the floor for his sword, the best he could, but before he had a chance to find it, the Nawg jumped toward him with his mouth wide open, showing very few but very sharp teeth.

Not knowing what else to do, Clearus put his hands up in front of him to help shield himself when, suddenly, a powerful force and a great beam of light emanated from his hands, which heaved the Nawg straight out of the tent with fierce energy.

"What the…" a stunned Clearus asked himself as he looked down at his hands to see this great light disappear back into his sweaty palms.

After another quick scuffle around the floor, Clearus managed to locate his sword. He quickly gathered it up along with his helmet before heading outside the tent to see a large group of Nawgs attacking the camp.

Standing out upon the field and looking over the attack, Clearus suddenly began to feel this energy flow through his veins, beginning from his toes and ending in what felt like his brain.

He felt power; power he had never felt before.

Electricity moved through his blood vessels like a fish down a stream. He was overcome with a feeling of great force and ability; he felt somewhat invincible. And without giving time to question it, he took full advantage of those feelings and rushed into the middle of the attack and began to slay the Nawgs by at least five at a time, using skills and moves that he did not know he possessed or was even capable of.

Guards and officers all took a step back and were all baffled and shocked to what they were witnessing, and within a matter of minutes, the Nawgs were obliterated almost single-handily by the hands of Prince Clearus and his new-found skills.

Mouths and eyes were wide open as Clearus stood in the middle of all the cut down creatures, not one person speaking a word, that was until Sir Payner stepped forward.

"What in the name of the spirits was that, Clearus?"

Prince Clearus released his bloodied sword, letting it drop to the ground. He turned his trembling hands round slowly to face his palms, whilst then proceeding to raise them in front of his face.

"I have no idea," he replied.

Instead of risking another possible attack, Prince Clearus, Sir Payner, and the rest of the camp decided to move onward through the night and on toward the next kingdom to visit the Elves.

As Clearus galloped along with the group, he was aware of everyone looking at him, muttering things under their breath, even his own Unit.

He had all the same thoughts the others did. He didn't know what to say, and he didn't know what to think. He had no explanation; he was just as confused as they all were.

Sir Payner galloped cautiously behind him.

CHAPTER SIX

WHISPERWOOD

Sir Payner

After many more miles of travelling, the group finally began to approach what was believed to be the land of the Elves.

Payner brought the group to a halt as he galloped in front of them all and spoke aloud. "Men, we are approaching the Elven land, be sure to keep all weapons holstered, unless we run in to any kind of trouble. Just remember when we enter their land, we are visitors, not hostiles; remember this and be on your best behaviour."

"How long would you have us wait out here?" asked Clearus.

"See through the remainder of the night plus another. If by then I do not return, go back to the city and inform the king. *Do not* carry on this mission alone."

Sir Payner then took his men on foot the remainder of the way toward the Elven Kingdom as Clearus waited behind for his return.

Just metres away from the camp, Payner and his Unit walked up cautiously toward a tall single silver gate that stood at the beginning of a long, winding, stone concrete bridge. The gate was merely hooked closed and was easily accessible; the Unit found this fortunate, whilst it concerned Payner.

Why would a land allow such easy access to outsiders? he thought.

Despite Payner's concerns, they unhooked the gate, and he and his Unit continued up the stone concrete bridge, hooking the gate closed behind them.

Payner had seven brave men following him up the bridge and into the unknown. Three of his other Unit members sadly died when a building collapsed in a little village on the far side of Ar'Gurd ten years ago. The day still haunts Payner, but he believes it has made his Unit stronger.

Portras was one; he suffered from a lazy eye. Deckern, Stringal, and Cartron, they made it four, all cousins once removed but more like brothers never separated. Keyomar and Barnagor make it six, those two were the brains of the Unit, always bouncing ideas and suggestions off of one another, trying to think of ways the Unit could improve, which then brings us to number seven, Leaden, the youngest of the group, only by a few months, but none of them let him forget it.

After a short walk, the group had finally reached the end of the bridge. There, they were faced with yet another tall single silver gate, and just like the first gate, this one was also unguarded, although this one appeared to be locked.

Concern still clouded Payner's mind, as easy as it seemed for the other races to make their way into Ar'Gurd, Payner was not expecting the same from the Elves.

"What is the plan now?" asked Cartron as the group stood huddled together, staring toward the gate. "We can't simply wait here to be greeted," he added.

"I could pick the lock," suggested Barnagor, who before he joined Payner's Unit was destined to follow in his father's footsteps and become one of the best locksmiths in the land.

"No. Definitely not! Remember, we come here as friends, not foes. When I say, 'be on your best behaviour,' that includes not breaking and entering into another race's kingdom and smuggling ourselves inside," replied a stern Payner as he then moved himself guardedly closer to the gate.

"Then, what is it you suggest we do?" replied Barnagor.

"We knock, of course."

Payner edged ever so closely toward the gate, taking every step with complete vigilance.

As the rest of the group remained where they were, Payner found himself close enough to the gate that he was able to touch it, fearing it might have a booby-trap of some kind. He carefully placed one hand around one of the single bolted rails of the gate; he then gave the gate a small shake to confirm it was locked.

Keeping his left hand wrapped around one of the bars, he clenched his right fist and knocked directly and clearly upon the gate three times, hesitating slightly before each single knock.

Within each second of hesitation, Payner stared warily through the bars of the gate and into the woodland that lay beyond it. The sound of his fist against the bars created a sort of elegant but rather deep echo throughout the trees.

Upon his third knock, Payner and his group heard nothing but silence. No wind was whistling, no leaves were falling, and no birds were singing; the group remained silent.

Payner clenched his fist one more time and raised his hand to knock upon the gate once more, but just as his hand began to swing toward the gate, an arrow came whistling through the trees, past the bars in the gate, and landed in the ground, dangerously close to Payner's feet.

Payner's eyes shot open in complete shock as he took a small step back away from the gate.

Upon seeing this, his Unit, still standing behind him, then drew their weapons.

"Holster your weapons!" ordered Payner.

"But they're attacking us," argued Leaden.

"They are not. The precision of that arrow through the bars to my feet wasn't by mistake. That would've been jammed into my head if they wanted it to be so. It was merely a warning, letting us know that they see us and that they have the upper hand."

"But how do you know this?" asked Portras.

"I don't. Now holster your weapons, all of you!"

Payner looked back through the bars and into the trees as his Unit holstered their weapons.

"Speak your purpose!" said a harsh and unwelcoming voice from within the trees.

"My name is Payner Dral-gon, son of Dangor Dral-gon. I know these names mean nothing to you. I am an aide to the great King Armish Hailguard of Ar'Gurd; he has sent me across the land on business to discuss an urgent matter with your king…or queen."

Silence once again fell throughout the woodland as Payner awaited a response, the silence was almost intimidating.

A few moments later, the voice within the trees returned.

"You may enter, on one condition. You must enter with only yourself and one other; all weapons must be returned back onto your own land, along with the rest of your men. Our land and our race have no problem with your kind, but our own precautions must be taken. Follow these steps and you may enter."

"Your rules we will respect, and your directions we will follow; thank you," replied Payner as he unbuckled his belt and threw it across to Barnagor, along with a small dagger that he kept hidden within his boot.

"Keyomar, you are to do the same. I want *you* with me in there."

"As you wish, Captain," replied Keyomar as he took his sword from his belt and also handed it over to Barnagor as he then moved toward Payner. "Are you sure about this?" he asked.

"The king wants this mission complete; we are not in danger now, and we are unsure if we ever will be, but the king will not be happy if we go back not having spoken to the Elves because we were worried. He sent us because he knew we could get the job done. We are worried about them, there is no denying that, so why should they not be worried about us?" stated Payner.

"So let's go. You guys head back to Clearus and we will be back before you know it."

Barnagor, along with the remainder of the group, then unwillingly headed back to Prince Clearus, still not happy with having to leave their leader behind.

Once they were gone, Keyomar and Payner faced the gate as it remained locked.

"Now what?" asked Keyomar.

Payner did not respond. Instead, he looked uneasily into the trees and called out, "We have followed the steps you have given us to take. Now, may we enter?"

The two of them were then kept waiting for several seconds by what could only have been described as a very unnerving silence, but that unnerving silence soon turned to befuddlement as Keyomar and Payner both watched as the locked gate suddenly swung open in front of them.

"That gate was locked tight," claimed a puzzled Payner.

"Magical Elves?" suggested a stunned Keyomar as they both looked at one another with great disbelief.

Sir Payner and Keyomar entered through the large silver gate, placing one foot in front of the other very carefully.

They stood for a moment and gazed upon the beauty of the woodland that stood before them.

There are no trees of this height in Ar'Gurd, just think of what you must be able to see from up there, thought Keyomar.

"I've seen smaller mountains," replied Payner as their eyes were fixated.

Suddenly, the two were jolted at the sound of the large silver gate slamming itself shut behind them.

"That is still freaking me out," added Payner.

"You were not invited in to stand and gaze. You were invited in to speak with our king," said a now-familiar voice from the trees.

"Please, tell us where we should go; we don't know this land, and we don't wish to get lost," said Payner.

"Enter the woodland; I will be your guide."

Payner and Keyomar anxiously moved forward, once again watching every step they took, trying hard not to draw any unwanted attention.

Payner began to feel the same sign of caution he received when he first gained access to the bridge; something just didn't feel right about this place.

They both walked for miles through what seemed like never-ending woodland, every inch looking identical to the other. When they looked up, they were not able to see the sky through the trees that stood so high.

Being unable to know when the light changes from day to night, the greenery and the leaves kept so bright and nourished that they illuminated throughout the whole woodland.

Time began to drag on as the two kept pushing forward, and the voice that was in the trees had now been silent for some time.

"Do you think he is still watching us?" asked Keyomar.

"Of course. I just don't think he cares all that much to talk to us."

Keyomar soon came to a sudden halt, putting his arm out in front of Payner.

"Keyomar, what is it?"

"Look over there, Captain; is that smoke?"

Both Keyomar and Payner then looked into the distance to see something covering the air, almost fog-like.

"I don't think it is smoke," answered Payner.

"That's because it's not. It is steam," corrected the voice from the trees.

"Steam?" questioned Keyomar.

"Steam, as in the whispering steam pond that you are going to make your way over to *now*."

"You're right, Payner; I don't think he cares for us at all."

The two then slowly made their way over to what was the most mesmerizingly numinous pond, surrounded by a great, shiny rock that looked as though it was crafted from some form of precious stone, formed in-between two large tropical palm trees and topped with a great glow from the steam that emanated from the very surface of the water.

"This is unbelievable," stated Keyomar.

"Is this where we wait for your king?" Payner asked aloud to the trees.

The voice from the trees responded quickly with the most displeasingly abrupt tone. "No. You will enter the pond through the stairway beneath the surface."

Suddenly, another arrow came flying from the trees and once again landed right beside Payner's feet, but this time, the arrow seemed to have a small note attached.

"Take this note with you and pass it on to a guard in the city; do not read it. Until next time, farewell."

Then, they heard a small flutter in the trees above them.

"Do you really think he has gone?"

"I'd rather not hang about to find out," replied Payner as he leant down and pulled the note from the arrow and headed to the edge of the pond.

Keyomar slowly came up and stood beside him. "What do you think the note says? Why would we not be allowed to read it?"

"I don't know, Keyomar, but he could still be watching us, so I'd rather avoid reading it. I don't want his next arrow to end up in my eye."

They both stood upon the edge of the pond and looked down into the steamy surface, where they could see an array of different fish flourishing through the water.

Payner got down on his knees and placed his hand into the pond. "It feels…like nothing, like air." He pulled his hand back from the pond only for it to be bone dry.

"Wait, are these Wizards or Elves because there is a lot of magic going on here? I never heard a single tale about Elves being magical," said Keyomar.

"Well, it appears as though there is only one way to find out."

Payner got back to his feet before slowly dipping his right foot into the water to find a step just below the surface. Once he found the step, his left foot soon followed.

One step after another, Keyomar looked on as Payner slowly disappeared into the pond. Not wanting to wait behind on his own, Keyomar reluctantly followed.

After a few cautious steps, Keyomar finally made his way into the lake, but just as he dipped his head below the surface, he found himself at the top of a large stairway met by four Elven guards all pointing arrows in his face.

"What the…" he muttered under his breath.

He looked down the stairway and saw Payner also being cordoned off by guards.

"What is your purpose here?" spoke one guard, who seemed to be leading the group.

"We are here to speak with your king on behalf of our own king, King Armish of Ar'Gurd; it is of great importance," answered Payner as he handed over the note that was given to him from their Elven guide.

The letter read,

Dear Chief Commander,

These two men were found by myself attempting to break into the city, they were armed and with reinforcements, I managed to send away the other troops before disarming these two men and luring them through the gate, they claim to have urgent matters with the king. I do not trust them, and neither will the king.

DAYLER [Head Tree Enforcement Trooper]

"Take these men to the dungeons," ordered the Guard Captain.

"Wait a minute. *What?*"

"The king is not around right now, and I can't allow strangers to be walking the streets alone until he returns."

"We understand your concerns, but we mean no harm. Can you not simply keep an eye on us rather than hold us captive? We are no threat to you; we've told you who we are, and our purpose here," bargained Payner.

"So you say, but with that being said, I'm sorry, but us keeping an eye on you as well as our own people would be a burden, not just for me, but for my men, and we do not care for burdens. We will notify you right away of the king's return, but until that time comes—dungeons."

The guards then cuffed Payner and Keyomar and escorted them to the bottom of the steps to two hefty, bolted doors, one leading left and one leading right, a guard opened up one of the doors as they were then taken inside.

They entered the dungeons and were met by nothing more than a small, damp, and darkened corridor, with four separate cells, two on the left and two on the right.

As they were led down the grimy corridor, they were baffled to see that they were the only two captives being held in the dungeons.

"Where are all the other prisoners?" asked Keyomar.

"All the people of this city like to abide by our laws; they dare not face these dungeons," answered one guard, grinning, as he opened up a cell and tossed Keyomar inside. After then locking the cell, he turned around as he then pushed Payner into the cell directly opposite, once again locking the door behind him.

"No need to be heavy-handed, we are still guests in your city, would your king want you to treat us this way?" enquired Payner.

"For now, you are captives in our city—not guests," replied the guard as he smirked back at Payner before leading the other guards out of the dungeon, leaving Payner and Keyomar to themselves.

"Now what?" asked Keyomar.

"Just try and relax, their king will be along shortly, and we can straighten this out."

"Try and relax? Have you seen this place? I mean…what is that smell?

"It's not me, I can tell you that much," joked Payner.

"How are you being so calm and cheerful? Look at where we are. I wish you had chosen Barnagor to come with you, for he has no sense of smell."

"Be calm, Keyomar; King Armish always told me that making the best of a bad situation is a great strength. It trains your mind, and to be honest, this is not the worst situation we could be in."

"Not the worst? Not the worst? Payner, listen to me, we are locked. In. A. Dungeon!"

"Only until the king returns, Keyomar. I agree, their council perhaps didn't make the best decision by locking us in here, but we bring no harm, and we are receiving no harm. Just try and stay positive and free-minded, we will be out of here before you know it."

And before they knew it, after just minutes, the dungeon door opened up, and the voices of guards could be heard.

"Here we go, Keyomar, out of here in no time at all."

But their hopes were beaten when they saw nothing more than a fat, malodorous, drunken Elf prisoner being escorted through the corridor, and instead of throwing him in a cell of his own, the guard took great pleasure in throwing the intoxicated Elf in with Keyomar.

"Here you go, man. A little friend for you to play with," joked the guard as he made his way back up through the corridor and out the door.

"Don't forget what I said, Keyomar. Make the best out of a bad situation," stated Payner as he was trying to keep himself from laughing at Keyomar's misfortune.

"And just how would I do that?"

"Make friends with it," replied Payner, jokingly.

Keyomar then looked back at his cellmate as he went on to belch and vomit more than any man or Elf should be able to. The prisoner then proceeded to pull down his pants before urinating in one large puddle on the floor.

Keyomar's jaw dropped in disgust as he tried to stay as far away from the Elf as he possibly could.

Meanwhile, in the opposite cell, Payner was in a fit of hysterics, as he found himself making the very best out of Keyomar's bad situation.

***

Before they knew it, Payner and Keyomar found themselves waiting endless hours for the large door at the end of the corridor to open once again, which after some time, it eventually did.

A light shone blazingly through the door, blinding both Payner and Keyomar as if the sun was lurking right outside. Whilst the light did not even faze the Elf, the other two began to see a large figure standing tall within the sun's glow, somewhat angel-like.

As the figure remained at the top of the stairs, four Elven guards came running in from behind as they made their way down the corridor, stationing one another outside both Keyomar and Payner's cells.

Once the guards were positioned, the figure began to slowly walk down the stairs, and with each step the figure took, the image of him became clearer.

The large Elf stood at least seven-foot-tall and dawned long, bright red hair. He wore a lengthy full-bodied, gold-sparkled gown.

As the figure now stood at the bottom of the steps, another two guards quickly came running in; one remained atop of the steps whilst the other stood by the side of the figure.

The figure turned his head toward the cell where Keyomar stood. "Guard, take this drunken Elf out of here and sober him up."

"How would I do that, my King?" asked the guard who stood beside him.

At that point, Payner and Keyomar looked over at one another, as they now knew that they stood in the presence of the Elven King.

The king then replied rather abruptly to the guard's question. "Is it not simple? Threaten him. Tell him to sober himself up; if he fails to comply, cut out his tongue."

The guard didn't say another word; he unlocked the cell and ran in to grab the drunken Elf. He grabbed him by the scruff of the neck then looked over at Keyomar, who had backed himself into the corner of the room. The guard then continued to say nothing; he just stared blankly into the eyes of Keyomar before dragging the drunken Elf out of the cell, through the corridor, up the stairs, and out the door.

Payner and Keyomar then continued to look over at each other but this time in complete repulsion and astonishment at the way the king had dealt with the drunk.

Payner then moved himself over to the cell bars and wrapped his arms around them.

One of the Elven guards outside of the cell then pulled out what appeared to be a small baton from his belt before then smashing it across Payner's fingers.

"Arghhh! Just wait until I get out of here!" cried Payner in agony.

"Is that a threat?" asked the king in a very deep and grisly tone as he stepped forward and look down upon Payner.

"No, it wasn't. He didn't mean it," shouted Keyomar from across the corridor.

"Was I talking to you, man? No, I wasn't, so I wouldn't talk to me if I were you," threatened the king as he turned his attention back to Payner. "Well?"

Payner took a few seconds to answer as he cupped his fingers with his other hand. "No, there was no threat, just an impulsive reaction. Are you the king?"

"Did I say you could ask me questions? I believe not, so don't. But tell me, what is your purpose here?"

Keyomar then spoke up to answer him. "We came to see you regarding a message from our kin—"

But Keyomar was soon interrupted by the king before he could finish. "This is your final warning, man. Do not speak to me when I'm not speaking to you. Do it again and I will cut off your head!"

The king then, once again, turned his attention back to Payner. "You—speak."

"Okay, King…"

"It's King Morrik Vale to you."

"Okay, sorry…King Morrik. My name is Sir Payner. I am a royal aid to the King of Ar'Gurd himself, King Armish Hailguard. He has sent us here before you today to invite you to a special meet that he intends to hold in a week and a day from today, a special meet that has never been done before, between Men, Wizards, Elves, and Dwarves. The meet will be held in the great hall of the king's fathers within our fair city of Carbaya. We mean no harm to you or your people, we are simply here to offer the invitation. Do I have your word?"

"Tell me, man. Why should I go? What will that do for me and my people? I already have the most powerful army any kingdom has ever seen, and your pathetic excuse for a king knows it!"

"Do not insult the king in front of me!" exclaimed Payner as he stared up into the eyes of King Morrik.

"Or what? What are you going to do? I hardly think you are in any kind of position to be making threats, man. Think of it, look at who your king has invited: Wizards? Dwarves? Pfft, give me a break. It is clear to me that they have only been invited along to give him extra support, but in all honesty, can you imagine anyone being intimidated by mystical freaks and hairy midgets? I will tell you this only once: I have *no* interest in attending this meet, and I have little interest in meeting your king. But I will say this—your king made a big mistake sending you two, as you have nothing of interest to me, and that means you are now trespassing, and that, that is treason!"

"What? You have to be kidding!" shouted Keyomar, which then provoked King Morrik, he swung his head round to Keyomar and stared at him with fierce daggers in his eyes.

"I believe, man, that I have warned you twice already. I couldn't have put it any clearer, talk to me again and I will cut off your head. Guards, bring him to me!"

CHAPTER SEVEN

A SORROWED EFFECT

Sir Payner

Thuds of a clattering baton against steel rails woke Sir Payner from a practically comatose state; his eyes trembled open as he smeared the sweat and blood away from his eyelids.

"Wake up, man. It's breakfast time," said an Elven guard who now stood tall outside of Payner's cell gate, glaring at him with an oversized smirk on his face. He flourished his baton in one hand along with a bowl of something in the other, something that didn't look the tiniest bit edible.

Payner slowly raised his head and locked eyes with the guard.

The guard then threw the bowl inside the gate, but looking into the guard's eyes had brought the flashbacks on; several hours after the incident, and Payner could still hear and see everything that had happened prior.

It began with just seeing Keyomar's face as the guards had stormed his cell.

After throwing the bowl into the cell, it was the guard who broke eye contact as he then proceeded to head back up the hallway.

"If only your companion had learnt to keep *his* mouth shut!"

Payner threw the bowl of food across the cell, smashing it to pieces against the wall; he stumbled and fell back into the corner and dropped to the floor. His head burrowed into his hands as tears began to fall from his eyes; flashing images of Keyomar once again clouded his mind.

Looking on as Keyomar managed to take down all four of the guards who stormed his cell then picking up and brandishing one of their batons, he left the bodies of the Elves behind him as he then ran straight toward King Morrik.

Voices within that moment came clear in Payner's head as though he was hearing them for the first time.

"Keyomar, what are you doing? Open my cell!"

"I got this, Captain!" reassured a positive Keyomar as he stormed down the corridor toward Morrik.

"Keyomar, I order you to stop!"

Keyomar disregarded the orders of Payner as he continued to run toward the Elven King. Keyomar raised the baton in the air as he neared him, whilst Morrik remained as solid as a statue, grinning back at him.

Payner momentarily snapped out of his visions; he raised his head from his arms ever so slightly and looked out into the dark and empty corridor. The tiniest bit of light entered the room from a small crack within the entrance door.

The tiny beam of light shimmered down on a small patch outside of Payner's cell door, but the light seemed somewhat outshone by a dark splatter of blood that lay within it.

Payner crawled across the dampened cell floor and over toward the steel rails, both of his fists clamped around the bars as he looked on at the blood-filled beam of light within the corridor.

Focusing his eyes a little, Payner began to see more blood splatter just outside of the light; he followed it in the corner of his eye for a moment before realising it wasn't a splatter of blood he was looking at. It was a trail.

He moved his head as far up against the cell as he possibly could, his eyes following the trail down the corridor the best his eyes could see.

As the trail got farther away, the darker the blood got, and the more it became lost within the shadows. Payner looked on as far as his eyes could focus, but he could not see the end of the trail.

Feeling a huge weight of aggravation and failure on his shoulders, Payner just released his clamp on the bars and dropped back to the floor with his back up against the cell door, his head once again falling into his hands.

With his head within his hands, he began to hear voices, but this time they were even clearer, these were not a part of his imagination.

He raised his head from his hands as the door at the end of the corridor swung open. Payner turned his head to see two Elven guards making their way down the steps and down the corridor toward his cell.

"Well, well, well. What have we got here?" said one Elven guard as they stood above Payner, who remained seated on the floor with his back to them.

Payner said nothing.

The first Elven guard then smashed his baton on the cell bars right next to Payner's head, forcing him to drop to the floor in complete shock.

He then looked up at the guards, who were now giggling to themselves at his misfortune.

"Still have nothing to say, huh?" asked the first guard.

Payner remained quiet as the two guards then approached the cell behind him that once played host to his fellow companion, Keyomar.

The guards then began to remove the bodies of the fallen guards whom Keyomar had previously taken down.

Payner did not take his eyes off of them the whole time they removed the bodies.

"Still lost for words, man?" asked the second Elven guard. "Are you upset that we have taken the bodies of our fallen guards away?" he added as the first guard walked up to the other end of the corridor.

Within a couple of seconds, the sound of dragging could be heard coming back toward them.

"Do not worry, we have still left you one body to look at," said the second Elf as the first Elf then dragged what appeared to be the body of a decapitated Keyomar.

Payner's head dropped in disgust as his visions began once more, envisioning the sight of Keyomar hanging from the end of a golden blade, a horrifying look of happiness on the face of King Morrik as Keyomar dropped to his knees.

Payner's mind went silent; he couldn't even hear the sound of his own screams, looking on as King Morrik pulled the blade from Keyomar's abdomen before swinging it toward his neck. But within that moment, when the blade connected with Keyomar, that was the moment Payner came back to reality, but in reality, another hour had passed.

Payner woke in a puddle of sweat looking up toward the corridor ceiling.

Bringing his eyes down ever so slowly to the body of his friend, it wasn't until he focused on the body of Keyomar that he suddenly saw something glistening within his pocket.

Payner, once again, pushed himself up against the cell as far as he could, this time squeezing one of his arms through the bars, as his face also pressed up tightly against the cell; his vision was limited.

He followed the touch of his hand until he felt the armoured garments around Keyomar's waist.

Once he found Keyomar's pocket, he stretched his fingers inside, and after a few seconds of rummaging, he managed to grab hold of something very small and jagged.

Payner quickly pulled his finger out of the pocket and then pulled his arm back through the cell bars. He sat back up against the cell door and slowly opened up his sweaty hand to only find himself looking back at a rusty golden key. Payner couldn't believe what he was staring back at. Feeling overwhelmed with admiration and surprise, Keyomar must have taken the key from one of the guards, or even King Morrik, as he knelt down in front of him, but one thing was for sure. If this was, in fact, a key to open the cell, then Keyomar had aided him one final time; he had given him a lifeline, at least.

Payner grasped onto the key tightly as he pulled himself up from the ground.

His hands shook anxiously as he slid the key into the lock, taking one huge breath before slowly turning it to his left.

Almost breaking down in complete joy when he heard the lock on the door click and seeing the door open up ever so slightly, Payner pushed the door open and fell straight down to his knees beside the body of Keyomar.

"I'm sorry, Keyomar, for all of this! If I didn't choose you to come with me, then this would never have happened to you. I'm sorry that I cannot take your body back with me; you deserve a lot more than this. And when I get out of here, everybody from this time and anytime onward will know what a hero you were and how you managed to save my life even after you were struck down. For now, I must move on, for I don't know how much time I have, I will see you again one day, my brother, may the spirits guide you. Farewell."

As one final tear dropped from his face, Payner grabbed hold of a baton that Keyomar still had grasped in his hand and with vengeance on his mind he headed straight for the entrance door.

Without any hesitation, Payner stormed through the door only to be hit in the eyes by a bright ray of light from the sun. Once his eyes began to focus, he soon began to see the land that lay before him, vaguely remembering the moment he was transported through here.

Before he could gather his thoughts, a foul voice came from the tower that stood tall over the dungeons. "Hey! Don't move! Stay where you are, prisoner! How have you escaped?"

"I am no prisoner; I carry that which no prisoner carries," replied Payner as he raised his hands in the air to reveal the baton.

"Do you see me for a fool? I was informed that all guards inside the dungeons were dead. I can see you're no Elf, I suggest you remain right where you are," ordered the guard.

Payner was caught. Suddenly, he began to hear voices and movements in the distance and had no doubt it was more guards.

"Sounds like the guards are on their way back," said the tower guard, Payner could almost sense the smirk on the guard's face at that statement.

He knew he had to do something quick; he knew whatever he tried couldn't be any worse than going back into that dungeon. He closed his eyes for a moment and listened to the sound of the guard above him.

"I can't wait to see what King Morrik is going to do to you when he finds out that you've tried to escape."

And with a split moment, Payner swung himself round and launched the baton up toward the guard. The baton smashed the guard in between the eyes, forcing him to stumble and drop from the edge of the tower and down to the floor; the fall must've killed him as he lay dead in front of Payner. The baton was gone, but instead, Payner equipped himself with the bow and arrow that had fallen from the tower.

Without waiting a single second longer, Payner ran straight through the trees and into the opposite direction of the oncoming guards.

Within a matter of seconds, the guards made their way to the dungeons, spotting the fallen tower guard immediately.

"One guard go and check the cells, now!" ordered the captain of the guards as he surveyed the body of the fallen guard. He looked up into the trees in front of him and saw the faint shadow of something moving in the distance.

After a few moments, the guard checking the dungeons came running back out with news of the escape. "He is gone, Captain. The prisoner, he has escaped!"

The captain remained focused on the trees. "I know exactly where he's heading," stated the captain to five Elven guards who stood behind him.

***

For what felt like hours, Payner had been storming through the woodland for what was actually all but ten minutes. He knew he could not last much longer, and he seemed to be finding no sign of an exit, but he just continued to run.

Although the soft grass of the woodland felt surprisingly cosy on his feet, he had no choice but to stop running. He knew, at this rate, he didn't need the guards to find him as he was already killing himself, gasping for as much air as he possibly could.

Payner found a nearby tree stump that looked awfully familiar to him. He was quick to throw that thought to the side, as his body was quick enough in telling him that he needed to rest. He took a few large breaths before waddling over to the stump to sit down.

After sitting for a few minutes to catch his breath, Payner began to hear the rustling leaves and the snapping of twigs behind him. He swung his head round in a shot, but he saw nothing.

Whilst still being focused on the noise behind him, he suddenly began to hear the same sound, but this time it was coming from in front of him. He swung his head back round to once again see nothing.

Payner quickly jumped back off the stump, as he knew he had to move on. One more time, he heard the noise coming from behind him. This time, a decision swarmed through his mind; turn around or ignore the noise and run.

His sense of knowing soon overcame his sense of logic. He swung his head round to investigate the noise once more, but this time, he came face-to-face with the Elven guard who was chasing him down. He locked eyes with the guard who appeared to be on his own. Payner quickly drew an arrow from his quiver and aimed straight for the captain, but was worryingly surprised when the captain began to grin back at him.

Payner tightened his pull on the drawstring, but as he was about to release the bow, for a split second, he heard the rustling of leaves behind him once more. But before he could react, he was soon met by a clubbing blow to the back of the head, knocking him straight to the ground and into a state of unconsciousness.

Soon enough, Payner began to awake back into consciousness but soon found himself trapped, tied to a tree like a horse at a hitching post. As he struggled to move, he looked out to see Whisperwood in a time that he had previously not seen it. It was dark; day had drawn to a close. The beautiful light that once was seemed as though it may not return; the woodland was unnerving, and the ground had become more swamp-like.

His attention drew away from the feel of the woodland when he soon smelt the burning of ash and the crackle of a campfire; he turned his head to the side to see the Elven captain along with now only four Elven guards, sitting amongst logs and battered down tree stumps.

They were talking to one another, but what the topic of conversation was, Payner didn't know.

"Let me out of here!" he cried as he tried to wriggle his way out of the ropes.

"What, and spoil all the fun?" replied the captain.

"What are you talking about? I'm of no use to you. To any of you."

"You are of use to our king!"

"Then, why is it you haven't returned me to him? I'm of no harm to your people; just allow me to leave in peace."

The captain grinned as he stood from his stump, shaking his head as he slowly made his way over to Payner.

"Where should I start? The king would have my head if I didn't return you to him! Invading our lands, bringing an army to our doorstep, killing one of our guards, one of our people, one of our friends. That says to me that you are of harm to us. I have sent a messenger to inform King Morrik of your escape and our recapture; the king would want you back alive, which we will see done. But that doesn't mean that we cannot exact some revenge for our friend ourselves."

"What are you talking about revenge? I killed the guard because your king killed my friend! We did not come to start a war."

The Elven captain then pulled a shiny dagger from his belt and moved in on Payner.

Payner wriggled and shook as much as he could, but the ropes were too tight, wrapped around the tree, covering his arms and his legs.

The captain wrapped his hand around Payner's throat with force, pushing his head back into the tree to keep him still before pushing his dagger into the side of his cheek.

"The king was the one who killed your friend, not the guard! Your vengeance should be with the king and the king alone. You became something you perceive us all to be— killers. Striking down an innocent Elf, an Elf that had a family, an Elf that had taken no lives, but you, man. You took it upon yourself to take his!" he shouted as he pushed his dagger farther into Payner's cheek before suddenly making a swift slice across his face.

The captain then moved a few yards away from Payner, leaving him to bleed as he then called over to two of his guards. "Dayn, Yayman."

The two guards hurried from their logs over toward Payner. The pair then proceeded to hold Payner securely to the tree as if the ropes weren't going to be enough.

With Payner not knowing what was happening, he tried to struggle, but at this point could only manage to move his head, and with his back still turned, the captain could still be seen cleaning the blood from his dagger.

"A few minutes ago, I said to you that I didn't know where to start. Well, now, I do," stated the captain as he turned back to Payner and stormed toward him with great intent.

As Dayn kept a tight grasp on Payner, Yayman managed to loosen one of his arms from the rope and pin his hand up against the tree.

The captain looked down the barrel of his nose and into the now anxious eyes of Payner and said only two words, "The fingers."

He then took the dagger to the pinned-down hand, and with complete force, he chopped off the two fingers that sat closest to the thumb.

"Aarghhhhhhhhhhhhhhhhhhhhh!" cried Payner in complete agony.

"Now, lay out his other hand!" ordered the captain.

But as Yayman moved on over to the other side, an arrow came flying from high within the trees, hitting him straight in the heart, shortly followed by a second one, which lodged itself into the back of Dayn's skull.

In complete shock, the captain dropped his dagger on the ground and instead he equipped his Elven Great Sword from its holster.

"Show yourself!"

But instead of the attacker making their physical presence known, they decided to send two more arrows down from the trees, hitting the two guards who stood indecisively around the campfire.

"Cowards! Do you not dare face me?" challenged the captain just before a fifth arrow came flying from the trees, piercing his chest plate, and dropping him to the ground.

Just as he fell, so did the rope that was wrapped tightly around Payner.

Payner dropped instantly to his knees, oblivious to the fact that he was now free, his body trembling as he held onto his wounded hand, blood streaming down his arm.

He looked down aimlessly at the ground until he saw that it started to become more distant. He began to rise above it.

Was he entering the spirit world? This was the thought that clouded his mind until he heard a voice from within the trees.

"Mind your *head*," came the voice, just seconds before Payner took another clubbing blow to the head, this time from a tree branch.

He continued to rise higher above the ground, through the leaves and past the branches, until the ground was no longer in sight.

His little trip through the trees soon came to a sudden halt when he found himself being pulled up onto a wooden platform by a very deceivingly scrawny Elf, followed by several other Elves who were helping to pull up the harness.

As Payner still clutched onto his wounded hand, he looked up at this scrawny Elf with great disbelief and praise. "Who are you? What is this place?"

"My name is Matine, and we are the rebel Elves of the treetop realm of Whisperwood. But that is all you should concern yourself with, for now, these Elves will take you to get patched up. And after that, I will take you to our queen, and there she will answer any questions that you may have."

After about an hour of pain, blood, and plenty of stitches Payner's hand was all but fixed, minus a couple of fingers, of course. But within that hour, all he could do was look around at the place he was in; it was magnificent, truly a place of wonder.

Just looking at what those Elves had built themselves so high up in the trees. There was platform after platform of Elven families, it was like a whole new kingdom.

"Are you ready to meet our queen?" asked Matine, interrupting Payner's deep train of thought.

"The sooner the better," replied Payner.

Just a few minutes walk across from the infirmary to where the queen was situated, Payner, with every step he took, was mesmerised by the way of life that had formed in the trees: great wooden huts, housing many families with a plentiful food resource, and species of colourful birds and insects he'd never seen before, some with wings as wide as bows. And being as close to the sky and the clouds as he could ever have dreamt to be.

"This place is incredible," said Payner.
Matine just smiled to himself and continued to lead the way.

After another couple of minutes, they suddenly came to a very elaborate curtain which draped from too large trees that stood above it, either side of a single platform.

Matine drew open the curtain and led Payner inside.

The sound of his heavy boots across each wooden plank echoed, bringing him closer and closer to a great golden throne that sit high above a mountain of sanded-down logs, draped in willow leaves and glitter corns. Payner was mesmerised. But what caught his eye the most, was the Elf who sat upon the throne, the queen.

She looked like no queen whom Payner had ever seen. She did not don dresses and gowns or sparkly frocks. She looked very much like a mercenary, leather boots, light chainmail armour, torn-up wrist guards, and a smile that would confuse any man.

Although, as battle prepared as she looked, she was still a lady, and she spoke in the gentlest tone.

"Greetings, Payner. I am Queen Angelar of the rebel Elves of the Whisperwood realm. You have been on some journey through these woods, haven't you?"

"All to lead up to this point, no doubt," replied Payner.

"We have been tracking you since they allowed you through the gates, but we are yet to know your purpose. The land Elves, they seem to have qualms with you; why is that?

"They allowed us to enter the land freely with no weapons. We were guided to a pond, where beneath it we were ambushed and imprisoned. We came on behalf of our own king, King Armish Hailguard. We are here because the Elves of this kingdom have been invited by the king himself for a special meeting to take place within Ar'Gurd along with the Wizards and the Dwarves. After turning down the invitation, we were put in the dungeons, where one of my companions was brutally and inhumanely struck down by your king!"

"He is not our king!" replied a stern queen.

Payner looked back at her with eyes of wonder and confusion. "Why did you save me?"

"Once we saw you, we had to determine who you were, so I had Matine follow you."

Matine then joined in the conversation. "I followed all the way from the bridge to the pond, I saw the tree trooper pass you the note, normal Elves do not know of the pond's passage; it is known only to the guards. And after they made you aware of it, I knew something wasn't right. Still using the trees as cover, I made my way around the pond and to the entrance of the dungeon. I heard guards talking about two men who were being held inside. I waited, and in that time, I saw Morrik enter with guards, and then I saw him leave, alone.

"He spoke to the tower guard of how he cut the head off your companion after he tried to escape and killed his guards. He mentioned that you were still alive and how he would return in due time to make you wish that you weren't. I ran back to Queen Angelar as fast as I could. She ordered me to come and rescue you and bring you to her, but when I got back to the dungeon, you had already escaped. I saw guards gathered around the dead tower guard before chasing you far into the trees. Unfortunately, they got to you before I did. I could get there no sooner. Once I finally found you, I did what I was ordered to do, and now here we are."

"And why is it you are rebels? Why do you have such hatred for your own people?" asked Payner from which Queen Angelar stood from her throne and made her way down the log stairs toward him.

"They are not *our* people—they're peasants, cowards! We were once ruled by a great king and queen, but one thing they never had was their own child. They tried and tried, but they had no luck. One particularly unfortunate day, the newest recruits for the Elven Huntsmen were in the city, and there was one recruit that stood out above the rest, a very skilled fighter, who was very handsome.

"The queen developed a soft spot for this recruit, and with a devilish look in his eye, he knew it. He befriended her, and he brainwashed her. One night, they got together. One thing soon led to another, and the queen, well…she fell pregnant. She knew the child was his and so did he, but he chose to steer clear from that point onward, that was until nine months later when the baby was born.

"The Huntsman came back into the fold with a cunning plan; he poisoned the king and once again brainwashed the queen. He made her believe that this was all for the best. She admitted to the kingdom that the child was in fact the Huntsman's. The two later married, and the Huntsman became king. Once he had all the power, he felt he had no need for a queen, so he cut off her head and he was left to rule the kingdom, just him and his son.

"If you're wondering where I fit into all of this, then you might be enlightened to know that the queen, she was my older sister. I was rightful heir to the throne until her son was born. The city became divided, followers of my sister became rebels with growing hate for the Huntsman. He banished all rebels from the kingdom under penalty of death, there were those that stood against him, but they did not survive.

"One of my sister's loyal friends, Brandol, he took me along with many rebels to the outskirts of Whisperwood before the Huntsman could track us down. We began building small shelters within the trees before eventually getting higher and higher until we could go no more. Brandol took over as leader of the rebels until I came of age and took over as the rightful queen of the Elves. Brandol died some years ago through old age, and so did the Huntsman, taking away any chance I had of redemption, but his son still lives, Morrik, and is just as cunning, just as ruthless, just as manipulative, and I will see his head hang from a pike before I meet my end!"

Payner was shocked, not normally was he lost for words, but at this point, he struggled. That was until he thought of the only right option. "You will see his head on a pike, I promise you that; I will make sure of it myself! But before that can happen, you must accept my king's invitation. Take on the role as the true leader of the Elves and attend the meet in their stead. Ally with us and we will see you retake what is rightfully yours; I will take on the task myself! The meet is in seven days' time, so what do you say?" asked Payner as he held out his hand to the queen.

"I can see passion in your eyes, Payner, but I also see wisdom. I do not doubt your word, and I will take it in good honour; I accept your king's invitation!" replied Queen Angelar as she then proceeded to confirm the agreement by shaking Payner's hand.

Bringing an abrupt end to the meeting, Payner bid a fond farewell to the queen of the treetop realm as Matine took him on a trip through the trees to show him the way out of the kingdom.

After about a ten-minute walk, Payner and Matine finally came to a small clearing balancing high above the trees on the edge of the land.

"Here we are, the way back into your land," said Matine.

"I guess this is goodbye, for now, Matine, and I truly cannot thank you enough for saving my life and patching me up afterward. I will see that your kingdom is returned to you."

"We are not just rebels, we are the eyemen of this kingdom, and we will see it restored to its former glory."

"Until then, my friend."

"Until then."

And after a very meaningful smile and handshake, Matine pulled an arrow from his quiver whilst then tying a small piece of rope around the arrow's head. He then fired the arrow straight into Ar'Gurd and into a tree on the other side.

Matine then passed Payner a large wooden bar so he could glide back into Ar'Gurd safely. And as Payner stood over the edge of the platform, hanging onto the piece of wood and looking on into Ar'Gurd, Matine moved in close and whispered to him, "Do not forget to remove the arrow from the tree and try not to scream too loud on your way down."

CHAPTER EIGHT

VALIANT CARNAGE

Maxin

As night drew all through the kingdom, Maxin gazed out from the tinted windows within his quarters of the castle, thinking back on the attack from the pirates.

The city was not ready for the attack, and Belthran wasn't the only one who thought so. Once the city fell to the pirates, what next? They would await the return of Prince Clearus and Sir Payner, and after slaying them, they would then move on through to the city of Paran-Dun, burning down any other small villages they may pass. The kingdom would soon belong to the pirates, all it needed was one more attack.

King Armish was adamant in his claim that he would not recall the troops. Maxin saw the look of certainty in his eyes, as did the queen.

Maxin wondered many things as he gazed upon the kingdom, but he knew one thing was true; they needed more troops, and they needed them now.

***

The hour was late when three solid knocks hit the door of Maxin's quarters, drowning out the sound of the crackling fire that lit up the room in the corner.

"Who is there?" asked Maxin.

"It is I, Brother, myself and Harnik; we have a matter of great urgency we wish to discuss with you."

Maxin hastily moved over to his big, bolted, wooden doors, unhooked the chains, and opened them to greet Belthran and Harnik.

"You scared of monsters getting in?" joked Harnik.

"Just pirates," replied a stern Maxin.

"Don't be scared, Cousin, I will slay them all before they even step foot within the castle."

"But Maxin has a right to be scared, Harnik, as do we all. We all know the danger that we face. The pirates have gotten smarter; they now know we're at our weakest, and they would be foolish not to strike again. Having no fear at all makes you thoughtless; a doom awaits us, which is why something needs to be done!"

"So what are you suggesting?" asked Maxin.

"Well, Brother, that is why we have come to you."

"Me? Why me? What can I do to help?"

"You can give us a chance," replied Belthran before then adding, "you already have four members in your Unit. Therefore, you still require six more. Me and Harnik, we know this city, we know it a lot better than you, and we know that you will not find much more here; you must expand your search."

"Expand my search?"

"It means search away from the city," explained Harnik.

"I know what it means. But how would me finding six more troops possibly help?"

"It'll give us a fighting chance, Brother. One skilled fighter can take down many pirates; just think how many six can do."

"But that is not all, Maxin," added Harnik. "Much like my own, your father is very stubborn; he will fall before he asks for any aid to help fight against pirates. Paran-Dun is a city full of great fighters. We suggest you start your search there. Give word to Paran-Dun of the attacks and they will spare some men to help us fight."

"And what of Mother and Father? They would never allow this," stated Maxin.

"You're right, Brother, they won't. That is why we have come to you now, that's why we are having this out-of-hours chat, and that's exactly why you need to leave, now!"

"Now?"

"Yes, now. If Mother and Father ask of your whereabouts, then me and Harnik will cover for you. We need the help as soon as we can get it, and the cover of darkness will help you leave the city unnoticed. Father is not allowing anyone to leave the city at this point, but you must be hasty; we have little time left. Take little in the way of provisions," instructed Belthran.

"We have also informed Scarlep, and we have sent word to Igor of the plan; they will be waiting for you down by the city gates. You cannot fail us, Maxin!" added Harnik.

"I will bring back help. I promise."

"Good, that's what I like to hear. Now, go!" ordered Belthran.

As Maxin hurried to the door, it wasn't long before he was stopped once more by Belthran. "Maxin, make sure nobody sees you leave the city. And if you fall, I promise you now that I will find your sorry, rotten carcass and I will kick it."

"I will return, I swear!"

Maxin then left the quarters and the castle with great haste to meet up with the rest of his troops at the city gates.

A luminous courtyard awaited Maxin and his troops as they remained hidden behind a nearby cobbled cottage.

Following the recent sneak attacks, the city at night was now lit up, making it extremely difficult to pass in and out without being noticed.

"Now what?" asked Scarlep as he looked on at the gates over Maxin's shoulder, trying to remain undetected.

"It's going to be impossible to sneak past them guards. Maxin, you're the prince. They cannot stop you," stated Igor.

"Actually, Igor, they can. My father's rule still leads over mine, and even if they were to let me go, there is still no doubt that they would inform him. There has to be another way."

"Perhaps there is," suggested Tamrin.

All eyes were fixated on Tamrin for an answer as he remained focused on the gates, and the ten guards that surrounded them.

"Tamrin, do you have a plan?" asked Maxin, urging him on.

But before Tamrin could let out an answer, they heard a voice in the courtyard that caught their attention.

"Guards!"

Maxin, Tamrin, Igor, and Scarlep peered around the cobbled cottage toward the gate to investigate the voice.

"It's Belthran!" confirmed Maxin.

"What is he doing?" asked Scarlep.

The four continued to look on as they suddenly began to see all the guards move away from the gate in a great hurry.

"What is happening?" asked Scarlep once more.

"Maybe there is an attack?" suggested Igor.

"No, the alarms would have been sounded, this distraction is meant for us," stated Maxin.

But they were all suddenly spooked when they heard another voice coming from right behind them.

"Of course."

"Harnik, don't sneak up on us like that," said Maxin.

"You're far too jumpy, Cousin. You and your little Unit will also need to be a bit more discreet and reclusive out there in the wild. Me and Belthran could spot you hiding away down here all the way from the brick alley bridge; how the guards never saw you, I don't know. We've caused a small distraction for you, but you must move now; they will not be gone for long, so go!"

Without wasting any more time, Maxin and the others gathered up their small duffel sacks and ran for the gates.

The four of them quickly made it to the gates, where they were greeted by Belthran and four horses.

"Hurry now, Brother, there is not much time!" stated Belthran.

Climbing up onto their horses, Tamrin, Igor, and Scarlep quickly fled from the city whilst Maxin remained where he was.

"Belthran, how did you…"

"Go, now!" interrupted Belthran before giving Maxin's horse a swift slap, prompting it to sprint away from the city in pursuit of the other three.

The journey toward Paran-Dun was not so much a long one, but an enduring one.

The two moons of the kingdom shone bright on this night, the air remained warm, and the dust blew thick. An open and desolate section of the land leading toward Paran-Dun looked almost derelict, whilst during the day it persisted on being a thriving plot for fruit to grow and plants to flourish.

***

Maxin and his Unit were riding for all but twenty minutes through the humid wilderness of Ar'Gurd before they eventually came to their first clearing, the woods of Faymanen.

Their horses slowed down as they proceeded into the woodland with great caution.

"What is this place?" asked Scarlep.

"You haven't been this far from the city before? This, my friend, is Faymanen, but you may know it more by its more commonly used name, Woodland Farm," explained Tamrin.

"This is Woodland Farm?" added Scarlep.

"Yes. One of the most amazing places of this land. For reasons yet unknown, the temperature of this woodland remains perfect all year round. The soil is but the best in the land, allowing the crops to continuously grow without any attention. All the farmers need to do is come and pick what they need; it really is a wonder," enlightened Tamrin.

"Great, magical crops—how wonderful," replied a sarcastic Igor, which was met by a very disheartened gaze from Tamrin.

They continued to move slowly through the dark woodland of Faymanen, the scent of freshly grown strawberries and corn apples brushing the noses of the group, forcing them to stop and fill up their duffel sacks as much as they could ahead of their journey.

Once they mounted their horses, they made their way through the woodland and out to the other side. Between the four of them, only Tamrin had ever ventured beyond Faymanen. It was even new territory for the young prince, being almost fourteen, he had not yet experienced the full depth of the kingdom.

"There is a canyon about five minutes from here, which to this day has been my farthest-reaching point, I dared not cross it," said Tamrin.

"Don't worry, my father has assured me on many occasions that these lands are perfectly safe, aside from the odd Zarnik or two, but I'm sure the four of us would have no problem dealing with one of them," reassured Maxin.

"There are many creatures other than Zarniks that patrol these lands, my Prince, you may find that there is a lot your father might not have told you," claimed Tamrin.

"Such as?" enquired Maxin.

"These lands might not be as safe as he makes out. I may not have travelled far, but I have heard things, stories of great creatures once spotted on these lands."

"They are but stories, Tamrin. I wouldn't listen to all that you hear. If there were great creatures that live on these lands, then I assure you, my father would have told me."

Tamrin looked on with doubtful eyes as Maxin and the rest of the Unit continued on through the dark wilderness and onto the resonant canyon.

The horses led them through the darkness and right to the very edge of the canyon, countless stones crumbling from the cliff face down to the not yet visible surface.

"Tamrin, when you said you dared not cross, did you really mean you could not cross?" asked Igor.

"Partly, the option to go around the canyon was always there, but it would take at least a two-day ride, something I wasn't at all committed to doing."

"Two days? We don't have that kind of time," stated Maxin.

"Then, what do you suggest?" Tamrin countered.

Maxin hopped off of his horse and walked ever so carefully through the darkness and to the canyon's edge. He looked down toward the bottom, but he couldn't see a thing; it looked like nothing more than a giant black hole.

But the fear of not knowing how big the canyon was didn't stop the young prince; he knew what had to be done. He looked back at Igor, Tamrin, and Scarlep, who were all still mounted.

"We climb down, cross the canyon and then climb up," he proposed.

"Are you crazy? We will fall to our early graves," confronted Igor.

"We have no other choice, Igor. It will take four days to go round and back again; that is time we don't have. We can either gather our courage and climb down, or we can cave into fear and go back to the city, burying our heads beneath our tails. I for one am going down, what say the rest of you?" asked Maxin.

"I didn't come this far to turn back now; I'm in," confirmed Scarlep.

"Me, too," added Tamrin.

Maxin then locked eyes with Igor once more. "Igor? What about you?" he asked.

Igor took a small moment, looking at Maxin with a deep unpleasantness. "Fine, I will do it. But someone else goes first," replied Igor as he then hopped from his horse, dragging his hammer off with him.

They sent their horses on their way as they then anxiously began to decline down the canyon with young Tamrin leading the way.

Still unable to see the bottom and with every step causing a freefall of small rocks, the group found themselves nearing forty feet from the surface. That was when they began to hear the noise of whooshing and crashing coming from beneath them.

"What is that?" shouted Scarlep.

"It's water. A stream flows through the bottom of this canyon, so I'm told," answered Tamrin.

They began to decline farther and farther down, and the sound soon became louder and louder.

Eventually, Tamrin reached far enough to be able to see the bottom. "Oh, no!" he cried.

"What? What is it, Tamrin?" Maxin asked, urgency lacing his voice.

"It is no stream."

"Then, what is it?" replied Igor as he carefully moved another step down, whilst his hammer rested heavily across his back.

Tamrin worryingly looked upward at the three of them and shouted, "Rapids!"

"You've got to be joking," Scarlep muttered to himself.

"Everybody, watch your step!" ordered Maxin.

"Oh, like we weren't already?" replied Igor, sarcastically.

Within a split moment, things suddenly went from bad to worse, as a rock that Tamrin grabbed hold of came loose. He lost his balance and fell straight from the wall, his screams echoing through the canyon as he fell.

"Tamrin!" cried Maxin, which was quickly followed by the sound of a great splash in the water below.

"Go everyone, climb down, quickly!" ordered Maxin.

And without any regard for their safety, the three of them began to hurry down toward the bottom.

"Tamrin? Are you okay?" shouted Maxin, but there was no response.

Igor was the first to touch safely down to the bottom, followed shortly by Maxin and then Scarlep.

They could see nothing but rapid water smashing into jagged rocks as it flowed downstream with great ferocity.

"Tamrin!" shouted Maxin once more.

"Where is he?" asked a worried Scarlep, when suddenly Tamrin shot to the surface of the water while he tried to stay afloat as the water dragged him downstream, narrowly avoiding several jagged rocks.

"Quickly, give me the bags of fruit that we packed from Woodland Farm, all of them!" ordered Igor.

Unaware and unsure of what Igor's plan was, Maxin and Scarlep quickly handed over their small leather fruit sacks.

Igor pulled a long piece of rope from his belt, and then he threaded it quickly through each sack and tying the end to his hammer. Creating some form of fishing pole, he swung the line into the water ahead of Tamrin, who was quickly heading toward a bay of rocks from which he had no way of avoiding.

Tamrin raised an arm out from the water and grabbed onto the sack at the end of the rope.

"Hold on, Tamrin, we'll pull you in!" shouted Maxin as he and Scarlep also grabbed hold of the hammer to reel him in.

But as Tamrin was being pulled with such force, it caused the sack he was holding to come loose and fall from the line, but quick to react in a state of panic, Tamrin managed to lunge himself close enough to be able to grab hold of the second sack and was then quickly pulled back to the bank and lifted from the water.

As Igor untied the rope from his hammer, Scarlep and Maxin were quick to gather around a drenched and breathless Tamrin.

"Tamrin, are you okay? Are you hurt?" asked Maxin.

"I'm okay. But that water is freezing," replied Tamrin.

Igor looked out across the rapids with a look of great stress, taking in a huge breath as he realised something of great importance.

"I think *you* three still seem to be forgetting something."

He turned his head toward the others. "There is still no way across the rapids. My rope will not be long enough to reach the other side."

Maxin and Scarlep looked on at one another with wondering thoughts, as they stood cold and wet upon the bank of the river, the sound of their thoughts blocked by the noise of crashing water as they strained hard to conjure up a plan in their minds so they could proceed forward.

As they continued to look on at one another without a single idea; they were soon side-tracked when a long, dampened rope was thrown to the gritty stone surface that surrounded the feet of the pair.

"Take my rope. You can attach it to Igor's and then you've got yourselves a way across," suggested Tamrin as he made his way up to his feet, trying to rinse the last few drops of water from his cloth.

Without any second-guessing, Igor tied a small knot to conjoin the two ropes. He then tied one end of the rope around a nearby boulder.

"There, steady as a rock," joked Igor as he then threw the other end to Tamrin, who attached it to one of his arrows before firing it over the rapids and into a wall on the other side.

"Is it safe?" asked a worried Maxin.

"It's one of my own knots, Maxin, you know there is nothing safer," replied Igor.

"We will see," said Tamrin as he lunged his arms and legs around the rope with no fear and began to scurry himself across to the other side.

After a short crawl, Tamrin safely made it to the ground on the opposite side of the rapids, then shouted across for the others to proceed.

Maxin was next to go, and as he touched down safely, he was then followed by Scarlep, who after a short while also made it across safely.

"It's your turn, Igor," shouted Scarlep, with the sound echoing through the canyon.

Igor was always a little heavier than most his age, and even some who were older than him, so he found himself a little on edge as he slowly pulled himself up onto the rope.

As he began to very slowly crawl across, the rope ever so slightly began to drape closer toward the water. He felt sploshes of water on his face as it crashed against the jagged rocks nearby.

Igor had just managed to make it a little over halfway across the rapids, just passing the small knot that joined the two ropes. As he moved his right hand forward to pull himself ahead, the knot that joined the ropes came loose, dropping Igor into the ice-cold rigorous water.

Luckily for Igor, apart from being a little on the heavy side, it made him just as strong, he hung on to the rope as it threw him into the water.

Much to their amusement, Maxin, Tamrin, and Scarlep were then just as quick to react as they grabbed hold of the rope and pulled him safely into the bank to join them.

"Y-y-you t-t-think this is f-f-funny?" stuttered Igor as he shivered and trembled back up to his feet.

He then looked at Tamrin with deep anger. "T-t-this is all y-y-your f-f-fault!" he claimed.

"*Me*? I don't see how I'm to blame for this?"

"You and your s-s-stupid r-rope!" replied Igor as he moved a step closer to Tamrin.

"My rope? Your knots!"

"I am not nuts!"

"*Knots*, I said your knots were the problem," continued to argue Tamrin. "*Oh, yeah, this is one of my own knots; nothing is stronger*," Tamrin imitated Igor's earlier words in a sarcastic tone, seeming to anger Igor a little bit too much, just enough that it made Igor retaliate in a way that nobody expected.

"Let's find out, shall we?" shouted Igor as he lunged toward Tamrin, grabbing hold of his garments and throwing him up against the nearest wall, pinning him there by his throat.

"Igor!" cried Maxin from behind him.

Suddenly, Igor felt a small cold blade rest on the right side of his neck; he turned his head ever so slightly to see Scarlep holding a dagger toward him.

"Get off him, Igor," he said, sternly.

"You're willing to kill me?" asked Igor.

"I don't want to, but at this moment, I don't quite know what you're capable of, and as long as you leave Tamrin unharmed, there won't be a problem."

Igor then looked back into the bloodshot eyes of Tamrin, who was just managing to remain on his tiptoes. Igor then began to see him struggle to breathe, which was the point he released his grip and allowed him to drop to his knees and catch his breath. As he did, he looked to his right and saw Scarlep lower his sword. He then looked to his left, and much to his shock, he saw his best friend, Maxin, holding up a sword toward him.

"Please, don't say you're aiming that thing at me, Maxin," said Igor.

"I thought you were going to kill him, Igor. I saw deep anger in your eyes, one I've only seen when you're caving a creature's head to dust. He is your Unit companion, and there should be no conflict!"

"You all honestly thought I was going to kill him? I may have killed a man before, but there is a difference between killing for what is right and being a murderer. I swore myself to this Unit and to protect everything in this land. I'm not about to murder its people, let alone my own companion. Maxin, you know I have a short fuse, and you also know I wouldn't kill one of my own men."

"Just apologize to him, Igor; shake hands and we can just move on. We are across the rapids now, and we must find somewhere to rest up for the night," suggested Maxin.

Igor then took a step toward Tamrin, who was still down on his knees, catching his breath. He held out his hand to him, and when Tamrin accepted the gesture, he was quickly pulled back up to his feet. "I am sorry, Tamrin, I did not mean to take it so far."

"So now what way do we go? We can't stay out in the open down here," Scarlep asked.

"We will keep west down the canyon bank, hopefully, we can find a small cave or burrow where we can lay for the night," suggested Maxin.

Throwing all disputes aside, Maxin and his Unit gathered their things and proceeded down the riverbank.

Still in complete darkness, each step on each wet and jagged rock was met with great caution, only being able to see patches of the ground around them. The air was warm and very humid down in the depths of the canyon.

The group kept moving down the bank a few more yards until Tamrin was soon halted by the sound of a different kind of water.

"Tamrin?" questioned Maxin.

"That sound of water in the distance, it is different to the rapids; it's less crashing against rocks and more of a heavy rush; the air feels different here," explained Tamrin.

Igor and Scarlep looked at one another, completely baffled. The way Tamrin spoke was almost foreign to them; it was the way folk would speak much further north of the city.

"What are you trying to say? Speak a language we can all understand," replied Igor.

Tamrin chose not to respond but instead continued to pass Maxin and head closer toward the new sound in the distance.

Maxin, Igor, and Scarlep carefully and reluctantly followed.

Sounds of rushing water became clearer and somewhat louder than the rapids. Maxin, Igor, and Scarlep soon lost Tamrin within the shadows as they tried to stay close, although the small chains that hung from his boots could still be heard with each step he took.

Suddenly, the sound of Tamrin's footsteps stopped.

"Tamrin?" Maxin called out, trying to make his voice heard over the water, but there was no response.

The three then moved a few steps farther through the darkness until they eventually caught up with Tamrin, just standing there staring up at this huge waterfall that was pouring down from a river at the top of the cliff wall that the group were planning to climb.

"How do we get past this?" asked Scarlep.

"Don't you now think we should have moved down the bank on the other side of the rapids first? There's no waterfall that side," added Igor.

"A little late for that now, my friend," replied Tamrin as he continued to glare up at the rocks within the falls. "But there could be somewhere for us to lay our heads," he added as he then pointed up to a small gap hidden behind a boulder and a patch of giant Mocker Leaves.

"What is that?" asked Maxin, squinting his eyes and attempting to see what Tamrin was pointing at.

"It looks like a hidden cave, how big it is, I don't know, but it could be worth a look," indicated Tamrin.

"And how is it you suggest we climb up through the heavy rush of water and the slippery mossed-up rocks?" enquired Igor.

"Easy," answered Tamrin as he moved a few steps to the side and parted a few Mocker Leaves that had been growing from within the cliff face, only to reveal a set of stone steps leading up in the direction of the cave.

"That is not right," stated Scarlep.

"Scarlep is right," added Maxin. "Steps don't just turn up leading into a cave for no reason; someone or something must have put them there, which means we weren't the first ones to step foot down here. But it also means that there could still be somebody in there, somebody who could help us."

Scarlep couldn't believe what he was hearing; he looked on at Maxin and Tamrin as though they were delusional. "You can't be serious. Who could possibly live in there? And if there was somebody in there, how could they possibly help us?"

"Where is your sense of interest, Scarlep? And if there is nobody up there, we still need a place to rest, and looking around, we don't have many other options," stated Tamrin.

"Tamrin is right," agreed Maxin. "We have little options left here, Scarlep. If you truly believe there is nobody up there, then you have nothing to worry about. Igor, what do you say?"

"Let's just get this done. It's going to be pitch black up there, anyway. So don't worry, Scarlep, if there is someone or something up there, you won't be able to see them," joked Igor as he pushed past Tamrin, taking it upon himself to lead the way up the cobbled steps, followed closely by Tamrin, Maxin, and then a very reluctant Scarlep.

After ten big steps up, the group moved beyond the Mocker Leaves at the top of the steps and into the entrance to the cave that was just big enough for them all to walk through. Moving one at a time, they all safely made it inside. But that's not without having the sight of a blind man, not being able to see their own hands in front of their faces.

"Now what? We can't even see where we are laying our heads. At least, outside we could see," argued Scarlep.

"Well, then, feel free to go back down the steps," stated Maxin.

But before anyone could respond, the group heard another voice, a voice neither of them recognised. It was a whispering tone that echoed gently through the caves.

"When trespassers come,
We will fight.
They will die;
They will not see the light,
Nobody has ever got out of here alive.
It is your turn now,
And you will not survive."

"Now, can we leave?" asked a worried Scarlep.
"No," replied Maxin, then turning his attention to the voice within the air, "Who are you? Show yourself!"
And it wasn't long before the whispering riddler spoke once more,

"My spear will be the last you see.
You trespassed here;
It is meant to be."

"Stop threatening me and present yourself!" ordered Maxin in great anger, drawing the voice to speak out again.

"You have a lot of anger inside.
When all your troops would run and hide,
I will cut off their heads, and they will see,

The devil they put inside of me."

"Just try it, you freak. I will pound your head to dust!" cried out Igor, whereas Tamrin answered the voice with a question rather than a threat.

"Wait, you said the devil we put inside of you? What do you mean by that?"
Then the voice, once again, was quick to respond,

"All these answers your kings will know.
Now, ready your weapons; let's start the show."

Anxiously keeping his weapon holstered, Maxin could only ponder on the questions his father may know the answer to, but also on the fact that he might not ever make it out of the cave to find out. He chose to speak up against the voice once more, this time in a less angered tone and, instead, a more direct one.

"Listen, my father is the king! I am Prince Maxin, and I know nothing of you and your situation. Please, present yourself, there'd be no need for a battle."

Suddenly, two wooden sticks struck the high walls of the cave, causing them to catch fire and create a small glint through the cave.

At that point, the size of the cave was insignificant to them. Neither of them spoke a word, nor could they see anyone; they glanced around looking for this figure, and it didn't take much longer for the whispering riddler to reveal himself.

Coming out from the shadows behind a dull glow and a small flicker of flames a little deeper into the cave, was a young, half-naked boy carrying a large wooden spear and donning long, dreaded hair, war paint, and tattered leather rags.

He looked at nobody but Maxin, staring at him with devil eyes, not a single flutter of his eyelids as sparks from the fire crackled across his face.

"If you are the king's son,
Then this should be fun.
Do not attempt to run;
I wouldn't even try.
As for being his son,
You'll be the first to die!"

The figure felt the glares on him, but his eyes remained solely on the young prince. His dirty face glimmering through the flames, eyes of hurt and anger with a grin to match.

Living a life in dark caves, the figure's sense of sound grew strong. He could hear the heavy boots of Igor scuffling across the floor, the blades of Scarlep's daggers chiming as they were pulled from his belt, the tightened grip of Maxin's hand around his sword, and the pulled drawstring of Tamrin's bow.

And for this figure, it was the latest of sounds that drew his interest. He knew all eyes were on him. He could feel the glares and he could hear the weapons being gripped tightly. And within an instant, the figure swung his small, flamed torch down to the floor in front of Tamrin, who stood yards across from him, causing the fire to spark and flash into the young archer's eyes.

Scarlep ran to his friend's aid in sharp fashion, no longer worried about his footing, whilst Maxin and Igor remained firmly where they were, keeping their eyes front and centre as sight of the figure was lost with the light. It dawned on them, at this point, that perhaps sound wasn't the figure's only sense that had been heightened.

Within moments, a faint shadow was soon spotted hurtling toward Maxin, warned by Igor, who quickly came barrelling in to help, but just as quickly went crashing to the dirt as his boot met the side of a heavy rock.

Quick and very fortunate to react, Maxin batted away the figure's spear from an incoming lunge but soon found himself on his back when that same spear was hooked behind the back of his ankles.

The figure placed his foot firmly over Maxin's sword hand, forcing him to release it. He stood atop the young prince menacingly, forcing his spearhead against his neck, slightly piercing the skin.

Seeing his prince and captain in danger, Scarlep grabbed the torch that lay at the feet of Tamrin and threw it back toward the figure, not enough to blind him, but enough to take his attention away from Maxin.

And as soon as that attention was drawn away, Maxin pulled his own dagger from his belt and struck across the ankle of the figure, causing him to drop to the floor in pain.

Igor was soon back on his feet, picking himself up like it was nothing and stomping over to the figure. He grabbed him viciously by his rags and pinned him up against a nearby wall, very much in a similar fashion as the Tamrin incident prior to entering the caves.

Maxin quickly joined Igor at the wall, resting his cold blade across the figure's throat. "Speak, now!" he ordered, but the figure said nothing.

"We can do this the easy way, or we can do it *my* way!" added Igor. But again, the figure remained a boy of silence.

"There is only one way this will end for you if you don't speak," warned Maxin, but instead of a response, he was just met by a serious glare of hate and anguish. Maxin had enough; he warned the boy, but he wasn't willing to cooperate.

"Then so be it," stated Maxin as he then pulled back his sword to swing at the neck of the mysterious boy but was quickly halted when he soon found his voice once more.

"Wait!" he cried.

"Oh, would you look at that, he remembers how to talk," joked Igor.

"Start with your name, boy! And why you tried to kill us," said Maxin, from which the boy reluctantly obliged, but this time in a gentler and less rhythmic tone.

"My name is Algo. If you're really unaware of our past, then I will enlighten you, but first, release me. You've sliced my ankle; I'm not in any condition to attempt to run."

"Igor, release him," ordered Maxin as Igor released his grasp, allowing Algo to stand freely on his one good leg, supporting himself up against the wall as he went on to enlighten Maxin and the group of their history.

"Years ago, as far back as man can go and your first king came to be, the land was a very different place, a lot different than what it is now. There was no equality throughout the land; you were rich or you were poor. Over time, the king grew a hatred for the poor and banished them all from the kingdom; he wouldn't even have them for slaves. To be poor was to be weak, and he had no time for the weak. Unless you made a great living being part of the king's army or being a sustainable worker like a farmer or a blacksmith, then he didn't want you.

"Back then, there was not a job for everyone, the king killed hundreds of poor people to prove a message to the rest of the kingdom. I don't know where he expected the poor people to go, but he said he will kill any poor person he would later lay his eyes on. The poor left the cities in flocks, unable to go to any village, town, or city, as they were all occupied by descendants of the crown.

"The poor gathered down within the canyons in an attempt to stay out of sight and live off the fish in the river, which is when the great leader of the poor, Baldruk Frowe, found the entrance to the cave; he single-handily carved the stairway into the canyon walls and saved our people from certain extinction. We have survived underground ever since, feeding off of the lake and other nearby resources. The cave goes through for miles, but the one thing you should know is there is only one way in and only one way out. So there you have it, a brief history of what your ancestors did to our people."

The group was stunned, neither of them expecting to hear anything of the sort.

"You mean to say there is a colony of you living within these caves?" questioned Maxin.

"Hundreds," replied Algo.

"Look, Algo, I cannot apologise enough for what you have all been through throughout the years, but know this; as you said, times have changed. My father would not stand for this now; your people are *our* people, and he would not have you forced to live a life underground. He will listen to reason; he is a good man. Let us help you."

"Wait a minute, this kid just tried to kill us! He almost blinded Tamrin," argued Igor.

"I'm sorry, we have been brought up to hate Landers and to kill on sight, me and my people, we know no other life. You have heard our story, and now my people must hear yours," stated Algo.

"What did he just call us? Landers?" groaned Igor before being interrupted by Scarlep.

"Say what? Why must they hear our story?"

"It is not enough to convince me to speak to your king. You must speak with my people; they must know of your willingness to right the wrongs of your ancestors," explained Algo.

"Why don't we just leave this place and forget about all of this? Let him and his people live down here like critters," suggested Igor.

"Did you not hear him?" asked Maxin. "They have hundreds of people in there. If we can make things right between us and get them on our side, just think of the extra aid the city could have," he added then turned his attention back to Algo.

"Algo, take us to your people."

CHAPTER NINE

IN THE DEEP, DARK DAMP

Maxin

Flaming torches in hand and an intrigued wonder in the back of their minds, the group, led by Algo, made their way into the tunnels of the cave, opening a whole new world that no other Lander had ever laid eyes on.

The tunnels were much smaller than the cave itself; they were cramped, dark, damp, and seemingly endless. But whilst Maxin and Tamrin saw this as a great opportunity, there were still buckets of doubt weighing down on the shoulders of Igor and Scarlep, who both happily kept themselves distanced at the back of the line as they moved through the cave.

"What if this is a trap? What if this is all a plan for that little caveman to ambush us?" whispered Igor to Scarlep.

"I don't like this, either, but we need to try and trust the prince's judgement on this. We are part of *his* Unit; we agreed to follow him, no matter what, and if it is a trap, then we will cut off their heads, regardless."

"I have known the prince for many years, he has a soft heart. If he is not careful, it will be his downfall. I should've just pummelled the caveman's head when I had the chance."

"You have too much hatred, Igor. If you're not careful, it will be *your* downfall," joked Scarlep as they continued onward through the tunnels.

As ember began to fall from the flaming torches, it began to signal the distance the group had already travelled through the caves; the air had become fouler, and the floor had become somewhat stickier. The light was beginning to fade, and the last thing the group wanted was to fall into darkness in an unknown cavern.

Much about Algo was still yet to be uncovered, but one thing was for sure, he wasn't quite the whispering riddler he portrayed himself to be at the cave's entrance.

"I must say, Algo, you're much more silent than our first encounter," said Maxin.

"From then, I had words to say. Now, there is not much I need to speak of or concern myself with," stated Algo.

"Is there not much you wish to know? Are you not in the slightest intrigued about the land outside? I like to think I'm a boy of interest, not so much through myself, by through the things I encounter and the people I have come across, and you interest me, Algo, you and your people; there is much I wish to find out."

"You can find out about my people from my people."

"And what of you? Nobody knows about you better than yourself."

"And I thought it was me that spoke in riddle-tongue. What is it you wish to know?" asked Algo from which many potential questions flew through the mind of the prince, but there was one, one that he so deeply desired to know the answer to.

"How old are you?"

"Fourteen and a half."

"Are you really? No kidding."

"Why would I lie? Why is it of importance?"

"It's not," replied Maxin before adding, "well, not yet at least. But do tell me this, why is it that a boy of fourteen was guarding the only way in and out of the cave? No offence to you, but with hundreds of people down here, was there not anyone more suitable for the job?"

"I am just as skilled as any man down here," replied a stern Algo.

"Then, we shouldn't have much to fear if things don't go right for us down here," interrupted Igor as he jokingly joined the conversation.

"And what exactly is that is that supposed to mean?"

"Oh, I'm sorry, Mr. Caveman, I forgot you have trouble speaking in proper tongue, so let me say that to you again, this time in a way you might understand,

"We came into the cave, and what did we find?
A half-naked boy who made Tamrin blind.
He came at us with a spear, and he started a bout.
But with all his skill and all his might,
It was never enough to keep the four of us out!"

Igor joked, which was met with an admirable snigger from Scarlep, but also an angered Algo.

Algo threw down the flaming torch as sparks burst out from the impact, using his spear as a walking stick for his injured ankle, turned around to Igor and glared furiously at him through the shadows.

"One more word from you, Lander, and the only thing you will have to keep out is my spear from your mouth!" threatened Algo, causing Igor to retaliate in typical Igor fashion, gripping his hammer in both hands and squeezing past Scarlep in the narrow tunnel to move closer to Algo.

"Just try it, you scrawny little cave peasant! I'll cave your head into dust before you could even lift your spear from the ground."

Maxin was caught in the middle, his best friend and companion against his guide and a possible potential Unit member in his eyes.

"Stop this!" he ordered. "Igor, I love you like a brother, but please, in the name of the spirits, shut up. Algo, I may not be your leader, but as we spared your life, I expect you to refrain from threatening ours and continue onward to your people. I think that concludes all else that needs to be said right now."

And as Igor lowered his hammer and moved back in position behind Scarlep, Algo picked up his fire torch and continued onward through the tunnel, leading the way to his people, without any one of the five boys saying another word to each other.

Lighting glimmered in the distance; the echoed sound of heavy-booted footsteps within the tunnels began to drown out with the sound of whispering voices up ahead.

The voices became louder as the group approached the light, the voices still very faint, but there was one that came through loud and clear, loud enough that it could've possibly been heard from back at the waterfall.

"Several bodies approach," echoed a voice through the tunnel.

The group gripped their weapons tightly as they edged closer toward the light.

"Holstering your weapons would be a great start toward getting us on your side," said Algo. "Just be prepared, they will have a deep hatred for you, and they will want to gut you at any given chance. I will take you through Cavetown and into the Hall of the Betters. There, you will then state your case in front of the council of the three Better Lords. Just try and be calm."

"Calm he says, he wasn't just told that a whole society wants to gut him," sniggered Igor to Scarlep.

As the group approached Cavetown, the entrance became clearer; it was a hole the size of a wagon wheel.

Bodies could be seen gathering around the hole to gaze through, almost blocking the light completely from the tunnel. Luckily, Algo still had hold of his fire torch.

A voice once again echoed through the tunnel; this time aimed directly toward the group. "Halt, all of you!"

"Who is it that approaches Cavetown? Present yourselves!"

"It is I…Algo."

"And who may it be that follows you, Algo?"

"Visitors to the Better Lords, and folk who spared my life after I fought to take theirs."

"They are Landers?" replied an outraged guard of Cavetown.

"They are Landers who could change all of our lives for the greater," argued Algo.

"I will not allow them to pass. I will have their heads!"

"As long as they remain alongside me, then you will have nothing! I am taking them to the Better Lords; they will decide what to do with them."

"Then, come on through," replied the guard.

Algo then took the last few steps toward the entrance before walking into Cavetown followed by Maxin, Tamrin, Scarlep, and Igor.

They were met by at least fifty folk of Cavetown, but immediately as they stepped through the entrance, the guard who spoke to them grabbed Algo and threw him to the floor and placed his large, dirty bare foot across his face whilst a few other guards stripped Maxin and his Unit of their weapons before holding their spears firmly aimed at them.

"Who do you think you are, Algo?" asked the guard as he pushed down harder onto Algo's face "I'll tell you who you are, shall I? You're a boy. You're a boy who is too big for his spear. You're a boy who doesn't tell me what to do. You're a boy who loses a battle with Landers. You're also a boy who then befriends Landers, which means you should pay the same price that they do. It means you're a boy who's about to become a corpse."

"Leave him alone!" shouted Maxin over to the guard.

The guard looked over at Maxin with daggers in his eyes but also a wicked grin on his face. "Tell me, Lander. If I stand here and threaten to kill one of my own for talking down to me and bringing Landers into our town, then what do you think I will do to a Lander that invades our town and talks down to me?"

"I do not care for your threats. I care only for the time and the understanding of your people," stated Maxin.

The area became silent, folk of Cavetown were looking on at the guard for a swift reaction, but what they saw was that grin turn crooked and the daggers in his eyes turn sharper.

Suddenly, voices amongst the commoners and the guards began to gather in the crowds.

"Make him pay, Torq!"

"Cut off his tongue and feed it to him!"

"Kill the Lander scum!"

Those were just a few of the threats that came Maxin's way.

The guard who seemed to go by the name of Torq pulled Algo up off of the ground and threw him across to a nearby guy, who held onto him. He then turned his attention back to Maxin as he vigorously paced his way over to him.

Torq stood tall over Maxin by at least a size and a half of himself.

"Know this, *boy*. I do not make threats, I make promises. The biggest mistake you made in your short little life was coming here, and I promise you, you'll regret it!"

"Do not threaten him in front of me. Otherwise, I'll be the one making the promises!" interrupted Igor, but this all seemed to come as a big joke to Torq; he looked as though this empowered him.

"And who might this fat little Lander be? Is he your lover? Do you go out skipping down by the river on a hot day?" he joked, upsetting Igor a little further.

"I'm going to enjoy caving *your* head in!" Igor replied.

"You are one courageous little boy, aren't you? Shall we see how far your courage takes you when your head hangs from my spear?" said Torq as he grabbed his spear from a scathed cotton holster he had hanging from his back, forcing Algo to once again speak up.

"Torq, you would be a fool to harm them; they must be taken to the Better Lords. The higher-dressed boy who you stand above, he is the Lander king's son. He is a Lander Prince!"

Torq lowered his spear.

Once again, the people who had gathered went quiet. Torq looked stunned, staring back at Algo before turning his head and looking down at the young prince, eventually showing that sick villainous grin he had previously shown.

"You're the son of the Lander King? Then, maybe cutting your head straight off from your shoulders and sending it to him in a box would be justified!" Torq grabbed Maxin from the small, buckled straps on his breastplate, with the guards then forcefully keeping Igor, Tamrin, Scarlep, and Algo restrained.

When, suddenly, a voice was once again heard coming from the crowds, but this one was stern, aggressive and direct. "Torq!"

The guards and commoners in the crowds stopped and turned toward the voice, whilst then dividing to create a small gap in the crowd, revealing a lone, armed man, dressed in rags like all the others, but his garments bore marks of some meaning; his cottons were finely stitched and properly cleaned.

"Drop the boy, Torq! Release them all from your grasps," the man ordered.

The man appeared to be of a higher power, Torq looked back at him with a disgusted look before releasing his grasp on Maxin.

"Come here to me, boy," ordered the man.

Maxin was trembling in terror; his hand shook, and his hairs raised on the back of his neck. He took a dry gulp in the back of his throat before slowly walking over to the man, trying his best to keep eye contact.

"And the others, too," stated the man as he gazed over at Torq.

The guards of the town then pulled their spears to the side, allowing Scarlep, Tamrin, Igor, and even Algo to hastily follow in Maxin's path.

Once Maxin reached the man, the man placed his hand on Maxin's shoulder and led him and his Unit through the crowds and into a small desolate cave alley, or in other words, a tunnel.

"You were foolish to bring them here, Algo!"

"If they didn't spare my life, then I wouldn't have returned here myself. The one you have in front of you is Prince Maxin, the Lander king's son, and as a favour for sparing my life, I said I would take him to speak with the Better Lords."

The man looked at Algo as though he wasn't given much choice, he then turned his gaze back to Maxin.

"Let's get this straight, boy, I may have saved your life, for now. But down here, we don't like your kind, I don't like your kind! And now, I'm the only thing that is stopping all those people out there from putting your heads on spikes. My name is Huunlow, I am cavern captain of the guardsmen here. In any other circumstance, I would have let Torq take your head, but number one, you're the Lander king's son; having you captured alive down here could work well for us. And number two, I overheard Algo mention to Torq that you spared his life. If that were true, then you meant us no harm. I will take you to the Better Lords, but do not expect them to greet you with open arms," stated Huunlow before leading Maxin and his group through the tunnels and into the Hall of the Betters.

Jagged rock and stone structured this cave, it was once not as big and as open as it remained now, the wide walls and the high ceilings that surrounded the cave town were crafted by hand, poorly, but still sturdy.

The rock had remained for hundreds of years, and the towns, the people, and the cave grew in number with each passing day. It seemed like a completely different world with small huts constructed from the rock taken from the expanding walls of the cave.

The people of this society were not in need of shops or farms; their food and water were fresh straight from the river. Their weapons were carved from wood and heated stone, and their clothes were made from the carcasses of wild animals who roam freely down into the canyons, from river wolves to wild cliffland cats.

Walking through dark alleyway after dark alleyway, Huunlow led Maxin and the group for more than a mile through the cave, until they came to a large clearing, a wooden arch inscribed with the words, '*For the Better,*' right above the entrance of the clearing. And lying beyond it at the end of the cave, a large carved circular hall, and in the middle lay a great rock and stone carved manor, something you wouldn't think of seeing the likes of underground, much to what the group had already seen.

"This is the Hall of the Betters?" asked Maxin.

"Well done, genius. Is that the type of common sense they teach you up top?" replied Huunlow, rather rudely and abruptly.

"You do not have to like me, sir, but all I ask is for you, along with everyone else, to hear me before you judge me."

"Just be prepared, little one, the Better Lords might not even want to waste their time on hearing you at all."

"Just who are these 'Better Lords'?" asked Scarlep.

Huunlow first looked down toward Algo, grinning at him as he knew Algo knew exactly who they were. His grin turned straight, and then so, too, did his head, looking down at the prince and his group with what looked like a look of despair; it was hard to tell with Huunlow, with his badly marked face and squinted eyes.

"Although I don't like you or your people, I cannot prepare you for the Better Lords; they are certainly unique, to say the least. In a way, I actually feel sorry for you, little lad."

"Why? What are we to expect?" asked Maxin after which Huunlow looked once more at Algo before once again switching his focus onto Maxin.

"There are three Better Lords: Lord Danlur, Lord Layzul, and Lord Pike. Lord Pike is the one you need to watch, for he is ruthless. I can tell you now, he will want off with your head as soon as he sees it; he will want your tongue from your mouth as soon as he hears it. Lord Danlur acts as a chief. Cavetown has always had three Better Lords, but everyone here knows that Lord Danlur is the righteous one. When you wish to seek guidance, you wish to hear it from him. He is wise. He disapproves of your people as much as the next

Caver, but if any one of them is to listen to reason, it is him. Which then leaves Lord Layzul."

"And what is he like?" asked Maxin.

"Lord Layzul is a she."

"Women cannot be lords. Any woman of power is a lady," replied Igor.

"Maybe in your little kingdom, but in these caves; we are not ruled by the Better Lords and Ladies, we are ruled by the Better *Lord*s, which, funnily enough, means that if you're elected to be a Better Lord, then you are in fact 'a Lord."

"So what of Lord Layzul; what is *she* like?" asked Maxin once more.

"She's fair; she is not vigorous, nor righteous; she is not high, nor mighty; she is much more of a commoner than the other two; she's very much for the people rather than herself."

"I think we've heard enough; take me to them," said Maxin, holding his head up high.

"You say it like you have a choice," joked Huunlow as he led Maxin, Algo, Igor, Scarlep, and Tamrin down the stony, cobbled pathway that led to the doors of the manor.

Upon reaching the end of the doorway, they were greeted by two guards, a quick whisper in the ear from Huunlow and the group were cleared to pass.

"Well, that was easy," said Tamrin.

"What have they to fear? Four unarmed boys? If you fear that, you have no reason to be a guard. Plus, they are most likely to believe they are sending you to your deaths by letting you pass," replied Huunlow as he guided the boys up the few steps that led up to the manor doors.

Two large, wooden doors now stood between the group and the jury for their lives. Huunlow gripped a hand around each pebbled doorknob and said, "I hope you little lads are ready," before turning the knobs and pushing the two doors wide open.

With their hearts in their mouths and their stomachs hanging from their arses, the boys stood, bemused with what they saw; from what looked like a well-crafted manor on the outside appeared to be nothing more than another dark and damp hole on the inside.

With a few flaming torches fixed upon the wall, all else that stood in the manor was a small rectangular table in the middle of the room where all three of the Better Lords were seated.

Lord Danlur was seated on the far left of the table, with well-groomed hair and the most serious eyes you'd ever wish to see.

Lord Pike you could have picked out in a room full of one-hundred people. He had long black hair tied into a ponytail, a long, devilish goatee, and a large scar on the left side of his face, from the corner of his nose to the bottom of his mouth. Lord Pike stood straight from his stool at first sight of the boys, slamming his fists on the table.

"You bring Landers into *our* halls?" he bellowed.

Then, there was Lord Layzul, sitting in-between the other two lords, keeping the peace between them. She sat with grace, somehow making leather rags look fashionable, but she had the heart and mind of a commoner, her long blonde hair braided like a common cave guard. Most of the time, she was the final decider in the arguments between Danlur and Pike.

"Sit down, Pike!" she spoke. "Seeing Algo amongst them, looking wounded and much like a prisoner himself, it appears to me that this is not your common Lander problem."

"Common problem, uncommon problem, what does it matter? They are Landers! We should have off with their heads!" stated Lord Pike as he remained on his feet, pulling his spear in front of him, and making the stomach of the boys curdle at the sight of it, and the possibility of it.

Lord Danlur then stood from his seat, also.

"Lord Pike, you were asked to sit. Whatever the problem, we shall have it resolved shortly, as they are but Landers; it should not take us long. The only thing that is currently keeping them alive is, as Lord Layzul put it, the look of young Algo; he seems to have purpose in all of this."

Lord Pike then grudgingly and hesitantly sat back down on his stool, scuffing his feet along the floor and his spear resting against the table, as he was then followed shortly by Lord Danlur.

"Huunlow, please, bring Algo before us," ordered Lord Layzul.

Huunlow placed his hand around Algo's shoulders, whispering to him, "Don't worry, boy, they will not harm you." He slowly led Algo into the centre of the hall, where he would then stand affront the Better Lords.

"Algo, you appear to be limping, my sweet, an injury sustained by training perhaps? By accident? Or by these Landers?" questioned Lord Layzul.

Algo was sweaty; he was nervous and felt sick to his stomach. He didn't want to tell of his failure to stop the Landers, he did not want the Better Lords to see him as weak.

179

"Speak, boy!" ordered Lord Pike.

Algo began to stutter, unable to get the words out of his mouth, but after a small nudge in the back from Huunlow, he began to talk.

"Usually, I would be partnered and trained by fellow Caver guard, Vorl, but he has been sick over the last week, and I was confident enough that I could cover these shifts on my own; today was my third one alone. Up until today, I had no problems, but then these four Landers entered the cave. I kept in the shadows, I used rhyming-tongue and threats to keep them away, but they continued to come. There was no time to send back for help; they were young boys, the same age as me. I thought I could take them; I was wrong, I underestimated them. They took me down, but then they spared my life. They were unaware that we ever existed," explained Algo as he then turned and pointed toward Maxin.

"This better-dressed boy right here, he is Maxin or Prince Maxin, should I say? He is the Lander King's son. He wanted an audience with our leaders; he has an offer to make you."

A look of intrigue and interest was then to be seen upon the faces of all the Better Lords as they all gazed their eyes toward Maxin, who remained by the doors, standing close to his group with his head still raised high.

The looks of interest differed between each lord; Lord Danlur looked intrigued as to why the young prince had wandered so far from the city and yet so far deep into the caves. Lord Layzul was interested in what offer the young prince could possibly offer them. As for Lord Pike, well, he was still only interested in one thing.

"Huunlow, may you bring the boy forward?" ordered Lord Danlur.

Huunlow then took a paced walk over to Maxin, grabbed him by the cuffs of his shoulder straps, and pulled him into a small circle that had been carved into the ground, front and centre of the three Better Lords.

"Just be thankful that we have not cut off your head already, boy. If not for Algo being in your presence, we most likely would've already done it," stated Lord Danlur.

Maxin stood as straight as a post; his head remained high, his eye contact was not faint, his out of body image showed the courage of a great prince. But on the inside, showed the fear of a young boy, his heartbeat smashing against his chest, his stomach curdling like he had not eaten in a month, and the small feeling of nerves slowly making their way down his body, reaching his legs, causing a very slight and unmanageable twitch.

"You stand before us as the son of the Lander king, is this statement true?" asked Lord Layzul.

"That it is, my Lord," replied Maxin, trying to stand as still as he could without showing weakness with the twitch in his legs.

"I am not your lord, nor are you mine. But what I would like to know is that, as prince of the land above, what could you possibly have to offer us? What could we possibly want from you?"

"I didn't know of your people until I stumbled across this cave. Our city is at war; I was out looking for men to help defend against the attacks. That is when we travelled down the canyons, which is how we came across your home. I knew nothing of your people, I can bet coins to say my father doesn't, either. I don't know when the stories of what happened here came to an end, but what I do know is that we can put this whole *thing* to an end. My ancestors and yours started this war a long time ago; we mean you no harm. Allow me to speak with my father, and I assure you, he *will* let you return to the lands above, leave this squalor, once again be men and women of Ar'Gurd!"

Lord Danlur and Lord Layzul turned heads and looked at one another in deep thought, whilst Lord Pike once again rose from his stool, this time kicking it to the floor as he rose and then slamming his palms on the table. "Let's get a few things straight! *Our* ancestors did *not* start this war. We also have *never* been men and women of Ar'Gurd, nor do we wish to be!"

Lord Danlur was then, once again, the second to rise from his stool, keeping his focus directed toward Maxin. "Lord Pike is right in what he says; only your Ancestors were at fault. But to say that we wouldn't like the opportunity for our people to live freely on the lands, that is absurd! We might not like you Landers, but we have no quarrel with the land itself. You can guarantee this, young Prince?"

"If I speak with my father, I'm sure I can pursua—" spoke Maxin before he was then viciously cut off by Lord Pike before he could finish.

"He can promise us nothing. If we let him go, then he will send the whole Lander Kingdom down here to wipe us out!"

Lord Layzul was then the third and final Lord to stand from her stool. "You speak with such strength and courage for such a young boy, but Lord Pike speaks of truth, as you're only a prince. Then, that means you're not the ruler of the land above; you cannot make decisions, you cannot make promises. If you speak with your father and he disagrees, then our whole town is compromised and put in danger. How can we trust you? I have been chosen as a Better Lord to keep our towns and our people safe. This doesn't sound like a safe option, perhaps cutting off your head would be the best move," she stated which of course was met by great agreement from Lord Pike.

But, however scared and worried Maxin felt, there was one feeling that overpowered all those emotions, his determination.

"I *can* make promises, and I will! If I had a motive to destroy your town and your people, do you not think I would have killed Algo and ran straight back to my father? I am risking my own life to help you, to reunite your people with the lands they haven't had the fortune to live upon. I may not be the king, but I am a prince of this kingdom, and whether you like it or not, you *are* people of this kingdom, and I would not have you live down here.

"My father has arranged a meet in the city in a week's time, between the four great kingdoms of this world; it would be an honour if you would join us there as my honoured guests. Speak with my father in person. We will give you your own lands to live off, or you can live within the city if you wish; there are always jobs available for anyone up on land. Times have changed, it is time we changed, too," spoke Maxin very wisely, forcing the Better Lords to look upon a boy who spoke like a nobleman three times his age.

This surprisingly drew a great smile upon the face of Lord Danlur. "I never thought I would say this, but I like you, lad. Yet I do not know whether we can trust you, but with that being said, I would rather die knowing that I tried to give our people and our children a better life rather than carrying on and keep wondering what could have been. I will meet with your king," accepted Lord Danlur.

Lord Layzul then spoke her peace, "Times have changed, you are right. Our people down here have adapted and evolved over time to their surroundings and life within the cave. We know nothing else, but even we know there is only so much adapting you can do within a cave. Our fathers and their fathers before them showed us their ways; it's now time we evolve that little bit more and show our great-grandchildren our own ways. I will meet with your king, also," agreed Lord Layzul, which then put all the attention on Lord Pike, still with an ugly frown smirched across his face. "You two are insane. These are Landers; they destroyed, besmirched, and banished our families into this place, and now you're going to parlay with them!"

Maxin felt the twitch inside him slowly leave his body; he felt the rush of courage and leadership rise up in its place, speaking up against Lord Pike's negativity before the other lords had their chance to.

"Those were the mistakes of our fathers, I wish to make right of their wrongs, and with that being said, I would like to start bringing you back into our society by adding one of your own to mine."

"What do you mean, boy?" asked Lord Pike.

"The law of the land would have me command my own ten-man army when I'm fourteen. I must find these men before my birthday; I have four of the ten soldiers already. I wish to recruit Algo as number five," answered Maxin as he looked over his shoulder toward Algo.

Seeing his eyes lighting up behind the dreaded locks that hung down his face, a small grin growing on him, something Maxin had not yet seen.

"This is a bold move for someone who is not king of the land! Tell me, boy, when is your birthday?" asked Lord Danlur.

Maxin threw his attention back to the Better Lords, taking a slight step forward, just stepping outside of the circle. "Tomorrow."

"You need to recruit six more men before tomorrow?" questioned Lord Layzul.

"Try to. But in the current state of our city, I will say that it's unlikely to happen, but that doesn't mean that I can't do my best to recruit who I can within that time. It took four of us to take down Algo. He is a skilled warrior with that spear; he has passion, and he has commitment. Bringing him into my Unit would not only be a great addition for me, but it would show you how committed I am to bring our people together once more."

Hatred for the Landers still burned bright in the eyes of all three of the Better Lords, perhaps none more so than Lord Pike. He grabbed hold of his spear as he slowly made his way around the table, dragging the bottom end of his spear across the floor, creating the most irritating noise. He closed in on

Maxin, who tried his best to remain upright and calm, developing a small lump in his throat.

Lord Pike looked down at Maxin before looking over his shoulder at Algo. "You know my hate for you grows strong, clearly stronger than any of these, but my love for my people grows even stronger. I will not stand in the way of Algo's decision to join you; it's his own doing. I will also join my fellow lords to this meet but just know this. I will never bow to your king; I will never serve your king, and if this meeting of yours turns sour and we're betrayed, I will make sure I cut off yours and your father's head before I lose mine," stated Lord Pike as he accepted the offer from the prince.

A proud and shaky smile lay upon the face of the young prince like a weight had been lifted from his shoulders. Knowing that he got to keep his life for another day longer at least, which then left him with only one thing left to ask. He turned around and drew his attention back in the direction of Algo. "What say you, Algo? Would your parents agree to such a thing?"

Algo brushed his hair from his eyes and looked the prince dead into his. "Probably not, but they're not around to rule it out. I am under the ruling, protection, and guidance of the Better Lords, and if it is approved by them, then it is approved by me. If my people are to once again become a part of the land, then it would still be in my duty to protect them. I do not condone what your ancestors have done, but I can see you are trying to atone for their crimes, so with that being said, I would be privileged in helping you to do just that, by not being a part of the past, but by being a part of the future."

Maxin's shaky smile quickly turned stern as he held out his hand to Algo in a sign of trust and acceptance into his Unit.

"Huunlow will escort you and your companions out of the cave and return to you your weapons. We are trusting you a great deal, Lander. You know the implications of a betrayal; do not let it come to that. Until the meet; we will see you," said Lord Danlur as Huunlow once again grabbed Maxin by the scuff of his garments, leading him and his now four companions out of the manor and safely back through the tunnels to the entrance of the cave, where Algo would show them to an easy to scale section of the cliff face.

CHAPTER TEN

CAMAROTH

Sir Payner

As the two moons lowered in the south, the two suns had just begun to rise in the north, glazing beautifully over the dry and desolate Greenland of Mulvan.

Sounds of chippering birds in the open skies were drowned out by the footsteps of a hundred horsemen galloping hastily through the lands. The greenest and cleanest of grass had soon become kicked up and trodden, in a vast and open section of Ar'Gurd where very few men had travelled. It was soon a dirt-filled pathway to the Dwarven Kingdom, led by Prince Clearus and Sir Payner.

"Stringal, take Deckern and ride ahead; come back to us with what you see," ordered Payner as Stringal and Deckern sped past them, kicking hard at their horses to see what lay on the road ahead.

As the pace of the group slowed down, Clearus thought it was time to bring something to the attention of Payner, something that even he thought was outlandish. "Payner, I keep having these visions when I sleep."

"What? You mean dreams," replied a muddled Payner.

"No, not dreams, more like nightmares, but reoccurring! They've been reoccurring ever since I came away from that Wizard World."

"And what happens in these *visions*?" Payner asked.

Clearus looked at Payner with serious eyes as he went on to explain the depth of his visions.

"I close my eyes and I find myself back in that land, and each time, I see their queen standing in front of me. Suddenly, she just ignites and turns into a pile of ash on the ground; the ash then begins to rise and spin around like a whirlpool, going faster and faster and faster and faster until, suddenly, it stops. It remains a big bundle of ash levitating in the air, there is a feeling of eyes watching me from within, and then I hear the voice."

"What voice?" questioned Payner.

"Her voice, the queen's: 'Our power belongs inside you,' is what she says. The ash then, once again, begins to spin before eventually smashing into me, and that point of contact is when I wake."

Payner was not sure what to think; he did not believe strongly in magic or the Almighty, especially those who can invade people's minds. But he saw something in Clearus's eyes. As he looked deeper, he saw fear, but not the kind of fear you get when you come face-to-face with an enemy, but the kind of fear that can tear a man up inside, a fear of not knowing.

"Nightmares, Clearus, that is all they are, just nightmares," he consoled, but Clearus did not stop there.

"That night, we were attacked by Nawgs, you saw what happened; everyone here saw what happened. I fought in a way that I'd never fought before, but right before that, in my tent, something else happened," Clearus explained as Payner continued to look on at him in puzzlement.

"Before I left my tent that night, a Nawg entered and slowly began to walk toward me with its raw ugly face and ogre expression. It was dark, causing me trouble when I tried to find my sword. The Nawg jumped straight toward me; there was nothing else I could do but put my hands out in front of me. But when I did, this great beam of light shot from my hands and threw the beast from my tent."

"You're crazy, Clearus. You *do not* have magical powers."

"No? Then watch this," commanded Clearus as he pulled his horse to a halt, causing Payner and the men behind them to do the same. He held out his hands in front of him as he then attempted to bring out the light he believed to be lying within them.

He concentrated vigorously under the hot sun, sweat dripping from his head and his mouth as dry as the air across Greenland. He focused on his hands, blinking only when the sweat dripped from his brows.

After a few short minutes, Payner began to find the whole thing rather amusing, even for him; he knew this was a new crazy low for Clearus.

He turned his head back to face the road ahead and gripped tightly onto the reins of his horse, ready to set off again for the Dwarven Kingdom. But just before he could, he was interrupted.

"Wait! Payner, look!" shouted Clearus, and as Payner turned to face him once more, a look of overwhelming disbelief covered his face as he looked down at Clearus's hands.

Clearus also looked on surprisingly shocked, seeing the tips of his fingers begin to grow luminous as the palms of his hands began to slowly sparkle and shine like the glow of a newly forged jewel.

Payner's jaw dropped immensely; every single hair on the back of his neck stood on end, but before the light could grow any stronger, a voice came from over the hills.

"My Lords, The Dwarven Kingdom is just a mile ahead. It's a straight road up to that point," shouted Stringal as he and Deckern came racing back to the group from over the hills.

Within that small moment, the split second when Clearus and Payner lost their focus, the light left his hands. They looked back at one another in certain awe.

They took a small moment of hesitance to take everything in.

"You men are to set up camp. Prince Clearus and I will ride on from here," ordered Payner as he then looked back at Clearus.

"We will speak about this when we get back; we will take the matter to your brother. Until then, we still have a job to do," stated Payner, and with a quick nod of agreeance from Clearus, they left their men behind in the Greenland of Mulvan as they proceeded forward to the Dwarven Kingdom.

An aged, declining, stone stairway was forged within pillars of ancient ruins, Dwarven ancestral patterns and runes carved into the stone, leading down the stairway to a lavish solid set of golden doors that stood guarding the bottom.

"I've never seen anything like this in my life, Payner. The Wizards were magical, but this...this is extraordinary, this is a true wonder for the eyes to behold," gushed Clearus.

Payner and Clearus stood at the top of the stairway as they gazed down upon the ruins and the doors.

Clearus was stopped by Sir Payner, who grabbed him tightly by the arm as he began to make his way down the first step.

"Be careful, Clearus, we know nothing of these Dwarves. These stairs could be boobytrapped. We need to proceed with caution."

"There is no other way down; if we are to proceed, then it is down these steps," stated Clearus.

"Then, one of us must go first. If they are boobytrapped, then it's best that only one of us takes the blow, so I will go, and you will follow a step behind me," instructed Payner.

So as Payner cautiously took the first step down; they were both relieved that nothing happened to them by doing so, but the worry wasn't over yet.

There were still at least another twenty steps to go down before they reached the golden doors.

Taking in all the runes carved into the walls with each step they took, they were mesmerised by all the history that was crafted within them.

"How long do you think this place has stood? Who was really the first to arrive on these lands?" asked Clearus as he followed a step closely behind Payner.

"There has been much talk through the years," replied Payner as he concentrated on the steps he was taking.

"There's just one thing I've never understood: as far as we know, men have never met or co-existed with Wizards, Elves, and Dwarves, so how is it we know they even exist and cohabit on these lands, if one has never seen one?" questioned Clearus.

"Have you never read the stories of the great explorer, Daryus S'Yaris?" asked Payner as he took another careful step down, just passing the halfway point, before then adding, "As the story goes, Daryus was the first and only man who travelled to each kingdom. There were many stories written about him, but the only fact that remained from his travels was that he never returned. Nobody knew what happened to him, or what he saw; all they found that was left of him were three small, torn-up parchments found within a small burrow in Killver Meadows. A lot of the inscriptions on the parchment were faint and smudged, but certain words could still be read, three words in particular: *Wizards*, *Elves,* and *Dwarves*, along with a badly drawn map that drew out their locations," explained Payner as he happened to reach the bottom of the stairway while he told the story.

"I don't believe in myths," said Clearus.

"Well, the maps and parchments have been right thus far," replied Payner. "His last trip was most likely to the Elves," he added as he sorely looked down at his mutilated hand.

"That reminds me, Payner, perhaps it is best that I knock, especially now that you have, how should I put it? *Hand deformities!*" joked Clearus as he then took his final step down and was met by a not so pleased look from Payner.

"Can I just remind you, Clearus, I'm not the only one here with *hand deformities*; why don't you just try and force the doors down with that light in *your* hands?" replied Payner as they both glanced at each other with stern looks. But as they looked into each other's eyes, the stern expressions soon turned to smiles on their faces as they then continued to laugh at one another's misfortunes in a way that only Payner and Clearus could, completely forgetting about being right outside the doorway to the Dwarven Kingdom.

Suddenly, their laughter was cut short when they heard a large, echoed thud on the other side of the door, like a gong or bell that had just been struck to signal a battle. Both Payner and Clearus then focused all of their attention on the door as they heard the large thud for a second time.

"Clear the way," came a deep voice from within as the thud was then heard for the third time, and as Payner and Clearus readily awaited, the doors then shuddered as they began to slowly open inward, a deep creaking noise echoing through the ears of the two, sounding like a large tree capsizing in the woods, sounding much like they had not been opened in some time.

As the doors opened fully, Clearus and Payner were met by a single armoured Dwarf with twenty more standing behind him, brandishing their axes and spears.

"Who are you?" spoke the Dwarf in a deep and strong tone.

"Pardon our intrusion on the doorstep of your kingdom, Master Dwarf, but we come bearing a message from *our* king to yours," explained Payner.

"I said 'Who are you?' not, 'What are you doing here?'" replied the Dwarf as he removed his fitted silver steel helmet, uncovering an aged, long-bearded, ginger Dwarf.

"My name is Sir Payner, and this here is Prince Clearus. Might I ask your name?"

The Dwarf turned to one of the guards standing behind him; he issued a slight nod before the guard then ran off in great haste back into the kingdom.

"My name is Kaldro, I am a Dwarven Higher Guard of Camaroth. We have been keeping a close watch on you two, from the moment you placed a foot on that first step. It signalled a trigger that rang through to us, and we watched you through a hidden hole we have above the doors. Our king knows you're here; he is now expecting you."

"Thank you kindly, Kaldro, we come in peace; we do not wish to carry out any attacking engagements," assured Payner.

"That's good, then," replied Kaldro. "We must ask you to leave your weapons down by the doors before you enter; it's completely precautionary. A couple of our guards will then collect them up and bring them inside; you will then have them handed back to you upon leaving Camaroth."

Payner and Clearus looked at one another in agreeance, as they then began to unbuckle their belts and then dropped their swords onto the floor next to their feet, along with the extra daggers and throwing knives they were both carrying.

"Great. Now, you may both enter. I'd like to welcome you to the greatest kingdom alive today. Welcome to Camaroth, home of the Dwarves," greeted Kaldro.

Payner and Clearus then without a single second thought, stepped over their bundled arsenal on the floor and followed Kaldro through the gates.

As they made their way forward, Payner just gave Clearus a small nudge as they did so. "Hey, I told you it was boobytrapped," he gloated.

Then, they passed on through the solid golden doors and just stood in awe of what they both saw.

A large hall lit up and crafted in a mix of the finest brick and granite and stems of gold built like veins into the walls, streaming through every crevice it could find.

Golden statues of what appeared to be previous kings and greater-known Dwarves stood high and mighty across each end of the hall, four on either side.

Floors coated in dark marble and forged over sandstone; they heard the metal and steel of each guard echoing through the hall as they marched. Looking ahead to the end of the hall, they saw a large set of wooden doors, locked tight with bolts and chains and crowned by a concrete arch.

However, their look of awe and admiration was soon cut short when they were interrupted and jolted by the solid golden doors being slammed shut and locked behind them.

They couldn't help but notice the small wooden watchtowers that stood on either side, with small holes drilled into the wall to allow the Dwarven guards to peer on through to the other side.

"If you please, follow me," guided Kaldro. "Open the gates," he added, shouting toward the guards.

The large wooden doors were soon then unbolted, unchained, and opened, requiring four guards to carry out this particular duty.

As the doors swung open, countless Dwarven commoners, along with several other Dwarven guards, came to greet them at the gates. None of them had ever seen a man before, and the Dwarves were much too curious, as were

Payner and Clearus. They had so much more to take in, seeing glimpses of buildings and monuments behind the crowds.

A whole new society, a whole new kingdom, and a whole new way of living just opening up before their very eyes.

"Move aside," shouted Kaldro toward the cluster of Dwarves who had assembled in front of them.

The Dwarves then parted, causing a small walkthrough that led into the streets of the kingdom.

"Follow me. Follow me," persisted Kaldro as he pushed through the crowds alongside Payner and Clearus as they made their way forward through the kingdom to meet the king.

Beautifully crafted concrete houses overlooked the busy streets of Camaroth; small gusts of smoke were blowing out from several chimneys, staining the air in a thick fog, whilst the ground remained lit up, vibrant and very lively.

Marketplaces selling exotic Dwarven fruit and ale and rich attire that wouldn't cater for a fully-grown man, or maybe even a man half that size.

Drunk and energetic buskers were parading through the streets with their steel drums and wooden flutes, spreading cheer, drinking ale, and collecting coins.

The kingdom was joyful, and it was lively. And as they passed through, it reminded Payner and Clearus of Ar'Gurd during their many municipal festivals throughout the year, from King's Day to the Unity Parade.

Walking past the bustling streets and the musically gifted, Kaldro finally stopped outside a concrete home that stood alone from all the rest, sitting above a small stairway, perched upon a solid stone and marble-built embankment, almost three times the size of any other home they had seen so far, enriched with several runes and jewel-infused linings that glistened through the creases in the walls.

Kaldro led Payner and Clearus up the small stairway, across the embankment, and to the entrance of the building; he turned to look at Payner and Clearus before pushing open the door and leading them both inside.

After almost both of them banging their heads on the doorframe on the way in, they made it safely inside, and once inside, they were met with three different directions to go in; a locked door to the right, a locked door up ahead, or a stairway to the left, each way being guarded by two Dwarven spearmen.

Kaldro led them to the left, toward the stairway, with the guards quick to block their path, creating a small gate with their spears.

"King Dunlin is expecting us," assured Kaldro.

"Very well, Master Kaldro, head on up," replied one of the guards as they removed their spears from the path and allowed Kaldro, Payner, and Clearus to make their way up.

Once they reached the top of the stairs, they found themselves in one large Dwarven king's office, surrounded by artefacts, books, axes, and the king himself. He had thick black braided hair with grey highlights and a shiny grey beard with highlights of black, groomed together nicely with several golden beads.

And he wasn't alone, a Dwarven woman stood beside him; much younger, red hair and no beard, donning a red and gold dress that brought a very admirable glow to her dark green eyes.

"My King, I bring before you Payner and Clearus from the Kingdom of Ar'Gurd, Kingdom of man," introduced Kaldro.

"Greetings, King Dunlin," greeted Payner, stepping forward, but the king spoke no words. So Payner proceeded to explain his presence.

"I am Sir Payner Dral-gon, right-hand man to King Armish Hailguard, King of Ar'Gurd. I'm joined by his brother, Prince Clearus Hailguard. We come to you today not as foes, but as allies; we come to deliver a message from the King of man to the King of Dwarves. He wishes to parlay with you, not only you, but Kings and Queens of Wizards and Elves, also, and the meet will take place in our city of Carbaya within the hall of our kings." Payner stepped farther toward King Dunlin, handing him a small scroll. "This parchment has all of the necessary information that you need, all we need from you is a response; can we count on your arrival?" he asked.

King Dunlin unravelled the scroll as his eyes drummed back and forth as he glanced through the small parchment.

His eyes rose slightly above the parchment as he looked on at Payner and Clearus, who were eagerly looking back at him for a response. He then lowered the parchment and spoke strongly and assertively to them both, "I will attend, but before I do, you must do something for me."

CHAPTER ELEVEN

ON COURSE

Maxin

Still travelling farther across Ar'Gurd, Maxin and his companions, which now included Algo, had now passed along the misty marshes of Penris and through the wooded creek of Elmanois and were now headed toward the second biggest city in Ar'Gurd, Paran-Dun, which was where Maxin hoped to find a few more companions, if not the rest of them.

"Do you not think it's funny, we hear nothing from Paran-Dun in the city, nothing of its villages, and nothing of its people, and here we are, heading straight for it. Has anyone here even met anyone from Paran-Dun?" asked Scarlep as they trotted through a stretch of dry terrain about a mile from the city.

"Don't worry yourself, Scarlep," assured Maxin. "Apart from the odd Zarnick here and there, I've never heard of any trouble emanating through these lands; we're perfectly safe, and I can't see the city being much different than our own. Has your brother, Rekken, ever been?"

"If he has, my Prince, he has never spoken to me about it."

"Well, I have actually seen a messenger from Paran-Dun; they deliver frequent news to my father of the people and its guards. I have never spoken to the messenger, but he looks normal enough," joked Maxin.

"I, too, have seen one," added Algo.

The rest of the group then came to a sudden halt, and every eye then turned to Algo.

"You have not," argued Igor. "Have you?"

"It was a long time ago. I was only a child at the time, and I was with my father and my uncle as they guarded the entrance on this particular night: the man, just like yourselves, wandered into the cave, just looking for a place to camp. He spoke little; he said his name was Brorey or Brairy, something like that. Anyway, he mentioned the fact that he lived in Paran-Dun across the way," explained Algo.

"And then what?" asked Maxin.

"My uncle planted a spear through his face; it was the first time that I'd ever seen anyone die," replied Algo with a slight grin on his face as he rekindled the memories of his younger days with his father. But he then looked up to see the shocked faces of his companions glaring in his direction, from which he remembered what a heinous crime it was to commit, killing an innocent traveller. The grin left his face as he tried to compensate for what he had just told them, "But as Maxin said, he seemed nice enough, just like this land of yours. I've never known anything so colourful and bright, and I have no doubt that this city will be no different."

Algo then marched forward, with the group then persisting to follow him, but before they could even travel another twenty yards, they were halted by Igor, who remained at the back.

"Hold up!"

Everyone turned to see Igor looking questionably back at Maxin.

"Igor, what's wrong?" asked Maxin.

"Guards," he replied.

"What?

"You said guards!" asserted Igor.

"What of it, Igor? I don't follow…"

"You said your father gets updates on the villagers and the guards? So why is it we're out here risking our hides when he has extra guards elsewhere in Ar'Gurd that he can call upon?" he asked.

"I got to say, Igor has a point, Maxin!" agreed Tamrin.

Maxin felt foolish and blinded that he didn't think of that sooner; why hadn't his father called upon the guards?

"I'm not sure, Igor," he replied, "perhaps he already has, perhaps he has them waiting on a whim so they can come in and surprise the enemy when they attack."

"A little far from the city to be waiting on a whim, don't you think?" disputed Igor.

"Look, as stubborn as he might be, I trust my father's judgement; he is a smart man. If he has not called upon them, then he must have good reason," explained Maxin.

"But if you trusted his judgement, then we wouldn't all be out here looking for more troops," contradicted Igor once more.

Maxin looked flustered. For the first time in a long time, he had no answer, but he wasn't about to stand back and lose a debate to Igor of all people.

"Whether my father had more troops or not, I still need to find my own, and that's what we're doing out here. So I suggest we keep on moving," stated Maxin as he then led the way toward the hill and back on course for Paran-Dun as Igor surprisingly kept back with no response.

***

After a short walk, large-structured concrete towers could soon be seen from over the hilltop. Two guards, suited head to toe in heavy-tailored armour, were guarding each watchtower insight.

As the group came over the dry and dusted hilltop, they then saw Paran-Dun in all its entirety, stretching almost a mile as they could only wonder how much farther it stretched back.

Walking down the hill, the gritty dirt slowly progressed into finely bladed grass that led all the way to the gate; the gate was a lot taller than the one that stood in Carbaya, as this one stood almost as tall as the city walls themselves.

Treading slowly, the group suddenly began to see something attached to the gate, which looked like a much smaller drawbridge that just so happened to be raised up in front of it, giving extra security and extra defence to the gate, making it much harder for anyone to penetrate.

Continuing to follow Maxin's lead and without any caution, the five of them continued to move to within just yards of the city, as the grass slowly began to grow finer as they ventured farther.

Maxin finally decided to bring the group to a halt with a slight raise of the hand.

A cloaked figure stood dark and brazen above the city gates, glaring down at the group, who could not see his face.

"We request entry into the city," shouted Maxin up at the figure, but there was no response; he just continued to glare until he made a very similar hand gesture of his own.

As the group stood wonderingly behind Maxin in their own version of a horizontal line, they were soon left staring with their eyes bulging from their sockets as dozens of arrows came flying from the city walls, landing directly at Maxin's feet.

With Maxin's heart then trying to cannonball from his chest, the hooded guard spoke down to him, abruptly and strongly. "As you can see, one wrong move and you're all dead! So tell me, what purpose would five equipped, mounted, and very strange-looking boys have in my city?"

"This is not your city; this my fathers' city!" informed Maxin. "I am Prince Maxin, son of the king."

"You lie! The king would never allow his youngest son to travel this far alone," stated the figure.

"I am not alone," argued Maxin. "Now, open the gate!" he then ordered, which surprisingly enough, seemed to work as suddenly the drawbridge began to lower, although the gate remained closed.

As the group then moved slightly closer, the figure spoke up once more. "You might be who you say you are, and you might not. Either way, what trouble could five boys really cause?" he joked before adding, "But as I previously said, one wrong move from either of you, then you will have an arrow in your head so fast that your body will hit the ground before the rest of you even realise what's happened! In this city, we're always watching."

After his cautious speech, the figure disappeared from atop the city wall as the gates to the city began to open. And without any regard for the caution and seizing the moment,

Maxin without any sign of hesitation, led his Unit through the burly wooden gates and into the city.

Once the gates closed behind them, they were sighted with a populous, labouring city. In every direction they looked, someone in the city was working, sweating, and grafting to the bone, from carrying lumbers of wood, to farming the fruit from the overgrown trees that shadowed some buildings, *everyone* was doing something. But then without another second to look upon Paran-Dun, which was the first time for either of the group, a cloaked figure jumped out in front of them from above.

"What the…" gasped a stunned Igor.

"We meet again," spoke the figure as he unhooded himself, revealing a middle-aged man with long black hair, a fine moustache with a chinstrap goatee, and a crooked grin that'd make any man look heinous.

"You're the cloaked man from the wall," confirmed Tamrin.

"Ten out of ten for observation, young one," replied the voice, sarcastically.

"You said this was your city; who are you?" asked Maxin.

"Why should I tell you?"

"Because I am the prince."

"So you say, but where is your proof?" questioned the man.

"I am wearing the city amour," replied Maxin, abruptly.

"Yes, that is city armour, all right, but it proves nothing," said the man. "This armour can be easily forged, stolen, or handed down. But I am not doubting where you are from; I am doubting who you are. And the fact that you do not know who I am, or what I represent, just makes me further believe that you're not the king's son!"

Taking a few heavy-footed steps across the dirt-dusted cobbles, the man grabbed hold of Maxin's face, gently squashing in each side of his mouth with one of his hands.

"You don't look much like the king, either!" stated the man.

Maxin vigorously shoved the man's hand away from his face, which was met by a cheeky grin from him before Maxin sternly replied, "I have my mother's looks."

But before the man could respond, Igor jumped in, feeling somewhat frustrated. "Look, I'm going to cut this short. This *is* Prince Maxin, and we stand here as part of his Unity. We left the city against his father's will in search of more troops to help protect the city from pirate attacks, *recent* pirate attacks! We need your help, Ar'Gurd needs your help, and the *king* needs your help. Will you not help us?"

"I was not informed of no pirate attacks!" replied the man.

"My father, he is in denial. He sent away Sir Payner, my uncle, Clearus, and over half of the city guards on some random quest whilst the city was being attacked, although they shall be back soon; he is adamant that he will not recall them. Carbaya will fall if there is no help to defend it," stated Maxin, looking worryingly up at the figure, who looked almost shocked as he stared back at him and the rest of Maxin's group.

"I'm sorry, but I can't help you, we are the king's driving force. If he has not called for us, then he has no need for us, I follow the king's orders."

"And what of a prince's orders?" suggested Tamrin as the man then looked back down at Maxin, who was now looking down at his feet in distress. The man then raised Maxin's chin up and spoke directly to him.

"Look, kid, there is still no solid evidence here to prove that you are who you say you are. I haven't stepped foot in Carbaya since, supposedly, you were six years old. I can't go off marching to defend a city that doesn't need defending because five little boys told me to. I will ride when the *king* tells me to!"

"Come along, guys, we move farther into the city; there is no help for us here," said a quietly spoken Maxin as he looked diminishingly into the eyes of the man, but as he attempted to walk away, the man grabbed Maxin's arm and pulled him back toward him.

"The name is Kaynar," he spoke.

"That has little interest to me now," replied Maxin as he continued to walk away, but that still didn't stop Igor from having the final say, marching angrily toward Kaynar as he released his anger on him.

"This is absurd. If Carbaya falls and you do nothing to stop it, then that's a lot of regret that you'd have to live with! You might just have to wear that cloak for the rest of your cowardly life!" he shouted as he stormed off into the city through a nearby alleyway.

"Igor, wait up," shouted Algo limping after him as the rest of the group were jogging behind to catch up with him, but Igor did not listen. As big as he was, he was also quicker than he looked, storming ahead of the group, smashing crates, and kicking rotten fruit as he coursed down the alleyway.

Scarlep and Tamrin then joined in to try and call for him back.

"Igor!" they shouted, but he just continued his path of destruction, ignoring them all along the way, that was until Maxin spoke up, bursting his way in front of Algo, Scarlep, and Tamrin.

"Igor! I order you to halt!" Which is exactly what he did. Maxin the Great ordered Igor to a sudden halt, which was met with great admiration from the others.

"It must feel good, being able to make him do what you like," joked Scarlep.

"It comes with more flaws than you could imagine," replied Maxin as he turned his attention back to Igor who still had his back to them.

"Igor, come back to us; we need to do this together," reassured Maxin.

Igor then, after taking a huge breath, turned around to face Maxin, but as he did, he turned straight into a female villager who was cutting through another alley that ran through this one, knocking her straight to the ground.

Without a second thought, Igor held out his hand to help her. "I'm sorry, please take my hand," he said in a tone that you wouldn't normally hear him speak.

She grabbed hold of his hand tightly as Igor then began to pull her up, that was until he made the mistake of looking straight into her eyes as he did so. He suddenly became as stiff as a statue, and his palms became instantly sweaty, causing him to lose his grip and allowing her to fall back onto the cobbled ground. In a world of his own, he looked on at her as she fell back onto the ground with her dark brown hair swinging from her shoulders, along with her glistening blue eyes, where there also lay a small spot below the right one.

"You are gentle, aren't you?" she joked, looking back up at him as he continued to glare over her in a comatose fashion.

Meanwhile, seeing a young lady being manhandled by Igor, the others ran over as fast as they could to help, with Scarlep being the one to offer his hand.

"No, no. I'm good, thanks; I don't fancy another fall," she said as she waved away Scarlep's help, dusting herself off and making her way gracefully back to her feet.

She did not look like a normal city girl; she wore a rich mixture of finely sewn suede and leather rags, with steel guards around her laced boots and a small dagger hiding in the cuff.

As she rose to her feet, she looked intriguingly around at the group.

"I've not seen you boys around here before, are you from out of town? Some of you even look like you've spent the last few seasons living underground," she said as she drew her eyes toward Algo. "And if I'm not mistaken, that there is Carbayan made armour," she added as she pointed at Maxin's wears.

"Actually, I have been underground, thanks to you and your peo—" replied an abrupt Algo before being cut off by Maxin.

"Algo! I'm sorry, Miss, what my companion here is trying to say is that you're right; we aren't from this city. But I've got to say, for a young girl of Paran-Dun, you sure know a lot about Carbayan armour."

"I visited there once with my father," the girl replied as she then began to look more in-depth toward Maxin, squinting her eyes slightly at him, "You may call me a liar here, but if I'm not mistaken, I swear I've seen you somewhere before," she said.

Maxin smiled back at her. "Perhaps you have on your travels," he replied.

The girl looked at him a little harder, moving her head in closer and just squinting her eyes a little bit more. All of a sudden, she jolted back and gasped, "Great mother of spirits! You're Prince Maxin!" she acknowledged.

"It's nice to see someone in this city recognises their prince," Maxin spoke sarcastically.

"You are speaking about Kaynar?" she asked as she then continued to speak, not allowing Maxin to answer her question, but she already knew the answer as her eyes filled with disgust and rage, "Urgh, I hate that guy. He has been the same the whole time I've known him. He believes he knows the answers to everything and will have nobody tell him otherwise, with that stupid little cloak that he wears, along with that maniacal grin that he bares on his face. He always looks as though he's up to something. He was the same way with my brother, Quenne. Quenne's recently turned old enough to be a part of the city guard; he's trained a lot, and he is a good fighter, but when he approached Kaynar, guess what happened? Kaynar knew best. He crushed his spirits and told Quenne that he wasn't good enough; my brother is more than good enough!"

"You say your brother has recently become old enough to join the city guard? You have to be fourteen for that?" said Maxin.

"He turned fourteen about nine months ago, why do you ask?" asked the girl.

Maxin didn't answer. With a small gleam in his eye, he turned to face the rest of his Unit, and as they all looked back at him, he quietly murmured to them, "He's of age." Which, unfortunately, couldn't escape the ears of the young girl.

"Of age for what?" she continued to question.

"Can you take us to him, your brother?" asked Maxin.

"Why? What are you all doing here?" The girl's mind began to wander for a brief moment; curiosity crept into her mind as a different style of squint came from her eyes as she scoured across the group.

"Take us to your brother and there we will explain everything," confirmed Maxin.

After a few seconds more of scouring the group, the girl tied up her hair in a scruffy bob as she then turned back into the direction she was previously heading.

"This way, then," she said in an agitated tone as she proceeded down the alleyway, followed immediately by Igor with Maxin and the others following soon after him.

After a quick jog through the dry and humid alleyways, the group were finally led to a row of three small stony cottages that sat opposite a grimy fishmonger; the stench was far from blossoming on the nostrils, making the boys crease their faces as they passed.

The girl made her way straight past the first cottage and came to a sudden stop outside the door of the middle one, which was also the smallest one.

"This is it, then?" asked Maxin.

"I wouldn't lead you astray now, Prince," she replied as she then began to slowly twist the creaky knob on the door before gently pushing it open and stepping inside.

Once inside, Maxin and his Unit looked around the small, warm, and surprisingly cosy cottage. The floorboards were smooth and sanded, the fireplace was roaring and crackling, and a small cat lounged on a tattered rug that lay in the corner of the room.

As they continued to look round, they saw a middle-aged woman in an apron stirring a pot, which smelt very much like pigeon stew and cheesy dumplings. There was another man, a little bit older than the woman, sitting in a very cushioned wooden armchair with his sweaty, bruised, and worn feet resting on a small stool in front of him, smoking on a long tobacco pipe, which along with the stew, seemed to drown out the smell of fish from the outside.

When they continued to scale the room a little more, they saw one more person, a young fair-haired boy. He was sitting on a small stool, leaning mindfully toward the crackling fireplace in full plates of scratched and used, light armour.

The three of them turned heads when they saw the girl enter the cottage with Maxin and the others.

"Sasha, you were meant to be home an hour ago. Where have you been? And who are your friends?"

Before she could answer, the elderly man, in pure shock and surprise, lay his pipe on a nearby table as he took his feet from his stool and rose quickly from his armchair. He looked Maxin square in the eyes with amazement; he knew exactly who he was.

"Melda, set more plates for supper, Prince Maxin is joining us!" he said.

The woman stopped stirring as soon as she heard those words leave the lips of the man.

The young boy also quickly rose from his seat. "You're Prince Maxin?" he questioned with complete astonishment.

"Minor details, kid," replied Tamrin.

"Trust us, you get used to it very quickly," joked Scarlep.

"Sasha, why are you in the company of the prince?" asked the elder man.

"His fat companion ran into me as I was on my way home. Prince Maxin was there, along with the others. He told me to bring him here so that he could speak to Quenne," Sasha explained.

"Speak to me? Why?" questioned Quenne, from which Maxin finally spoke up and greeted his hosts as he did so.

"I am sorry to intrude on your home like this. Allow me to introduce us; the bowman just to my right is Tamrin from the village of Malba, the cheeky chappie just to my left is Scarlep from the capital city of Carbaya, the so-called fat companion to my far left is Igor from the outskirts of Carbaya, and then finally the rough and ready looking spearman to my far right is Algo, he is from…a town.

"When we spoke to Sasha earlier, we were on the topic of the guard captain of the city, Kaynar, and she spoke of how he let Quenne down when he requested to join the city guard. What we never spoke about was the reason I was here in the city, which is why I asked her to bring me here. As you may know, as a prince, I have certain obligations to uphold, one of them is forming my Unit before my fourteenth birthday. Five of these members I have already, I've searched all I can in Carbaya, but nobody there has quite what I'm looking for, so we decided to venture east to this fair city of Paran-Dun, which is where we found you, Quenne, and I hear that you're still of age."

Complete shock was bestowed upon the face of not only Quenne but his mother, father and Sasha, also.

"You want me to join your Unit?"

"Not so hasty, Quenne, as much as I would love for you to join, I can't allow that just from your sister's word alone; I need you to prove to me that you're capable enough to be a part of all this."

"Well, I've never killed a man, but I've taken my fair share. Since I was eight, I trained to be a city guard, picking fights with anyone I could find, and when I found kids my own age, it wasn't challenging me enough, I'd go out and I'd find older kids who would. You might not see me as the brightest, quickest, or strongest of the group, but I can tell you now, I'm the most determined, and determination powers over all of that, and that is why I am capable enough," stated Quenne.

With a huge smile on his face and a nod from each member of his Unit, Maxin turned back to Quenne with an admirable look upon his face. "It looks to me like you need to grab your sword and take a position behind me, Quenne, I hope your skill is as true as your words," said Maxin.

"Wait," shouted Sasha, bringing an abrupt end to the pleasantries, "What about me?" she asked, turning her attention to Maxin.

"What about you?" replied Maxin.

"Where's my offer to join your Unit?"

"You're kidding, right?" replied Scarlep, which was met with a very stern look from Sasha.

"I'm as good a soldier as any girl or boy my age. As you can see, I am not your typical frolicking-in-the-flowers-kind of girl; I love the thrill of combat and beating down on someone," she explained, valiantly.

"I'm sure you're a great fighter, Sasha, but the truth is, there's never been a female Uniteer. I'm not even sure it's allowed; there is no rule for it," replied Maxin.

"Nor against it," argued Sasha.

Silence filled the overcrowded cottage, just sounds of overboiled stew, a crackling fire, and a faint purring from the cat in the corner was all that stood over the uneasy air.

Maxin looked at Sasha deeply before looking at Quenne and then switching his focus to their parents.

"And how do you two feel about this?" he asked, and it was the father who answered.

"If you came to me and asked me about Quenne, then I would have agreed with no hesitation, but Sasha, she's my daughter, my, young, beautiful daughter. It's true, she has never been much of a girl, always wanting to cause trouble and always wanting to make her own decisions. Quenne had that chance, I see it only fair that Sasha is allowed the same." The man walked calmly over to Sasha and gave her the gentlest of kisses on the forehead before putting his arm around her as his eyes began to well.

"I still don't know," pondered Maxin.

"Just let her join!" shouted Igor, which was then met with sudden and very curious looks from everyone in the room.

"I think what Igor is trying to say is perhaps she deserves a chance. We cannot afford to be picky here, Maxin. If her own father believes in her, then so should we. If there is no rule for it, then perhaps we should make one," consoled Tamrin.

Maxin then looked around at Scarlep and Algo, receiving a nod of agreement from them both, but then he turned to Quenne. "You're a part of this team now, Quenne, what is your say on this? This is your Unit, and this is your sister," said Maxin.

"Sasha is a good fighter, I can vouch for that, and the truth is I would love my sister to be as far away from trouble as she possibly could be, but she seems to find trouble wherever she goes. At least if she is part of this Unit, then I could still keep a brotherly eye on her."

Maxin then turned swiftly to Sasha, "Your father said you should make your own decision, which you've clearly already made. And my five Uniteers, including your brother, have all agreed that you should join, some more abruptly than others," he said as he looked toward Igor, "so it is with great duty and honour that I welcome you into my Unit, making you the first-ever female Uniteer!"

A large smile formed on Sasha's face as she hugged her father with great pride, along with her mother.

Maxin felt good, as he had brought another two recruits into the Unit whilst making a small family very proud.

"Okay, we will be leaving for Carbaya in two hours' time, this gives you both a chance to have one final meal together as a celebration, and to say your goodbyes. If I'm right, today is now my birthday and the day of the initiation. We need to get back to Carbaya before my parents realise I'm gone; we will wait for you both at the front gates. It's good to have you both on board," commended the prince.

Upon hearing this, Sasha left the side of her parents as she ran straight over to Maxin and gave him a huge hug of appreciation, whilst whispering into his ear, "Thank you so much, I understand how difficult of a decision that was. I promise I will not let you down." Then, as she left the arms of Maxin, she was met by Igor who also had his arms out for a hug, but instead, he received a warm-hearted handshake.

The group then left the hut in great haste, only to be hit with the stench of rotten fish once more.

"Another two members down. We have only a couple of hours left to go, so let's go and see who else we can find," suggested Maxin.

"We have but one goal in mind.
With three hours left,
We have only three members to find," Algo rhymed.

"Oh, no. Not this again," said Igor.
"Why do you speak in rhyme, Algo?" asked Scarlep.
"It is something us Cavers like to do; it is much like singing; it takes the bore away from normal speech," explained Algo.

"Algo is crazy, that is for sure,
He goes around saying that speech is a bore," Igor mocked.

He then added in a jokey tone, "You're right, Algo, it is more fun."

But before Algo could retaliate, Maxin cut the chat short; there was still a job that needed doing, and it was no time to lose focus.

"Guys, we have more important things to concern ourselves with right now, we *need* to find three new members, and we are not going to do that here, bickering with one another as we inhale bucket loads of rotten fish fumes. Once this task is complete, then you lot can riddle war as much as you like, but for now, we got to keep moving," commanded Maxin as he led the group away from the cottages and the rotten fish and farther into the city in search of more Uniteers.

CHAPTER TWELVE

A DWARVEN MATTER

Prince Clearus

Glares of interest and restraint flickered between both Clearus and Payner, as King Dunlin awaited *his* response.

"What is it you ask of us?" asked a sceptical Payner.

"We ask you to prove yourself allies," replied King Dunlin.

"And just how is it we do that?" Payner added.

King Dunlin then placed his hand across the back of the female Dwarf and gently pushed her forward. "I'd like to introduce you both to my sister, Princess Sawndra. Before you men arrived here, my sister and I were discussing something very serious and problematic for us and our kingdom. It's a problem we've had to deal with for many years, and we would appreciate your assistance in helping us end it."

"What sort of problem are we talking about here?" asked Clearus as he stepped forward to, once again, stand alongside Payner. "Are we talking about settling a debate? Or getting violent?"

"The king speaks of Vankerrians," stated Kaldro.

"I'm sorry, what?" questioned Clearus.

"We have an ongoing conflict with Vankerrians," added Kaldro.

Payner turned back to the king and looked him dead in the eye as he took another step forward. "What is a Vankerrian?" he asked.

"Wait, you're saying you don't have Vankerrians on your land?" questioned Princess Sawndra.

"If we did, then we wouldn't be asking," replied a stern Clearus.

"What is a Vankerrian? And what is it you want us to do?" asked Payner once more.

King Dunlin took a small walk around his stone-built office table and planted himself just inches from Payner; he then went on to answer his questions.

"Until a few years ago, us Dwarves were just like you, we didn't know what Vankerrians were, that was until they forced us to know *who* and *what* they were—cannibalistic, vicious, mutilated, demonic creatures. We have no idea where they came from, and now they will not leave. For the last three years, they have struck fear, anger, and pain all throughout Camaroth and into the hearts of us Dwarves and we do not know how to stop them.

"Our first meeting with them was one nobody here will ever forget. It was the eve of our annual gold mining scavenge; music was heard loud and the ale was drunk often. I looked over the marketplace from the embankment outside and heard the laughter, the music, the cheer, and then the screams! They came from nowhere. We saw Dwarves, commoners, and guards alike, being lifted through the air by nothing; the blood of these Dwarves then pouring over the marketplace like showers of water as two large spikes penetrated their bodies and cut them in two.

"Nobody knew what was happening; there was panic, Dwarves running aimlessly through the villages, women hanging onto their children, and the men hanging on to their axes. Then, we saw them. They appeared from nothing, from the very air itself, grabbing me by the throat. Six of them stood tall, hairless heads and pale blue skin, with a face that would give any man nightmares, eyes as big as their mouths and teeth as big as fingers. They stood, barely clothed, with just a tattered rag to cover their waists, but the scariest thing to see was the two large-boned spikes that grew out from the top of each hand, and as I thought I was about to meet an early end in front of my followers, something truly unexpected happened; they spoke to us."

"They spoke? And what did they say?" questioned Clearus before King Dunlin continued to explain.

"I remember it word for word as if I was reading it from a parchment, much like this one," he said as he threw the scroll from Payner onto his office table, "the leader, the one who had me by the throat, he lifted me off my feet and pulled me toward him so I could feel the stench of his breath coursing its way through my nostrils. He looked at me with his large, blank, bold eyes and said in the foulest of voices, 'We have taken your kingdom for our own! We have taken many lives for our own. We hunt for our own. We will not stop until you're all gone, and we will finish with your king, just so you can see your kingdom fall and your people suffer. It will be slow, and it will be painful, but it *will* fall!'

"And then he dropped me and disappeared. In those three years, we have suffered over thirty attacks, at least once a month. They enjoy what they are doing, and they have no plan in stopping anytime soon. The Dwarves here, they put on brave faces, but they look to me for answers, those which I don't have."

Payner and Clearus looked back at one another in complete shock and astonishment from what they heard; the Vankerrians made King Morrik sound almost friendly. There was fear in the eyes of the two just hearing about them, but both had different forms of fear.

Payner feared what might happen with the Vankerrians once they finished with the Dwarves, whilst Clearus feared what King Dunlin was going to ask of them.

"Tell me, King, what is it you're actually expecting us to do here? If you've had no success in three years, then what are two men going to do?" argued Clearus.

"The princess and I were thinking of a plan to try and stop these Vankerrians, moments before you arrived. We've had many failed attempts over the years, and this one would probably have been another, but we have to try. We were planning on sending a group of Dwarf guards into a cave where we believe the Vankerrians to be camping. We will draw them out, whether it be with force, fire, or just simply teasing them. Once drawn out, we attack them in full force," explained King Dunlin.

"But we have many doubts about the plan," added Princess Sawndra.

"Such as?" questioned Payner, from which the princess replied.

"The group of Dwarves wouldn't make it. The Vankerrians would kill the Dwarven guards, realise what we were planning, and then come into town and kill even more Dwarves just to prove a point."

King Dunlin then added on top of that before Payner or Clearus had a chance to respond. "When we heard that two men had entered the kingdom, we were curious, could this be a sign of aid? My sister and I discussed this at length, and when you told us that you come as an ally, that was a big enough sign for me. Now, the Dwarves, we would send into the caves might not have been able to escape, but you two, you might just."

Payner looked back at Clearus as Clearus looked on at the king and princess with overwhelming frustration and defiance. "No. No way am I going to sacrifice myself!" he argued.

"Clearus, hear them out," requested Payner.

Clearus's look of overwhelmed frustration then turned its attention to Payner. "Hear them out? Hear them out? It is because I heard them out that I'm reacting in the way that I am! You heard what he said about these things; they are vicious, non-stop killing, demonic murderers who, just as it happens, can turn themselves invisible and sneak up on you. I think I've *heard* enough."

"Do you think it will end here, Clearus?" argued Payner. "Do you think it will stop with the Dwarves? What do you think will happen when these creatures are finished here? Perhaps they will find another kingdom that they can try and conquer, or perhaps they might not, but I'm not willing to take that chance," he said as he turned back toward the king and princess. "I will carry out this task for you, but we must first prepare a plan."

"Did that crazy Elven King cut out a slice of your brain, also? This is crazy. Why can this king not come back with us to Ar'Gurd for the meet and we can send many men back here to help with their cause?"

"I will not leave my people, not whilst this threat remains! If you and your king want me at this meet, then you must help us!"

Clearus looked around the room in great stress, almost causing his hands to light up. He had no intention of sacrificing himself, but he also knew that he could not let Payner go alone, but that's when it came to him; his look of stress soon turned to a look of great thought and brilliance, a smirk appeared across his face.

"Okay, you win. I will help you. And I have just the plan to do just that."

CHAPTER THIRTEEN

THE BATTLE FOR CAMAROTH

Prince Clearus

"Are you sure you want to go through with this, Clearus?" Payner asked as Clearus slammed shut the entrance door to King Dunlin's home.

"It is the only chance we have, Payner. I'm not happy about doing this, but if it means leaving here as soon as we can, then this is the best way."

"It's an optimistic plan," added Kaldro as he led the two of them back down the stairway of the embankment, this time leaving the guards behind.

"Optimistic?" questioned Clearus. "How can you doubt my plan, considering none of yours have worked so far?"

Kaldro remained silent, not having a chance to reply before he was asked another question.

"Just how far away is this tunnel where you think they are hiding?" asked Payner.

"It is about two miles in this direction," confirmed Kaldro as he continued to lead Payner and Clearus through the city.

"And what if you fail with this plan, Clearus, then what?" asked Payner as he changed his focus, stepping over a drunken Dwarf lying in the middle of the streets.

The surrounding Dwarven commoners more concerned with why Payner and Clearus were here.

"*If* I fail, then I'll be lucky enough to already be dead whilst these creatures destroy our kingdom. Either way, I win," joked Clearus as he also looked aimlessly around the town and its streets as they passed through, trying to take in as much as they possibly could as they continued to move further and further through Camaroth and toward the Vankerrian tunnel.

Every street corner, every building window, and every alleyway, they found Dwarves standing in great number, eyeing up Clearus and Payner as they passed through, not speaking a word, just glaring intriguingly at them.

After a couple of miles of walking, they cut through a nearby alleyway reaching only a few yards long but wide enough to fit only one man through at a time.

As the three of them made their way through the tight alleyway, they found themselves standing within a small, derelict courtyard, several run-down houses on either side, leaves and vines infesting each building.

A beaten-down fountain no longer flowing took centre stage of the courtyard, covered in grime, vines, and mountains of moss.

"So this is the small village your king spoke of?" asked Clearus as his eyes wandered around.

"Yes. It's hard to believe that less than a year ago, *this* village was one of our most thriving. When the villagers discovered the Vankerrians may be coming from a tunnel just over there, right in between the two stately homes, they all fled. The people of this village always seemed to be the first and last to get attacked, and after sending our own guards in, we soon found out that it was the truth," explained Kaldro.

Kaldro then slowly led them over to the small tunnel that was settled in between the two large Dwarven homes, only a few bushes and branches stood in front of it blocking the way, and as soon as Payner pushed them to the side, the way was clear.

"Now, are you sure you want to do this?" asked Payner to Clearus once more.

"Tell me if there is a better way and we will do it," replied Clearus, which was met with silence from both Payner and Kaldro before he then added, "exactly, there isn't a better plan. Yes, it's risky, but if it works, then it's foolproof."

"Then, let's just hope it works," nodded Payner as he then turned to Kaldro. "You know what to do, don't you? If we aren't out in twenty minutes, then presume we're dead. You'll need to gather your men and prepare for their retaliation. Hopefully, we'll see you very soon."

Payner and Clearus shook the hand of Kaldro, who thanked them before heading back into the busy streets to prepare his troops, and with Kaldro now gone, Clearus and Payner looked in toward the tunnel, where they saw a faint red light in the distance followed by an obscure, eerie movement from within the shadows. The two then looked back at one another with a sense of deep regret.

"Why are none of these kingdoms straightforward?" questioned Clearus. "Why could we not walk in, get them to agree to attend my brother's meet, and then walk straight back out with no complications?" he added.

"It's not too late for you, Clearus, nobody would think any less of you if you were to turn back now," replied Payner.

"I'm doing this," stated a reluctant Clearus as they both then sucked in their guts and proceeded into the tunnel.

As the two moved farther into the tunnel and closer to the red light, they could still see no sign of a candle or flame anywhere, all they felt was their boots cushioning heavily against the dense, muddy surface along with a very unnerving presence surrounding them.

"Just where exactly is this light coming from?" asked Clearus.

"Heat," came a voice through the air.

"What did you say?" questioned Clearus.

Payner came to a halt in front of him, just staring around at the ceiling above.

"That was not me," replied Payner as his eyes continued to scout.

"It wasn't you? Of course, it was you, Payner. If it wasn't you, then who else could it of b…" Clearus stopped what he was saying as soon as he realised where the voice could've come from. "Payner, we've made a mistake; we're out of our depth here," added a jittery Clearus.

"I think you're right," agreed Payner as he turned back to face Clearus. "We shouldn't have come alo…" and it was Payner this time who stopped what he was saying, but that was only when he turned to face Clearus only to see a Vankerrian standing tall and vacant behind him.

Payner quickly drew his sword.

"Whoa, Payner, what are you doing?" asked a now panicked Clearus.

"Clearus, just slowly walk toward me, and whatever you do, don't turn around!"

"There's one behind me, isn't there?" asked Clearus as his lips began to jitter.

Suddenly, the unnerving presence in the air soon allowed Clearus to come to the realisation when he felt an uneasy and chilling breath fall past his shoulder, causing every single hair on his body to stand on end.

Clearus was shocked, standing in a panic and frozen to the ground where he stood.

Payner, now with his sword drawn, began to hurl himself toward Clearus in great haste, when he saw the Vankerrian standing behind him, raising his right hand revealing his two predatory spikes.

With Payner not being as quick as he could, scuffing clumps of mud between his boots with each step, Clearus looked on, stunned and worried, as he then saw Payner caught in his tracks before he could reach him. Seeing Payner lifted through the air by nothing, he was then held up against the wall.

As Payner dangled from the wall, another Vankerrian became visible with his hand wrapped around Payner's throat.

Almost forgetting about the one who stood behind him, Clearus, with adrenaline now taking over, drew his own sword and began to run to Payner, taking only three steps before he was then lifted off his feet and pinned up against the wall beside him.

"Please, we do not mean you harm," pleaded Payner as he looked into the giant bug eyes of the soulless beast.

"Your swords tell a different story," came a foul voice from the beast who held up Clearus.

"I thought you were going to kill my friend," replied Payner.

"Why are you here? The two of you are either brave or very foolish!" spoke the Vankerrian.

"We are here to try and sort this problem between yourselves and the Dwarves, all this doesn't need to happen," said Payner as he continued to plead as he struggled for breath, whilst Clearus remained silent and panicked.

"We've no quarrel with men; Dwarves are the problem, and nothing you can say will change that, so you can either die or help us kill them!"

"Kill the Dwarves? We can't," replied Payner. "We promised we would help them."

"Payner, are you stupid!" argued Clearus. "Who are you more afraid of? The Dwarves? Or these...these, things?" he added.

Payner looked at Clearus for a second out of the corner of his eye before turning his attention back to the Vankerrian. "So what, you're just going to let me and Clearus go, we then help you kill some Dwarves, and then what? Once the Dwarves are all gone, who's to say that you won't then enter Ar'Gurd and slaughter *our* families?"

"Can you not provoke them, please?" pleaded an anxious Clearus toward Payner as sweat dripped from his brows.

"This is not a hard decision to make. Listen to your companion, he knows. You either help us in the hope no harm will come to your people or your lands, or you choose the side of the Dwarves and die right now, leaving us with the thought that man also tried to kill us. And with you gone, who then would protect your people? We have more power and more force than either of you, *and we are everywhere!*" stated the beast.

Much to Payner and Clearus's horror, four more Vankerrians then became visible, standing statuesque and vacant as though their bodies were there, but their minds were not.

The first Vankerrian spoke up again. "We have many powers, but would you like to know the way that I'm going to kill you if you wish to help the Dwarves? I'm going to climb into your body through your mouth and then climb back out whilst pulling every working organ out with me…"

"Do you take me for a coward?" argued Payner.

"I take you for a *fool*," replied the beast.

"Payner, are you mad? They are going to kill you!" warned Clearus.

"Listen to your friend; he speaks truth! But it is only truth if helping the Dwarves is what you desire."

"It's what I desire, you ugly freak," he replied.

The Vankerrian looked on at Payner with his basic vacant expression until what appeared to be a glimmer of a grin appear on its face. "Good," he replied. "Then, we shall start with your friend over here," added the beast as it tightened its grip around Clearus's throat, causing the boned spikes in his hand to glisten slightly.

"Wait. I'm on your side," said Clearus as he struggled to speak through the grip around his jugular.

"Clearus!" shouted Payner as he looked on in fear.

"You did this. Your friend's death is going to be on your hands. But don't worry, after you've seen him die, you'll have your turn."

The Vankerrian lunged toward Clearus with great force whilst Clearus tried to keep his mouth closed. Clearus grabbed hold of the creature's hand that was wrapped around his throat, when suddenly, he saw that small light flicker from his hands. The Vankerrian immediately stopped what he was doing and looked at Clearus, this time with an expression that was not vacant.

"What was that?" he asked, abruptly, but Clearus didn't respond. All he heard was the voice of Payner flowing through his ears as a feeling of great energy flowed through his bloodstream.

"Do it, Clearus. I believe it; you can do it."

Clearus continued to stare down at the beast, who was looking back at him with a slight restraint.

"I will ask this only once more. What was that?" asked the angry Vankerrian as he loosened his grip on Clearus enough so he could talk.

Trying to catch up with a few big breaths, Clearus smiled back at the slender beast. "You want to see what it is?" he said before feeling this huge force of energy flow from his gut, up his chest, down his arms, and then into his hands.

A light flickered slightly from them. Clearus closed his eyes for a slight second to try and concentrate his mind on his body, and when he soon felt like his hands were about to explode, he pushed them straight toward the upper body of the Vankerrian, imploding all this energy onto him and launching him across the other end of the tunnel.

The remaining beasts stood stunned, as well as Payner. Neither of them had ever seen a man with such abilities before. And now that Payner had seen it in full force, he was in awe, but he also knew an opportunity when he saw one. Whilst the Vankerrian who had him held was focused on Clearus, Payner managed to lift his right leg up and stretch far enough that he was able to grab a small dagger he had tucked away in his boot, after the Dwarves allowed them back their weapons for this quest.

He pulled out the dagger and stuck it straight into the neck of the Vankerrian, causing him to lose his grip as he bellowed out a huge demonic roar.

Payner quickly got back to his feet after he dropped to the floor and headed straight for Clearus.

"Let's get out of here!" commanded Payner as they started to run back through the tunnel for the exit, but they only took about five steps through the thick surface before they heard several bellowed screeches from behind them. They both stopped and turned to see all six of the Vankerrians standing in a straight formation, one of them still with a dagger through his neck.

Suddenly, one by one, each of the creatures became invisible and out of sight.

"Run, quickly!" shouted Payner as he and Clearus turned back around and sprinted as fast and as best they could.

"What happened to completing the task?" asked Payner, running side by side with Clearus, feeling like the distance to the exit had trebled.

"We can still do it," replied Clearus as he came to a sudden halt allowing Payner to go a few steps ahead before stopping himself.

"Clearus? What are you doing? Come on."

Clearus leant forward and placed his hands on his legs to catch his breath, taking one deep breath after the other.

Payner began to jog back to him in quick haste, pulling on his arm to drag him along. Clearus shook his head as he continued to breathe heavily, pushing Payner's hand from him.

"You must continue alone, Payner. The plan can still go ahead, but you must trust me. I can't run anymore; that light seemed to have taken a lot from me. In this state, we will both die. Prepare the Dwarves, and I will be along shortly, trust me. Now, go!" muttered Clearus under a deep breath as he pushed Payner toward the direction of the exit.

Reluctant to leave, Payner knew Clearus was right; he wasn't going to make it much longer. Without saying another word and giving Clearus a very honourable nod, Payner then turned back in the other direction and sprinted as fast as he could to the end of the tunnel.

Losing the sight of Payner in the distance, Clearus suddenly realised he wasn't the only one in the cave breathing heavily.

Feeling light footsteps in a circle around him, he closed his eyes tight and listened to the noises, the heavy breathing echoing through the tunnel and bouncing from the walls and back into his ears, a sound of demonic growling just inches from each eardrum. He was feeling as though he was in a nightmarish world just by closing his eyes.

Now standing up straight, with his eyes closed as tight as they could be and his arms quivering down either side of his body, he suddenly heard the tunnel go quiet, only being able to hear the sound of his own worried breath. He gathered his thoughts and composed himself for a second before then shooting his eyes open, and surprisingly to him, he saw nothing.

Confused and completely baffled, he spun his head round to face the way he had just come, but again, he saw nothing.

Continuing to breathe heavy and in a panic, he began to wonder about where the Vankerrians had gone. They were definitely there; he felt their breath run across the back of his neck. Thoughts ran through his mind at that point; he even contemplated that the Vankerrians could've skipped him and proceeded to chase down Payner, from which they would then come and finish off Clearus once they were done with Payner.

Clearus, fearing now for Payner's life, quickly spun his head back round to face the direction of the exit once more, but as he did, he found himself completely stunned when he came nose to mouth with a Vankerrian.

Breathing stench and anger into his nostrils, Clearus scoured his head to the side in an unbearable tension, realising then that the other five Vankerrians were also there, standing one by one in front of him.

"I do not mean you any harm," muttered Clearus, nervously.

"You attacked us. That shows different. Your companion put a dagger into one of our necks; we will not allow this!" exclaimed the Vankerrian as he grabbed Clearus by the throat once again and lifted him from the ground so that their eyes met.

"Please, I was always on your side, you know that. I only attacked you to stop you from killing me. It was my companion who stabbed yours, it was my companion who almost got me killed, and it was my companion who left me here to die when I could not run anymore. Let me help you bring them down," pleaded Clearus.

With a ghostly snarl, the Vankerrian released him back to his feet. "Just how can you help us?" asked the Vankerrian.

"You know how," replied a now confident Clearus as he created a small ball of light in his hands.

"What are you?" asked the mystified Vankerrian as his large, bold eyes drew to the light like a moth to a flame.

"I'm a man who is going to help you, a man who has power beyond reason, a man with vengeance on his mind. There is no reason why we should be enemies when we would make much stronger allies, something my companion failed to see. So what do you say? Do we have a deal?" asked Clearus as he allowed the ball of light to fade away, forcing the Vankerrian to look him in the eyes once more.

"We have a deal," agreed the Vankerrian before adding one simple clause, "But when we attack the Dwarves, you leave your companion to me."

Clearus looked up at the Vankerrian with a huge smile on his face, along with a small chuckle to himself. "That's a deal. But on one condition of my own, you make him suffer," stated Clearus, which was then met by a large roar from the Vankerrian, followed in sequence then by the other five.

Making themselves invisible once more, they then allowed Clearus to lead the way back to the village for a vengeful attack.

So leading the way and still hearing the footsteps of the Vankerrians following behind him, Clearus finally made his way back into the Dwarven village. But when they eventually reached the village, it was just as derelict as the last time they saw it. But, this time, it had one small change, Payner.

Payner stood alone and just ahead of the moss-filled fountain of the courtyard.

Suddenly, the Vankerrians, one by one, became visible once more, each bearing a ferocious growl as they did so, with what appeared to be their leader stepping forward, slightly ahead of Clearus.

"Again, you are either very brave or very foolish to be waiting for us."

Payner stood valiantly, and as brave as any man could, he held his head up high with a huge grin on his face as he glanced back at the Vankerrians.

"I thought these little monsters would have killed you by now, Clearus. I was hoping they would save me the trouble. I abandoned you to die. That is a true crime in our lands, which means there is only one way to move past this now, me versus you. One on one," offered Payner.

Clearus looked up at the Vankerrian, as he knew he wanted Payner for himself. He rose up on his tiptoes and whispered gently into the creature's ear, "Let me take him. I won't kill him, but with this power I possess, I could bring him straight to his knees."

The Vankerrian looked at Payner in great anguish and hate, without taking his eyes off of him. He replied back to Clearus in a forcefully abrupt tone, "Bring him to me."

Clearus nodded back at the Vankerrian in agreeance as he walked out into the courtyard with his hands held out together in front of him; it didn't take long for the ball of light to ignite in his hands. As he walked closer and closer toward Payner through the cracked and weeded surface, the light began to grow bigger and wilder as Payner remained where he stood, holding his sword cautiously down the side of his leg, appearing to be waiting for Clearus to strike first.

Just yards away from one another, Payner still remained solid, looking on as Clearus approached farther, but as he got closer, Payner formed another big grin on his face.

Clearus came to a halt. The big ball of energy in his hands was the biggest he had ever seen it, but at that point, it went to the back of his mind as he stared back blankly at Payner.

"Do it! Do it now!" shouted the Vankerrian from across the courtyard, remaining just outside of the tunnel.

Payner, then with a grin still on his face, he muttered to Clearus, "You heard him, Clearus; do it now."

Clearus then formed a big smile on his face as he spun around with the big ball of energy in his hands and launched it toward the tunnel behind the Vankerrians, causing the whole thing to cave in on impact, blocking the only way in or out.

"You fool!" cried the Vankerrian as he looked frustratingly back at Clearus, who now stood alongside Payner, now with his sword drawn, also.

"You think this is a victory?" asked the Vankerrian. "This is far from it; this is your demise. With all of that energy, it is still not enough to stop us!"

Payner, still bearing his huge grin, then moved a heavy step forward before shouting across the courtyard. "This ends now!" And before the Vankerrians knew what was happening, a small throwing axe came from beyond a nearby building and planted into one of the Vankerrian's heads.

The Vankerrians looked on in shock as they saw large groups of Dwarves come running from the buildings to join Payner and Clearus.

The head Vankerrian then let out the most ferocious and demonic roar before the remaining five of them became invisible once more.

"Stand in formation!" yelled Kaldro.

Prince Clearus and Sir Payner stood back-to-back at that point, knowing that they were prime targets for the Vankerrians but had no clue where they were.

"Well, your plan worked, Clearus. You smoked them out, and just as we thought, we're now being hunted," said Payner feeling a slight tremble, not knowing whether it was from himself or Clearus.

Suddenly, the two were jolted when they heard a huge crash come from the northeast side of the village; several Dwarves were seen being tossed onto the already damaged huts.

Reckless Dwarves were poking spears, throwing axes, and launching arrows any which way they could to try and hit one of the Vankerrians, almost hitting their own people on several occasions.

Spears scraped armour, arrows pierced barrels, and axes created whistles as they flew past ears. Everything looked like a mess; the Dwarves couldn't see what they were fighting, and they feared for their lives.

Payner and Clearus heard the crashing and saw the panic and sprinted over to the small group as fast as they could.

Payner, as well as carrying the most armour, still managed to be the much quicker of the two and led the way.

With Clearus trailing behind, Payner went crashing into the huddle of Dwarves. He pushed them out to form a circle around him, leaving himself in the middle.

"I am the bait. Let them come to me and then strike. But please, in the name of all spirits, try not to hit me," commanded Payner. Knowing who the Vankerrians wanted, Payner had his plan, but that wasn't to say that everything would go according to plan.

As Clearus ran for the small circle of Dwarves that Payner had formed, he was forcefully tripped up and dragged back toward the fountain, scraping his chin across the grimy floor in the process.

Attention from Payner and the Dwarves drew to Clearus, causing them to forget about the other four Vankerrians who still roamed the village undetected.

The circle was soon smashed into a carnage-filled heap of Dwarves, leaving Payner alone in the middle. He raised his sword high when he saw the Vankerrian appear in front of him, brandishing the large, bony spikes that adorned each hand, striking instant fear into any enemies' eyes.

As Payner locked eyes with one Vankerrian, Clearus was still having his hands full with another, being dragged across the ramshackle surface.

Holding on to a small concrete slab that had come loose from the surface, Clearus managed to bring a short halt to the dragging. With the Vankerrian still having a firm grip around his ankle, Clearus managed to turn himself around onto his back, but not before letting go of the slab.

The Vankerrian looked on at him with a tilted head and a much more exasperated expression than what they were used to seeing.

Clearus, with a little bit of built-up antagonism of his own after dropping his sword and being used like a rag doll, formed up another ball of light in his hands, much to the Vankerrian's irritation. The Vankerrian bellowed out a deep cry before dropping Clearus's leg, but before the Vankerrian could react in any way, Clearus fired the ball of light, tossing the Vankerrian metres up into the air.

"Archers, axe throwers, fire!" shouted Clearus as he pointed up toward the airborne Vankerrian who, unfortunately for him, found himself implanted with countless arrows and axes before he collided back with the concrete floor.

Another one down, only four more to go.

Clearus picked himself back up to his feet and brushed himself off before looking back in worry at Payner, who was now duelling with a ravenous Vankerrian of his own.

The Vankerrian swung at Payner with each claw, frustratingly seeing him duck underneath each swing with ease. The Vankerrian then drew a small haunting hiss toward Payner before barrelling into him with no regard for itself.

Payner dropped to the floor like a sack of bricks as the Vankerrian passed quickly over him, taking a small slice to his right arm from Payner's blade, much to the appraisal of Clearus, who continued to look onward with a small glance as he proceeded to be vigilant for the rest of the creatures.

Payner scoured the floor with his hands, looking for his sword, which had fallen loose from his grasp, not once taking his eyes off the Vankerrian, who now viciously stalked him.

The Vankerrian moved from side to side, atop of Payner as though he had an evil plan but was just waiting for the perfect time to execute it, hissing every time Payner neared his weapon.

As Clearus looked on through the corner of his eye, heavy breath and heart racing, he could see Payner struggle for his sword, but he could also see the Dwarves having their hands full with another Vankerrian on the other side of the courtyard.

Clanging steel and armour were silenced out in Clearus's mind, focusing on where the other two Vankerrians might be. If he let his guard down, it could be the last thing he ever did.

He stood tall near the fountain, trying to draw the Vankerrians in like easy meat.

Clearus suddenly heard yet another hiss from the Vankerrian who stalked Payner, but this time, the hiss had intensity, Clearus threw his attention to Payner, who remained on the floor but finally with his hand gripped on his sword.

Clearus looked on as Payner tried to pull his sword from the floor, but it remained stuck to the concrete like a ten-tonne weight.

Payner pulled and pulled, but still no luck.

Another hiss was heard, but this time, it wasn't from the Vankerrian who still stood atop him.

Clearus turned his full focus to the situation, as he saw another Vankerrian become visible standing tall above

Payner's head with a long, bony foot placed solidly over his sword.

Payner was in trouble, and Clearus knew he now needed to help. He sprinted with what energy he had left, but before he knew what was happening, Clearus was soon dragged back through the air by a tight clutch around his throat before being slammed to the floor with great force, causing him to become immobile for a short period of time as he continued to feel the power of the grip around his throat, from which a Vankerrian then slowly appeared, partially piercing parts of Clearus's neck with his sharp, claw-like fingers.

Clearus gripped one hand around the Vankerrian's wrist, just trying to pull him off with what energy he had left.

He began to turn as pale as the Vankerrians themselves as his hand slowly unhooked from its wrist; he collapsed to the ground, leaving him in a state of defeat and almost certain death.

As Clearus began to briefly fade in and out of consciousness, the figure of the Vankerrian who dominated him became hazy. As the grip tightened, Clearus could feel the light leaving his body as he came close to his end.

His eyes begun to feel heavy, as they shuttered into a final close.

As Clearus's eyes inevitably closed, a young Dwarf suddenly came swinging in from a nearby rope that draped from a near lighting post.

The young Dwarf then released himself from the rope, kicking the Vankerrian in the face, forcing him to loosen his grip on Clearus.

The Dwarf now stood axe in hand, face-to-face with a raging Vankerrian.

The Vankerrian now opened his gigantically bloodshot eyes wide as he stood tall over the youngling.

A brave young Dwarf, merely a child, with slight facial hair and long braided ginger locks, he donned the eyes of someone who had seen far too much for someone of his age. He looked back at the Vankerrian, who stood almost four times his size above him with eyes of confidence.

The Vankerrian hissed at the young Dwarf before lunging forward and taking a swing at him. The youngling rolled under the attack and came up behind the Vankerrian. He found himself within a perfect moment to strike from behind.

As he raised his axe to embed it into the lower spine of the Vankerrian, he saw a helpless Payner out of the corner of his eye being taunted by two others, one whose bony foot remained solidly over Payner's sword.

In a moment of weakness and desperation, the young Dwarf turned in the direction of Payner and launched his axe, which landed perfectly into the skull of the Vankerrian who held Payner's sword.

In quick haste and retaliation, as soon as Payner's sword was released, he claimed a firm grip on the handle and lifted himself up onto one knee before lunging himself upward and forcing his sword through the throat of the second Vankerrian.

With his focus now away from the other Vankerrian, the young Dwarven saviour found himself being stalked, whilst Clearus still remained lifeless on the floor behind him.

The young Dwarf looked on in respect toward Payner.

Suddenly, everything through the young Dwarf's eyes moved slowly; his vision became a haze. He looked on as Payner's expression turned from admirable to stunned.

He found his body levitating above the rest, all eyes looking up at him. He looked down to his own bitter surprise when he saw two large spikes pierced through his gut.

The Vankerrian looked back at Payner without a single ounce of remorse.

Payner, with a hell-bent look in his eyes, sprinted as fast as he could toward the Vankerrian, who then slammed the body of the young Dwarf down to the ground in front of him.

The Vankerrian readied himself as Payner continued to surge toward him. As the other remaining Vankerrian who was still battling the Dwarves over the other end soon became invisible, all eyes were now on the impending collision.

Payner tightened the grip on his sword as he pulled it back, ready for a large strike.

Taking his last few strides, Payner gave out a huge roar toward the Vankerrian, who in return opened his mouth as wide as he could, showing his dagger-like teeth in an attempt to intimidate him.

Payner did not stop. He continued his pursuit. That was until he unexpectedly saw the tip of a sword pushed through the mouth of the Vankerrian from behind.

As the gaping eyes of the Vankerrian became bloodshot and more lifeless, his body plummeted to the floor just yards away from Payner. And to his surprise, there stood Clearus atop of him in a shrine of battered victory, with his sword draped down by his leg, with no more energy left to lift it.

Payner and the Dwarves donned smiles around him, until one Dwarf yelled out, catching the attention of everyone around. "He's still alive!"

Payner and Clearus turned to see a Dwarven soldier cradling the body of the young Dwarf who had saved their lives.

They rushed to his body in great urgency.

"Please, you must do something," pleaded the Dwarven soldier

"Like what? We're not doctors or healers. He needs more skilled hands. These hands are only good for creating wounds, not treating them," replied Clearus.

"We must try something, Clearus, this Dwarf saved both of our lives. Maybe you can…No, forget it, it's a crazy idea," uttered Payner.

"Maybe I can what?"

"Well, I was going to say, perhaps you can try and use your 'magic hands'?"

"What? Are you crazy? And how am I meant to do that? I don't think that's quite how this magic works."

"Can you not try?" pleaded Kaldro.

"Try, how?" argued Clearus. "These aren't healing hands. They're a curse given to me by the Wizard Queen."

"They haven't been cursed tonight. They have helped to save our lives; embrace them," replied Kaldro.

"Clearus…" continued Payner.

"Okay. I will try. But if I end up blowing him into oblivion, then that's not my fault."

Clearus knelt down beside the young Dwarf and placed his hand firmly over his abdomen. He pressed down hard and concentrated the best he could, but nothing happened.

"Nothing is happening," stated Clearus.

"Keep trying, Clearus," demanded Payner. "Close your eyes, block everything else out, focus all of your energy. Dig deep," he added. And as he did, a hypnotising, bright blue glow emanated from the palms of Clearus's hands which still lay pressed down on the young Dwarf.

Stunned faces filled the courtyard; none of them had seen anything like this up close.

The eyelids of the young Dwarf started to flutter as his heartbeat began to steady. Dripping blood began to dry and stain the body as the wounds suffered began to close up and heal.

The glowing blue light shot back into the body of Clearus once he removed his hands from the Dwarf, taking much energy out of him and dropping him down on his arse.

As Payner rushed to help Clearus, several Dwarves rushed to the aid of the young Dwarf, draping his arms around their shoulders and helping to lead him back into the heart of Camaroth.

Payner held out his hand to help Clearus up, but before Clearus had a chance to accept it, he saw Payner get flung into the side of one of the nearby buildings and hitting the dirt with great force.

With little strength left, Clearus pulled himself back onto his feet, only to be knocked straight back down again but this time surrounded by a circular wall of golden flame.

As Payner shrugged off the dirt and dragged himself back to his feet, he looked on as the remaining Vankerrian stood tall above a helpless Clearus.

Payner and several remaining Dwarves ran toward the flames, but they could do nothing more. Clearus was hurt, and he was stuck.

Payner paced a line outside the circle just trying to think of a way to help, but he was all out of ideas.

"Get up on your feet!" ordered the Vankerrian toward Clearus.

But Clearus just stared blankly back at him, all out of breath and focus.

"I will tell you once more, get on your feet!" yelled the Vankerrian, but he got the same response.

In great ferocity, the Vankerrian grasped his hand around the neck of Clearus and pulled him up to his feet with great ease.

With his grasp wrapped firmly around Clearus's neck, the Vankerrian creepily turned his head around toward Payner and looked on at him with vicious eyes, before speaking aloud to him.

"He made this mistake. He turned his back on us, to help you and to help these Dwarves. He has himself to blame; that is why he will die on this day. You sided with the Dwarves from the very beginning. You did not care what we had to say, and you corrupted this man into turning his back on us and help you. You have yourself to blame, which is why you will watch him die on this day."

"Nobody else has to die! We've shown you our strength, and you have shown us yours. There doesn't need to be any more bloodshed. We can all still walk away from this; you don't have to kill him," argued Payner.

"Strength? This man is your strength. Without him, you would've died back in the cave. You may have killed my siblings, but there are always more. And even on my own, I could tear this kingdom apart! And I'm going to start by taking away its only strength."

The Vankerrian then turned his head back toward Clearus. With great, gaping eyes, his mouth opened wide as it gave out a huge screech.

"Nooo!" cried Payner as he desperately tried to battle the golden flames.

Within a second, Payner and the remaining Dwarves were taken back in great shock as they saw the Vankerrian enter the body of Clearus through his mouth.

"Clearus!" cried Payner once more.

Clearus closed his eyes as his body remained standing. The same hypnotising glow once again began to emanate from his palms as a fiery glow appeared around the rest of his body.

"What is it doing to him?" said Kaldro in great disbelief.

As he remained standing, movement could be seen within the gut of Clearus, as though something was trying to break out. His mouth began to open once more, much wider than any mouth was able to. The fiery glow began to shine from within the mouth of Clearus when suddenly, in the blink of an eye, the Vankerrian flew back from his mouth and blasted through the golden flames, setting himself ablaze.

The Vankerrian squirmed and screeched on the floor in great agony for several seconds before suddenly disintegrating into nothing, but a pile of ash surrounded by a flutter of fiery glow.

The Vankerrians were gone, and so then was the circle of golden flames. The body of Clearus left lying in a motionless heap was all that remained.

Payner ran straight for him, kneeling down beside his body, slightly frightened at the thought of what might happen if he were to touch him.

"Clearus, are you still with us?" he asked, gently.

Clearus's eyes fluttered, licking the broken skin on his dry lips, just then managing to relay a response. "Did I just explode?"

A grin of relief appeared on Payner's face as he helped Clearus get back to his feet, surrounded by a group of admiring Dwarves.

"Your quest is complete, the Vankerrians of Camaroth are no more. Let's get you patched up, for tonight, my friends, we celebrate!" hailed Kaldro.

Great applause swept through the caves of Camaroth as Clearus was helped to his feet, his arm draped over Payner's shoulder.

"Heroes of Camaroth," applauded King Dunlin as he made his way through the crowds toward the pair, accompanied by Princess Sawndra. "You have both risked your lives to defend this kingdom and its people, the least I can do is attend this meet with your king in time to come; but this still feels like a small prize. If there is anything else I can do for you, if it is in my power, then I will see it done."

With Clearus still looking somewhat distant, Payner's eyes prowled the crowds of Dwarves, but there was one face he couldn't see.

"Where is the young Dwarf? The Dwarf who helped to save *our* lives? He was here just now; I owe him a great deal of gratitude, as does this kingdom."

A small voice was then heard in and amongst the crowds, pushing his way to the front was the young Dwarf himself. "You speak of me."

Payner's eyes grew with admiration for this young Dwarf as he appeared. "If not for this young Master Dwarf, I would not be here; he played just as big a part in this victory."

"Ahh, yes! Young Sprock," replied Kaldro. "He is a fine young warrior in the making."

Payner's attention turned back to King Dunlin with a courageous idea rattling around his head.

"King Dwarf, this young Sprock has exceeding potential; I have an idea that could work well for both of us, but first there are a few things we must discuss."

CHAPTER FOURTEEN

SURPRISE VISIT

Belthran

"Belthran! Come here, my son!" ordered King Armish as he spotted Belthran darting down the long castle corridor ahead of him.

Belthran stopped in his tracks, refusing to turn and face his father. "If this is another one of your brilliant plans, then I would rather not know it."

"Don't patronise me, Belthran!" said the king in such a deep tone that it forced Belthran to turn instantly, looking back at his father, whose presence down the corridor made the walls look narrow. "I'm here to talk of your brother," he added in a much calmer tone.

"Well, then, maybe you should speak to him instead because he's not too happy with you, either."

"I would if I could find him. Your mother said he wanted to leave the city, and after she refused him, he's suddenly nowhere to be found; would you know anything about that?"

"And why would I know anything about that?" replied Belthran, sternly, as he slowly made his way through the corridor to his father.

When he stood in front of him, King Armish looked down on him with a serious expression of doubt on his face as his voice became stricter. "Because you're incredibly calm for someone whose brother I just said is missing, If I find out you're lying to me, Belthran, then I will…"

"Then, you'll what, Father?" Belthran responded, fighting fire with fire. "You'll keep me held up like a prisoner in a barely armed city whilst pirates attack? You know what, Father, if Maxin did get out, then good on him; he's probably safer out there, anyway!"

King Armish grabbed Belthran by the buckle of his posh, leather shoulder straps, pulling him in closer, looking back at him with an irritable look in his eye.

"I've had just about enough of you, Belthran. You take me for a fool? Maxin would not go against your mother's will, unless he was urged to do so, so where has he gone?" Armish asked as he gave Belthran a slight shake. "Tell me!"

For the first time in his life, Belthran was staring back at his father and seeing a man he didn't recognise. He wriggled loose from his father's grasp, and without speaking a word, he ran back down the corridor and headed toward the palace courtyard as quickly as he could, barging past an oncoming guard and snubbing the sound of his father calling after him.

King Armish was left standing at the end of the corridor, embarrassed by his actions, but also felt they were somewhat justified. He was worried about everything that was happening around him, wondering how he could keep the backing of the city and its people, if he couldn't even keep the backing of his own family.

King Armish shouted over to the nearby guard, instructing him to follow Belthran to bring him back to the palace. Without any hesitation, the guard obliged his king's orders and marched off in hasty pursuit.

Just outside of the palace, within the courtyard, the guard finally caught up to Belthran, calling out to him as he was storming ahead. "Master Belthran, you must come with me. Your father wishes for me to escort you back into the castle."

"Get lost," replied a stern Belthran as he continued to march forward toward the palace gate, but much to his annoyance, the guard, following his king's orders, continued to follow.

"Please, my Prince, I can't leave until you come with me."

Belthran stopped in a huff and turned to face the guard, who edged slightly closer toward him.

"Yes, that's right, I am your prince, and you *will* leave because I order you to do so."

"I can't do that, Master Belthran…"

"Are you defying my orders? I can have you put in a dungeon for that, you know. Now, do as I say!"

The guard gulped at the thought of upsetting Belthran, as he knew he couldn't turn back without him. "I must do what your father commands; the will of the king outweighs the will of a prince, and as a guard of his kingdom, I can't let him down," pleaded the guard.

But still, Belthran was having none of it. He grinned back at the guard in admiration for his courage, but that grin soon turned back to a stern look of arrogance. "Well, you're going to have to let him down because I'm not coming with you."

As Belthran turned to walk off, the guard hurried back after him; eventually catching up with him and grabbing the prince by the arm. "Please, my Prince, you must come with me."

Belthran struggled, but unlike with his father back in the palace, this time he couldn't break free.

"I demand you let me go at once!" he ordered, but the guard's grip was tight; he didn't say anything back to Belthran as he fought to pull him back to the castle.

Belthran wasn't giving up so easily, as he began to pull the guard back toward him, engaging in a small tug of war style confrontation. As a small crowd began to gather, overcome with frustration, Belthran pulled the guard as hard as he could toward him whilst connecting with a swift headbutt to the nose on the way in.

The guard let go of his grasp as he held onto his face with both hands whilst Belthran lost his footing and fell to the courtyard floor.

Gathering his breath, Belthran looked up at the guard as he removed his hands from his face to reveal a very bloody and broken nose.

The guard stood over him, pulling his sword from his holster.

The small crowd was in shock, shouting absurdities at the guard who now aimed his sword toward their prince.

"Get back on your feet. You need to come with me," spoke the guard with a surprisingly humble tone considering Belthran just broke his nose.

The guard then holstered his weapon and held out his hand toward Belthran to help him up.

Although he was the prince, Belthran was still quite surprised as to why the guard remained so calm. "What is your name?" asked the prince as he remained dormant on the courtyard floor.

"Brayle," the guard replied, keeping his hand held out, but becoming seemingly nervous about the raucous crowd that had gathered.

"I'm sorry for the headbutt, Brayle, I admire your composure," praised Belthran.

"I live to serve the crown, my young Prince. Believe it or not, it comes with its fair share of bumps and bruises; failing the king is not something I wish to do. Now, please, I beg you, take my hand."

As stubborn as Belthran was, he gained quick respect for that guard and had no further wishes for him to fail in his father's task. Belthran nodded back at him in admiration, as he then leaned forward to grab the guard's hand. And as the pair locked hands, the guard pulled Belthran straight back to his feet.

"You won't fail the crown today, Brayle; we're lucky to have a guard like you at our service," commended Belthran, raising an honourable smile toward the guard. But that smile soon turned to shock and horror when Belthran came face-to-face with an arrowhead skewered straight through the back of Brayle's head.

Screams were heard from the gathering crowd that was looking on.

Belthran now looking back into lifeless eyes of Brayle, the young guard's tight grip on Belthran's hand became loose as his body beneath him gave way.

A tear strolled down the face of the young prince as he let go of the guard's hand. He quickly turned around to see more villagers running away from their homes and toward the palace.

Smoke was rising in the east of the city whilst screams were heard from all around.

Belthran was stood in a trance as he saw a bombardment of arrows come down around him, taking down more villagers and surrounding guards; he was soon knocked from his daze as another guard grabbed hold of his arm.

"Master Belthran, you must get out of here, now!"

"No, help get the villagers into the palace and keep them safe, alert my father! I must gather what troops we have left and fight against this. Otherwise, the city will fall tonight!"

Following orders, the guard left to alert the king.

Belthran then gathered a group of nearby guards and ran toward the smoke east of the city.

Heading down the eastern bank, Belthran and the guards soon come across a small village market, deprived of any life at all.

There was a very eerie calmness in the air. Belthran sensed something was off, and it wasn't just the left-behind fish on the market stalls, either.

They all came to a halt in front of a large, wooden bell tower that stood tall above any of the buildings surrounding it.

Belthran dispersed the five guards whom he had taken with him; two of them to his left, two of them to his right, and the fifth guard sat just in front of him.

Belthran was drawn to this bell tower as the bell began to slowly swing side to side, so gently that it never made a chime.

"Be on your guard," he spoke gently, along with a few hand gestures directing the guards toward the entrance of the bell tower. As the first four guards slowly crept over to cover the left and right sides of the door, Belthran then gave his orders to the spearman, who stood in front of him. "Now, you, open that door! I will be right behind you."

With a nervous gulp, the guard then edged closer to the door, with Belthran following just yards behind him, sword in hand.

Once the guard reached the door, Belthran made sure he kept a safe distance behind him, especially with not knowing what could be on the other side.

The guard reached for the doorknob, and as he placed his hand around it, the young prince looked up at the bell with a puzzled mind, as it began to swing faster and faster, picking up speed with each swing. Suddenly, Belthran's eyes shot open as an uneasy feeling hit the pit of his stomach.

As the guard twisted the doorknob, the bell gave out a huge chime that could be heard through most parts of the city.

"Run!" screamed Belthran toward the guards, but before any of them knew what was happening, the whole building exploded into a hundred shards of wood, the great bell crashing down with it as the blast threw Belthran back across the market floor.

With his ears ringing and his body battered from the blast, Belthran slightly raised his head from the ground and looked on at the carnage that now lay before him. Planks of wood now covered large portions of the courtyard as the great golden bell now sat statuesque in the middle of it all. The bodies of the guards were nowhere to be seen.

As the ringing in Belthran's ears faded away, he began to hear the sounds of footsteps in the distance, making their way toward him. But it wasn't this that made his ears twitch, that came from a soft voice just to the right of him.

"Over here. This way, quickly!"

He tilted his head to the right and fixated his eyes on a young woman cowering in the doorway of a nearby hut.

"Quickly! They're coming!" she added, raising her voice ever so slightly.

Belthran heard the footsteps getting louder and louder. He quickly tossed himself over onto his belly before bringing himself up to one knee, barely catching his breath.

"Over here," came a foul voice from an alleyway close to where the bell tower once stood.

"Run!" cried the woman across to the prince, trying not to make her voice heard. Belthran hobbled back to his feet as he then hastily darted over to the woman, who immediately pulled him inside and slammed the door closed behind him.

Belthran immediately fell to the floor with his back against the door as the woman bolted the door above him. He looked around the small, darkened room, locking eyes with a much younger girl standing in the doorway of a bedroom.

"Come here, Ye'ara," spoke the older woman quietly to the young girl.

As the scared young girl ran across the room, she wrapped her arms around the legs of the woman, crying gently into her lap.

"It's okay, my daughter, you're safe," comforted the woman, stroking the girl's hair.

The two were then startled, when suddenly, the incoming footsteps could now be heard just outside the door.

"Get down out of the way and be quiet," ordered Belthran quietly as he then shuffled over to a nearby window before slowly and carefully raising his head to peer outside.

A distraught look grew upon the face of Belthran at this point, as he saw at least twenty pirates scavenging the market.

"How many?" asked the woman, clutching on to her child.

"Too many!" replied Belthran as he sunk back to the floor. "Is there any other way out of here?" he added.

"Only through that door on the right; it leads out into the alleyway that runs down the side of the hut."

"That's no good, they will still see us leave."

Amongst the rummaging outside and trying to conjure up any kind of plan, Belthran unexpectedly heard a voice he recognised moving toward them from the alleyway.

"The explosion came from down this way," spoke the voice as it moved closer.

Belthran donned a smile of hope after hearing the voice of his Unit member, Saxon. But that smile soon became dampened when he heard two more words, this time coming from the market area. "Ready, aim!"

He boosted his head to peer through the window once more to see all of the pirates now aiming arrows toward the alleyway, just waiting for Saxon and whoever else he was with.

Saxon and his party were walking into a death trap. Belthran rattled his brain as hard as he could, but as the footsteps of Saxon grew worryingly closer. Belthran hopped up from the ground and moved over toward the alleyway door. He then closed his eyes and took a few deep breaths.

Upon hearing the sudden command of, "Fire!" from the pirates, Belthran kicked open the door as hard as he could, stopping Saxon and other Unit members, Anamaforth and Panagor, in their tracks; the door was then used as a shield, taking the brunt of many sharp arrows. Belthran then pulled his Unit members inside and slammed the door shut behind him.

"Prince Belthran. What are you doing here?" asked a stunned Saxon.

"You're Prince Belthran?" questioned an even more startled woman.

Belthran glanced over at the woman, but he was weary of the time they now had left. "You saved our lives, my Prince!" hailed Panagor.

"For how long? They now know we're in here," stated Belthran as he wedged a nearby chair up against the previously kicked down door.

All four men were then unsettled when they heard a deafening scream from the young daughter. They looked toward the young girl to see her trembling in her mother's arms whilst pointing toward the window.

Belthran and his men then turned to face the window and were taken back in fear when they saw the scarred flesh of a partially burnt pirate staring back at them; half of his hair had been singed, whilst one eye was covered with a poorly frayed patch.

The pirate had a sinister grin on his face as he stared back at the prince through the window with his one extremely bloodshot eye.

As the burnt pirate continued to creepily stare back at Belthran, they were soon called into action when the other pirates began to barge and hack away at doors. Saxon and Anamaforth shifted a nearby table and bookcase in front of the main door for extra support whilst Belthran and Panagor covered the alleyway door, pushing their bodies up against it to keep it closed.

With the woman and her daughter screaming in the corner, Belthran and his Unit were trying desperately to stop the pirates from entering, but just as it looked as though the door were about to be smashed down, the barrage suddenly stopped, and everything went quiet. Belthran looked over at the window and the burnt pirate had also disappeared.

"What's going on?" questioned Anamaforth.

Belthran moved his body away from the door before edging over to the window to take another peek outside. As he crept in front of the window, he stood confused when he looked out to see all the pirates standing in a line outside, gazing on at the hut. Anamaforth crept up behind Belthran and looked out the window over his broad shoulder, "What are they doing?" he asked, but before anyone could answer that question, they soon began to realise that the room was slowly filling up with smoke.

"They've set fire to the hut; they're trying to smoke us out!" claimed Belthran.

"So we're dead either way," said Saxon. "Well, we can either storm out there and get skewered, or we stay in here and get cooked," he added.

As they bickered amongst each other about what to do, a small section of the roof began to crumble; dust and soot fell from overhead as a slight piece of roofing caved in, narrowly avoiding the woman and her daughter.

"There must be another way out," suggested Panagor.

Belthran scoured the room as the others continued to panic.

He scurried over the wall adjacent to where the woman and her daughter cowered. "There is another hut that joins on to this one, right?" he questioned.

"A run-down tapestry seller, the merchant moved to the west side a few months back," answered the woman.

A small explosion on the rooftop then caused ash and ember to rain down from above.

"Saxon, Anamaforth, Panagor. Help me hack away at this wall, if we can make a hole big enough, then we can escape this hut before it kills us all!"

The four of them then persisted to slash away at this wall with their longswords, daggers and anything else they could use.

As a small hole began to form within the wall, they were all shaken by a small rumbling.

"It's about to come down!" shouted Saxon as the building continued to creek.

"Keep going!" ordered Belthran as the four then resulted in kicking, punching, and clawing at this hole to make it big enough to crawl through, which it eventually was.

Belthran allowed his troops to go through the hole first which, without a thought, they rapidly did. With one foot already in the hole, he then turned to face the mother and daughter across from him and held out his hand. "Come now, quickly!"

The woman picked up her daughter and hurried over to Belthran, holding out her hand to grab his. But just as she reached out, another section of the roof caved in, narrowly avoiding Belthran, causing a plank of flaming wood to drop between them.

Leaving the smallest of gaps to crawl through, this obstacle was only big enough to squeeze through one at a time. The woman placed her crying daughter down and kissed her on the head. "You move, quickly now, Ye'ara!" she said as she helped guide her underneath the burning plank and toward Belthran, who immediately sent her through the hole to join the others,

"Now, you," he said as he looked back through the rapid flames at the woman.

As the woman now lay on her belly, quickly trying to drag her way through to the other side, avoiding the falling debris, another rumble came from above, this one louder than the last. She stopped dragging herself toward Belthran and stared upsettingly back at him.

"What are you doing? Come on, move!" he commanded as he was then blown back into the wall by a short blast as a large section of the roof came down, collapsing on top of the mother. Whilst the building continued to cave in around him, Belthran continued to look on at the woman with a distraught look on his face, drowning out the cry of Ye'ara behind him and the screams of his troops.

Just as another falling plank then broke his sight, Belthran looked directly above him as the ceiling began to cave in on top of him. Fortunately for him, his troops had his back and dragged him through the hole just in time as the roof collapsed down, blocking the gap.

Taking a few moments to capture his breath, Belthran looked on at the worried look on the faces of his troops and Ye'ara, who was being comforted by Panagor.

"Master Belthran. The only way out leads back into the marketplace, and the fire is continuing to spread; we're still not safe here," stated Saxon as smoke slowly started to gather in the room.

"Start on the wall at the back of the shop, it must lead on to somewhere," ordered Belthran, but just as he gave the order, he heard another order coming from outside.

"Into positions!"

But it wasn't a voice he was expecting to hear. He looked up at his troops, who looked back at him with a glimmer of hope.

Saxon spoke aloud, "That voice. Was that…"

Belthran looked back at him with the biggest smile on his face as he made his way back to his feet and hobbled over to the window to look outside and at that point, one name left Belthran's lips, "Harnik!"

Harnik stood courageous across the marketplace with his troops, staring down the army of pirates. Much to Belthran's surprise, Harnik was also being supported by several of the city guards, plus the remaining members of his own Unit: Belarear, Vinagey, Kroyl, Angelio, and Rekken.

Belthran turned to Panagor at that point and urged him to take young Ye'ara back to the palace and keep her safe, from which he then kicked down the door of the tapestry store, much to the dismay of the pirates, and stood alongside

Harnik as Panagor ran in the opposite direction toward the palace with Ye'ara.

"Do you mind if I cut in?" said Belthran to Harnik, who just smirked back at him.

Not amused in the slightest, the burnt pirate bellowed out a huge roar from which twenty more pirates appeared from the rooftops around them, whilst Belthran and Harnik stood with only thirty men of their own.

"Were there not more guards?" asked Belthran. "No, Cousin, there was another small attack not far from here; they'd set fire to Kelby Mickens' Tavern. Fortunately, there were only a few casualties, but these were the only guards that were there. Once we cleared the area, we heard this huge explosion, which led us here."

Troops of both armies then stared grudgingly at one another, scoping each other out, that was until the burnt pirate raised one hand in the air, which was then followed by all the rooftop pirates aiming arrows at them from above, as the pirates on the ground swapped their bows for their rusty swords and their trailing point daggers.

Belthran swiftly gave the same orders to the troops behind him, but unfortunately for them, they only had seven archers on their side.

A tense, unnerving feeling coursed through the air, leaving a silence that spoke louder than any noise could. The look on the burnt pirate was deranged as he stood with a small hunch, ready to charge forward, staring back at Belthran and Harnik with his one bloodshot eye and a sickening smile to match.

As Belthran, Harnik, and the men behind them anxiously readied their weapons to fight, they suddenly heard a large command coming from the direction of the pirates, "Charge!"

But even the burnt pirate was puzzled, as this order did not come from him. The pirate turned to face behind him and saw none other than King Armish leading eight city guards toward him.

"Father," muttered Belthran to himself before he and Harnik then seized the opportunity and charged at the pirates whilst they were distracted.

Before the burnt pirate could give another command, the two groups of men then clashed with the pirates, hitting them from both sides. And the battle between men and pirates was finally underway.

Within seconds, bodies were dropping, arrows were flying, and blood was filling the streets; but amongst all of the carnage, Belthran had his sights set on one person, the burnt pirate; he wanted vengeance for Ye'ara's mother.

Belthran had the burnt pirate in his sights, swiftly taking down a couple of pirates just to get closer to him.

As he eventually got close enough, the pirate's back was turned. Belthran saw this as the perfect opportunity to strike, and with a firm grasp around the handle of his sword, he lunged toward the pirate, swinging at his neck with such power and accuracy that he wished to take off his head. But his swing was quickly interrupted by another pirate, jumping in the way of his leader and clashing swords with the young prince, catching the attention of the burnt pirate.

Belthran made quick work of the pirate who stood in his way but now found himself locking eyes with the very man whose head he tried to take.

King Armish spotted the altercation in the distance and instantly began to push forward through the battle to aid his son, but his easy passage through was short-lived when another large group of pirates jumped from the surrounding rooftops and joined the battle, and the men were quickly outnumbered again.

Seeing this, King Armish grabbed one of the city guards who was fighting beside him. "Head back to the castle, find the queen and tell her to send 'The Bird', then tell her to take Layna and hide until I come for them! Go, now."

And off went the guard to send word to the queen.

After sending away the guard, King Armish looked on to see Belthran locking swords with the burnt pirate, who appeared to be very confident and very skilled with a blade. Belthran was in way over his head, and King Armish knew it. And it wasn't long before he saw it.

Belthran was suddenly knocked to the ground by a passing guard, and the burnt pirate now stood tall above him, once again donning that sickening grin.

King Armish was desperately trying to race through the crowd, but he didn't look like he was going to make it in time; he looked on worryingly as the pirate's sword came barrelling down toward a defenceless Belthran.

Belthran kept his eyes open wide as he saw the sword coming down, but it was at that point when he saw another sword cut across his path to stop the pirate; it was Harnik, much to the relief of Belthran and King Armish.

Infuriated with the interruption, the burnt pirate pulled his sword back up before then ramming the handle into the face of Harnik, knocking him to the ground. Not too concerned with Harnik at this point, the pirate then switched his attention back to Belthran, who was trying to make his way back to his feet. The pirate, once again, chose to capitalise on a defenceless prince and swung his sword down toward him once more.

But King Armish did make it in time, clashing swords with the pirate and pushing him back a few steps.

With built-up anger and rage emanating profusely from both the king and the burnt pirate, they both charged toward each other with great velocity.

This particular pirate fought well and with remarkable skill, even up against such a formidable foe as King Armish. Armish had never dealt with or seen a pirate so skilled.

Belthran got back to his feet quickly and ran across to help his father, who had drifted off from him slightly.

Once Belthran got back to the clash, he swung his sword straight at the pirate, who saw the attack coming and calmly ducked out the way, leaving Belthran to clash swords with his father, who also went in for a high strike.

Taking full advantage, the burnt pirate punched the king in the gut and then proceeded to attack Belthran.

As King Armish pulled himself up, he found himself faced with three pirates who now blocked the way between him and re-joining the clash. For the time being, the king focused on the three pirates in front of him, but he wasn't alone.

Harnik regained his footing and found himself now standing alongside the king. "I can't let you and Belthran have all the fun now, Uncle." And within seconds, King Armish and Harnik slaughtered the three pirates who stood in their way. But by that point, Belthran and the burnt pirate had now drifted a lot farther away.

Strikes from the burnt pirate were getting stronger and more powerful, forcing Belthran to backpedal as King Armish and Harnik ran as fast as they could to catch up. Battling through more pirates along the way, they glanced on as things soon turned incredibly bad.

As the burnt pirate battered down on Belthran with a barrage of powerful strikes, Belthran's sword suddenly flew straight from his grasp, and before he knew what had happened, the burnt pirate pushed his sword straight through his gut.

Belthran's eyes opened wide, and his pupils dilated as blood began to exit his mouth. His arms went limp as his body hung from the end of the pirate's sword.

CHAPTER FIFTEEN

FIGHT TODAY TO LIVE TOMORROW

Prince Harnik

"Noooo!" screamed Armish with a cry so loud it could be heard from the palace, and it was certainly heard from the burnt pirate, who pulled his sword from Belthran, who dropped straight to his knees before hitting the dirt like a sack of bricks.

"Belthran!" shouted Harnik as he also stormed forward, followed by Belthran's Unit members, who also witnessed the incident nearby.

The burnt pirate turned to them all with that criminal grin on his face before perversely licking the blood of the young prince off of his sword.

However, the burnt pirate didn't have too much time to gloat and celebrate, as King Armish broke through the crowds and stormed toward him. The pirate got back in position, ready to fight, but nothing could prepare him for the monster he had just released inside the king.

King Armish raged toward him with nothing but hatred and anger, staring at the pirate with daggers in his eyes, not taking his eyes off of him for a second.

The pirate charged forward and swung at the king, but Armish ducked underneath the swing, coming up behind the pirate and slicing the back of his knees, forcing him to drop to the floor. Suddenly, without another moment's thought, King Armish swung back around at the pirate, taking his head clean from his shoulders, and as the pirate's head rolled away, his body dropped to the ground, landing in a pool of his own blood.

After the quick kill, King Armish holstered his sword and then sprinted across to Belthran, along with Harnik and the rest of Belthran's troops. Armish turned Belthran onto his back and just cradled him in his arms. "I'm so sorry, my son, I have failed you!" sobbed the king burying his head into Belthran's chest, but that's when he heard the very faintest of voices in his ear.

"Father…"

"He's still alive!" hollered Saxon.

"Belthran! Can you hear me, my son?" whimpered the king as he witnessed his son's eyes roll into the back of his head as he lost more and more blood.

"He's still alive now, but he won't be for long unless he gets help," stated Harnik.

King Armish then picked up Belthran in his arms and held him closely, "I will take him to the infirmary at once! Though, with my sword to wield, I'm defenceless."

"Have Belthran's Unit escort you back to the infirmary, Uncle; I will hold out here until they return."

Then, with a nod of agreement from King Armish, Saxon led the way with the rest of Belthran's troops to escort the king back to the palace, leaving Harnik to defend the area with what troops he had left, which consisted of his Unit members plus a handful of guards.

Harnik regrouped with his men as they stood facing off with the remaining pirates, several of whom still remained atop the nearby roofs, now without a leader. Outnumbered as they already were, Harnik and his men stood defiant and determined to defend their city.

He turned to face the men that stood behind him, "On days like this, it's courage that separates the men from the boys. We're all here by choice; any one of you could've run and scarpered, and who would've blamed you? But you stayed, not because you had to, but because you wanted to and because you know those who stand against you.

"They burned down your homes, pillaged your stock, and harmed your families. They wish to take the city for their own, lay their heads in *your* beds, drink *your* ale, and fill *your* streets with their filth. Not only that, they took down your prince, your future king, skewered him like a prize pig. Today, we get our vengeance!" Harnik was soon cut off by the sounds of more footsteps as he turned to see another large group of pirates storming the marketplace, taking their number of troops to at least fifty.

Harnik's head sunk for a short moment before he then turned and saw the faces of all the brave soldiers behind him who were counting on him to lead. He gave an admirable nod to his troops, took a deep breath, and pulled out his sword before charging straight at the pirates, howling at the top of his lungs, "For Belthran!"

CHAPTER SIXTEEN

THE KINGDOM'S CRUSADE

Maxin

"How long does it take to say goodbye?" murmured Algo as Maxin and his Unit continued to wait for Sasha and Quenne at the gates of Paran-dun, "It's not like they're never going to return," he added, huffing as he took a seat on a nearby ledge.

"Leave Sasha alone. She'll be here when she's ready," Igor quarrelled.

"And what of Quenne?" asked Tamrin.

"Who's Quenne?"

"Quenne would be Sasha's brother."

"Oh, him. Yes, he is taking his time, isn't he?"

"I give up," groaned Algo. "How much longer are we going to have to wait here?" he added, aggravatingly banging the bottom of his spear into the dirt.

***

Meanwhile, atop the city walls, Maxin stood anxiously, gazing out into the open plains of Ar'Gurd.

"Are you okay, Maxin?" enquired Scarlep, who had gone to join him.

"I did the right thing, didn't I? With Sasha and Quenne?"

"It was a tough choice to make, and if the circumstances were different and you put them through tests first, I'm confident they both would've succeeded. And in time, they will prove to you that the choice you made, was the right choice."

"We *need* more men, Scarlep, I feel like we're running out of time." Maxin looked on out into the distance, seeing the stars slowly begin to glisten in the sky as the great sun lowered in the north and two moons rose in the south.

"My father once told me that this whole kingdom *is* my home; I can't fail it! I won't fai…" Maxin stopped speaking; he squinted toward the muddy terrain, just outside the gates.

"What is that?" asked Maxin, looking on at a small man digging about in the dirt below.

A guard standing beside them heard what Maxin said, also then spotting the man himself, alerting the nearby guards and Kaynar as they ran to the top of the city wall to investigate, along with Algo, Tamrin, and Igor following closely behind.

"What is he doing?" muttered Scarlep, as the man was still unaware that all eyes were now fixated on him.

"Fire a warning shot!" ordered Kaynar.

A shot was quickly fired from a nearby archer; it flew at some speed and stuck into the ground right next to the man's feet. He shot up in a panic and turned his head toward the city in shock, lingering on his tiptoes, looking as though he was about to run away.

"Don't move," ordered Kaynar, "If you do, then you won't live to see the sunset!"

Kaynar then ordered all archers to aim down on that man.

"Slowly move yourself toward us!"

As the man nervously moved closer, Maxin was as surprised as everyone when he realised this man wasn't exactly what he seemed. "That's not a man," stated Maxin, "it's a boy."

The boy suddenly stopped in his tracks as he moved into the light, where he could be seen a lot clearer. He stood with long blonde hair, a very scrawny build, a narrow chin, and a slender neck, dressed in garments of blue and green cloth.

"Keep moving," Maxin ordered, but the boy remained dormant where he was.

"He doesn't look of this land," stated Tamrin, who also had an arrow drawn.

Kaynar ordered another warning shot, this time with the arrow flying right past the boy's head, but he didn't even twitch.

Becoming aggravated and feeling somewhat humiliated, Kaynar snatched the bow from a nearby guard and aimed it toward the figure himself, pulling back tightly on the drawstring.

"This is your final warning, kid. Move, now, or this next arrow is going straight through your skull!"

With a slight glance through the strands of hair that covered his eyes, the young boy then slowly continued to move forward toward the city, as the gates gradually opened below with several guards waiting to apprehend him.

As the boy moved edgingly closer, Tamrin noticed something else, something very distinct about the boy that was sticking out from his hair.

"Wait, look at his ears. They're all pointy."

"Tamrin is right. He has big ears. Ten out of ten for observation, Tam," teased Igor.

"Big to us, yes," stated Kaynar.

"What do you mean?" enquired Maxin with a look of uncertainty upon his face, "I can't believe I'm about to say this, but I think this boy might be of Elven descent."

"He's an Elf?" replied Scarlep in a high-pitched tone.

"He can't be. It's impossible," added Maxin.

"It's not impossible, it's just not known to happen. It's the only explanation for his pointed ears," asserted Kaynar.

"But how do you know that Elves have pointy ears if you've never seen one?" asked Maxin, and Kaynar looked as though he was caught off guard, turning his attention quickly back to the matter at hand and shouting back down toward the young boy who was still moving sluggishly toward the gate, "Move, now. Quickly!"

But Maxin was persistent. He knew something wasn't right; he continued to question. "Have you seen Elves before, Kaynar?"

"I *do not* have to explain myself to you when you still haven't provided me with any proof that you're the king's son. So what I suggest is that, when we have this creature safely inside, you grab your weapons and belongings and get out of my city. Or you, too, will face the consequences."

"Just try it!" replied Igor, sternly, raising his hammer and standing bravely in front of Kaynar.

The guards quickly turned their attention away from the boy and rapidly drew their bows toward Igor.

Sparking a sudden urge of allegiance, Algo, Scarlep, and Tamrin in return, pointed their weapons at Kaynar.

"Stand down, all of you! There doesn't need to be any confrontation or acts of violence here. We will be on our way as soon as my new recruits get here, but until then, I just want to know what you know, Kaynar," said Maxin in his attempt to defuse the situation.

Kaynar's mouth twitched, staring down Maxin with a malevolent glare. "You have no right to ask me anything! You're a boy. Nothing more. Just because you come in here, say you're Prince Maxin, and walk around gathering soldiers, I'm just meant to roll over and believe you? What kind of captain would that make me?"

"A smart one," provoked Igor.

Kaynar growled at Igor as he raised a hand signal to his archers. "Kill the fat one first."

"Nooo!" cried Maxin in a panic, also pulling out his sword.

"Halt!" ordered Kaynar as he gazed upon Maxin's sword, mesmerised by the glistening steel as he looked upon it; he had a keen eye drawn toward a particular part of the sword, the engraved pommel.

"Bray'manoor," he uttered to himself.

"What?" questioned Maxin, still fearfully holding his sword out in front of him.

"The sword of spirits gone. You *are* Prince Maxin!"

Kaynar suddenly ordered his men to lower their weapons, still with eyes fixated upon this sword. But with a very puzzled mind, Maxin didn't have a chance to ask questions, as a voice came from the sanded courtyard below.

"The young boy for you, Captain!"

Maxin holstered his sword, forcing Kaynar to break his fixation like he was under some form of spell from the sword.

His attention drew back to the young boy as the group made their way back down to the courtyard.

As they reached the bottom of the steps, Sasha and Quenne were also seen making their way into the grounds.

"Are we ready to go?" asked Sasha.

"Not just yet," replied Maxin, not taking his eyes of the young Elf.

Sasha and Quenne soon joined the circle that now surrounded the young Elf, along with a large group of townsfolk.

Whispers and murmurs echoed around the circle, as the Elf was bound by thick rope and forced to his knees.

"Get all of these people away from here," ordered Kaynar as the guards pushed the crowds back into the city's streets to continue going about their business.

Maxin circled the young Elf, scouring his clothing and his wares before eventually kneeling down right in front of him. "What do you suppose we should ask him first? I mean, does he understand us?"

Kaynar pulled up behind the young Elf, before yanking him upright and pushing him in the hands of a nearby guard. "You won't get answers from him here," he said to Maxin. Then, he switched his attention back to the guard who held him. "Take him to the dungeon and prepare the interrogation chamber."

"Wait! Interrogation what? You don't mean to torture him?

"I do what I must to get answers."

"This is wrong!" cried Algo, pulling his spear ahead of him once more, with the rest of the Unit members uncertain on whether to bear arms.

"I think it's time you all left!" barked Kaynar.

"Not before you answer my questions," ordered Maxin, glaring over at the guard who had hold of the Elf. "I order you to bring the Elf to me," he said, but the guard remained still.

"You're not in charge of these men, you foolish little prince, nor will you ever be! You do not command these troops, and you do not command this city. You may have your father's blood, and you may carry the sword of your ancestors, but that doesn't give you the right to demand or order anything; do you hear me? All that does is give you the privilege of me not being able to kill you where you stand! Now, leave my city. Otherwise, that might be a privilege you no longer have."

"You can't talk to the prince like that!" argued Sasha.

"A girl? You brought a girl into your Unity? Are you also planning on riding a cow into battle?" joked Kaynar, which then forced the rest of Maxin's Unit to draw their weapons once again.

"You're hiding something, Kaynar; I know you are. I'm not leaving this Elf with you."

Anger and agitation flooded the mind of Kaynar; with the city guards aiming their weapons at Maxin's troops. They were helpless when Kaynar grabbed hold of the prince and threw him up against a nearby post, even to the shock of the surrounding guards.

"Unhand him!" shouted Algo.

"You're going to pay for this!" added Igor, with just a couple of the insults and threats flying Kaynar's way. But his mind was focused; clutching his hand tightly around Maxin's throat, lifting him from the ground, with his feet inches from the floor, being unable to utter anything. All Maxin could do was squirm and listen.

"Don't even think about reaching for your sword, Prince, because I can gut you before you even grasp its handle." But Kaynar's attention was clearly drawn, as was everyone else's, when the sound of a great horn blasted its way toward the city.

Kaynar lost his grip on Maxin, who dropped to the floor holding his throat as Sasha and Scarlep ran to help him up.

But at that point, Maxin's focus was no longer on Kaynar or the Elf who remained apprehended, but it was on the familiar horn that was heading their way.

"It's the horn of Carbaya," Maxin gasped.

"Open the gates!" ordered Kaynar.

Thick metal and chain clanked together as the large gates of the city drew open once more, making way for a lone horseman galloping at pace, before coming to a sudden halt in the courtyard.

"What's the meaning of all this?" barked Kaynar.

"I'm here for Sir Kaynar, Captain of the wolf order of Paran-Dun!" gasped the rider as he still attempted to regain his breath.

"That is me! Now, speak of your wishes!"

Maxin looked on at the rider, baffled, hearing him speak of this secret order on top of Kaynar's earlier comments about his sword that he knew nothing about, and not forgetting the Elf that Kaynar seemed to know a lot more about than he was letting on. As Maxin stared vaguely at the rider, the rider, in turn, clocked Maxin looking on.

"Prince Maxin. What're you doing here?" But now was not the time for Maxin to be explaining himself; it was not every day a rider was sent with such haste to Paran-Dun, blowing the horn of Carbaya.

Maxin had only ever heard the horn once before, back when he was a child, during one of the most vibrant festivals in Carbaya, a festival to celebrate the creation of the city. The horn was played as an instrument on this day behind a fiddle and a flute, but Maxin knew, this time, the horn was not being used for such festivities.

"Please, rider, I wish for you to answer Kaynar."

"Yes, pardon me, my Prince; I'm here on behalf of the king. He requires urgent aid against a pirate attack."

"It's about time. I knew my father had a backup plan for when the pirates' next attack."

"I think you've mistaken me, Master Maxin, for I wish I've not spoken so clearly. The attack from the pirates is not forthcoming, it is present!"

Maxin's face dropped.

Kaynar instantly began barking orders left right and centre to any guards within the area. "I will be leaving in five minutes. Make sure that these gates are locked down tight, and nobody is to leave or enter until I return. Do you hear me?"

"Excuse me, Sir Kaynar," spoke the rider. "The message was for you to bring your men, not for them to stay here."

Kaynar sniggered to himself. "These are not *my* men!"

Suddenly, Kaynar pulled out a small whistle that he had hung around his neck, and within seconds of him blowing into it, the clanking and banging of another gate could be heard, this time coming from a nearby tunnel.

A dark and damp passage that could easily be mistaken for a sewage tunnel was soon filled with the echoed sound of chainmail and horseshoes.

Nine horsemen appeared from within the tunnel, dressed in all black velvet garments layered over a coat of thick chainmail, every one of them donning a closed-faced, rounded bascinet; armed with long spears, broadswords, and great steel shields that were each masked with a tribal depiction of a white wolf.

Every one of the nine horsemen halted in a pyramid style formation behind Kaynar, who then whistled for his own horse.

"We move out!" he shouted to his men, but as he turned to mount his horse, he was met with a spearhead pointing directly at his throat.

"Algo!" shouted Maxin.

"What about the Elf?" he questioned.

"The Elf stays in Paran-dun until my men and I return. Now, get that spear away from my face before I use it to cut you a new hole to piss out of," Kaynar warned, but the threats didn't concern Algo, as he pushed the spear farther toward the throat, slightly piercing the skin, allowing for a drizzle of blood to trickle down the spearhead.

"The Elf comes with us!"

"Algo, this is not the time," argued Maxin, but Algo continued to plead with him.

"If the Elf stays here, then they will torture him whilst we're gone. Don't you want answers from your father or not? Take the Elf with us and present him at your father's feet."

Kaynar looked back at Algo with murderous eyes, but he also knew they didn't have time for this, and he couldn't start killing the prince's troops in front of the king's messenger.

"Just do it!" he grunted.

"Put the Elf with Igor and he can tie him to a hitching post just outside the city, but we must leave. *Now!*"

And as quickly as that, Algo removed his spear from Kaynar's throat and with the help of Scarlep, he secured the Elf to the back of Igor's horse, which Igor wasn't best pleased about.

Once secured, Maxin and his Unit then rode out in great haste toward Carbaya, trailing just behind Kaynar and the Wolf Order.

CHAPTER SEVENTEEN

A HERO'S RETURN

Grendel

"Somebody, help my son!" cried King Amish, barrelling through the doors of the infirmary, Belthran in arms.

The med bay was frantic, doctors were running around like chickens in a coop, just trying to keep on top of the countless bodies piling up. Soldiers were sprawled on top of made-up wooden beds on the floor, every square inch covered. Bodies were lying either broken, limbless, or dead. Screams were infesting the ears of every surrounding body, but none more so than the king himself.

"Over here, my King, you can have my bed."

King Armish followed the voice to his right and saw young Grendel standing at his bedside, crutches under each arm. The king moved quickly, placing Belthran gently onto the bed as Belthran's Unit scurried through the ward to grab anybody who could help them.

"How bad is it out there?" Grendel asked the king.

"It's death, and it's all my fault! They had this all planned, and who, let alone a king, gets outsmarted by pirates? I have failed this city, and if Belthran dies, then I have failed him, too!"

"This is not your fault; this is nobody's fault. If the city was fully guarded, the pirates would've still attacked; Belthran may have still been struck down. This is not your doing, my King, this is the will of the spirits."

Suddenly, a barrage of footsteps and voices were heard from behind as Belthran's Unit returned with a young, panicked doctor, covered in blood-soaked rags and pores dripping with sweat.

King Armish grabbed the young man by the medicinal bandolier that was slung over his shoulders. "Help my son; save your prince!"

"I will do my best to save him, my Liege, but I need space to do so," stated the doctor as he gestured for the men to move back.

As King Armish and the others anxiously took a few steps back, Grendel hobbled past in great stead. "My prayers are with Belthran, my King!" he said as he began to make his way to the med bay doors.

"Where're you going? It isn't safe out there!"

"No, it's not, but if the pirates break through our forces, then it won't be much safer in here, either; the least I can do is meet them halfway! I can't walk too well, but it doesn't mean I can't fight. Plus, I have my own vengeance to claim with the pirates, my King!"

"You have a courageous heart, young one; Maxin is lucky to have you."

"And I him."

"Take Belthran's Unit with you, for they are not needed at his bedside." King Armish then turned to Belthran's Unit and spoke aloud to them all, "Take your leave, look after this young one, fight for your city and fight for your prince."

Without anything more to say or hear, Grendel, accompanied by Belthran's Unit, hastily made their way back into the city streets to rejoin the fight, leaving the king alone with the prince.

As the battle within the city grew, and more pirates continued to scale the walls in great numbers, victory for the pirates looked almost imminent. Harnik was struggling to keep his men and remaining city guards alive. For every pirate he took down, two more would appear.

Rain began to pour down heavily on the square, mixing with pools of mud and blood across the courtyard cobbles. Swords and spears swinging left and right as arrows flew down from above like the raindrops that showered them.

Harnik's grip started to become looser on his sword as the handle began to wear his gloves thin, causing a slight blistering on his hands. As he struck down a few more oncoming pirates, he wiped the blood and grime from his eyes to see no more pirates running toward him and no more arrows flying past him; the pirates were all fleeing back toward the centre of the city.

Cheers and roars were heard from the remaining city guards as panic grew in the mind of Harnik.

Grendel and Belthran's troops soon caught up to sounds of victory with huge smiles upon their faces.

"They're retreating, my Lord," praised Draydor, one of Harnik's men.

"They're not retreating, why would they? They're winning this fight and they have us outnumbered. They're either finding another way through to the palace or they're wanting us to follow them into a trap."

"Can't we just go back and guard the palace?" suggested Grendel as he hobbled to the front of the group.

"We must keep the fight as far away from the palace as possible, it's too risky. Which means we must follow them deeper into the city centre, it's most certainly a trap, but we must defend it at all costs!"

"Then, we defend!" replied Grendel.

After agreeing to what appeared to be a suicide march, Harnik, Grendel, the remaining Unit members and city guards bore arms and trekked farther into the city in pursuit of the fleeing pirates.

Chasing through a shortcut along Huxon Bank Bridge, the troops finally caught up with a handful of pirates, who were stood waiting for them in the city centre gardens, just in front of a large-scale fountain adorned with a bronzed sculpture of the great King Belmun II, architect of the great city itself.

Harnik and the troops came to a sudden halt ahead of the few pirates that stood before them.

"Are they here to slow us down?" whispered Amrex, another one of Harnik's men.

"No, they're here to distract us," said Harnik as he quickly turned back toward the bridge to see the entryway was now blocked by the enemy. Bearing a blockade of spears and shields, he faced the front once more, and his face dropped when he saw every rooftop, alleyway, and exit now also covered by pirates.

"Surrender all of your weapons!" commanded one of the pirates ahead of them as he stepped away from the fountain, taking a few strides in great confidence. "One by one, move toward me and lay down your arms."

A few of the city guards edged forward but were stopped when Harnik held out his sword to the side to prevent them from passing, "Move back into position! There will be no surrender from us, not while we're still breathing and are still men of this kingdom! Do you think they're just going to let us go? If we are to die, then we will die heroically and honourably, with our weapons in hand!"

The pirate laughed aloud, sniggering to the other pirates on either side of him before turning his attention back to Harnik, "If you move one step, then you're all dead. Look around you, kid. You wouldn't make it halfway up this footpath without us turning you into a pincushion. Now, you did speak some truth to your men. We are still going to kill you, but being unarmed, we would've given you the honour of a quick death. So the choice is all on you," spoke the pirate as his men closed in behind the group with their spears raised out in front of them. The pirate continued to stare down Harnik and his men like lambs to the slaughter, just waiting to tuck into his prey as he continued to taunt.

"Now, here we are. Let's be honest, we're the last faces any of you expected to see today, but we're certainly going to be the last you see in your lifetime. You mustn't blame yourselves for what is happening. The age of pirates had been looming for years. You weren't to know that it would come to pass in your lifetime, you didn't have the fortune of choosing the age in which you were born, so it's only right that you don't get to choose the time in which you're taken out of it. The moment my mouth draws silence, and my sword is pulled from my holster to taste the tainted air of this land for the first time, then and only then, will you meet your end."

The pirate's mouth closed as he drew silence through the gardens; only the sounds of rain battering against steel armour and the deep exhales of anxious men surrounded them. He pulled his body straight as he stared intently at the group of helpless men ahead of him. With a victorious grin upon his face, the pirate grasped the handle of his rusted blade before pulling it out from his holster about a quarter-inch to tease the men, but the teasing didn't last too long, as he yanked the sword out fully with great force, raising it high up in the air above him.

The deep exhale of men grew short, but no arrows flew.

Harnik and his men were unharmed and baffled; they looked ahead as spears pierced through the back of two pirates on either side of their leader. With the pirate now stunned, Harnik seized an opportunity and sprinted forcefully toward him. Without a moment to spare and a few swings of his sword so quick and precise, Harnik took the arms of the pirate before then taking the legs, leaving him in a pool of his own blood; just a torso and a head were all that remained. But before the pirate bled out completely, Harnik stood over him, sword in hand.

"When my sword breaks through your skull for the first time, then and only then, will your time on this land end!" he uttered as he then drove his royal blade through the pirate's skull, almost cracking it in two.

Completely enthralled within himself, Harnik was oblivious to the battle that had now commenced around him, that was until he heard the sound of a very familiar voice.

"Just the way your father does it."

He turned his attention upward to see Prince Clearus sitting proudly upon his horse. "Father!"

"It's great to see you, my boy, and just in time, clearly! You've done me proud, but for now, that can wait, there's more fighting to be done."

And as those words left the lips of Clearus, Harnik pulled out his sword that was still embedded into the pirate's skull and followed his father into battle.

Batting away oncoming arrows with his crutches and trying his best to stay afoot amongst the carnage, Grendel couldn't believe his luck, as he had cheated death once again. Seeing Sir Payner and Prince Clearus barrage their way through the pirates, accompanied by a young Dwarf and the rest of the city guards, was nothing short of astonishing in his eyes, but now was not the time to gaze upon the pools of admiration, the pirates still greatly outnumbered the men.

Flesh cut deep and blood spilled thick through the gardens of the city, whilst outnumbered, the men of Carbaya were showing the pirates why they have been the superior race for thousands of years. Stunned and taken back by the ambush, the pirates were dropping like flies from the onslaught.

Victory drew near for a time but was soon shattered into uncertainty as the second wave of pirates emerged from the alleyways and the rooftops, shortly followed by the third and fourth wave of bloodthirsty cutthroats.

Fights spilled into surrounding streets and markets as the pirates aimed to thin the herds and segregate groups.

Remembering the good times he had with his father, Grendel took great pride in cutting down any pirate who stepped in his way. Using only one good leg, he continued to fend them off with impeccable skill, that was until he found himself edged away from battle and backed into a tight corner by three pirates.

"Would you get a load of this creature?" spoke one pirate.

"Don't come any closer, you will regret it!"

"The thing speaks," joked another pirate. "He has courage, it almost seems a shame to have to gut it out of him, but then again, we could be doing him a great favour; he's an abomination, after all, he should've been gutted at birth!"

The three pirates closed in on Grendel as his hands began to shake, crutch in one hand and small dagger in the other. His attempts at escape were cut short when one of the pirates chopped the crutch from under his arm, leaving him unbalanced.

"Swords away! There's only one way this ends for him," stated the first pirate as they each holstered their swords. Grendel's dagger was swiped from his grasps as the pirates proceeded to beat down on him, one heavy punch after another. Sounds of each pirate's knuckles crunched against his face as blood and spit coursed from his mouth.

Every time Grendel fell, he would pull himself straight back up and endure the beating some more.

As his eye began to swell into a newly deformed part of his face, the punching unexpectedly stopped, a ringing in his ears was silenced by the thunderous horn of a long-awaited cavalry.

Grendel heard the sounds of bodies dropping around him. He squinted through his swollen eye toward a figure that stood atop a nearby roof, longbow in hand. As the moon drew over the city, its light glistened upon the figure, and despite his beatdown. It was at this moment Grendel knew all was going to be okay, as he saw a young man firing shots from above as well as another figure who stood above him, holding out a hand.

"Maxin?"

"You can't seem to stay out of trouble can you, my friend?" joked Maxin as he helped Grendel back to his feet, reuniting him with his lost crutch. "What're you even doing out here, Grendel? You're not fit to fight."

"I am here as your father's replacement."

"My father? Where is he? Is he okay? And what of my mother and sister? And where is Belthran? I thought he would be the first one I saw in battle."

"Prince Maxin, I don't know how to tell you this, but there's been an incident."

"Death?"

"No, my Prince, not yet. The doctors are doing everything they can to help."

Maxin felt his stomach sink to its lowest pit as the question he didn't want to know the answer to, began to tremble from his lips. "Who?"

"It's Belthran, my Prince, he was gutted by a pirate."

"I-I need to get to him!" stuttered Maxin as tears ran down his face.

"You shouldn't do that."

"W-Why not? He is my brother; I must!"

"You being there will not help him, you probably won't even find space around his bedside. Your father is there with him, and these people, they all need you out here. You're the king's son, Maxin; it will serve these men well to know you are out here fighting alongside them, and how else can you avenge what they have done to Prince Belthran?"

Maxin with a little sniffle, wiped the tears away from his eyes and drew his sword passionately. "You're right, Grendel! He isn't dead yet, and if I know Belthran, he'll be on his feet and ready to fight again by sunrise. Plus, these pirates need to learn first-hand what happens when you piss off the wrong prince! Head back to my father and inform him of our returning troops, I'm sure he will be glad to hear it."

And off went Grendel, hobbling away from the battle in a hurry to get word back to King Armish.

CHAPTER EIGHTEEN

THE GLORY OF THE NIGHT

Maxin

As Maxin teetered on the edge of battle, he bore witness to a few first experiences. It was the first time he had encountered a full-scale war unfolding before his very eyes, it was the first time he had seen the pirates alive, in the flesh and in full force, and it was also the first time he witnessed his Unit members in combat together against a real threat. It was the first chance Maxin really had to see what his Unit was made of, and he couldn't have been happier.

His eyes drew first to his newest recruits, Sasha and Quenne, watching them work together as a formidable brother and sister duo, using remarkable sword skills to take down the pirates with ease. His attention then fell on Tamrin, who remained atop the nearby buildings, picking off pirates with such precise accuracy that any archer would find difficult to match. Just to his left, he saw Algo using his spear in such a fearful way, that for a moment, Maxin wondered how he ever overcame him back in the cave. Ahead of Algo, he spotted Scarlep with two small daggers to hand taking down several pirates at a time as if they were beginners. But Maxin formed the biggest grin on his face when his eyes locked onto Igor, who had only one strategy when it came to fighting, 'Hit hard and don't stop,' and he did that better than any other boy Maxin knew.

At that point, Maxin truly believed he was on his way to having the strongest Unit of them all.

Prince Maxin was never the strongest fighter and was normally much more equipped to holding a book than a blade. And as the battle longed on through the night, that weakness in him stuck out from the crowd like a fish in distress, drawing a handful of pirates to single him out in an attempt to drive him away from the crowds.

As one pirate engaged in a battle with the young prince, he used minimal skill and a slight force just to keep Maxin at bay and to force him to backpedal. Another pirate then joined the fray to block the sight of Maxin from nearby troops and to force him on the back foot a bit quicker.

Once edged toward a nearby alleyway, a third pirate crept up behind Maxin, placing his hand over his mouth and dragging him inward, followed closely by the other two pirates.

They smashed the sword from Maxin's grasp as he was then thrown down to the wet, muddy terrain.

He scurried back to one knee before being humiliatingly kicked back down to the dirt.

"I've never met anyone whose clothes are fancier than their sword skills. Who taught you to fight, kid? The maid?" joked one of the pirates. "See, this is where it gets interesting, you don't fight like a soldier, and you barely dress like one, which leads me to believe that you're much more than that. Who are you?" he added.

Maxin looked up at his attackers and their sadistic grins, seeming almost proud of themselves for bullying a young boy.

He believed in his heart that he was a very fortuitous boy and that everything happened by chance; on his short trip through the caves and into Paran-Dun, he stumbled across his courage, and he wasn't about to let go of it now.

"If you think my skills are lacking, then why take away my sword and surround me in numbers?"

The pirates laughed mockingly amongst themselves, "Tell me who you are, and I will return your sword to you," bargained the pirate.

A bargain was made, but could they be trusted? If Maxin was to tell them he was the prince, would he be worse off for it? The only chance he had at this point was a fighting one and he needed to reclaim his sword. The battle was too loud and distant for anyone to hear his pleas.

"Do we have a deal?" pressed the pirate.

"My name is Lowan," replied the prince, acting off his instinct. "I come from the next town over, born into a wealthy family. My brother and my father, they are the swordsmen, but I'm still obliged to do my bit to help the city."

The pirate looked back at Maxin with broad emotion, then proceeding to kick his sword back to him, "Pick it up; let's end this!"

Maxin lunged for his sword, but found trouble picking it up when one of the pirates forced his filthy boot down onto the blade; and as Maxin yanked at the sword in anxious desperation, he was soon blindsided when a fist came hammering down from above, knocking him face-first into the mud, where he bordered on unconsciousness.

With a pounding head and eyes filled with mud, Maxin heard a scuffle from above him. Why hadn't they killed him yet? What were they planning? His eyes fluttered, opening to a slight squint, allowing him to see the lifeless eyes of a pirate lying beside him. He rolled over onto his back and opened his eyes more, and was shocked when he saw the young Elf prisoner shadowing over him.

"Are you okay?" asked the young Elf in the softest voice.

"You killed them?" questioned Maxin.

"You saved my life earlier; I had a debt to repay."

Maxin shuffled back to his feet, cautiously raising his sword in front of him. "You're meant to be tied up."

"Your stocky companion, as strong as he is, his knots are not."

"What is your name? That's if Elves have them?"

"We do, Krawsin is mine."

"What're you doing here?"

"Your city is infested with war and you think now is time for questions?"

Maxin knew the Elf was right; he had to get back and help in the fight, but he couldn't leave the Elf alone, especially untethered. Surprisingly to Maxin, Krawsin willingly raised out his hands toward him so he could bind them together once more. Stunned by Krawsin's admirable gesture, Maxin quickly roped his hands together and led him to a hitching post alongside a nearby butcher shop located a few metres away from the battle. And just as Maxin began to tie a knot around the post, a huge roar came from beyond the adjacent cottages.

"They're fleeing!"

Maxin looked back at Krawsin and quickly unravelled the knot from the post.

"We must go, quickly. I think the battle is won!" claimed Maxin with a delightful grin upon his face.

Whilst keeping Krawsin's hands bound, Maxin quickly led the way back to the battlefield.

Cheers soon echoed far throughout the city as the scurrying footsteps of the defeated pirates fled south toward the harbour.

"Victory!" cried the men of the city.

As several city guards chased down the fleeing pirates, the rest of the men rejoiced, some singing songs of great victory whilst others helped up their wounded and exhausted brethren. But victory celebrations were cut short as the rigorous cry, of "Elf," drew from the mouth of Kaynar as he spotted Maxin and Krawsin entering the body-filled gardens.

Despite the darkness of war and the blood-stained walls, the garden still flourished with colour, from the yellow and pink tulips to the fluorescent bluebells that circled the fountain. But there was one colour that shone brightest, and that was the angered red in Kaynar's eyes as he glared down at the two boys.

All eyes in the gardens were on Krawsin as the men gasped at what they saw.

"Is that really an Elf?" questioned Harnik.

"Yes," snapped Kaynar, quick to make his voice heard. "He is believed to be very dangerous; we brought him here before the king, but he is meant to have been tied up outside until the battle was won."

"I'm sorry, and, who are you?" Harnik continued to question.

"This is Sir Kaynar Cornall," interrupted Sir Payner. "He is the captain of a great order, one close to the king. Guards, do as Sir Kaynar commands and apprehend that Elf! Prince Maxin, Sir, please step aside," ordered Payner as two guards edged toward the young Elf.

"Should I make a run for it?" whispered Krawsin.

"No," commanded Maxin, "You will stay where you are. Let them see that you're no threat to them; let Sir Kaynar think he has the upper hand. I won't let him harm you. You will stand before my father, and I will defend you. You will tell us why you inhabit our lands, but you must do it willingly if you're to stand a chance; these men here have witnessed far too much action for one day."

And with that said, Krawsin, still with his hands bound, moved forward ahead of Maxin and toward the couple of guards that waited apprehensively.

"He's not running. Why isn't he running?" Scarlep muttered to the group.

Krawsin was soon seized by the guards but was quickly halted when Kaynar stormed through the gardens, striking the young Elf in the gut.

"Kaynar, no!" shouted Maxin.

"You think you still hold all the cards, don't you, Elf? You might be able to trick the young prince here, but you won't trick me," stated Kaynar as he struck Krawsin once more, this time across the face. As the surrounding fighters looked on in astonishment, Kaynar raised his hand once again, clenching his fist tightly, and as his hand swung down, the gathering troops' jaws dropped, but it wasn't due to a third strike, it was seeing young Prince Maxin barrelling ahead of Krawsin and shoving Kaynar backward with unknown force.

"Leave him alone!"

The anger and hatred grew in Kaynar like a great demon had gained control of his soul. His nostrils flared and his eyebrows furrowed. He drew his sword and stampeded toward Prince Maxin, raising his arm in the air, but before anyone else could react, Kaynar was stopped in his tracks when a firm hand clutched his forearm.

"If you touch a single hair on Maxin's head, then I will not hesitate to slit your throat!" warned Sir Payner.

"Release me!" ordered Kaynar before Payner loosened his grasp.

Kaynar grew up with Payner, and he knew that Payner was bigger and stronger, and his influence on the king was much greater. He holstered his sword and stormed off in a huff, taking his men with him.

"Guards, take this Elf to the cells," ordered Payner.

As the guards escorted Krawsin to the holding cells, attention was soon taken away from one race and drawn toward another, when Igor spotted an unfamiliar figure standing beside him, of what appeared to be a much hairier version of himself.

"I don't wish to confuse anyone else more than they already are, but there appears to be what I can only imagine is a Dwarf standing beside me, either that or this kid's hormones are through the roof!"

"Yes, Master Igor, he is a Dwarf. His name is Sprock, a very talented fighter; he saved my life in the Dwarven Kingdom of Camaroth, and I brought him here for him to stand ahead of Prince Maxin as a potential member of his Unit, and with a support of confidence from myself and Prince Clearus…If there is still space, of course," spoke Payner, turning his focus back toward Maxin, but the prince had his mind set on other things.

"Thank you for bringing him forward, Sir Payner; your word means a great deal. My Unit will keep him company until I have a chance to speak with him at a more convenient time, but I must head to the infirmary to check on Belthran at once!"

"Wait, what is Belthran doing in the infirmary?" questioned Payner.

CHAPTER NINETEEN

UNDERLYING POWER OF MAN

Maxin

As bodies were counted and cleared from the city gardens throughout the night, a glumness filled the infirmary ward, as the state of Belthran grew no stronger.

It wasn't long before Maxin, Harnik, Payner, and Clearus hurried through the doors of the infirmary, much to the delight of the king.

"Father!"

"Maxin! I heard of your return, I'm just so glad you're safe!" said the king, wrapping his body around his son with great affection, looking beyond Maxin's shoulder with a huge grin, seeing his best friend and his brother also standing behind him.

"Payner, Clearus! Your return is most fortunate, I'm glad to see your faces."

"We have much to discuss, my friend, but for now, it can wait. How is Belthran doing?" Payner empathised.

"He is still in critical condition. This wasn't meant to happen," cried the king, looking back at Belthran's unmoving body.

"Belthran is strong, Brother, he will pull through. If death wanted him, then he wouldn't be lying on that bed still breathing," consoled Clearus.

A large thud broke the consolation as a jug of water smashed on the floor from Belthran's bedside, the room quickly filling with panic as the young prince began to shake uncontrollably.

A couple of nearby doctors rushed over to the bedside as King Armish and Sir Payner fought to hold him down.

"Doctor! What is happening?" wept the king.

"I'm not sure, it seems like his body is rejecting our treatments."

Everyone began to fluster helplessly around Belthran's bedside, worried and anxious, unable to help him.

After seconds of uncontrollable shaking, it suddenly stopped, and within an instant, Belthran's body fell flat, and tears fell from the eyes of all those who had gathered.

"Belthran, no," whimpered Prince Maxin.

Payner removed his hands from the body of the young prince as he consoled the king with a gentle arm across his back.

"Do something!" demanded King Armish toward the doctors.

"There is nothing more we can do, my King. He has stopped fighting; his heart rate is decreasing at an alarming rate, and we have no other way of giving him the boost of power that he needs. He will be dead within the next few minutes; I am sorry."

"Nooooo!" cried the king with such anger in his heart that it could've most likely have been heard across the foggy sea.

As Maxin, Harnik, Clearus, and Belthran's troops shed floods of tears, Payner, whilst holding the king tightly, had a great thought as his eyes began to glow with a theoretical intent, spinning his head round to Prince Clearus, who had his head buried into the shoulder of Harnik.

"Clearus, you can save him!"

Heads lifted and ears listened closely.

"What?" questioned King Armish.

"The doctor said that they can't give Belthran the power he needs to increase his heart rate, but I believe Clearus can!"

"How?"

"Payner, no , I can't," interrupted Clearus.

"Clearus, what is he talking about?" probed the king some more with a look of intrigue and hope.

"We don't have time to explain, but Clearus can do things, things he couldn't do before, he has power, a light, an energy inside him, he can help Belthran."

Eyes fixated on Clearus, Harnik took a slight step back from his father.

"You have to try, Clearus!" pleaded Payner.

The room was confused, all of them feeling like they were stuck in some kind of fairytale nightmare. Belthran was lying on the brink of death, and Payner claimed that Prince Clearus has powers. King Armish looked at his brother with an open mouth and broad eyes, unable to mutter any words.

Clearus closed his eyes and drew a large exhale before moving across to Belthran's bedside. Rolling up the sleeves of his undergarments, he placed his hand steadily and firmly over the chest of Belthran, closing his eyes once more, but nothing happened.

"What is happening here?" asked King Armish.

"Please, my friend, trust me, Clearus can do this," answered Payner. "Focus your mind, just like you did in

Camaroth; Belthran needs you," added Payner toward Clearus, who stayed focused with his hand remaining on Belthran's chest.

As Clearus closed out the sounds of everyone around him, he allowed himself to focus on the slow beat of Belthran's heart, feeling the steady flow of his blood begin to settle beneath his skin. He cleared his mind and focused on the energy he had flowing through his own body, feeling his skin cells draw in electricity like a natural current and each bone inside him feeling like the yearning flames of a well-logged firepit.

He heard the mystique voices in his head, urging him to believe, to focus, and to ignite his power.

The group stood in overwhelming awe as an ominous blue light grew from the palms of Clearus, creating a power surged barrier around the body of Belthran.

Seconds passed, and as Clearus continued to focus, the beat of Belthran's heart began to beat harder and faster. Clearus could now feel the electricity coursing through his nephew's veins. Clearus opened his eyes wide as he slowly began to retract the energy back into his body. And much to the shock of everyone around, as soon as Clearus removed his hand from Belthran's chest, the young prince sat straight up in a jolt, before instantly dropping straight back down, along with Clearus, who fell to the floor beside him.

"Father!" yelled Harnik as he ran to help Clearus back to his feet with the aid of Sir Payner.

"Astonishing!" said one of the doctors as he checked Belthran's pulse.

"What is it, doctor?" asked an anxious king.

"His heart rate is steady, above average in fact. I think he's going to be okay."

After hearing this news, the king hurried across to Clearus and wrapped his arms around his brother, tighter than he ever had before.

"Thank you, Brother! I am forever in your debt. Although, I think you and Payner have a lot of talking to do after this."

And with a nod of acceptance and no energy for Clearus to muster a word, Sir Payner spoke. "That we do, my King. I shall go and fetch the queen and escort her here. Upon my return, me, you, and Clearus have a lot to discuss."

After a kind hand on the king's broad shoulder, Payner left to locate the queen, accompanied by Belthran's Unit, who allowed space for their captain to rest.

With a feeling of nervous tension and a numb mind, Maxin gathered his bearings, just trying to wrap his mind with what he just witnessed.

"For I must leave, too, Father. I hate to leave Belthran at this time, and I know the hour is late, but I have another Unit member I must meet. I will be back shortly, as I also have urgent matters I must discuss with you. Uncle Clearus, thank you for what you have done." Maxin nodded as he scarpered in a hurry toward the palace gates, with Grendel following closely behind.

Entering the courtyard of the palace, just outside the infirmary doors, Maxin and Grendel heard the sounds of playful jibes coming from beyond the gate which linked to the city. The moon shone bright on this particular section, hitting the south of the city like a great spotlight as it began to slowly decline behind the palace towers.

They were voices of those familiar to him, of Tamrin and Scarlep, and a young lady's chuckle that could only belong to Sasha.

Maxin and Grendel moved beyond the gate to see his troops gathered in a circle surrounding Sprock.

Sprock stood slightly smaller than the rest of the Unit, but he was wider than the rest, except for Igor.

"What is going on here?" enquired Maxin.

"Prince Maxin, sir, how is Prince Belthran?" asked Scarlep.

"He will live to see another day."

Eyes drew beyond the shoulder of Maxin, engrossed onto the disfigured face of Grendel, who stood cowering behind him.

Embarrassed by the group's repelled expressions, Maxin stood to the side to allow Grendel to step forward, which he did with some hesitance.

Grendel's head hunched down as he glared back at them all with his one good eye, which was still pretty bruised.

He scaled the group from left to right until he came across Tamrin who stood second from the right.

"You! You're the one who saved my life from the rooftop!"

The group remained silent.

Tamrin offered an apprehensive smile, lost for words.

"Guys, and Sasha, this is Grendel. He is a member of this Unit, and he was the first one of us to ever take down a pirate. Yes, he is different, but that's what makes him special and what makes him a crucial part of this team; as much as Algo is different, as much as Sasha is the first girl in our history to ever join Unity, as much as Igor is fat. Grendel is one of us; he is a brother to you all and should be treated as such," stated Maxin.

"Welcome, Grendel," said Sasha taking the first step forward to greet him.

And, one by one, they all shook his hand.

Maxin looked up to see Sprock still standing where he was.

"Sprock, is it?"

"Yes."

"What was happening a second ago? Why were they all circling you?"

"I was showing them a game I grew up playing in Camaroth, all about being quick on your feet; it's called 'Wheel'."

"And?"

"And what?"

"Were they quick on their feet?"

"Surprisingly so, Master Prince."

Maxin took a quick glance back at his troops with a cheeky smile bestowed upon his face.

"Good," he said, turning his attention quickly back to Sprock. "Sir Payner speaks highly of you, and my Uncle Clearus, too."

"They are good men. I'm glad they were the first men I ever had the pleasure of meeting, and I'm sure they would say the Dwarves were the best race they had the pleasure of coming across, as well."

"What do you mean?"

"Well, with the Wizards giving your uncle some kind of magic power, the Dwarves must've been a welcoming sight for them."

"Wait. What? The Wizards did this to my uncle?" asked Maxin, causing a confused look upon the faces of his unit members.

"Apparently so, and have you seen Payner's missing fingers? The Elves took them right off."

"Elves?"

"Yeah, he claimed their king killed one of his men, and one of the guards chopped off his fingers; it's not really a story to tell the kids before bed."

Maxin began to breathe heavily and rapidly.

"Prince Maxin, what's wrong?" asked Scarlep.

"I have to go. All of you go and get some rest, and Sprock, welcome to the team," stated Maxin as he sprinted as quickly as he could back to the palace.

Barrelling through the doors of the palace into the long, winding hallway, Maxin searched room by room, corridor by corridor in hunt of Payner, going through studies, washrooms, mess rooms and pantries, until he eventually saw Payner leaving the war room that was located at the end of the third corridor on the ground floor.

"Sir Payner!"

"Ah, if it isn't the young prince of the hour, did you catch up with Sprock?" Payner asked as he closed the doors to the war room firmly behind him.

"Yes, I did. And it is my meeting with Sprock that has led me to you now; he told me about the Elves," said Maxin as he grabbed the hand of Payner to look upon his amputated fingers.

"It's true," muttered Maxin as Payner swiped his hand away from Maxin, then squeezed it into a fitted leather glove with threaded stitching across where his fingers used to be.

"Maxin, I just spent the last few minutes explaining everything to your father and Sir Kaynar; I'm not prepared to repeat myself again tonight. We have a big day ahead of us tomorrow, and I am in need of some much-needed rest. Can this not wait until morning?"

"Wait. You told Sir Kaynar?"

"Yes. Why?" asked Payner with a puzzled face.

Maxin looked dazed, like he had just been given the death penalty.

"Maxin, what is wrong?" questioned Payner.

"Krawsin!" replied Maxin as he stormed back down the hallway with great speed, followed by Sir Payner chasing urgently behind him.

"Maxin, wait!"

Making his way east of the palace at an extraordinary pace, Maxin barrelled into the holding cells only to find four stationary guards and eight vacant cells.

"Maxin, what are you doing?" panted Payner as he caught up to the young prince.

"Where is he? Where is the Elf?"

"When we left the war room, your father took Kaynar to trial the Elf before sunrise."

"With no witnesses?"

"What's going on, Maxin? You're acting kind of crazy."

"Kaynar wants to kill the Elf, and he will twist my father into doing so; the Elf isn't a threat to anybody!"

"How do you know this?"

"I was in Paran-Dun when the Elf was captured."

"You left the city? What were you thinking?"

"The city needed help, and I needed men. I don't have time to explain this, Sir Payner. Please, you have to take me to them!"

Payner bore the face of an uncertain man as he looked down at Maxin.

"Please, Sir Payner, you saw what Kaynar was like in the gardens; he won't stop until this Elf is dead!"

Feeling like he would later come to regret this decision, Payner reluctantly agreed to help Maxin as he led him to where Krawsin was to stand trial.

***

King Armish

In a small, desolate corner of the city, situated just behind the palace, a trial was about to take place, one that had never before taken place on the city grounds.

Kaynar threw Krawsin to his knees, wrists still bound, this time by a strong leather strapping. The muzzle was removed from his mouth as the king approached, towering over him with eyes of wonder and intrigue.

"You kneel before us on this night, accused of trespassing and endangerment on our lands and the city of

Paran-Dun; what do you have to say for yourself?" interrogated King Armish.

But much to the king's annoyance, and a slightly flickered grin on the face of Kaynar, Krawsin didn't speak a word. He continued to suffer in silence, staring a hole into the floor he was placed upon.

"I told you, my King, he doesn't say a word. He is of no use to us. He is a tyrant and a felon, and I think we should just have off with his head!" suggested Kaynar as he continued to rant, not giving King Armish a chance to ask any more questions, "If what Payner said is true, then there are other Elves out there who will speak to you or can provide us with information. This Elf has no purpose left to offer; he won't even speak to save his own life."

King Armish was in deep thought, battering his gaze between Kaynar and Krawsin as he struggled to reach a culminating decision. He stopped for a moment, keeping his final gaze upon Kaynar, followed by a slight gestured nod. Kaynar's grin multiplied, stretching from one side of his face to the other, thrusting his foot into Krawsin's back, forcing him onto his hands.

Kaynar drew his longsword, a sight Krawsin was becoming too familiar with seeing. Kaynar rested the cold steel of his blade across Krawsin's pale neck as he satisfyingly licked his dry lips, eager to slice to head off the young Elf. Kaynar took one more look up at King Armish as he readied his sword, with both hands gripped tightly around the handle.

"Do you have anything left to say before this trial meets its end?" asked King Armish toward Krawsin as one last attempt to make him speak, but Krawsin drew out his final moments in silence. Feeling the blade slowly lifting from his neck, Krawsin could only hear the sounds of his own deep breath coursing through his ears.

"Noo!" bellowed the voice of a young prince, dashing in-between the concrete columns that surround them.

"Maxin! What are you doing here?" questioned the king.

Kaynar's eyes grew wide, and with a slight lump in his throat, he swung his sword down with great aim, but his blade never found his mark. His sword was halted, once again by the hand of Payner being gripped around his arm.

"I wouldn't do that just yet," stated Payner.

"What is the meaning of all this? Maxin, Payner; explain yourselves!" exclaimed King Armish.

"You can't kill Krawsin, Father!"

"Wait…How do you know his name?"

"He doesn't, my King," argued Kaynar "He's making it up to try and save this Elf for some reason!"

"Shut up, Kaynar!" warned Payner, releasing his grip from Kaynar's arm.

"This Elf saved my life, Father, when the pirates attacked the city; he isn't a threat!"

"Is this true, Elf?" asked King Armish.

Krawsin lifted his head slightly, giving the king a slight glare. "What your son says is the truth; he saved my life, so I had a debt to repay."

The men stood, bewildered, hearing the Elf talk for the first time.

"Why did you not speak of this before?" the king continued to question.

"Every life has its own path to take; who am I to question mine? Your son was meant to save me, maybe for the reason that I was meant to save him. Destiny is certain, and so is my fate, and no word I could utter would change that.

"That's not to confuse destiny with fate, for they are not always the same. Destiny is a path in which you're born to take, and fate is the path to which you're drawn to. Don't go down the path you're drawn to; you must walk down the path you're born to. My destiny brought me here for what purpose, I don't yet know, but the fate of my destiny lies in your hands, King; only your destiny will force you into making the right decision."

"He speaks in riddles, an Elven tongue of lies and deceit; don't believe what he says, my King!" argued Kaynar.

"He speaks words of wisdom, Father," countered Maxin. "His destiny did bring him here, the same reason it brought me and Krawsin together, and because of that, I now know what has to be done."

Maxin could feel the fierce stare of Kaynar beating against the back of his head as he dealt with the pondering glare of his father from the front.

"What has to be done?" asked the king.

"I'd like to invoke Unity upon Krawsin; I wish to make him a soldier under my command."

"You cannot be serious? My King, my smart and noble King, you cannot allow this Elf to be unified! It's a disgrace!"

King Armish didn't take his eyes off of Maxin, seeing the willingness and the passion in his eyes to do what is right and not let anything or anyone stand in his way. The king kept a broad face, hiding a proud smile for his son in his mind.

"If this is what you wish, my son, I shall trust your judgment and you will take this Elf in your Unity. Although, I will still need to speak with him at a later time concerning his original motives on this land. Until that time, he is under your guidance; do not make me regret this."

"Am I dreaming right now?" argued Kaynar. "You don't know this Elf's motives, Armish, and you're just going to let him roam freely through the lands; we can't trust him."

"I don't trust him; I trust my son."

"Do you trust *me*, my King? Then, trust me when I say that this Elf needs to die."

"You've wanted him dead from the start. You even threatened me when I tried to help him back in Paran-Dun," claimed Maxin as he helped Krawsin off the floor, cutting his bonds.

"That's a lie!" defended Kaynar, looking over at King Armish, who now had eyes of great intensity baring down on him. "It's all lies, my King; I would never threaten your son!"

"I also have reason to believe Maxin's story, my friend," added Payner.

"What?" murmured a panicked Kaynar as Payner continued to question the intent of the king's captain, "Just now wasn't the first time I caught Kaynar's sword in mid-swing. Just earlier, I stopped the same sword from swinging down on top of Maxin's head, also."

"They both lie, my King; you must trust me!"

"I do trust you, Kaynar," stated King Armish. "But you have to understand, I also trust the two of them more!" And as the words left the mouth of the king, Sir Payner, Maxin, and Krawsin stood in complete shock as Kayner's head flew straight from his shoulders, hitting the floor with his body dropping straight after.

An eerie calmness shadowed the small corner of the city as King Armish stood tall above Kaynar's decapitated corpse, brandishing his sword tightly.

"Sir Payner, take Krawsin to the palace and give him a bed for the night, and send someone to clean up this mess."

"Yes, sir," replied a shocked Payner, not taking his eyes off the body for a second.

"Now!" pushed the king, from which Payner grabbed the arm of Krawsin and led him back to the palace.

King Armish then turned to face Maxin, only to find that he had taken a few steps back from him, panicked and scared. Maxin always imagined what his father was capable of, and as he looked on at him standing above Kaynar's body and showing no emotion, he finally bore witness to it.

"Maxin, my son, please, don't cower," pleaded the king as he moved over to a nearby step, patting a small space next to him for Maxin to join him, but Maxin remained where he was, with a body like jelly and a mind of great worry.

"Why did you kill him?"

"Kaynar was a good fighter and a good captain. I had known him since I was a child. Before today, I had not seen Kaynar for a while, and I could see a change in him tonight. I didn't see a man I once knew. When I looked into his eyes, whoever he was before, no longer lived within him. Something has corrupted him over the last few years, and it had finally taken over his soul. I agreed with him in his decision about the Elf, but when he threatens my family or anyone else for that matter, I will not hesitate to put them down. It was a foolish thing what you did, disobeying your mother and I, leaving the city in a time like this; it could've gotten you killed!"

"For that, I apologise, Father, for I thought it was the right choice to make, and that choice helped save this city."

"There are worse things than Zarnicks and pirates that infest these lands, and maybe one day, I will tell you all about them. But for now, you must understand the seriousness of what you did!"

Maxin moved over to his father slowly, sitting down anxiously beside him, still keeping some space between them.

A thousand questions entered the mind of the young prince at that point, questions that he had been waiting for the opportunity to ask, but was unsure on where to start. Should he speak of Algo and his people? Or of his sword which bore the name Bray'manoor? Or even how, according to Kaynar, Krawsin was not the first Elf to have been spotted in their lands. In the end, Maxin looked on at Kaynar's body, and only one thought entered his mind, who was now going to lead the King's Unit? Which led him on the path to his first question.

"What is the King's Order, Father? You sent for them, I fought alongside them, but in my lifetime, I have never heard a story or song about them."

"The King's Unit is an army of great standing and one bound only to the king; it was unfortunate that this was the way they were presented to you. But under the circumstances, I had no choice but to call for them. Sir Kaynar was once a member of my royal Unit when I turned fourteen, as was Sir Payner. When I became king, I always felt like the King's Unit should be above the rest, in power, strength, ability, and size.

"I realised that, as a king, it was near impossible to check on every city, town, or village in this land; messengers were not enough. One day, I was passing alone through the rocky caverns of Dramadoi, and I came across a lone wolf, or at least what I thought was one. The wolf howled, and I suddenly found myself surrounded by six of them, each one as vicious and as hungry as the next. I stood atop my horse and climbed onto a nearby ledge, hanging over the top of them like a prized meat, looking on as three of them devoured my horse. The other three were nowhere to be found. I looked up over the rock that roofed over my head, and I saw the Valleyian river just yards away and I knew if I crossed that river then I'd be safe…"

Completely involved in his father's story, Maxin had forgotten the feeling of fear and anxiety he had felt moments before.

King Armish shuffled across to Maxin, placing his arm around his shoulder as he continued to pass on his experiences. "I took my chances. Whilst the wolves were feasting on my horse, I scaled up over the rock, and that is when I came face-to-face with one lone wolf, stalking me, biding its time to come up with a plan, hearing my racing heart and my every breath, looking on at the sweat dripping from my brows; the worst thing I did was stop running. Before I knew it, the other five wolves were now standing right behind me. I pulled out a small dagger, and with adrenaline at the helm, I ran straight for the lone wolf, hitting him right in the eyes.

"I left the dagger and carried on running as fast as I could without looking back until I eventually crossed the river. I collapsed down on the stony ground and looked back across to see all five remaining wolves staring back at me, unable to cross. I looked down at my robes, seeing the bite marks and the scratches, realising then how close I was to death. It was during that moment, looking back at them, that I realised that is how I wanted my army to be.

"They knew the area, they were tactical, they were fierce. They had scouts, fighters, sending signals across to one another, making their enemy want to run and hide; they were the perfect army, so I made it. I scattered my Unit across the land, each one becoming a captain of the Unit based in that city, town, or village. But why stop there; we have three other kingdoms on our doorstep. If we come together and join forces, then never again will anything threaten these lands. Men, Elves, Wizards, and Dwarves, if we can co-exist and fight together, then we will become The Wolves of War."

"So who will be captain of Paran-Dun now?" asked Maxin, completely indulged in his father's plan. That look of fear he once had turned to a glistening gaze of admiration toward what his father was trying to achieve.

"Now, that is a big decision. One of the troops will get a promotion, but I have tests in place for this, but don't you see the bigger picture, my son. This is one Unit that can never disband; it can only expand. Every time a king dies, his predecessor will seize control. This land is stuck in a dark age; it's time we worked toward building a more advanced future. This is just a small step toward achieving that. I'm sorry you had to witness that with Kaynar, but in the end, he was too far gone; the future had no place for him. Now, the hour is late, it's your birthday tomorrow and your mother will be at

Belthran's bedside, wondering where I've gone. She doesn't know of you disobeying her, and just this one time, I will make sure it stays that way because truth be told, when your mother is upset, she scares me more than those wolves did. The only difference is, I can't run away from her."

Then giving his son a heart-warming hug, King Armish walked Maxin back to the palace to rest ahead of big preparations for the next morning.

***

King Armish

As the sun rose over the city on the morning of the great meet, the streets were already flooded with city folk and other villagers from towns over who had heard word of the historic meet.

Streets were cleared of bodies and blood throughout the night, making way for the villagers to turn the city into a great spectacle. Banners and fireworks were prepared around Carbaya to welcome their new visitors as each walkway was lined with streams of decoration and dressing. The great hall was being scrubbed and cleaned three times over by a hundred handmaids to have it sparkling for the meet.

Back in the palace, King Armish was preparing himself, along with Queen Neva, Prince Maxin, and the young Princess Layna. The king stood tall and proud on this day as he draped his kingly white attire with a velvet blue cloak and furry white hem that cuddled around his shoulders.

Blue and white were the colours of great celebration and festivities across Ar'Gurd, and for this day, their attires were each specially made. The colour blue agreed well with the queen, dressing in a vibrant blue gown which would light up any room, the pair of them crowning each other with solid gold crowns, infused with blue rubies and white crystals.

"It is unfortunate Belthran is going to miss the meet, he is missing history," stated Maxin as his mother arranged the buttons on his lavishly sewn tunic.

"Your brother is alive, that is the most fortunate thing we could've asked for," replied Neva.

"And Belthran will continue the line of history when he takes the reins as king; his moment will come," added King Armish.

A sudden knock of intent drummed against the doors of the royal cabinet room.

"Enter!" instructed King Armish.

"My King," spoke a guard in a great rush, "there are men at the gates, men in worn rags, bearing spears and cleavers!"

"What?"

Maxin knew exactly who these men were, but for the sake of his mother finding out he disobeyed her, he remained in nervous silence.

"What is their will?" King Armish asked the guard.

"They say they were invited to the meet by Master Maxin here…"

"What?" This time, the vicious tone was coming from the queen as she glared down at Maxin in utter infuriation.

"My wife, I know of our son's betrayal, and I have spoke with him on the matter, he will not do it again."

"Maxin, what were you thinking?" she continued to nag.

"Who are these people, Maxin?" asked King Armish, attempting to somehow divert the attention away from the scalding that his mother was about to hand him.

"I went to Paran-Dun to find troops to help the city. On my way, myself and three other members of my Unit stumbled across a cave in the great canyon beyond Woodland Farm. We found people living inside, people of a very hostile nature, ruled by three people who call themselves the Better Lords. They have lived underground for some time, thriving on the water that flows beneath, banished and segregated there many moons ago by the first king of this land, hunted under the penalty of death for the reason of being poor. They let me go on the promise that you would allow them to return to land and live their lives free."

"They let you go? They kept you captive? Did they threaten you?" questioned King Armish, switching from his previously abiding tone to a much more vigorous one, and fearing an aggressive reaction to the people of Cavetown.

Maxin responded abruptly, "Can you not blame them, Father? Growing up believing that everyone on land loathed them? They did not know who I was at first sight. You said you were working toward a better future involving Elves, Wizards, and Dwarves, then why not reunite these people with the lands that their ancestors before them used to inhabit. I, too, have made a start, recruiting one of their own into my Unit."

"You do have a very diverse Unit, don't you, my son?" spoke the king in a subtle admiration, "Fine, I will meet with them at the gates. Neva, escort Layna to the great hall, make sure everything is in order there; I will take Maxin with me."

Neva escorted Layna over to the great hall, but not before giving Maxin a look that made him, for a time, regret ever disobeying her.

King Armish then led Maxin to the gates in great urgency.

Maxin's Unit had already surrounded the inner gate, thirty feet high, steel chained and impenetrable. The pirates always found ways over the walls, but never through the gate. Beyond it, lay the outer greenland of Carbaya with a darkened shadow of a hundred men of Cavetown bearing arms, staring through the bars in the gate, led by the Better Lords.

"Algo, it is good to see you, boy," greeted Lord Danlur.

"And you, my Lord."

"Open the gate, Algo!" ordered Lord Pike.

"Only I have that power here!" spoke King Armish, bustling through the crowds that had gathered. "Do you all not have work to be doing?" he added, separating the villagers from the area.

"You come bearing arms, ordering us to open our gates. That doesn't seem like a peaceful negotiation to me. I know of your story, for my son has enlightened me. Holster your weapons and the archers on the wall will lower theirs. I will open the gates and we can discuss this in a more appropriate manner."

Lord Danlur raised his hand, gesturing for his men to follow the command.

Lord Pike remained spear in hand and a face like thunder.

"Do we have an issue here?" doubted the king, staring back into the eyes of Lord Pike.

Lord Layzul commanded Lord Pike to stand down, as did Lord Danlur, eventually leading the proud lord to hesitantly holster his spear into a torn sack he had hanging from his back.

King Armish gave the signal, and with a small rattle and sharp shudder, the gate began to rise, and the king stepped forward, showing his empty hands as a sign of peace.

The three Better Lords then moving forward, mirroring his movements.

"Firstly, I would like to welcome you to the city. Secondly, I would like to apologise for you being shunned away from it by my forefathers. I don't wish for any man, woman, or child of this land to be treated in such ways, and I will not condone it to continue."

"We appreciate your apology. After meeting your son, we understand that there is maybe hope left in this land, and we only wish to rejoin it," pleaded Lord Danlur as Lord Layzul then proceeded to continue the plea.

"It will take time for us to adjust and to trust, but we feel this is what is needed for our people to evolve and—"

But Lord Layzul was cut short, interrupted by the ever-growing irritation that was Lord Pike, "And we will never call you, 'King!'"

"Excuse me?" gasped King Armish.

"We have led our people through generations of Better Lords. We are giving them hope that they may return to land, but we cannot ask them to bow to a new ruler, especially not one with your bloodline."

"As much as Lord Pike acts with stupidity and aggression, he also spoke with truth and honesty; we will ask to live upon the lands once again, but we will not ask for you to be our king," added Lord Danlur.

King Armish was stunned but was somewhat understanding. The men in that cave had a history, and not a great one, thanks to the ruling of his ancestors. The whole meet was about change and evolution, and he was being provided with an opportunity to expand on his vision, even if it did mean siding with those who refused to call him, "King."

"There's a space of land, just west of the Meadow Marshes, beyond the Lochland River, it is yours to call home and for you to live life as you see fit, under the rule of your Better Lords, under one circumstance."

"And that is?" asked Lord Layzul.

"You join us in the great hall. Attend the meet I have put together and hear my proposition for the races of this world, which will include yourselves and your people."

The three Better Lords agreed correspondingly, easing the tension that surrounded the city gate, then leading their people through the gates with a certain Lord Pike, non-admittingly having a newfound respect for King Armish and his judgment.

As they made their way through the gates, King Armish held out his hand in a show of respect to shake the hands of the three Better Lords to show that he now witnessed them as significant rulers in this land, much to the acceptance of Maxin and Algo as they looked on in deep love and admiration of their people finally coming together. But this admirable welcoming was soon disrupted when a deafening thud burst through the eardrums of everyone in the city, a vibration echoing through the floor with every beat.

"What is that?" muttered Igor.

"That is the Dwarves!" replied Sprock, with a smile so proud it could've lit up the sky.

As a crowd once again gathered, to King Armish's annoyance, the thud also brought in Prince Clearus, Sir Payner, Prince Harnik, and their respective troops. Archers on the wall signalled down to King Armish to acknowledge that Dwarves were closing in.

Maxin and his Unit hurried up a cluster of nearby steps to top the city walls, looking out ahead as hundreds of well-armed Dwarves marched over the hill in the most satisfyingly synchronised march with two Dwarves standing atop an open metal carriage, laced with chains of silver and gold, being pulled along by a handful of the strongest Dwarven soldiers.

The beat of tens of thuds simultaneously crashing against the great drums, bestowed upon a line of Dwarves marching behind the carriage, playing to the beat of every footstep.

At once, the beat stopped, and the Dwarves halted at a safe distance beyond the gate. King Dunlin standing proud and strong atop his carriage like a great god of some sorts, speaking loud and true.

"King in the city, I am King Dunlin of Camaroth, and this here is my sister, Princess Sawndra. We come bearing no grudge against you and your people, and no plans of war. We stand here proudly upon the soil of your great ancestors for the first time, feeling the rays of that luminous being in the sky upon our skin. We come to repay a debt we owe to two of your own and to sit with you in the great halls of your fair city."

King Armish, once again, pulled away from the crowds, signalling Prince Clearus and Sir Payner to step forward with him. "Great Dwarven King of Camaroth, allow me to introduce myself formally. I am King Armish Hailguard, King of man, and it is an honour to bear witness to an awe-inspiring race such as yourselves. Standing with me, I have Sir Payner and Prince Clearus, two people who have already made your acquaintance and speak highly of your ruling. If you turn your gaze atop the city walls to my left, you will see there one of your own, fighting Unity alongside my son. No harm has come to him from us, and it never shall. I welcome you as an ally to our great city of Carbaya, you and your people are free to enter," welcomed the king with such grace, standing to the side and holding out his arm toward the city, gesturing for the Dwarves to pass invitingly.

As King Armish once again scattered the gathering villagers, space was cleared for the mass of Dwarves to enter the kingdom, squeezing through the gateway six at a time, King Dunlin's carriage just about cramming through.

King Dunlin stepped from his carriage to a bow of respect from Armish, Payner, and Clearus, helping his sister down from the carriage steps with a gentle hand.

King Armish stood up straight and shook the hand of the Dwarven King, but a cloud loomed over them, a misted fog grew thick throughout the courtyard.

"I think it's about rain," warned Sir Payner.

Prince Clearus grew thoughtful for a moment, feeling an energy surrounding the place like a huge weight was bearing down on him, only to be lifted with the click of a finger or the banging of a staff. He wrenched down, holding his head in searing pain.

"Clearus, are you all right?" asked Payner.

"Brother?" added King Armish with everyone looking on in worry and distress.

"It's the Wizards; they are here," uttered Clearus as a bolt of lightning struck the floor behind them, not once but twice, each one revealing a guardian of the night, standing firm and desolate. They raised their staffs as one and brought them down together, driving them into the floor like a spear before battle. The moment the staffs connected with the floor, Clearus's pain went away, forcing him to drop to one knee, panting in relief.

Smoke in the area cleared, everyone including King Armish mesmerised at what drew from the fog, a woman dressed in gowns brighter than the sun and more glistening than the blue sea to the north. Queen Kandriel had arrived and in some style.

Those who had gathered from the men, to the Dwarves, to the people of Cavetown, shared a reaction of great astonishment, open jaws, and unblinking eyes.

Prince Clearus rose to his feet, looking around at the catatonic state of everyone around, looking as though they were all tranced with some spell. As scared as Clearus was of this woman, the option to greet her kindly was forced to the back of his mind, he only wanted one thing from her, and that was answers. "What have you done to me?"

Kandriel grinned deviously back at him, uttering words in a calm tone that put Clearus on edge the moment they left her lips. "I still have time for you, Master Clearus, but it is not for this moment," she spoke as her gaze flickered past his shoulder and into the sight of King Armish.

"*Velnaar, li sawnra la Kandriel,*" she spoke with such grace in her more common tongue of Amren'oir, but for Clearus, he did not know, for he unknowingly understood everything she said, which is why it confused him when she repeated herself, this time using a language they all understood.

"Greetings, my name is Kandriel."

Everyone listened to every word she spoke, ears opening up like freshly blossomed flowers.

"There is no need to fear us; we mean you no harm. If we did, then you would certainly know it. It is a wonder for myself to look upon your manmade kingdom and see through my own eyes the lives you have made for yourselves. But I am disillusioned, I was invited to this meet, and the nature of this coming together pulled me with a sense of intrigue, but did I come on false pretences? Was I not informed that all four kingdoms would be here? I see those of men and Dwarves, but I don't see those of Elves."

The aura surrounding them all depleted, allowing them to feel some sense of normality, each baring a slight tingle through their fingertips, a feeling they wouldn't forget in such a hurry.

King Armish stepped ahead of Prince Clearus, presenting himself to Kandriel, "I wish you greetings, and may I start by saying that your entrance was truly a spectacle to behold, and it is a great honour to have you here in our presence. As for the Elves, they seem to be last to arrive."

But King Armish was interrupted, but not by a voice he had heard before, this voice came from the walls above the gate, drawing attention to the archers who stood atop the wall, one of them turning to face the gathering; a female of fair standing, not of this land, but dressed in the armour of a city guard.

"I believe we actually got here first," she spoke.

"Angelar!" gasped Payner as twenty archers on either side of her turned around to face them all, each of them dressed in Carbayan armour.

"Where are my archers? Why are you in city armour?" roared the king, not the first words he would've liked to have uttered to the Elves.

The rebel Queen Angelar removed her helmet, her plum hair draping gracefully over one shoulder, her beautiful Elven ears now having room to breathe. "King Armish, it is an honour to meet you, as it is King Dunlin of the Dwarves and the very glamourous Wizard Queen Kandriel. We are masters of movement, and it's only fair that we got to make a grand entrance, too.

"We arrived here bright and early, and one of your guard captains above the gates was very deceptive, and my right-hand Elf, Matine, he plays the part of a man very well, his performance was one of a kind. After he snuck into the city and located the armoury for himself, he brought word to one of your guards located nearby, instructing all of your archers to go and aid with the decoration of the city, and that order came straight from the king, of course. Once the archers fled, that allowed us to sneak in ourselves and play dress up in your armoury. In full uniform, we made our way back to the wall and waited, and after several hours, we were able to make our entrance."

King Armish stood in shock.

"Can anyone just break into the city now?" questioned Harnik.

"I appreciate your attendance, Queen of the Elves, but what I don't appreciate is you breaking into my city and deceiving my guards."

"We weren't breaking in," defended Queen Angelar with a certain charm, "we were invited, after all, and I believe the invite on the day was not time specific. It is true, we saved Payner's life, but that was only one man from a whole kingdom. We didn't know what we were walking into, so for the safety of my people, we scouted ahead."

King Armish turned his focus to Payner, who in return gave him a nod of acceptance, allowing King Armish to bite his tongue from saying anything further and giving him the push to move forward with proceedings. "Welcome to the city, it is an honour to meet with you and a pleasure that you have agreed to join us. Once Sir Payner collects the archers who should be stationed here, we will then escort you to the great hall, and this meet should get underway at once."

After a short time, Sir Payner returned with the archers, much to a very unpleasing look from King Armish. And the armour that Angelar and her Elves stole was returned back to the armoury. Each race was then escorted respectfully through the city, passing countless crowds of captivated villagers and onto the great hall that stood tall in the south of the city.

CHAPTER TWENTY

THE MEET

King Armish

It had been many years since the great hall of Carbaya had
been filled to this magnitude. This last was to celebrate the
birth of a princess, but it was the first time in history that the
halls had been filled with that of men, Elves, Wizards, and
Dwarves. The great hall sat upon a high rise of land within the
city, just metres away from the palace itself, casting a glorious
shadow over a small section of the city. The building's great
history was on constant display, as the untouched outer walls
grew worn and cracked from a time gone by, but remaining
ever so stunning from the pillars that supported it all, being
built with the finest stone and brick that the kingdom had to
offer.

Inside the great hall, visitors would be greeted by statues
of the greatest kings to rule these lands. The interior covered
in blinding white granite streamed with pure gold trim, and a
great golden throne taking centre stage upon a block of marble
steps sited at the far end of the hall, this great hall really was a
wondrous sight to behold.

Before the meet took place, King Armish allowed the
groups to converse within the halls in a gracious manner.
Dwarves learnt the mysteries and tales of the Elves, the Elves
learnt of man's ever-growing passion for fruits and strong ales,
Wizards learnt of the daunting history that had befallen the
Kingdom of Camaroth through the years, and the men learnt

of the constant ignorance of Wizards, none more so than Prince Clearus, necking his third cup of bitter ale as his focus remained solely on Queen Kandriel, staring at her from across the room.

Once Clearus swallowed the last drop of his favourite brewing, he slammed his cup on the table, rose from his seat, and marched across the hall and toward Kandriel, learning the art of ignorance himself as he surpassed many great Elves and Dwarves who were interested in greeting him.

As he approached her with driven intent, he was stopped in his tracks by one of the guardians who had accompanied her.

"And how may I be of help to you, outsider?" spoke the guardian, looking down at Clearus, whose gaze had still not left the Wizard Queen, now seeing her looking back at him as he was caught behind the guardian.

"You want to know how you can help me? Then, move out of my way!" spoke Clearus, and surprisingly to him, the guardian stepped aside, not speaking another word.

The eyes of Kandriel grew with amazement as she witnessed his power over the guardian, something anyone other than a Wizard should have.

"It cannot be," she uttered under her breath as Clearus approached her. "What is happening to me? Something I thought not possible."

"And what did you think not possible?" asked Clearus, growing tired of short answers. "I need to know what is happening to *me*!"

"Time is a power you can't control, a force of will and regret, it is that which your life moves along with and thus it has to be respected, you cannot change what was and you cannot see what awaits you."

"Stop speaking in tongue. Tell me what you have done to me."

Kandriel rose from her seat, standing slightly taller than Clearus, but making him feel half a foot smaller. "Many things, I believe, but now is not the time to share them with you, Master Clearus."

Anger coursed through the body of the prince; he was trying to not let his frustrations ruin the historic day.

Before Clearus could react to Queen Kandriel, King Armish rose from his seat, causing a surrounding hush, speaking aloud while those who stood took their seats.

"I look out upon you all, and I feel like I am in a dream as races from all corners of this world, have come together as one for the first time. It feels somewhat inspiring, but at the same time, it feels like it's something that should've happened many moons ago. We sit in wonder and awe of one another, hearing stories of lavish histories, but there is much more history to be written, and I ask, why can that history not be written together from this moment on? We each have threats that curse our lands, from the pirates to corrupt Elven Kings. I wish for peace for my people, as I hope you all wish the same. Then why can we not have it? Why can we not come together and band as one? Open up your lands freely, allow for wondering travellers with no hostility, expand our trading resources, and help one another. Allow for aid when our kingdoms are threatened."

A city guard, moved up the steps toward King Armish, handing him a sealed scroll.

Armish pulled open the scroll, grinning to himself as he looked upon it before raising it high above his head so everyone in the hall bore witness to it.

"Here in my hand, I hold a treaty. Not just any treaty, but '*the*' treaty. If the great leaders of all kingdoms sign their names upon this parchment, then that will seal all of our futures with good tidings and prosperous relations. If I may read out the terms of this agreement,

"I hereby accept and adhere to the terms set by the four great kingdoms of men, Wizards, Elves and Dwarves.

- Each kingdom should be ready and willing to fight and aid one another if called upon by another kingdom in peril.

- Neither one of the four kingdoms should wage war against another.

- All races are permitted and given access to travel to and from each of the four kingdoms.

- Any person who causes trouble of any kind, will stand trial and will be punished accordingly by the kingdom in which the person belongs and also by the kingdom from which the trouble occurs.

"These are the terms in which we must abide if the treaty is signed. I know this is a big step for all of you, so please take a moment to discuss this with your people before we proceed," instructed King Armish as he took an almost exhausting drop back onto his throne, huffing in anticipation as the groups of men, Wizards, Elves, and Dwarves discussed the treaty amongst themselves, hundreds of whispers filling the halls like the tune of a great song.

As moments passed and the muttering tunes of the four races grew quiet, King Armish rose from his throne once more, laying the treaty across a stone table that sat in front of him, inking into it the first signature of rulers. King Dunlin was the first to step forward, proudly with Princess Sawndra by his side.

"Long have we waited to gaze upon the structures of another kingdom, to build houses, not of strong stone, but of great allies. You proved to be strong allies when two of your own helped aid my people in a crisis against such demonic creatures that taunted our kingdom. In return, we agree to uphold that allegiance," stated King Dunlin, taking the last few big steps up the platform to reach the parchment, wrapping his stubby hands around a quill that rested on the table and etching his name in history.

As King Dunlin took a stand alongside King Armish, Queen Kandriel was the next to move forward, parting the guardians and standing brazen at the bottom of the steps, "I find it rather charming that you've written up these rules alone, Master Armish, thinking to yourself that we would be happy to sign along with these terms, but I also find it irrational that you have not considered all possibilities. Our Kingdom of Amren'oir is not accessible to outsiders, it is walled by a great spell of armour and protection that cannot be undone. Prince Clearus was fortunate to have survived, and it is he who is now left with a troublesome fate. Our kingdom is not to be travelled to, and if this is in agreement, then we will oblige."

"The treaty will be amended to support this," respected King Armish, and with an endearing smile, Kandriel raised her gown above her ankles and gracefully made her way to the top of the steps. She refused the quill from a guard, using her own finger on the parchment like a pen, ink staining the paper from her mere touch. She then stood proudly alongside King Armish and King Dunlin.

Everyone focused their eyes across the hall toward Queen Angelar as she rose solemnly from her seat, moving keenly toward the others, each step she took, feeling like a thunderous clap, echoing through the halls as the people fell silent in anticipation. She stopped suddenly, halfway up the marble steps. "How can I not agree to help those who are willing to help rid my land of evil?" she asked, taking a few more strides to top the steps, turning around to face the crowds that were looking on in overwhelming pride.

"This day will seize to exist in the memory of you all, as well as in the minds of your children and their children after them from the stories that we tell. King Armish has taken the first step to a greater, more diverse future. I, for one, am honoured to be the ruler and representative of the Elves as this piece of history is created and cemented in eternity."

And as Queen Angelar signed the treaty and took her place proudly next to the other three great rulers, the four of them were met with outstanding applause and admiration; cheers echoed true throughout the halls as music played fair, songs in honour of the great occasion as the festivities continued long through the night.

Songs of heroes and legends fed the ears of people throughout the city. Ale and wine ran thick and fast down the throats of all, even the special brewing that the Dwarves brought along with them. Pleasant conversation and games of friendly competition were enjoyed by all and Maxin's birthday was celebrated amongst the chaos, with a toast being raised throughout the halls for him and his coming of age; and although he could not get the inauguration for his Unit until he had all ten warriors, the night in whole, was a success, and the four rulers conversed atop the stairs; queues of people eagerly waiting to show their appreciation to the two kings and the two queens of these lands.

Some kneeling before them with words of praise and great fortune, others bowing at the sight of such things, many relishing in the aura of great kings and queens. Questions were asked to all of them, and answers were given back to each person with honour and humbleness.

The queues stretched far and wide throughout the kingdom with everyone having the opportunity to bask in this moment; as the night grew dark, the queues had no sign of growing shorter.

King Dunlin and Queen Angelar sat on the right of King Armish and his throne, and Queen Kandriel sat just to his left, each in their own hand-carved stools that were prepared before their arrival. Queen Neva, Princess Layna, and the princes, Maxin, Clearus and Harnik also joined the four rulers atop the platform, seated on an extended table that formed just behind them.

The three Better Lords of Cavetown came forward during this time to express their gratitude once again to King Armish and to look into the eyes of those whom they now shared their lands with.

Young Krawsin stepped forward to show his appreciation to King Armish for eventually showing great mercy on him and to also greet the great Elven Queen Angelar, whom he was brought up to believe was dead. Hearing stories of Morrik's Elven guards about how she was slain some time ago. Krawsin saw the will and the beauty in Angelar's eyes, feeling hope that maybe now, peace would one day reach the Kingdom of Whisperwood once again, a time he only ever dreamed of.

"What is your purpose on these lands, young Elf? You've found yourself in the services of the young prince in a time before this meet took place?" questioned Angelar.

Krawsin put himself in the position he was fully expecting, and with Maxin in attendance also, he was able to explain himself to all, no matter how much damage and confusion it may cause. "King Morrik, he saw weakness in this land, one for the taking, no guard stations or watchtowers around any of the entrances toward this kingdom, he thought King Armish to be too blindsided by possible threats, but he would not risk his life or the life of his guards to prove it. He took those who were young with no families left and no commitments. He forced them out into this kingdom to scout for him. Either you head back with information or you're caught in this land with no reason for being here, too young to have any information on King Morrik and his plans, you'd either be caught and imprisoned or you would die, he has nothing to lose and everything to gain."

"Have you given him any information?" asked King Armish.

"No, I had only been in the lands for a few days, but I have seen other scouts come and go from Whisperwood, unknowing to what information they may hold. He wants these lands. He manipulates and corrupts those who follow him; those who speak up against him, die. I had no choice; it was risk dying here, or die at his hands. If you're to take back the Kingdom of Whisperwood from his rule, then I wish to help!"

"I thank you for your honesty, young Elf. Once the threat of pirates has been diminished, then Whisperwood will have the help it so truly desires. This King Morrik has taken rule over your lands. He killed one of our men and wishes to scout our lands for his taking. I can assure you this, he will be dealt with," assured King Armish.

Queen Angelar rose from her seat and spoke down to Krawsin, but with great strength in her voice that the whole hall stopped to listen to a poem, a tune of great standing with the rebel Elves, and Krawsin listening avidly,

"Through mountains of grass and rivers of fog,
The tides of land are changing.
Over years and years of burning logs,
The time of evil is ageing.
From trees of whisper and an ever-growing wood,
The kingdom will rise with the power of good."

Queen Angelar took her seat once more smiling back at Krawsin, causing him to blush at the mere sight of her. He bowed to the kings and queens graciously before moving on over to his nearby Unit members, who were waiting aside to greet him.

"Morrik is a danger to us all, I hope the rest of you can see this now," stated King Armish.

"He won't dare attempt to penetrate Camaroth, but let's not give him a chance to try," said King Dunlin.

"He knows this meet is going ahead; there's a chance he knows we've joined forces already," added King Armish.

"Then he knows the threat he faces; he has no other allies! But he still won't go down without a fight; he is too proud," indicated Angelar.

"Then, let him come," replied a stern Kandriel, "we have nothing to fear from him, and he has everything to fear from us. If he is foolish enough to challenge us, then I say let him," she added.

But before the conversation could continue, another Elf stepped forward to the head of the queue, one who drew many gazes from Queen Angelar, he stood with an overpowering gaze and scars of battle on his face.

"Who are you, Elf? Your face is not one I recognise," she said.

"My name is Ma'hk-lochlen Harrows."

The name of harrows made the ear of a nearby Krawsin twitch at the sound of it.

"I come on behalf of King Morrik!"

Those words drawing attention from all, King Armish and Queen Angelar standing forcefully from their seats, brandishing their swords as the Elf continued to speak aloud.

"You think the swords frighten me? I am merely a messenger. I come bearing words, and a gift from the king. A prisoner escaped his dungeons after wrongfully trespassing on our lands, and instead of facing rightful justice, that prisoner escaped, claiming many Elven lives. It darkens King Morrik's heart to know that this monster is now sitting freely back within the walls of his city, with the backing of his king. King Morrik is hurt by this lack of lawfulness, and therefore, King Armish is also a traitor to the Kingdom of Whisperwood and shall therefore be punished by penalty of death!" The Elf then pulled a small dagger from an inside pocket of his woven jacket and launched it; it passed the ear of King Armish.

"You missed," sniggered the king, but much to his surprise, the Elf stood smiling, pulling another dagger from his jacket.

"I don't miss, and King Morrik sends his kindest regards," replied the Elf before lifting the dagger and slicing his own throat.

Screams fell through the great hall but not for the Elf; it was the unnerving screams of a young girl and the cries of an adolescent prince. Everyone looked up in shock toward King Armish, but they were not on him.

The faint sound of Prince Clearus called over to him in a sympathetic tone.

King Armish turned to face his brother and immediately dropped to his knees in grave distress, as he saw the Elven dagger pierced through the skull of Queen Neva.

The great halls were cleared as villagers were sent home and guards patrolled the streets.

Queen Neva's body was covered as Prince Harnik escorted Maxin and Layna back to the palace with the help of his troops.

King Armish sat in a trance, resting upon the back of his throne, staring at the body of his wife, now draped in curtains pulled from a nearby hanging.

Clearus crouched in front of him, speaking words of no sound, being blocked out by King Armish, whose mind remained distant.

Queen Angelar scoured the body of the fallen Elf whose life had led to such disarray, wondering how he had escaped her knowledge upon her travels.

King Dunlin and Sir Payner spoke to each other of King Morrik's fate, whilst Queen Kandriel disappeared from the city altogether shortly after the chaos of it all began, faint-heartedly escaping the halls in quick fashion.

King Armish began to hear voices all around him, none of them making sense, but each of them getting louder and louder. The face of Prince Clearus was dipping in and out of focus in front of him. The beat of his heart was crashing against his chest like a great battering ram, and his mouth was twitching as he reimagined that dagger in his wife's head over and over again in his mind. A deep exhale brought him back to reality, hearing the bickering of everyone around him as Queen Neva lay lifeless on the bloodstained marble flooring.

"Get out," he uttered under his breath, only enough for Clearus to hear. "Get out!" he spoke once more, this time a little louder, reaching the bottom of the stairs. "GET OUT!"

he screamed for a third time, this time in at full volume, pulling himself up from the floor, pushing Clearus aside. "Get out, all of you! Get out, get out, get out!"

"Brother, please…" pleaded Clearus, leaning over to Armish, who had now knelt next to the body of Neva. King Armish turned his head slowly toward Clearus, speaking quietly, but with much anger in his heart, "I said get out!"

After some resilience, they all respectively left the halls, allowing King Armish to grieve alone.

***

Hours had passed, and the night air fell calm as a fog spread thick throughout the city. Guards of men, Elves, and Dwarves all patrolling the city with lanterns of solid flame, making sure every villager was kept safe. Messengers were sent in great haste toward neighbouring villages and towns with news of the possible threat that stalked them and the devastating attack that had befallen the city of Carbaya which left their kingdom without a queen. Neither sight nor sound came from King Armish within the great halls, and Sir Payner and Prince Clearus grew worried.

"He was not himself. I looked into the eyes of my brother, and for the first time in my life, I saw a part of him no longer existed. Something in him left the moment Queen Neva drew her last breath."

"Then, why did we leave him?" argued Payner.

"It was a bad idea leaving him alone, but it would've been even worse staying with him at a time when we were not wanted."

"Morrik is going to pay for this! With the spirits as my witness, he will suffer!" raged Payner.

"And what of Queen Kandriel? She and her guardians puffed out of there the moment things got crazy," stated King Dunlin.

"She will answer for her disappearance, amongst other things. But we have bigger problems. We have mobs of pirates coming in from the south, a corrupt king who toys with us from the east, and a king here whom I strongly fear for," said Clearus, which was met with a crashing thump that came from inside the great halls.

In a panic, the four of them broke through the doors to the halls only to find them empty of any life. King Armish was gone.

"I told you we shouldn't have left him alone! He couldn't have gotten far," spoke Payner, running out of the halls to alert guards of the king's disappearance.

Queen Angelar walked awkwardly across to the body of the fallen Elf with a small lump in her throat, looking down in revulsion as his head was removed from his body and impaled onto a corner of the king's throne with one eye removed, and the words, *'eye for an eye,'* carved into the Elf's chest.

The thud was the sound of the fallen hanging pole that once donned a curtain that now draped over the body of the queen. King Armish had left the great halls some time ago, through a back entrance that didn't seem to enter the minds of the others. He was four miles gone, in fact, racing east through the night at an alarming pace upon his trusted steed.

In between the sound of each hoof hammering against the mud, the cries and screams of his children tainted his eardrums, filling his heart with more anger as he rode on. It was only when the sun began to rise in the north that King Armish brought his horse to a halt, dismounting upon the gates at Whisperwood, staring down the narrow bridgeway with overpowering intent. He removed only a long sword and small bolted weapon from his sack before slapping the rear of his horse, signalling it to flee.

He stormed the first gate, barrelling through it with immense force. He walked the long, winding bridge until he reached the second gate, soon enough finding an arrow fired directly between his feet.

"What is it you seek from this land?" spoke a voice from the trees.

King Armish looked up with a sadistic grin, muttering beneath his breath, "Oh, I've heard all about you!" Then, he aimed his bolted weapon up toward the trees and pulled a small trigger that burrowed on the inside, firing a small arrowed bolt at some pace. As the bolt flew into the trees, King Armish heard a slight scuffle and a rustle before the body of an Elf dropped to the ground below like a sack of rocks. The king then proceeded to break through the second gate and enter the Elven Kingdom of Whisperwood in search of King Morrik.

CHAPTER TWENTY-ONE

THE LONE WOLF WEATHERS THE STORM

Belthran

Belthran's eyes flickered and opened for the first time since his escape from death, unaware of his dead mother and his missing father, seeing the blurred figures of Prince Maxin and Princess Layna standing distressed along his bedside as he woke.

"Brother, you have returned," he uttered as his eyes began to focus, creasing his face in agony. But before Maxin could say a word, Belthran spotted Sir Payner standing next to them, along with Prince Clearus and Prince Harnik to his right.

"Sir Payner? Cousin Harnik? Uncle Clearus? How long have I been here? Where are Father and Mother? And what happened to the pirates?"

***

King Armish

As the news was broken to Belthran of the passing tragedy of his mother, King Armish was marching forward through the Woodlands of Whisperwood. The unnerving void of life within the woodland bypassed the king's mind as he set out to find the pond that Sir Payner had previously spoken to him of.

But he lost his way, his view north looking almost identical as his view east, west, and south. He stood for a moment to gather his thoughts, watching the sun as it began to beam through the branches of every tree, leaves falling but evaporating before they hit the ground, no sounds of birds or other wildlife.

He focused his squinted gaze up into the trees, trying to see the tree Elves whom Queen Angelar commanded, but he could see nothing but a glowing sun in his eyes. He pondered the idea of whether to shout out for them or not, would his voice reach their ears? Would they trust him without the rule of their queen? How could he prove who he was, or if the allegiances were formed? As those thoughts flew through his already crowded mind, he began to hear a sound coming from the trees ahead of him, one he knew meant trouble. It sounded like tens of armoured footsteps racing his way. He gripped his longsword tightly in his right hand and kept his bolted weapon covered against the side of his left leg.

As the sound of clattering boots grew stronger, another sound of rustled branches was heard from above, drawing in the king's attention. And for the first time, he saw movement, shadows of beings leaping past the glare of the sun, jumping from branch to branch, three or four of them, at least. He wondered whether to breathe a sigh of relief. As much as it could've been the rebel Elves looking down on him, it just so easily could've been more or King Morrik's tree troopers.

He pulled his head down to face the front as a group of well-armoured Elves bustled through the trees, forming an intimidating circle around him. King Armish remained silent as an Elf broke from the group and met him head-on. He looked the king up and down in some disgust, knowing he was of the human race.

"How is it that a man is found wandering alone through our woodlands?"

"Easy, I broke through the gates, put an arrow through one of the Elves in the trees, and now, I'm on my way to put my sword through the face of your king!" exclaimed King Armish in fearless confidence, a small part of him hoping the Elves in the trees were listening in and watching keenly.

The Elf who stood in front of him had an overpowering look on his face. He knew he was in control, and he knew that they had him outnumbered. "You must be the great leader of men. I can tell by the overbearing need to look like a man of importance. King Morrik said you would arrive at some point. It's a shame he's going to get blood all over your nice white dress."

King Armish remained standing with great confidence, unfazed by the Elf's threats. The Elf looked the king up and down again, already seeing splatters of blood on the shirt King Armish wore, forcing a sadistic grin upon his face as he began to taunt. "Or maybe he will just add to that which you already bear; it's nice to see you taking a piece of your wife with you on your travels."

The look of confidence left the king, changing into a fearsome look of vengeance and hatred, staring daggers at the Elf as he continued to smirk, slowly drawing his bolted weapon up in front of him, pulling the trigger, and satisfyingly watching as a small bolt flew through the eye of the Elf, causing the circle of Elves to step back in shock. King Armish then followed on from his attack, firing another arrow through the face of another Elf in front of him, forcing the surrounding Elves to draw their weapons and charge him.

He quickly took out three with two precise swings of his sword and firing another bolt to his left. Feeling a course of adrenaline and hate flowing through his veins, he turned with rage to continue his attack, only to find the Elves were gone.

Hearing the sounds of rustling in the trees above yet again, he yelled, "Show yourselves!" But there was no response. "Do not hide away in fear, whether friend or foe, either trust me or fight me; it's not a difficult decision to make!" he added, holding his arms out wide as he stared back into the trees.

Within a moment, the body of the missing Elves fell from above, their corpses smashing against the perfectly trimmed grass. But their bodies were quickly followed by others, three others to be exact, who landed on the ground perfectly, feet first, and very much alive, dressed in amour somewhat thinner and less protected than that of the Elves who just attacked.

"You're the King of Ar'Gurd?"

"Yes. And who might you be?"

"We're the Elves who just saved your life, and we are loyal to Queen Angelar, rightful ruler of Whisperwood! But tell me this, she leaves to meet with you in your kingdom then we find you wandering our lands, with no sign of our queen; where is she?"

"Your queen remains on our lands, unaware that I am here. I trust you heard some of what these Elves said? King Morrik sent a mercenary to kill my wife, with great success. I came to your lands seeking vengeance, and to make him suffer for his crimes! Can you not take me to him?"

The Elves looked at one another in question of King Armish's story.

"I'm having trouble with the fact that what you say is true. You come in here and slaughter any Elves you come across, trying to fight an army on your own. If what you say is true, then why come without an army, side by side with Queen Angelar and hers?" one spoke.

"Because his head is mine and nobody else's!" exclaimed King Armish with great passion. "I've not come here to take on an army, I have come here to kill him, and anyone who stands in my way of that, shouldn't plan to leave this place alive!"

The Elves saw truth through the hurt in King Armish's voice and the desire in his eyes. They agreed to help, but only so far as to guide him to the location of the pond. As much as they wanted Morrik dead, they knew that his army was still too big for them to take on, and King Armish had no chance of surviving past nightfall. Even if he managed to somehow get to King Morrik and slay him, he would be surrounded by a city of vengeful Elves, and the rebel Elves did not wish to end their lives, also.

After a small trek east, and keeping to the trees, the Elves safely guided King Armish to the pond, leaving him with a few words of advice. "Morrik's men guard every entranceway, from the steps to the dungeon. His troops are large in number and loyal to him beyond belief. Do not try to trick or bribe them; they will not fall for such things. Keep your wits about you, and may our wishes of luck guide you."

King Armish thanked the Elven rebels without hearing a word back, knowing then they had gone, and he was back to being on his own from this point onward.

Armish lingered for a moment, circling the pond, struggling to compose himself, and trying to think of a plan to penetrate somewhere he had no visual of. He closed his eyes for a short while, feeling a light breeze whisk through his beard, experiencing the embodiment of spiritual light roaming his body, the spirits of his ancestors and the newly created divine entity of Queen Neva. He felt them within him, not by voices in his head, but by the warmth that hugged his heart.

A tear of loss and sorrow fell from his eye; his head sunk and his lips quivered. The feeling of warmth in his heart was soon gone, suddenly feeling like someone had clamped their hand around it, forcing him to grab hold of his chest, his mind once again filling with the vision of his wife with a dagger in her skull. He released his hand from his chest, and the air fell flat. The thought for a plan erased from his mind. He drew his sword, and with no sense of hesitation, climbed into the pond. Feeling the first step underneath his heavy boot, he braced himself as he began to decline farther and farther into the water until his whole body was completely under.

As King Armish dipped below the surface of the water, feeling the loose droplets leave his skin, he came upon a sight that he resentfully anticipated, streams of Elven troops aiming arrows and spears toward him as he bottomed the stairs. He felt somewhat conflicted, he knew it was going to be highly impossible to get to Morrik without bumping into any guards, but a hurdle of this magnitude really put a sharp thorn in his side. He stood his ground, aiming his sword and bolted weapon out in front of him.

"I want Morrik! Either you lead me to him and he accepts my challenge, or I cut through all of you and find him myself!" threatened King Armish, forcing a middle-aged Elf to step forward, placing his arrow back in his quiver, pushing the surrounding Elves to withdraw their weapons, also.

King Armish remained on edge, weapons still in hand, resting his eyes on the Elf who stood dormant in front of him.

"You want Morrik? He's been waiting for you! Follow me," relayed the Elf as the Elves around him split apart, forming a pathway behind him. The Elf began to move down the pathway, signalling for King Armish to follow him.

He reluctantly did so, looking into the eyes of every Elf whom he passed, as they sniggered and hissed back at him, and saying words that bore no meaning in his mind.

Being steered through trenches of spiteful Elves, the Elf who led the way came to a halt; ahead of him was another great circle of Elves armed head to toe in armour and weapons. As King Armish stepped forward into the circle, he saw a large wooden hut, situated at the head of the gathering troops.

"Where is King Morrik?" he screamed at the top of his lungs, pacing the inside of the circle, but he got no answers; all he got was the beat of heavy boots knocking against the deck inside the wooden cabin, each one getting closer to the door. Armish turned to face the hut just as the sound of each footstep stopped. He held his breath for a moment, but just a short moment because he drew a deep huff of rage when the door of the cabin was kicked open. There was the silhouette of a tall daunting figure covering the doorway, followed by a gritty voice.

"If it isn't 'King' Armish. I must say, I was expecting you to be slightly more, what's the word? Charming."

King Armish knew now he was standing in the presence of King Morrik, with his brows burrowed deep and his eyes flamed with venom, he rapidly raising his bolted weapon toward the Elven King and pulled the trigger, firing a small bolt directed between his eyes.

The bolt was quickly batted away from Morrik, much to his amusement. "Why, I thank you greatly for humouring me with your poor attempt at assassination. I thank you more for your help in bringing justice to me! I told you of the crimes you committed, and your wife paid the cost. In turn, you force entry into *my* lands, kill more of *my* people, and threaten *my* life! The punishment for this is death!"

"Do not mention my wife with your murderous tongue! If you want me dead, then you must do it yourself! I'm here to claim justice of my own. Me against you. The victor gets their justice!"

King Morrik donned a sickening smile that would frighten any child, or any man for that matter, and one thing the Elves feared more than that vile smirk was when it turned into a menacing sneer; vindictive and wrathful acts would most surely follow.

The two great rulers locked eyes with one another, each of them picturing the sweet serenity of ending the other one's life.

Morrik walked down the few steps that led to the cabin and stood a few feet away from King Armish, who held his position without a flinch of any kind. "I must admit, there is nothing better than piercing through unlawful flesh, that sweet aroma of divine justice," spoke Morrik, raising his nostrils to the air, "and to have the kill of a treacherous king, well, that is divine in itself. Although, being responsible for the death of a queen comes pretty close."

King Armish could stand to hear no more, he rapidly fired another bolt toward Morrik whilst sprinting fiercely at him. As expected, Morrik once again knocked the bolt out the way. But this time, he had no time to gloat as Armish came in swinging his sword forcefully from the right.

The two locked swords and were embroiled in a fight of great will and strength, this time, good prevailing over evil as Armish hammered his sword down on top of Morrik, which was met by constant blocks. He was quickly forced to his knees from the strikes, but this wasn't so much of a disadvantage for Morrik, as he kept a decent height, even on his knees.

They continued to clash swords several more times before Armish was punched in the gut, forcing him to take a step back.

As Morrik made his way back to his feet, they clashed swords again, this time with so much power and intent from both of them that they both lost their grip on their swords.

Morrik pulled a small baton from his belt and charged back toward Armish, but Armish was too quick and conniving in this case; he grabbed the incoming forearm of Morrik whilst then proceeding to punt him in the groin, making him drop to his knees in agony.

"Different races, same body placement!" taunted Armish, who still had hold of Morrik's arm as he fell. Then, he capitalised on the compromising position he had him in by bringing up his bolted weapon and aiming it straight at the Elven King's head, "Divine justice, indeed!" growled Armish as his finger began to squeeze the trigger. But what he didn't expect was the Elven arrow that flew through his hand, causing him to drop his weapon. The Elves didn't like to play fair.

Piercing the nerves in his hand, Armish acted quickly as he ran to grab his sword from the ground nearby, holding his injured hand close to his chest, still with the arrow buried deep in it. He grabbed his sword and looked on as Morrik began to pick himself back up. Armish charged back at him before he had a chance to recover, but was soon halted when he was struck with another arrow, this time through the back of his knee.

He fell to the ground in grave distress, trying to fight through the pain, planting his sword deep in the ground as he tried to make his way back to his feet with great struggle. As he started to rise, he looked up to see King Morrik standing tall above him, bearing his sickening grin as he launched a fist at King Armish, knocking him unconscious to the ground.

CHAPTER TWENTY-TWO

LIGHTING THE FLAMES OF WAR

Belthran

"Belthran, what are you doing? The doctor said you should be resting!" said Maxin, cradling their younger sister in his arms as he entered Belthran's quarters, looking worryingly at him as he tied up the loose straps on the armoured plates around his arms.

"Resting? How can I rest?" he replied angrily with a slight tremor in his lips as his eyes began to well, throwing a nearby cup to the floor in frustration. "Mother is dead, Maxin, and Father is missing! I will give you one guess as to where he's gone; the troops should've followed him the moment they realised he had left! It was his choice to go this alone, but it is our choice to let him."

"You're not fit to fight, Brother! And what if the pirates attack in our absence?"

"Our? No, Maxin, you will stay; you will care for Layna. Now is not the time for her to be alone. I will take my troops, along with Uncle Clearus, Cousin Harnik, and Sir Payner. I will speak with this Elven Queen, also. She can show us the way and give aid with her army. The city guards will remain with the army of Dwarves, which should be plenty to keep the city standing."

A double knock thumped against the already open door of Belthran's quarters; there stood the allied group of Clearus,

Payner, Harnik, King Dunlin, and Queen Angelar, one by one entering without an invite.

"I don't believe we have been formally introduced, I am Angelar," spoke the Elven Queen as she held out her hand to shake the hand of Belthran's.

He clutched her hand with his, gently, not wanting to crush her delicate fingers with his heavy grip.

"I would like to express my deepest sympathies for your loss," she added as she kept hold of his hand. Belthran was lost in the beauty of her eyes for an instant. Seeing an Elf for the first time was a wonder for him, especially when it was one so beautiful as Queen Angelar.

But this didn't go unnoticed, King Dunlin broke the gaze of the young prince, forcing him to divert his gaze and release his grip on her hand. "And I am King Dunlin of Camaroth, pleasure to meet you, young man," he said as he stomped across the wooden floorboards, grabbing the hand of Belthran and shaking it before it was offered to him.

"How long were you all eavesdropping?" Belthran asked the group aloud.

"Long enough," replied Clearus, "and we are with you. You're acting King of Ar'Gurd until your father's return; we will follow you in any way you see fit!"

"Your father is a passionate man," spoke Payner, "but he was never a foolish one."

"Death can change a man, it can be the sole difference between good and evil taking over your mind, whether you're the one holding that blade, or if you're the one witnessing it. It can change a man in many ways. My father wouldn't have left without word, not unless he had a strong intent in his heart!"

"If he has left for Whisperwood, then he will not have aid, even my troops would be cautious of him, and there are not enough of my Elves to fight against Morrik alone," stated Angelar.

"Then we must be quick. We will find my father and Unite our forces! By the end of the day, Morrik's head will be used as a door knocker, hanging from the door of these quarters!" swore Belthran with fire in his belly.

Suddenly, the walls of the palace began to shake like an earthquake just struck, waking Layna from a sleep in Maxin's arms. Thunderous repetitive beats smashing against the floor in a harmony of one beat, one beat then two beats. A great horn bellowed throughout the kingdom, synchronizing with the beats in a great march, one that felt familiar in Angelar's mind.

"Oh, no!" she uttered in a stutter of worry, all eyes drawing on her for answers. "What is it?" stressed Payner.

Angelar listened to the beats through one more round as she looked up and answered with deep concern, "Morrik!"

The name Morrik sparked a flame of anger in each of them.

"Get all troops to the gate!" ordered Belthran in befuddled haste. "Maxin, take Layna to the hidden shelter in Mother and Father's quarters and keep her safe!"

"I should be there with you, Belthran! What if Father did go there? With Morrik on his way, does that mean he didn't succeed?"

"It means nothing. Have your troops take Layna in your stead; have them guard her with their lives. She is their priority from this moment on. Then, you can join me at the gates!"

As Maxin left with his sister in his arms, he ran with her to the safety of a small cubby built into the flooring of his parents' bedroom, also accompanied by Princess Sawndra of Camaroth and his troops who he had gathered in the palace's mess hall nearby. The room was barricaded with the troops inside as Maxin then rushed toward the city gates as the thunderous march of a vast battalion of Elves closed in on the city.

Villagers rushed to the palace for safety, and those who didn't, locked themselves in their huts, cowered away in crawl spaces and under staircases.

Although the city had not been breached, warriors of men, Dwarves, and Elves hurried through the city toward the gates.

Belthran topped the wall with Maxin following closely by his side. Clearus, Harnik, and Sir Payner also stood nearby, all with their troops stationed below. Queen Angelar positioned what troops she had across the wall to assist the cities archers as ordered by Belthran.

As for the Dwarves, King Dunlin arranged them in a formation just inside the gate and the connecting courtyard. He looked on at the incoming army through the gate's metal bars, seeing the first line of Elves escalate slowly over a hill in the distance.

Floods of red and gold illuminated the land outside the city as eight thousand Elves marched on the walls. Towers of wood and leaf being pulled along, carrying clusters of troops.

The beat of metal drums and the war cry of a winded horn followed the march louder and louder as they gained on the city. The clink and clank of Elvish metal armour created a lavishly harmonized beat of its own, intimidating the worried archers upon the wall.

Prince Clearus readied the surrounded men as Belthran, Payner, and Maxin anticipatingly awaited for King Morrik to reveal himself.

Angelar paced the top of the wall, knowing the strength and will that Morrik possessed, trying to keep her Elves alert.

As the army drew near, the march resembled the sound of a severe thunderstorm, the orders and commands of those around were drowned out by the noise. The beat of the drums quickened as the steps became few, the army of Elves coming to a complete halt, just a spear's throw away from the city walls, continuing the deafening roar of an intimidating force, proceeding to smash their shields to the floor in great sequence, in some form of pre-war ritual.

Movement became statuesque above the wall, listening to the shields of Elves crashing against the Ar'Gurdian lands, before stopping in complete silence moments later, forcing an eerie hush as the sounds of a whaling wind took over.

The sound of single heavy footsteps broke through the army of Elves as they parted to form a walkway through the middle. And there he was, King Morrik with a walk of such confidence and eyes of a winning man, cloaked in less armour than the rest, believing he didn't need it.

Clearus grabbed the arm of Sir Payner in quick purpose as he saw a riled-up look form on his face, uttering words of rational thinking in his ears. "He will not survive this war,

Payner. You need to bide your time, you will find your moment; do not do anything rash, now!"

Payner settled his shaky arms as he looked to his left at the king's sons, Belthran with eyes of fire, seeing the man who enforced the attack that killed his mother, and just beyond him, Maxin, who stood tall, trying hard to hide the fact he was petrified looking on at an army of eight-thousand Elves waiting to storm the gates, a look that was not so easily hidden.

The Elves parted in half as King Morrik took centre stage, holding out a large golden bludgeon as he drew his gaze to those who topped the wall. "Men of this city!" he said aloud, before taking a slight pause and a moment of thought, "Does that sound right to you—men? Because it is of my belief that there are more than just men who occupy these grounds. I hear that there are Dwarves there, also. No doubt, your city is already filled with an even fouler stench because of it."

It was a comment not met too gracefully with King Dunlin and his Dwarves, as a roar of resentment bled from within the confounds of the city gates. But Morrik continued to taunt, "And if my Elven eyes have not deceived me, is that the Elven traitor, Angelar, trying to make friends outside her own kingdom? How pleasant it is to see you again. Tell me, how is your sister?" he asked, chuckling to himself.

But Angelar remained strong-willed, forcing no reaction from her.

"Give me the word, my Queen, and I will put an arrow through his eye!" proposed Matine.

"You will do no such thing; he will suffer more than an arrow through the eye for what he has done!" she replied.

"Ahh, the traitor Payner still stands with you, I see. And answer me this, also, who is the unsightly pubescent who stands at the helm?"

And it was at that point when the silence was broken. Belthran was suffering deep, trying to keep his lips filled, but Morrik perfected the art of forcing reactions. Belthran raged, a gritty, overwhelming passion in his voice as Morrik looked back at him with a patronising and humorous glare. "You murdered my mother! We have more than enough men, Elves, and Dwarves in here who wish to cut off your head."

"And I have enough Elves here to destroy your city," disputed Morrik, who once again continued to taunt. "Don't try and play big boy games until you can fit into big boy armour. You're not the only ones with allies, the formed partnership of Elves and pirates has seemed more than worth the time."

Faces dropped; minds wandered. The pirates had been working for Morrik the whole time; he had instigated every attack.

"My scouts provided me with information of every pirate attack on this city throughout the years, so I formed my own meet; they fight for me, and they can have the city. In a few moments' time, the pirates will attack the city from the south."

"Harnik! Take your men and race to the south wall, now, and take my men with you!" ordered Belthran.

"I just have one more question for you all," yelled Morrik, "but this question I will happily answer myself: where is your king?" And as those words left the Elven King's lips, the Elven army formed another parting, this time the beaten down but still conscious body of King Armish was dragged through the middle and displayed in front of everyone.

"Father!" cried Maxin, as Angelar rushed to ready her archers.

Belthran remained in a state of shock, looking on as his hero and father lay defeated at the feet of an Elven King.

Payner and Clearus bellowed orders left and right as spears and arrows were drawn in plenty.

Dwarves crowded the gate like a herd of cows, awaiting the order for them to be opened, desiring the urge to take down as many Elves as they could.

"I'm going to destroy you all!" promised Morrik as he moved just behind Armish, brandishing a brass jug. "With the pirates, we have four times your army. And by the sunset, your kingdom will be looking for a new ruler," he said as he proceeded to douse Armish in a liquid substance.

"Archers, fire!" ordered Sir Payner, with a worry of knowing exactly what Morrik had in mind.

One-hundred arrows were fired from atop the walls but were frustratingly deflected by Elven shields who had stormed ahead of King Morrik in an impressive defensive manoeuvre.

After blocking the arrows, the Elven front line moved back into positions.

King Armish was stripped of everything but his rich quilted trousers, and symbolically, his crown. His arms were bound by some of the strongest Elvish rope, being pulled and stretched out wide by two Elven guards as Morrik was handed a flaming torch. He raised the torch with one hand above his head, allowing the flames to meet the heat from the sun.

"From the fire that draws its strength from the sun, spirits will bear witness to the coming of a new king in these lands, a king with the name of Morrik! Especially as your current king is somewhat…occu-fried!"

Screams broke louder than that of the beaten drums. Flocks of crows and bush-hounds fled the scene from the sounds; a flaming torch lighting the drenched skin of a king, sending his body ablaze, his screams of agony, overshadowed by the cries of his countrymen and his family who looked on.

Maxin broke down in the arms of his uncle and Payner, and Angelar signalled for the archers to continue fire.

Belthran had fallen into a trance, seeing his father's body going up in smoke, breaking free from the paralysed state as he bore sight to the maliciously pleased grin of Morrik standing proud, leaning down and replacing his crown with that of King Armish's, rescuing it from further damage and char, only to crown himself with it.

Belthran drew his sword and stormed the stairs to the city gates.

"Belthran, what are you doing?" yelled Clearus down to him, still cradling Maxin in a clump on the floor.

"Open the gates!" ordered Belthran amongst the riled-up Dwarves, feeling like he was in the middle of a pack of tormented wolves.

"Belthran, no!" yelled Clearus once more, releasing Maxin from his grasps, commanding him to get back to the palace and protect his sister.

Clearus rushed down the steps toward the gate, but it was too late. The gate of the city had been lifted, and Belthran with a few hundred Dwarves at his tail, charged the eight thousand Elves who stood before them.

As Belthran and the Dwarves neared the Elves, King Morrik backed into his sea of troops, getting lost in the crowds and disappearing from sight.

The Elves lowered their defences from the incoming arrows, as they threw their attention toward Belthran and the Dwarves, culminating in a collision of the armies and a battle was underway.

Circled by a considerable amount of Elves, Belthran and King Dunlin were trapped, holding off against the army the best they could, with Payner and Clearus looking on in worry at a sight no different to ants swarming a mud hill.

Payner instructed Angelar to continue her fire from above as he and Clearus boldly dared to join the fight that had ensued, to help aid Belthran and to capture the head of Morrik.

Arrows and spears flew in by the thousands as bodies of Elves and Dwarves dropped in rapid proportions. Sounds of explosions and roars came from back in the city, halting Payner and Clearus, who had gathered with their troops at the gate.

"Harnik?" pondered Clearus.

"Go and aid your son. Keep the pirates from the palace! I will rally what guards we have here and take the fight to Morrik," planned Payner. And as Clearus ran as quickly as he could to the south of the city, Payner led his troops and a bombardment of city guards toward the Elves, ordering the gate to be closed behind him.

***

Back in the city, Harnik and his men, with the aid of Belthran's Unit, battled hard against a few forty pirates who had scaled the south walls over the passage to the harbour.

But in timely pirate fashion, a few dozen more leapt from the rooftops, undetected, surpassing the group and sprinting toward the palace.

Maxin reached the palace some seconds before, banging on the bulky wooden doors that had been barricaded from the inside.

"Hurry up, now!" he yelled, hearing the moving of chains and wooden boards from the inside. As he waited anxiously, bobbing about on the spot with a continuous knock on the door to push the process along, an arrow flew past his ear, burrowing into the door, causing him to jump out of the way in shock. He turned around to face where it had come from, and he wished he never did. He could hear the rambunctious rustling of boards from inside the door, whilst on the outside, he faced a much deadlier sight, at least forty pirate mercenaries eyeing him up and down with predatory eyes.

They moved in, stalking him like prey, forcing him to push his back up against the door.

"Hurry up! Let me in!" he squealed.

The pirates created a barrier surrounding the doorway, giving Maxin nowhere to go.

He looked on at them with sickness in his stomach, seeing their murderous eyes and their grimy teeth buried between sickening frowns with tethered clothes that resembled anything but comfort. The young prince drew his sword in fear, too panicked to even comprehend using it. He lowered his body to a crouch, cowering against the door as the pirates raised their cleavers and rusted axes above them. He panted to himself in terrified distress. He could hear the barricade behind him still being removed, knowing he would be long dead before they reached him.

Suddenly, a spear flew into the door above his head, even causing the pirates to look on in puzzlement, but they didn't have long to ponder over the spear when a huge bellow came from behind them as they were met with a flurry of spears and rock-carved swords, plunging through their faint armour. The people of Cavetown had arrived, the three Better Lords, joining the battle just in the nick of time, much to the trembling relief of Prince Maxin.

As Clearus caught up with Harnik, the current pirate threat was quickly taken care of as they hurried back to the palace to meet up with the others.

"Uncle Clearus, where is my brother?"

"He and the Dwarves took the fight to Morrik, but they are greatly outnumbered, even with help from Sir Payner and the city guards."

"Then, we *must* go and help!"

"And who will protect your sister? The matrons? You need to stay here, Maxin. Get in the palace and barricade the door, you and your troops will be fine. I will take Harnik and these men of the caves here, and we will pull our forces back into the city to regroup."

After the fright he had just received, Maxin was more than happy to oblige whilst still trying to act like he was missing out on a fight.

And without a second thought, Clearus led the men back to the city gates as Maxin was dragged inside by his troops, and the door barricaded once again.

As the great battle escalated, Sir Payner and the city guards collided with the first line of Elves, just trying to break through the circle that surrounded Belthran, but he was having no such luck.

The towers of wood, vine, and leaf broke free from the scuffle, being pushed toward the walls with great force by packs of Elven soldiers. Angelar and the archers drew fire at the towers, but they were built with the strongest of Elven Wood, Mayrebone, the same wood Angelar used to build platforms and houses within the trees; it was impenetrable by any object; sword, spear, axe, or arrow.

Clearus and Harnik arrived back at the gate, ordering for it to be opened once more as he led his own charge toward the Elves, leaving Angelar to keep her leadership atop the wall and to bring down the towers by any means necessary.

Once Clearus caught up with Payner, they forced an opening through to the middle, catching up with Belthran and King Dunlin who were dripping with sweat and covered in blood-stained armour, not seeming to have made a dent in the enemies' forces.

Belthran continued to strike down Elf by Elf, remaining in a focused rage whilst King Dunlin seemed to be loving every minute of it, looking like he was about to burst into song and rhyme with every Elf he took down.

With the forces of Payner, Clearus, Harnik, and the Better Lords joining them, the Elven forces began to slowly deplete, but not because they had been killed. They seemed to have disappeared, and so had Morrik, much to Belthran's dismay. He drove his sword into the next Elf he came across with such ferocity, screaming at the top of his lungs as his attempt at catching Morrik slipped away from him.

"Where has he gone?" he called out to Clearus and Payner as they continue to strike down the enemy.

"As far as I'm aware, these Elves aren't magical but they're crafty; he couldn't have gone far," stated Payner, but it was at that point when Clearus felt a feeling of unease, remembering the towers that were heading toward the city, filled to the brim with Elves. He looked back toward them, looking on as they reached the city, crashing against them, surpassing the resilient arrows Angelar and the archers fired at them. Before they knew it, floods of Elves bled into the city from atop the walls as the archers tried their best to hold them off, but the forces were too large.

"He's in the city!" uttered Clearus as Belthran rapidly barged past him in great haste.

"Maxin!" he exclaimed, leaving the others to follow whilst fending off the pirates who remained outside the city. The archers on the wall were no longer an aid for the men and Dwarves outside, as their troubles now lay within the walls.

The men ran back as fast as they could with the Dwarves trailing just behind, pushing up against the gates that remained closed whilst the Elves chased them down.

A guard on the inside began to open the gate slowly as it was normally a job much more equipped for two people. As the gate slowly raised, Belthran, Harnik, Clearus, and Payner scurried under the gates, pulling through as many men as they could with them. King Dunlin came through next, followed by a handful of Dwarves and two of the Better Lords, Lord Danlur and Lord Layzul.

As men and Dwarves began to crawl under the partially opened gate, Elves atop the wall jumped down in front of them, forcing them into another battle inside the walls, causing the guard who was raising the gate to release the rope, slamming the gate shut and leaving a handful of men and Dwarves trapped outside, including Lord Pike of Cavetown.

"Pike!" yelled Lord Danlur.

"Don't you worry about me. These Elves are unfortunate that I'm one of the men left on this side!" he said with grit in his voice, a slam of his spear, and a confident wink, but that didn't fair him well. When he turned, he and the others who were trapped outside were struck with a bombardment of arrows, a carnage that no man or Dwarf was walking away from, much to the despair of those inside.

"Back to the palace!" commanded Belthran as he took down an oncoming Elf.

CHAPTER TWENTY-THREE

A MOMENTS WILL

Maxin

Leaving the inner parts of the city unguarded for some time, the south city was soon overrun by pirates, attempting to lure Maxin and his Unit out of the palace, ransacking townhouses and stores, slaughtering any villager they could find cowering away.

"We have to get out there!" urged Igor.

"I can't leave my sister!"

"Villagers are dying out there, Maxin! The city is outnumbered, they need our help," pleaded Grendel.

"The Dwarves are my family and my friends; they shouldn't fight this alone," agreed Sprock.

"You brought the people of Cavetown here, you offered them hope and a new life. They just risked theirs to save yours, now we need to do the same for them," added Algo.

"If the Elves and the pirates win here today, then they will do the same to neighbouring villages and towns; nowhere is safe, unless we stop this now!" said Quenne.

"As soon as we open these doors, the pirates will come flooding in and then we'll all be dead! It's what they're hoping we do," argued Maxin.

"Maxin is right," agreed Tamrin, peering through a hole in a nearby stained-glass window. "We cannot go kicking open the palace doors, that'd just be inviting them in! But I agree with the others, also. We can't sit here and do nothing. If the city is lost, then the princess won't be protected for long. The best way to protect her is to deal with the threat head-on."

"Then, what do you suggest we do?" questioned Maxin, hearing the screams of more and more villagers outside.

Tamrin gathered the Unit and relayed to them a deceivable plan.

***

Layna was kept safe in the cubby, and the matrons and villagers who found shelter in the palace, bore arms with vintage weapons hanging from the walls and any other objects they could find. They were barricaded inside the bedroom to guard the princess at all costs.

From a window on the highest floor of the place, Tamrin, Grendel, and Scarlep scaled the walls to stand high upon the roof, taunting the pirates who pillaged nearby, drawing their attention whilst Maxin and the others scaled down the walls and into the palace gardens around the back.

The plan worked perfectly, luring the pirates in as Tamrin, Scarlep, and Grendel fired arrows and daggers toward them with a deceptive distraction that worked all too well, humbling the pirates long enough for the others to sneak in behind and catch them off guard.

Maxin roared out at the pirates, turning their attention toward him, seeing a prince in his royal robes and expensive armour standing before them, theirs for the taking; they looked like a pack of hungry hyenas. Knowing attention was now on them, Maxin and his company hurried further into the city, leaving the pirates to follow in a hasty pursuit.

The pirates were drawn as far as the city gardens, a battleground known all too well, allowing chance for Tamrin, Grendel, and Scarlep to catch up. The Unit came to a halt, outnumbered three to one, but they all stood tall and headstrong, brandishing their weapons as the pirates approached cautiously and eagerly.

An arrow flew in from behind, catching a pirate in the back of the neck. Tamrin, Scarlep, and Grendel had arrived. Amongst the scurry of puzzled pirates, Maxin signalled an attack and his Unit charged from both ends, putting their true courage, strength, and teamwork to the test.

The young prince felt just as frightened as before, but with his team behind him, the fire in his belly grew, thinking of those whom he had lost in front of his eyes, the innocents who were butchered and what might happen if they didn't win this fight. Blood once again stained the city gardens as Maxin, and his Unit battled strongly, eventually forcing the pirates into a corner.

"You have lost!" yelled Igor as he forced his hammer into the gut of a pirate, pushing him into the corner.

"Beaten by kids!" laughed Scarlep.

Maxin forced his way to the front, holding his sword brazenly in front of him, with a short huff and puff to catch his breath; a gleam of victory bestowed upon his face, proud of what he and his Unit just achieved. "The people you have killed from your attacks on this city will now find justice. You almost succeeded in killing my brother, you killed the father of my friend here, and you support an Elf who murdered my mother and father, for what!?" yelled Maxin, but the reaction he received from the pirates was not one he and his Unit were expecting, sniggers and laughs, spit flying through the gaps in their teeth at the amusement of it all, seemingly not affected by their current standing.

"What is it? What's so funny?"

The chuckles continued, "We don't want to kill you, Princey; we only wanted to catch you for him," stated one of the pirates, pointing behind Maxin as he continued to join in with his fellow buccaneers in a fit of hysterics.

Maxin and his men turned in the pointed direction, and there was Morrik, standing shameless and arrogant, backed by an overwhelming number of Elves who had found their way into the city.

"Guys, go back to the palace!" ordered Maxin, not taking his eyes off of Morrik for a second.

"But Prince Maxin, we aren't going to leave you!" said Grendel.

"You will, because I order you to do so! My sister will need your protection! Now, go" he ordered once more, and one by one, his Unit reluctantly fled the scene as they were then chased down by the pirates and the Elves who had accompanied Morrik over the wall in a race toward the palace.

"You will not have me, and you will not have this city" exclaimed Maxin as he held his body up straight, looking on at an unresponsive Morrik, who bore a devilish stare.

Eyes locked onto eyes; hands gripped to swords. One warrior was weighed down by a menacing anger as the other was upbeat with a vision of annihilation.

Maxin was the first to raise his sword, still without a blink.

Morrik kept his sword down, showing his confidence and dominance over the young prince. A battle could still be heard coming from the direction of the wall, clattering steel and the collapse of brick and stone.

This pleased Morrik greatly, feeling an ease of enjoyment from the army he had conjured up and bestowed upon the lands.

Eliminating fear from his mind and being driven by pure hatred, Maxin charged Morrik, with both hands clutched around the grip of his sword.

Morrik sidestepped the young prince with ease, causing him to swing and miss, his mouth filling with dirt after he hit the ground.

Maxin scuffled back to his feet, but his sword was knocked from his hand by the baton that Morrik carried in his right.

Morrik holstered his weapons and grabbed Maxin by the throat, dragging him through the bloodstained flowerbeds before pinning him up against a cottage wall with one firm hand gripped around his throat.

Maxin kicked his legs as he struggled for breath, wrapping his arms around the forearm of King Morrik, but Maxin became faint, and his legs fell loose, his eyes squinting as he began to fall into darkness.

Morrik leaned in close to him, his lips up against Maxin's ears as he whispered softly, "Men are weak. Your bloodline will fade, and I will be the one great ruler of these lands!" But Morrik's attention was quickly diverted when a company of panicked Elves came rushing through the gardens, heaps of mud being kicked through the air. Morrik dropped his grip on Maxin, leaving the prince to plummet to the floor. "What is going on here?"

But within a moment, he had his answer, bolts of light came beaming from a street across the way, throwing Elves far and wide across the city.

Morrik's jaw dropped. This was magic even he wasn't accustomed to, and he himself couldn't prepare for it.

Prince Clearus ran first from the street ahead, thrusting the bolts of light in the cluster of runaway Elves, followed closely behind by Belthran, Payner, Harnik, Dunlin, Angelar, the two Better Lords, and all of their combined troops.

Morrik was stunned but had no time to act before Clearus stormed toward him. Morrik pulled out his sword but could do nothing with it, as Clearus sent him flying across the courtyard with a heavy bolt of blue lightning, sending Morrik barrelling into a nearby building, winding him as he crashed to the ground.

With just about having enough strength to crawl into an alleyway close by, Morrik dragged his body out of harm's way whilst his Elves scrambled around the gardens trying to escape the blasts themselves. But this did not go unnoticed by Belthran, who stormed through the bustling battle and chased down the Elven King whilst the others pursued the runaway Elves who had scarpered toward the palace.

CHAPTER TWENTY-FOUR

A HARROWED DISDAIN

Igor

Whilst the Elves fled from the gardens, the Elves and pirates who pursued Maxin's Unit were still unaware of what was happening elsewhere. The Unit, temporarily led by Igor, was caught up in a side road that led to the palace, as the pirates and Elves that chased them, ended up in the main street adjacent to them.

"How did they get in front of us?" asked Igor.

"You tell us, you said this was a shortcut!" quabbled Scarlep.

"I did not!" argued Igor as he and Scarlep continued to bicker, drawing the attention of their followers.

"Did you hear something?" spoke one of the Elven soldiers, forcing the Unit to hush.

The army of Elves and pirates halted and scoured the area. There was a small alleyway in-between the buildings ahead of the side road. If the Unit could make it to there, then they would be on a straight course back to the palace.

"Would they not see us?" whispered Quenne.

"Not if we're quick enough," replied Krawsin. "The time taken to visualise, and act is somewhat different than the time taken to run," he added.

"What?" replied a confused Scarlep, to which Sasha explained, "I think what he means is, the time it would take them to act after seeing us, we would already have made it across to the alleyway."

"Then we must go, now! They're getting closer!" warned Grendel, as he clutched onto his still injured leg.

And with wishes of good luck whispered throughout the group, they all plucked up their courage and sprinted for the alleyway ahead. Tamrin and Scarlep led the way first, as they were the quickest, followed by Sasha, Krawsin, Quenne, Algo, and Grendel, who were then supported by the two stocky troops who were Sprock and Igor. The first seven made it through just as they were noticed by the enemy. They drew their arrows and fired a bombardment upon the passage, narrowly missing Sprock as he dove into the alley. But with that, a stray arrow connected into the left leg of Igor dropping him to one knee.

"Igor!" cried Sasha as she ran from the alleyway to help him.

"Sasha, no!" screamed Quenne as he was held back by Sprock.

The pirates were sent to chase down those in the alley as Sasha remained in the street, trying to help Igor to his feet, urging her brother to proceed toward the palace. As the pirates flocked into the alleyway, Sasha and Igor were left to fend for themselves, feeling a sense of unnerving tension as the sounds of armoured boots circled them, and the tight drawstrings of bows were drawn back.

Igor was too heavy for Sasha to lift on her own, and he collapsed back to one knee with her knelt beside him, looking into each other's eyes, seeing the growing affection they secretly bore for one another turn to a dilution of life as arrows were fired, piercing them both as they fell to ground, hand in hand.

***

Belthran

Back east of the city, Belthran was still in hot pursuit of King Morrik as he ran to the enclosed embankment connected to the city river.

Morrik came to a sudden halt, standing over the embankment and looking into the filthy river, not being able to see his reflection, knowing Belthran was standing readily behind him. "Perhaps your father should've taken the man with the fireworks in his hands when he chose to infiltrate my lands, at least then he may have stood a chance." He turned his body to face Belthran, with the same type of grin he had upon his face when he burnt King Armish alive.

Belthran didn't speak a word, not for the thought of not knowing what to say, but more for the desire he had blazing through his mind, eyes of daggers, and a face of steel, but that still wasn't enough to frighten Morrik. Belthran was still only a young boy, after all, and the Elven King still had an ambition to rid the lands of the royal bloodline.

"Then raise your sword, little man. You've taken down many soldiers of mine, which is a great achievement, bringing an even tide to this great battle. One perfect swing of a sword from either of us, swings that balance in our favour! I've assassinated too many queens and cooked too many kings to turn back now," stated Morrik as he drew his Elven blade in one hand and bore his golden bludgeon in the other.

Belthran, already with his sword in hand, bolted toward King Morrik, taking him slightly off guard, causing them to clash swords with much ferocity, sounding like the crashing together of two armoured wagons.

Morrik was rather surprised with Belthran's skills with a blade, not knowing whether it was natural or if it was all brought on from inner desire.

Powerful swings and near misses left both of them with plenty of scratches and cuts on their armour and skin. But Morrik would continue to taunt Belthran throughout, trying devious tricks to try and get him to slip up or lose his focus, but the more Morrik would taunt, the harder Belthran would strike.

They clashed swords for what would be the last time, Belthran pressing with such strength that Morrik had to drop his bludgeon and grip his sword with both hands.

The great Elven King stood tall over Belthran, so he tried to use this to his advantage, forcing his weight down onto him, bringing his face in close enough that they could smell what each other had for supper. "This is it, little lad, the end of your short little reign as king!" Morrik jibed as the force of his push weighed Belthran down to his knees.

Belthran looked up at him in a great struggle, as his arms began to shake from his resistance. The power of Morrik's push suddenly fell flat as a sword pierced his chest, spurting blood across the face of Belthran. His eyes grew in shock as he rose quickly from the ground in envy, witnessing Payner on the end of the sword that impaled Morrik.

Payner released his sword, watching the body of the Elven ruler plummet to the ground. "What have you done?" mumbled Belthran, staring down at the fallen king.

"I've ended this! Now come, Belthran, your uncle has pushed enemy forces to the palace; he has taken your brother with him, and the enemy is trapped and surrounded. This all ends now!"

Payner left the body of Morrik behind as he left for the palace, with Belthran following begrudgingly behind, and it wasn't long before the battle was finished. Signals were sent across all four kingdoms to all who could hear it. The remaining Elven soldiers were apprehended outside the palace and were to be imprisoned by Queen Angelar. The pirates fled the city in terror and were chased down by Harnik and his troops, who ended up at the city harbour.

"They've gotten away from us," said Amrex.

"Not so easily this time!" replied Harnik as he stormed the docks, boarding a ship that was left behind.

"My Prince, what're you doing?" asked Manrik, another one of Harnik's troops.

"We are following them; they won't get away this time!" stated Harnik.

"But, my Prince, we don't know how to sail a boat," argued Amrex.

"We didn't know how to fight against an army of Elves before today, but we achieved that. We cannot let these pirates escape, not this time!" spoke Harnik, forcing his men on the boat as they pulled up the ship's anchor and very amateurly sailed away from the docks in a worrying pursuit across the foggy sea.

Plenty of emotions carried deep across the city; an unharmed princess was embraced by her loved ones, two prince brothers shared a hug of pure love and compassion, a sister and a best friend were found buried under a cascade of Elven arrows, a prince who couldn't find his son after he was spotted chasing pirates out of the city, and husbands, wives and children of many were discovered slaughtered in their homes, tears ran for fallen Dwarves, Elves, and the people of Cavetown as the remnants of the biggest battle the lands had ever faced buried deep in the hearts and minds of all.

Belthran escaped the doom and gloom for a moment, knowing eyes would all be on him soon, to stand high upon the Palace of Kings as the new King of Ar'Gurd and speak to the people of the tragedy that fell upon them. He pottered through the hallways of the palace, scathing over old paintings and artefacts as he passed, eventually finding himself in his father's study, looking around the room at the pictures, the walls, the decorations; they all brought tearful memories to him, and it pondered the question in Belthran's mind about what his father would say during this time of great tragedy. As he contemplated, he saw a scroll still within its seal, resting upon a pile of books on the desk. The top of the scroll bore the handwriting of his father, and it was addressed to, "*Sir Payner, my dearest friend.*"

Belthran moved over to the scroll quickly with a sense of intrigue, staring down at it with a want of knowing. As he reached over to grab it, he heard a humbling voice coming from the doorway, "Master Belthran, it's almost time for your speech."

"Yes, thank you, Sir Payner," replied Belthran, snatching the scroll from the desk before Payner had a chance of seeing.

As Belthran began to leave the room, he still had the impulsive urge of wanting to know what was written on the scroll Payner had awaiting him. The impulse grew over him, forcing him to blurt out, "My father left this for you." He slowly pulled his hand from behind his back, revealing the scroll to Payner. "But as king now, I would very much like to know what my father was thinking before he left. He had time to write a letter, but not to tell us his intentions. Please, Payner, can you tell me what it says?"

Payner grabbed the scroll from Belthran, breaking the seal and unravelling it in front of him. Payner was not normally one for revealing private matters, but he understood the need from Belthran, so in this case, offered to read aloud,

"To my good friend, Sir Payner, I trust this letter with you and only you."

Payner paused for a moment, looking up at Belthran with unsure eyes.

"What is it?" questioned Belthran.

"If your father was trusting me and only me with what's in this letter, then perhaps it is not something to be shared."

Belthran knew he couldn't go on always wondering what was in the letter. He licked his dry lips, his intrigue grew stronger, "I respect you, Sir Payner, but as your new king, I demand you share with me my father's words!"

Payner didn't reply, he felt no need to cause more dispute, so he continued to read, his eyes growing in shock as he did so,

"If you're reading this, then I didn't survive my pursuit of the Elven King, Morrik, the understanding of what he took from me is all I need from you to forgive my decision. I have full confidence that Ar'Gurd will continue to thrive under the leadership of Belthran, I have no doubt he will make a great king, but I have no doubts that Maxin will do the same.

Right now, you're probably wondering what the meaning of this letter is, as my last command as King Armish Hailguard of Ar'Gurd, I have thus decided that the kingdom should from this point be ruled by my two sons, both as kings in their own right. Belthran has the skill, the power, and the strength of a great king, whereas Maxin, will provide the lands with logic and reason.

They both have great qualities, and Ar'Gurd will thrive that much more with them both at the helm.

This is my final wish. See it be done.

It has been an honour serving with you my friend, until we meet again."

The room was silent. Sir Payner was speechless, as was Belthran, feeling betrayed by his father, shocked, confused, and angry. His face went as red as the blood that boiled inside him before he lashed out in stress toward Payner. "It cannot be. This kingdom is mine! I am king!"

"Yes, you are. But so is King Maxin."

Belthran let out a slight squeal hearing those words leave Payner's lips. "Do not call him that! You're enjoying this, aren't you? First, you take the opportunity of killing Morrik away from me, and now you're quick to jump into such a ridiculous request!"

"Enjoying this? King Morrik killed your father, my best friend since before you were born. He killed your mother and Keyomar, also. And if I hadn't shoved my blade through his chest, then he probably would've killed you, too! As for the request, as crazy as it sounds, it is your father's last wish, and I owe it to him to respect that," argued Payner.

Belthran's temper calmed as he realised the state of his actions. "I'm sorry, Sir Payner. I have been through a lot, and I know you are only trying to do right by father." He spoke with deep regret as a sorrowed tear fell from his eye. He held his arms out to Payner to accept his apology.

Payner had no qualms with that; he wrapped his arms around Belthran and held him tight, patting him on the back in admiration. But he found himself locked, Belthran's grip so tight that he could not release himself. "Belthran, that's enough! What're you doing?" gasped Payner as he tried to break free.

Belthran pushed his face up against Payner's ear and whispered demonically into it, "This kingdom is *mine*!" He planted a small dagger through Payner's heart before letting him go, allowing him to bleed out over the floor.

As he lay dying on the floor, Payner tried to muster words, but couldn't find the strength to speak to them, looking up and seeing the sight of Belthran standing freakishly over him and grinning in a way that mirrored King Morrik, a tear then fell from the eye of Sir Payner as he lay in a pool of blood, and he closed his eyes for the final time.

So on this day of reckoning, who really did prevail, good or evil? Only one thing was for sure, it was only *The Beckoning.*

ABOUT THE AUTHOR

Born in Canterbury, England. I was never sure on what I wanted to be when I grew up.
From early childhood fantasies of becoming a Cowboy or a Wrestler, to developing a real desire for wanting to become a Fireman.

Unfortunately, due to colour-blindness, becoming a Fireman was never an option for me, so I had to look elsewhere.

I always had a wild and vivid imagination from early childhood. Drawing inspiration from what I'd seen in movies of my favourite franchise, The Lord of The Rings. The world was my playground and every day objects would take on a life of their own in fantasy battles across my bedroom floor.
I knew I wanted a career where I could express myself freely.

During high school, I was tasked for one of my English assignments to write a story about a day in the life of me. This wasn't for me. Instead I picked up a pen and I wrote a short horror story. I handed in my paper, and although my spelling and grammar wasn't the greatest, the teacher said something to me that day that stuck with me. After thinking she was going to tell me off for not doing the work that was asked of me, she actually praised me and told me that I had a great imagination. Wanting to use that in any way that I possibly could, I explored the idea of performing arts. I enjoyed acting and the freedom that it gave me to nurture my imagination. Unfortunately, due to not getting the grades that I needed, the performing arts college would not take me. So I choose a different path gaining qualifications in animal care and marine biology.

I've moved about a lot in my life and never really settled in one place. But after moving up to the North of England, that's when I rediscovered my passion for writing. I moved into a new property with my mum and my sister, and we had little to live off at first, so boredom crept in quickly. Not long after the move, upon finding a partially used notepad in the kitchen drawer, I found my escape. I took the notepad and a pen to my bedroom, and without a seconds thought, instinct took over and I began to write. 7 years later and after a lot of stoppages and life getting in the way, that book that I started all that time ago, is finished. But as for its story and mine, that's only the beginning.